Of
NOBLE
BIRTH

ALSO BY BRENDA NOVAK

Of
NOBLE
BIRTH

A NOVEL

BRENDA
NOVAK

NEW YORK TIMES BESTSELLING AUTHOR

Montlake
Romance

Text copyright © 1999 Brenda Novak

Published by Montlake Romance, Seattle

www.apub.com

Amazon, the Amazon logo, and Montlake are trademarks of Amazon.com, Inc., or its affiliates.

ISBN-13: 9781477824825
ISBN-10: 1477824820

Cover design by Laura Klynstra

Library of Congress Control Number: 2014905353

Printed in the United States of America

To my husband, Ted.
After thirty years and five wonderful children,
I still see fireworks.

PROLOGUE

Bridlewood Manor
Clifton, England
December 2, 1829

"The babe's deformed," the midwife gasped, nearly dropping the slippery newborn.

"What do ye mean?" Martha Haverson rounded the bed in alarm.

"Look at 'is arm. 'Tis no more than a stump."

The housekeeper stared at Mrs. Telford's moon-shaped face before letting her gaze slide down to the squalling child. Just as the midwife had said, one tiny limb flapped about, ending just above the elbow, as though a surgeon had amputated the rest.

"What?" The mother of the newborn craned her neck to see the child. A moment earlier she had seemed oblivious as she moved listlessly on the bed, all color gone from her fine-boned face, her lips a pallid gray. Now her eyes sprang open with a look of panic in their violet depths. "Deformed did you say? My son's deformed?"

Martha watched anxiously as Her Grace's eyes sought the child in the midwife's hands. After five years and as many miscarriages, the duchess had finally produced an heir. And what a long, difficult birth it had been! Martha thought her mistress deserved a moment of triumph before further worries beset her, but Her Grace spotted the baby's clublike limb before the midwife could shield it from her view.

"No! No!" she moaned. "My husband hates me already. What will he do?"

Martha took the baby into her strong arms, and she and Mrs. Telford exchanged a meaningful look, sharing the lady's trepidation.

"'E won't do anythin' but be glad the wee babe's a sweet, 'ealthy boy," Martha assured her, reaching down to squeeze her mistress's hand.

The baby let out a piercing howl that seemed to contradict her words.

"You don't know him," the duchess whispered. The revelation of the baby's flaw seemed to sap what little strength she had left. She let her

1

head fall back and her eyes close as a tear rolled back into her thick, dark hair.

"Don't fret so, Yer Grace," Mrs. Telford advised. "Yer in a bad way an' need yer rest. 'Tis not good for ye to stew so."

But Martha knew that the duchess no longer heard, much less understood, either of them. She remained somewhere inside herself. Her lips moved without making a sound, as if in prayerful supplication, and she tossed restlessly on her pillow.

"Don't just stand there. Help me." The midwife scowled at Martha, making her realize she'd been standing motionless, staring at the duchess. Her mistress did not look well. The housekeeper doubted she would last the night.

"Will she live?" Martha whispered.

Mrs. Telford sent an appraising glance at the duchess's face, the harsh lines around her own mouth deepening into grooves. "I don't know. But 'tis not doin' 'er a bit of good, ye standin' there like that. 'Tis time to clean the whelp up."

Sternly reminded of her duty, Martha pulled away from her mistress's bedside and headed off to bathe the new arrival. His small weight felt good in her arms. She had been unable to bear children herself, at least any that lived beyond their first month, and had been looking forward to having a little one in the house. But when she reached the small antechamber where a bowl of tepid water waited and began to sponge the child off, she couldn't escape a heavy sense of loss. Poor Duchess. Heaven only knew that her life had not been easy since her marriage to the Duke of Greystone.

"Mrs. 'Averson?" It was the tweenie, the least among the least of the maids.

"Yes, Jane?" The housekeeper paused from her ministrations to look up at the gangly young girl. Only twelve, Jane was all arms and legs and as shy as she was young.

"The master would like to see 'is son," she said, slightly out of breath.

Martha could tell by the uncertainty in Jane's eyes that all was not well. *So the duke already knows,* she thought, wishing Mrs. Telford had kept her voice down. The walls had ears. Evidently someone had already carried tale of the baby's arm to the master.

"An' where is 'e?" she asked. "I've barely begun to bathe the babe. An' 'e should be allowed to suckle before—"

"I'm beggin' yer pardon, Mrs. 'Averson," the jittery girl interrupted. "'Is Grace demands we bring the child right away, lest we both lose our positions. 'E's waitin' in the library. Mrs. Telford is on 'er way there."

Martha bit her lip and glanced over her shoulder in the direction of the duchess's room. "Very well. Fetch a blanket. It won't do for the babe to catch a chill, poor little love."

Albert Kimbolten, Duke of Greystone, was pacing across an exquisite gold-and-blue Turkish rug when Martha entered. Massive mahogany bookshelves crowded with leather-bound volumes lined three walls. They were dusted once a week, though rarely used. A fire crackled comfortably in the fireplace. The midwife sat in a Chippendale chair near a long, rectangular table, the fingertips of both hands pressed together, her lips pursed.

At Martha's entry, the duke turned to face her. His brows knitted together, a solid black line atop flashing blue eyes, making Martha shiver as though a cold draft suddenly swept the room. The heir had been born, and she was to present him to his father. But this was nothing like the moment she had long anticipated. There were no smiles of delight, no proud glances—only anger, seething from the man before her with all the force of a tidal wave.

Martha drew a shaky breath. "Yer son, Yer Grace."

"Lay it on the table." Greystone did not bother to watch as Martha reluctantly deposited her charge as directed. Instead, he stared into the black night beyond the window that mirrored his savage-looking visage. "That will be all."

Martha backed away. Only the fear of making matters worse forced her to take one step and then another until she passed into the hall. After closing the door, she paused on the other side to listen to the words floating to her ears from within the library.

"What are you telling me?"

Martha could hear the tremor in the duke's voice even through the door.

"As I said before, yer son is deformed," the midwife explained. "'Tis not uncommon. Such things happen now an' again. From the look of it, the babe will never 'ave the use of 'is right arm."

"And his mind? Is it similarly . . . defective?"

An interminable pause.

"I cannot tell, Yer Grace. 'Twas such a difficult birth . . ."

"I see. Will he ride? Hunt?"

"'E may do neither. I 'ave no way of knowin' 'ow the child will develop. In all 'onesty, Yer Grace, I am far more concerned with yer lady—"

"My *lady*? After five years, this is what she gives me. A cripple. A laughingstock!"

The sound of shattering glass made Martha jump. The baby began to wail, and she fought the urge to march in and fetch him.

"But Yer Grace, the duchess 'ad no—"

"Leave me!" he shouted above the cries of his son.

Something—his fist?—crashed down onto a table. A startled yelp escaped the midwife, followed by the thud of other articles being hurled against the walls or fireplace. Then the midwife scuttled from the room, slamming the door behind her.

Martha acted as though she were just approaching. "Mrs. Telford, is somethin' wrong?"

"'E's gone mad, I tell ye. Simply mad." The midwife threw up her hands. "Ye'd best leave 'im for a time. I've got my work cut out for me with the duchess."

Martha wavered as Mrs. Telford fled down the hall. She longed to enter the room and rescue the crying infant, but was loath to further fuel His Grace's anger, for the baby's sake as much as her own.

Silence jolted Martha out of her quandary. One minute the baby had been wailing uncontrollably; the next, nothing. She pressed closer to the door, holding her breath. Not a single sound reached her ears.

Panic propelled her forward. She burst into the room and her eyes took in the tall, immaculately dressed duke leaning over his son. One large hand covered both nose and mouth of the newborn infant.

He's killing the lad. He's killing him! her mind shrieked as she flew at her master. Scratching and clawing at Greystone's manicured hand, she tried to provide the child with air.

"Get away!" he snarled.

But Martha fought for the child's life with the same desperate longing she felt for her own dead sons, and finally the infant let out a howl.

The duke backed away, his face red, the veins in his neck bulging above a white collar. "I'll kill you for this!"

"Please," Martha gasped. "'E's yer son."

Greystone gave a derisive snort. "I could not have fathered this . . . this deformity. I will not have him. Do you hear? He will never be my heir."

Martha gulped air into her lungs as the duke's words registered in her mind. How could a man be so cruel? Finally she asked softly, "May I take 'im, then?"

Crimson suffused the duke's face. "Without me, without my reference, you will be unable to find work. How will you provide for a sick husband and a deformed babe?"

"I don't know."

"Fool! I'm tempted to let you starve the child for me, let you watch him die a slow death, but I cannot take that chance. Should you manage it somehow, as soon as he grew old enough, the two of you would be on my doorstep crying 'Inheritance!' 'Heir!'" He lunged at her. "Never!"

The air stirred near her ear as Martha whirled away. She fully expected to feel the duke's long fingers close about her neck, pinching off her own breath, when suddenly she heard an odd gasp and turned in time to see him trip on the plush rug. His head struck the corner of the table as he toppled over like a felled tree.

Martha stared at the limp body lying unnaturally at her feet. Blood oozed from a wound at his temple. *What now?* she thought as panic rose like bile in her throat.

Bending to search for a pulse, she felt a faint beat at his throat and slowly let out her breath. But the fact that he yet lived posed another problem. Suppose when he awoke, he blamed her for his fall—blamed her and the baby.

Martha's gaze left the duke's ashen face and moved to the squirming bundle atop the table. Its cries registered in her mind. Greystone had tried to kill the baby. The duchess was likely dead already.

Without further deliberation, Martha pulled the infant into her arms and fled the room. She ran through the long halls of Bridlewood Manor, past bedrooms and sitting rooms and libraries, to the back stairs and down, and finally through the kitchen and beyond into the cold winter's night.

Chapter 1

Manchester, England
March 5, 1854

"Let me out! Please, Willy, let me out!"

Alexandra's voice rose to an unnatural, high-pitched scream. The walls and lid of the trunk pressed in upon her like a coffin, the heavy darkness crushing her chest like a thousand pounds of sand. Stifling. Suffocating. Terror gripped her as she struggled for breath, pounding her fists on the locked lid of the old steamer trunk.

In her panic, she almost failed to notice the sliver of light that penetrated the blackness. When she did see it, her gaze clung to it as tightly as a drowning man might clasp a life preserver to his breast. Age and use had left the dome-shaped lid slightly warped. Surely air could pass as well as light. Still, Alexandra had to force herself to breathe slowly, to resist the hysteria that threatened to overwhelm her.

She ceased her pounding.

"Papa?" she wept. She hadn't called Willy "Papa" for years, but she felt like a child again, like the little girl who used to love him, trust him. "Are you still there?"

Silence. Alexandra concentrated on the beam of light. The tiny slit didn't provide much air. She could hardly breathe. Where was he? There had been no sound for several minutes. Had he left her?

"Oh no, please," she whispered. Certainly even Willy wouldn't abandon her this way. Her stepfather never hurt her when sober, rarely spoke to her, in fact, but his love of gin exposed another side of his nature.

The beatings that had begun shortly after her mother's death five years ago had become increasingly common and more violent as Willy's dependence upon alcohol grew. Now drunkenness was his way of life.

Alexandra tried to shift her weight, but the trunk was too small to hold a nineteen-year-old. She was crammed into it with her long legs tucked under her chin, her arms squeezed tightly against her sides. Her right hip supported the whole of her weight, causing pain to shoot down her leg until, mercifully, the restricted blood flow made it go numb. Still, her head throbbed; whether from the punishing blow Willy had landed when he had first set upon her, or from the fit of weeping that had overtaken her when he had forced her inside her mother's steamer trunk, she did not know.

A shuffling sound alerted her to the fact that she was not alone after all. She tried to hold her breath so she could hear from whence the movement came, but her involuntary gasps continued.

"Willy? Please, open the lock." Alexandra hoped a calm appeal would evoke some response, but she received no answer. She felt as though she were walking a tightrope of sanity. One wrong word could turn her stepfather away and send her plummeting into panic once again.

"Are you still there? Don't leave. Please. If you don't let me out, how will I work? You know we have a half-dozen shirts to finish today." She paused. "Don't you want to get paid?"

"Shut your trap, wench," Willy growled. "I can't stand the sight of you."

"But I'll go directly upstairs. I promise. You won't so much as see me." Her body ran with sweat, but Alexandra fought to control her fear. At least Willy was there. At least he was talking to her. So far, she was managing to keep her precarious balance.

"We've got only until noon to finish the shirts. The skirts for Madame Fobart's are due right after. You said so yourself," Alexandra pleaded. "I'm the quickest seamstress you've got, aren't I? I'll work hard, you'll see."

Willy cursed, but Alexandra could tell his anger had lost its edge. Her approach was working, it seemed. "Madame Fobart gives us the bulk of our work. We certainly don't want to lose her."

"To hell with bloody Madame Fobart!"

Willy kicked the trunk, causing Alexandra to yelp in surprise as he bellowed in pain. "To hell with it all!" he croaked.

"You don't mean that." Alexandra forced the words out above the heavy thumping of her heart. "We've got a lot of business now, and soon we'll be making good money. But I can't finish our orders if you don't let me go."

For the briefest moment, she wondered if they could finish their work on time in any event. The order Willy had brought from Madame Fobart's was double the usual, and with the work came the demand that the skirts be made up and delivered in less than two days. Though Alexandra and the other needlewomen had sewn well into the night, they still had much to do. But how would Willy know that? He had left for the tavern while the candles yet burned in the garret above, and she and the other women worked tenaciously on. Could he even begin to comprehend the mounting pressure of each new deadline when his time was spent sleeping off the effects of the previous night's bottle? Willy never appeared until late in the day, and then only to criticize, grumble and complain. That he procured any clients at all was indeed a great wonder.

Silence again.

"Willy?" Rational thought bled slowly from Alexandra's mind as her head began to spin. There was so little air. Work. She had been talking about work. But why? She no longer remembered, except that her life was one monotonous round of stitch, stitch, stitch. Even now her mind called her fingers to sew—but it was so dark.

The lamp is out, she thought. *I must relight it.*

"Someday," Willy said, his voice grating low and cutting through her fuzzy thoughts, "someday I'll snuff out the light in those eyes that are so much like your mother's."

Alexandra had long since given up trying to understand the unrelenting anger that poured out of Willy when he was in his cups. What had she done to deserve such punishment? And Willy had loved Elizabeth. More than loved her. He had worshipped her. On her deathbed, her mother had asked Alexandra to look after him.

A roaring, like the sound of the sea, filled Alexandra's head, and she felt as though her body were being gently buffeted by the water's currents. *I don't care what he says . . . I only want to sleep.*

Then another thought surfaced. *The others will be here soon.* Of course! That's what she had been trying to remember: the six women who climbed the rickety stairs to the workroom garret each day before dawn.

They would soon arrive to begin the long day's work of sewing trousers, linen shirts and skirts. The pittance they received for their labor, along with the demands placed upon them by Willy and his impatient buyers, required that they work sometimes eighteen or more hours in a day. Alexandra knew she could depend on them to help her if she could only last a few minutes more. But a peaceful, black abyss beckoned, and she began to move toward it.

The lock clicked. Alexandra heard it above the crashing of the waves in her ears, though the sound had no meaning until the battered lid was thrown open. Then the cool morning air rushed upon her like a good strong slap in the face.

Her chest heaving as she sucked air into her lungs, Alexandra glanced wildly about until she saw Willy.

He stood not three feet away, the imprint of a hat still matting his gray hair above a heavily lined face. Bloodshot eyes, yellowed with age and bad living, peered at her with loathing. He seemed to stare into her very soul, then he staggered away toward his own room, a string of epithets spewing from his alcohol-numbed tongue.

It was over, for now. Alexandra closed her eyes and breathed deeply, her nails curling into her palms. *No,* she promised herself. *Not for now. For always.*

By the time Miss Harper arrived, Alexandra had composed herself. Though the others knew about the beatings, she did her best to conceal what she could for fear her fellow seamstresses would jeopardize themselves on her behalf. After all, they were powerless to offer any real help. They needed every penny they earned for the most basic wants—food, clothing, shelter. And it was a fortunate needlewoman indeed whose income provided enough for all three.

As the aging spinster entered the small attic with its peaked ceiling, sloping walls and single window, Alexandra was already hard at work on a full-dress shirt with a pleated front. Shirts required some of the most exacting needlework, forcing her to bend toward the tallow candle to better see each intricate stitch.

"Good day." Alexandra glanced up to smile at the woman with a cheer she did not feel. She was in charge of the small shop, and felt obligated to greet each needlewoman in a welcoming manner, though today that simple duty contended with a strong desire for comforting. Those with whom she worked were her only friends. Had anyone but Myrtle Harper been the first to arrive, Alexandra might have blurted out the whole terrifying experience. But the sight of her feeble comrade, whose steady decline she witnessed day by day, stemmed the tide of her self-pity.

Miss Harper tilted her head in acknowledgment, but did not speak.

Noticing how drawn she looked, Alexandra halted her work despite the pressing deadlines. "You're ailing again?"

The spinster nodded as she crossed the room to hang her bonnet and shawl on a hook before settling down at the large deal table that stood in the center of the floor, surrounded by seven chairs. The only other furnishings were an old clock, a coal stove and two tallow candles.

"What we got?" Miss Harper flexed her fingers before taking up her thimble and needle.

"Skirts." Alexandra pointed to a pile of burgundy velvet in the corner. Skirts were comparatively quick and easy, so Alexandra had set aside her share for the ill woman.

"Morning," several soft female voices called as the other seamstresses entered the room in a knot, and the room shrank instantly to the stuffy quarters to which they were all well accustomed. It was barely large enough for its scant furnishings, let alone the women who had to work in it. But they jostled about and managed to slip into their seats and position their few belongings in a relatively short time.

Alexandra worked quietly as the other women chatted and laughed, her own thoughts returning to the morning's episode with Willy. He was getting worse, she realized as anger and humiliation flooded her senses. Through her early years, she could have accused her stepfather of nothing beyond indifference. But he was becoming truly vindictive. She had hoped that his antipathy would go away. She'd blamed his behavior on the bottle, his bad knee, his unhappiness since her mother had died. After this morning, however, she knew such hopes were childish fantasy. He hated her.

"Another beatin', Alexandra?"

Alexandra glanced up to see Libby, a frail-looking widow with five children, focus her all-knowing eyes her way.

She shook her head.

"Then what?"

The others paused in their stitching to gaze expectantly at them both.

"Come on, dear, spit it out," Libby prodded. "Ye can't 'ide it from us. There might not be any telltale scrapes or bruises this time, but that devil of a man's done somethin'."

Alexandra swallowed against the lump that swelled in her throat. "I have to get away from him, that's all."

"An' we've been tellin' ye that for months. 'E's not goin' to get any better, livin' on the bottle the way 'e is," Libby agreed.

Miss Harper made a tsking sound. "I knew Elizabeth. Yer mother would never 'old ye to a promise to care for 'im if 'e wasn't returnin' the favor. 'E uses ye to earn 'is bread, that's all. An' abuses ye in the bargain."

Any mention of her mother evoked a poignant longing in Alexandra. Everything had been so different when Elizabeth was alive. Alexandra's mother had been kind and beautiful. She'd taught her only child to read and write and speak like a lady. And when Willy had finally intervened, insisting Alexandra leave books to the lads, Elizabeth had taught her to sew. Though they stitched endless hours together, those times had been nothing like the drudgery of the present. Her mother only picked up piecework when Willy fell from a ladder at work, badly injuring his right knee. When he couldn't stand for any length of time, the mill let him go, and finding new employment was difficult. But the worst was yet to come. On the heels of his accident, Elizabeth succumbed to scarlet fever and died, turning Alexandra's life upside down. Without her mother, the pillar of strength who had kept the family together and reasonably happy, her stepfather was not the same man.

"He thinks he earns our living by lining up our accounts," Alexandra said.

"Any God-fearin' man wouldn't be able to justify takin' the lion's share of our meager profits for an 'our's work 'ere an' there," Miss Harper replied.

The others nodded as Libby jammed her needle into the shirt she was sewing. "'E 'eld back 'alf my pay last week because Mary Jane got sick an' I came in a few minutes late, remember? Someday, I'd like to—"

"We'd all like to take a stick to Willy," interrupted Sarah, a young woman trying to earn enough with her needle to provide for three younger siblings. "But we can 'andle 'is miserly ways because 'e keeps 'is distance from everythin' but our money. That's not true for Alexandra."

"Don't ye 'ave any relatives who can 'elp?" asked Merna, a new hire.

Alexandra bowed closer to her work. "Not many I know," she said, not wanting to announce that her mother had been banished from her wealthy family when she'd found herself pregnant, at fifteen, by the village baker's son. Elizabeth had gone to her young lover, hoping he'd run away with her, but her father had gotten to him first. For a few pounds and the promise of his own bakeshop someday, the boy turned his back on Elizabeth. So she left on her own, made her way to Liverpool and went to work in a cloth mill, where she met Willy.

"Willy has family here, but they keep to themselves. They didn't like my mother, accused her of thinking herself above them."

"If they're anythin' like Willy, she *was* above them," Miss Harper snapped.

Alexandra smiled at the spinster's matter-of-fact tone. "I do have an aunt on my mother's side."

"The one Willy chased away when she came to visit?" Libby asked.

With a nod, Alexandra continued, "I hear from her every once in a while, but not often."

"Where does she live?" asked Eliza, the young mother.

"In London right now. I received a letter not long ago saying her husband, who's a military man, just received a post in India. The entire family is moving there—"

"When?" Libby pounced on the question so quickly, Alexandra paused from her work to look up in surprise.

She did a quick mental computation. "In less than a week."

A sparkle entered the widow's eyes at the same time a smile curved her cracked lips, and Alexandra began to shake her head. "No. I know what you're thinking. I can't go with them. I've thought of it and thought and thought, and I wouldn't dare burden Aunt Pauline by foisting myself upon her. Besides, it's probably the first place Willy would look—"

"They're leavin' the country. Ye just said so yerself," Sarah put in.

"And ye could always work," Miss Harper added. "Ye could be their servant, or the children's governess, or just stay with them for a short while until ye found a post elsewhere—"

Alexandra held up her hand, trying to get them to stop because she feared the hope that their excitement fostered in her soul. "And how would I pay for my passage to India? I'll not expect my aunt to carry the cost!"

Libby and Miss Harper looked at each other, then at the others, and soon smiles curled everyone's lips. "'Tis almost noon," Libby announced as Alexandra became the center of attention again. "The shirts for Mr. Cophagen are to be delivered after lunch, less than an 'our away. Madame Fobart's skirts are due shortly after. Payment on such an order would be significant, if ye get my meanin'." The widow fell silent, letting the suggestion of her words hang in the air.

Alexandra's heart doubled its pace, even though her head still insisted she could never run to Aunt Pauline. "I only deliver our completed orders. Willy collects the money. You all know that."

"Convince Fobart's manager that Willy sent ye to collect for 'im," Miss Harper said. "That mother of yers trained ye well. Ye could pass yerself off as a real lady if ye wanted to."

"But Fobart's manager has seen me dozens of times. He knows who I am. And I have no time to arrange anything with my aunt," Alexandra argued. "She's leaving in less than a week. It could easily take a letter longer than that to reach her."

"Then ye'll simply 'ave to convince Fobart's manager that Willy's ill an' needs the money. An' ye'll 'ave to travel directly to London, and catch yer aunt an' 'er 'usband before they set sail," Libby replied.

"What better chance 'ave ye got?" asked Miss Harper.

A lump of fear congealed in Alexandra's stomach because she knew Miss Harper and the others were right. Aunt Pauline might be her only hope. But what if the manager at Fobart's refused her and told Willy what she had done? What if she didn't make it to London in time?

She shuddered at the memory of the beating she'd received the last time she'd gotten the crazy idea to escape her stepfather, but slowly, she nodded and gave the others a shaky smile. Though the risks of their plan were great, it offered her a chance at freedom. A very slim chance. "All right," she said at last. "I'll try it."

Nathaniel Kent strode boldly to the bow, his good arm gripping a rope cable to help him keep his balance on the heaving deck, the other arm hanging useless at his side. The thrill of the chase surged through his body, heightening his senses and causing his heart to pound within his chest. His quarry was close to surrendering. It had to be. The merchant brig had tried to run, but there was no escaping the sleek, fast-cutting *Royal Vengeance*, not on a day like this, when the sun was high in the sky, the water as smooth as satin and the wind as steady as a camel plodding through the desert.

Still, Nathaniel wondered why the *Nightingale* didn't return their fire; he knew she carried at least four thirty-two-pound cannons.

"What's going on?" Mystified, he turned to Trenton, his lanky first mate.

Trenton shrugged. "Damned if I can say. I know we come as quite a surprise, but even the first ship we took offered up a better fight than this."

"Still, I don't see a white flag."

"Should we blast 'em again?"

Nathaniel thought for a moment. "Aye, maybe a direct hit will convince them."

The deafening roar of cannon clamored above the shouts of his men as four twenty-five-pound steel balls plunged into the sea somewhere near the stern of the *Nightingale*, sending large, drenching sprays of seawater across her decks. Smoke obscured Nathaniel's view but soon cleared, rising like the ascension of a million ghosts.

"We got 'er!" someone cried.

A chorus of cheers resounded.

Nathaniel glanced back over his shoulder. His men were busy cleaning cannon muzzles so they could reload. He doubted such action would be necessary. Since the invention of the steam engine, pirates were a thing of the past, but the tales of their bygone era were not forgotten. Any good sailor could recount, and usually did, at least a dozen hair-raising stories supposedly experienced by someone in his ancestral tree.

Banking on the fear those tales engendered, Nathaniel knew it would only be a matter of time before the *Nightingale* surrendered. He smiled, enjoying the feel of the deck moving beneath his feet, the wind rushing through his hair, even the smell of battle—especially the smell of battle, for it brought him that much closer to his goal.

"There's the flag," Richard shouted, pointing toward the other ship. As unpredictable as a wild boar and twice as mad, Richard had been a member of Nathaniel's crew for less than a year. "We got the bloody bastards!"

Nathaniel turned to look. Sure enough, a white flag rippled wildly in the afternoon wind, hoisted high on the brig's mainmast. "Good girl," he murmured to himself. "Now for your cargo."

Moving quickly, he headed to the side of the ship where his men lowered a boat. He heard it splash in the water only seconds before he climbed over the side and jumped in. Trenton stayed behind to take charge of the *Vengeance*, but Richard and Tiny, a man the size of a bear, came with him.

Nathaniel listened to the rhythmic slap of the oars hitting the water as Tiny pulled for the other ship. The whine of voices from the *Nightingale* shifted on the wind. He couldn't determine the words, but he could guess that expressions of surprise and dismay were chief among them.

When they reached her hull, Nathaniel turned to his men. "Are you ready?"

"I'm as eager as a sailor with his first woman," Richard exclaimed. The barrel-chested Tiny merely nodded.

"Let's go."

Nathaniel scaled the rope that dangled to the water, climbing with the ease and grace that came only from experience, despite his bad arm. He was the first to stretch his long legs on deck. Richard and Tiny came behind.

An older man with iron-gray hair and long sideburns, evidently the captain of the *Nightingale*, separated himself from his crew almost immediately. He wore a new frock coat, but his face and hands were as crusty and battered as an old sea chest. "What in damnation do you think you're doing, firing on this ship?" he asked.

Nathaniel hesitated before making his reply, letting silence establish his dominance better than any amount of talking could ever do.

Evidently the *Nightingale* carried passengers. Trunks, stacked in front of the artillery in great rows several feet deep, rendered the cannon useless in an emergency, making it little wonder that the other ship hadn't returned the *Vengeance*'s fire.

"I'll have an answer."

Turning back, Nathaniel focused on the man who addressed him. "You're hardly in a position to make demands," he said smoothly, motioning toward the plethora of baggage stowed in front of the cannons and allowing his lips to curl into a smile.

The captain's face reddened. "You're a fool if you're doing what I think you're doing. There haven't been pirates in these waters for nearly thirty years, and for damn good reason."

Nathaniel's smile turned cold as he let the hostility that smoldered inside him show in his eyes. "Considering your vulnerable situation, I'd certainly be careful who I called a fool, Captain—"

"Merriweather. Captain Thaddaeus C. Merriweather, and I've likely been sailing since before you were born." The old gentleman opened his mouth to say more, then clamped it shut again, obviously struggling to contain the emotions that occasioned this unwelcome boarding.

"I am Dragonslayer," Nathaniel replied. He was tempted to chuckle at the name, but he could hardly identify himself. Sobering, he scanned the faces of the *Nightingale*'s crew once again. He didn't want any surprises. Captain Merriweather behaved like a proud old tar, and his men, collectively a hodgepodge of whiskers, tattoos and handmade clothing, looked almost as tough. Nathaniel wondered how they would have reacted had passengers and their attendant baggage not been a consideration.

"I'm glad you were sensible enough to surrender before there was any loss of life or limb," Nathaniel said. "Especially because I mean no harm to your passengers or your crew. That is to say, we will harm no one as long as you cooperate," he clarified, liking the old man in spite of himself. Obviously a relic from the old school, Merriweather cared about duty and honor. Men like him were entirely too rare.

Captain Merriweather's chest expanded as if to draw one last breath before hearing the worst of it. "Providing your requests are within reason, we'll cooperate," he said reluctantly.

"Your destination is?"

"Liverpool."

"As I thought. Your men will stand aside and keep all passengers out of the way. Some of my crew will board and unload what we can carry of your cargo. When we have what we want, we will leave. Peacefully." Nathaniel gave the man a benign smile. "You will then be free to repair your ship and continue on your way. And of course, to carry the tale of our visit to your benefactor, the most fearsome and noble Duke of Greystone."

Surprise lighted the old man's pale blue eyes. "How did you know who owned—"

"I make it my business to know," Nathaniel interrupted. He turned to Richard. "Send the signal."

On the deck of the pirate ship, Nathaniel braced against the roll and pitch of the waves, listening to the hoots and hollers of his crew as they celebrated their victory. Rum flowed freely among them as first Richard, then his brother John, toasted everything from the speed of the *Vengeance* to Nathaniel's estranged father, the very nobleman they had just confounded.

Nathaniel shook his head when Trenton brought him a mug. "Nay, I'll not ask for a throbbing head come morning," he laughed. "I'm sure the rest of you will drink enough for me."

"Come on. 'Tis only our third ship. Certainly you've got a bit of celebrating left in you."

Nathaniel smiled and relented, taking the proffered cup. "To future successes," he said, and another cheer burst from those who heard him.

"To Mary. We owe what success we've had to her," Richard added.

Lifting his cup high, Nathaniel took a long sip of the warm brew, then reached out to stop Richard before he could volunteer yet another toast. "Speaking of Mary," he said to the burly, redheaded Scotsman, "when do we learn the position of our next target?"

Richard's freckled face took on a mournful pout. "Ah, Mary. I'm afraid the lass is being a wee bit stubborn."

"What do you mean?" Nathaniel asked in alarm. "You said she'd do anything for money."

"Och, well." Richard looked longingly into his drink, as though reluctant to be sidetracked at this particular juncture. "Now she claims the money does her little good. She can't spend it, or her father will know she's up to something and give her a thrashing."

"Why did you not mention this before?"

"Because I think she'll still help us. She just wants something more than money, ye ken?"

"Like what?"

Richard exchanged a look with his brother John, who had come to stand beside them, before turning back to Nathaniel. "She wants to meet you."

"What, does she think I can simply ring the front bell at Bridlewood and introduce myself?" Nathaniel asked.

Richard shook his head, apparently taking Nathaniel's words at face value. "I'd not ask you to do that. Just come with me once. That's all it would take."

"But why does she want to meet me?"

"She's heard rumblings among the older servants about your mother and you, and she says she wants to know that you're real."

"No doubt she wants to have something to gossip about," John put in. "She ain't but seventeen or eighteen. Her days get long in that big house with nothing to break them up but a spot of tea and a juicy tidbit. What else could she want with you? She's in this as deep as we are. If the duke ever discovers that she's been stealing his controller's books and schedules and letting us take a look, he'll send her to Newgate right along with us." He grimaced at the reminder of prison. "Still I, for one, understand if you think it's an unnecessary risk."

Richard glanced at his brother. "I'd say Mary's made it necessary enough. Unless we find another way to get the information we need, we're out of a job. And nothing could be more simple than what we got going—"

"Of course Richard doesn't want to lose Mary. He likes what she gives him along with the information," John exclaimed.

Richard laughed, but Nathaniel didn't find anything to do with his father amusing. "So what do you suggest?" he asked Richard. He had visited the duke's lavish Clifton estate only once, when he was seven, but that day held enough painful memories to last him a lifetime. He had no wish to probe the wound.

"Mary always meets me in the woods near the pond. She can't read, so she brings the books with her. It takes me a few minutes to find out what we need to know, then I pay her and send her on her way . . . or I would if you were with me," Richard added with a devilish grin.

Nathaniel thought for a moment. It wouldn't be easy to replace Mary. As one of the housemaids, she had access to every room in Bridlewood Manor. And being uneducated, she remained above suspicion. "Very well, when we put in at Bristol, send her a message telling her I'll come."

Turning and finding Trenton gone, Nathaniel left Tiny and John to their revelry and went below, where his first mate was already scratching numbers in a large black book.

"Not bad," Trenton said as Nathaniel entered the captain's cabin. "Eighty crates of tobacco. Should bring a good price."

Nathaniel didn't answer. He was still thinking about Mary and Bridlewood and, as always, his father. "What?" he asked, glancing up.

"I said, according to the ledgers, we're doing well. If every ship goes like the *Nightingale* and the one we took a few days ago, it won't be long before we're both rich."

Nathaniel smiled. *Rich* had a pleasant ring to it. Not that he knew from experience. Before Martha was killed, he had grown up in a small shack with her sister, Beatrice, and Bee's eight children. Bee's husband had run off after the birth of their last son—Nathaniel had never known why—but the formula of so many living off so few, namely Martha, destined all to a life of poverty. Though he loathed thinking of it, Nathaniel would never forget the hard, stale bread, the cold winter days without any coal and the dark nights when they'd been too poor to buy candles.

Yes, Nathaniel thought, *if one couldn't be loved, one could at least be warm, comfortable and full, always.* "But it won't be this easy for long," he replied. "These ships were no challenge because their crews hadn't any prior warning. They were at sea before we took our first ship. But word will have gone out now, and things will begin to change."

Trenton grunted. "Nothing ever stays easy for long."

"Like Mary, for instance." Nathaniel stretched out on his bed, propping his arm behind his head.

"What's that supposed to mean?" Trenton's face showed concern.

"She wants to meet me."

His first mate's chair scraped the floor as he shoved the ledgers away and stood up. "Don't tell me you're going to go along with that. If your father catches you at Bridlewood—"

"I know, but we can't lose her. Our whole operation depends on the information she gives us."

"To hell with the operation. You go to Bridlewood, and your life will depend on her, too."

Nathaniel shrugged and gave Trenton a grin. "You, my friend, have a problem with trust."

The hilltop village of Clifton, famous for its pure air and picturesque vistas of the Severn Estuary and the Welsh hills, sat one mile to the west of Bristol, high above the River Frome. Nathaniel had long admired its beauty, and he was not alone. Some of Bristol's wealthiest residents, most of them Quakers, owned homes in Clifton.

Nathaniel and Richard made their way through Bristol, up to Clifton, and then to the duke's country estate where they waited by the pond to meet Mary. They stood in silence, patting the noses of their hired mounts to keep them quiet, as the moon's light peeked through the crooked branches of the many oak trees surrounding the water. Mary was supposed to arrive at midnight, but it was well past that, and Nathaniel was becoming uneasy.

"Does she usually come on time?" He tried to see through the trunks and limbs and leaves that completely blocked his view of the house.

"She's not the most punctual girl I've ever met," Richard responded. "But then, she's never in much of a hurry to get back, either, ye ken?"

Nathaniel saw the gleam of Richard's teeth as his mouth spread into a smile. "I'd find another maid to dally with, if I were you," he replied. "There's no telling what my father would do if he found you here. He's certainly not a man of conscience."

"You worry too much," Richard said. "How could he prove my connection to you?"

"Entirely too easily. You're not nameless and faceless when you board his ships, you know—"

The snap of a twig made Nathaniel fall silent. Someone was coming. His eyes bored into the darkness, but still he jumped when Mary popped out of the trees behind them.

"'Ere I am," she laughed. "Did I scare ye?"

Nathaniel didn't answer. Mary was a wiry young girl with medium-brown hair and a heart-shaped face. She had sharp little teeth and a flat, shapeless figure; nothing much to recommend her, but Richard gave her a hug.

"Did you miss me?"

"No, an' I know better than to believe ye missed me." She laughed again, her eyes turning to Nathaniel with apparent interest. "Oooo, ye did bring 'im. But ye never told me 'e was so 'andsome."

"That's because he's an ugly bloke in the light," Richard responded. "His hair's as black as one of those American savages everyone talks about, not the flaming red of me own, and while I admit his eyes are blue, they sometimes look as pale as ice. You should see him when he gets angry, which I must admit, he does, and entirely too often."

Nathaniel couldn't resist a smile at this quick accounting of his attributes, or lack of them, but he hadn't come to be inspected like a horse. He was ready to get hold of the heavy book Mary hugged to her breast, and doubly eager to be away from Bridlewood.

"Well, 'e wouldn't be 'is father's son if 'e didn't 'ave a temper," Mary responded. "The duke's been a miserable soul ever since the two of ye took that first ship. I can scarcely keep a straight face when 'e starts rantin'. I swear, the mention of ye makes 'im apo-apo . . . what's the word?"

"Apoplectic," Nathaniel replied dryly, deriving a small bit of pleasure from picturing his arrogant father out of his mind with rage.

"That's it. 'E's apoplectic near 'alf the time."

Nathaniel felt the maid's hand on his forearm.

"But 'ow did ye get so tall?" she asked. "Yer a full 'ead taller than yer father."

"Perhaps I've my mother to thank," Nathaniel responded. "May I?" He put his hand out for the book she still held to her flat chest, and finally she shrugged and relinquished it.

"'E's in an awful 'urry," she remarked to Richard, a grimace claiming her plain face.

Nathaniel quickly lit one of the candles he had brought in his pack and laid the book open, searching for the information he needed. The pages were filled with the names of ships; the dates, times and locations of their departures; their destinations; even a list of their anticipated cargo.

Nathaniel smiled as he memorized the schedule for the following two weeks, but the smile froze on his face when he heard voices, men's voices, coming through the trees.

"There's someone at the pond," a stranger shouted. "Come on!"

Running feet pounded the ground, making apprehension prickle down Nathaniel's spine. Whoever it was, they were close. And they were coming closer still.

He glanced up to see a look of shock, then fear, cross Mary's face. Snapping the book closed, he shoved it into her arms and pushed her back into the cover of the trees. "Run," he whispered. "Go back another way and return this. The sound of our horses will draw them after us and keep you safe for a bit, but you must hurry."

Nathaniel leaped onto his horse as Richard did the same, then he glanced around, wondering which direction to go. The water was on one side, their pursuers were on the other, and he had no idea what he might encounter in front or behind him.

"How do we get out of here?" he asked Richard.

Richard shrugged and pointed. "I'll go this way, you go that way. We'll meet back at the tavern, where Trenton is waiting for us." Then he dashed away, leaving Nathaniel to charge ahead in the direction specified and to pray they could both escape.

Chapter 2

Tree branches clawed at Nathaniel's face and clothing as he goaded his horse through the thickest part of the forest. Whoever he had heard back at the lake sounded as though they were on foot, but there was no way to know for sure. God willing, even if they had mounts, he could outdistance them.

After climbing a rocky hill and descending an embankment on the other side, Nathaniel came to a stream. He couldn't hear anyone behind him, but he wasn't about to wait to see if he was being followed. Nudging his horse with his heels, he spurred it into the stream, then gasped as the icy water soaked him almost to his thighs.

Heading up a small dale and around the outskirts of the village, Nathaniel hoped to find Richard as he circled back to the east. But except for a few rambling carriages heading home from some dinner party or play, the road remained empty. Perhaps Richard was ahead of him.

Known for its hot wells and the medicinal spring rising out of Saint Vincent's Rocks, Bristol drew tourists by the droves, and Nathaniel encountered more carriages as he came into the city. He passed Queen's Square, then turned left, heading to Farley's Tavern.

Trenton was waiting there, as planned, when he arrived.

"Where's Richard?" Nathaniel asked, still breathless with excitement.

Trenton looked up from the table in surprise. "What do you mean? He was with you."

Nathaniel glanced around, still wary, then slipped into the booth. "Someone surprised us, and we had to split up."

"Then he'll come." Trenton stared at Nathaniel for a few moments, his fingers drumming agitatedly on the table, then added, "Maybe you should head back to the ship and get ready to sail. With that arm of yours, you'll hardly go unnoticed. I'll wait for Richard."

Trenton's logic made sense. Nathaniel's arm would only increase the chances of getting them all caught if he stayed. Nodding, he stood and tried to imbue his next words with a conviction he didn't feel. "If he hasn't come by three o'clock, we'll have to sail without him."

"God willing, he'll be here by then."

"God willing," Nathaniel repeated, and headed out.

Nathaniel encountered nothing more exciting than a drunk beggar lying amid the garbage in the gutters as he wound through the back alleys of the city toward the wharf.

The ships waiting at the docks tugged and swayed against their ropes, groaning loudly, as if protesting their captivity, while the familiar scents of salt, guano and rotting wood rose to Nathaniel's nostrils. He easily spotted the *Vengeance* and hurried aboard, but the wait proved agonizing.

When Trenton finally arrived at the ship, it was after four in the morning. Unfortunately, he was alone.

"What happened?" Nathaniel asked as soon as his first mate climbed aboard.

"Let's get out of here. Mary sent a note to the tavern. The duke's got Richard."

Nathaniel groaned and dropped his head in his hand. "Did they catch her, too?" he asked, looking up.

"Evidently not. With over fifty servants in the house and on the grounds, it could be some time before your father figures out who you were there to meet. With any luck, he never will."

"We can't leave Richard," Nathaniel said, watching Richard's brother, John, make his way over to them. "I've changed my mind."

"Well change it back. There's nothing we can do for him now," Trenton argued. "The duke has hired some men, and they're scouring the city looking for us."

Nathaniel glanced back at the lights of Bristol and cursed. What now? He hadn't known Richard long, but the man had already proven himself a loyal friend. Still, getting them all caught served no purpose. "Raise anchor," he said at last.

"Wait! We have to go back," John exclaimed.

"No, Trenton's right," Nathaniel told him. "No doubt my father hopes we'll do just that. We've got to outsmart him somehow, get Richard back another way."

"And how are we supposed to do that?" John asked incredulously.

"By using our heads." Nathaniel pinched the bridge of his nose, hoping some brilliant idea would occur to him. "Anything is possible with a little bit of leverage," he said at last. "What if we took something the duke wanted badly enough that he'd be willing, even eager, to trade—"

"Yes!" Trenton slammed a fist into his hand and looked excitedly at Nathaniel. "That could work. What about the cargo from his last ship?"

Nathaniel shook his head. "He's too rich and too angry to give Richard up for money. It has to be something else . . . something he simply can't refuse."

"Wait." A gleam entered Trenton's eye. "Your father has a daughter, doesn't he?"

"Aye." Nathaniel watched Trenton's face split into a smile as his friend's thoughts became obvious. Then a grin tempted the corners of his own mouth. "Aye," he repeated softly, "that he does."

Manchester was famous for its spinning mills. More than seventy sprawled off its wide streets, kingpins amid the pubs, pawnbrokers, rambling warehouses and surrounding slums. Some were four or even five stories high and housed as many as a thousand workers. All were ugly, irregularly shaped giants that hummed and whirred and belched soot into the air through long snouts that turned everything a dismal gray.

Alexandra hardly noticed. She was too accustomed to the factories and the soot they produced to condemn their existence. And she could think of little besides her goal. Would Fobart's manager give her the money? What could she say to convince him?

She cast a furtive glance over her shoulder. Willy had been deeply asleep on the couch when she left, his stubble-covered jaw slack, snores and grunts resounding. But her fear of her stepfather was strong enough to make her believe he would catch her no matter what, and only by taking a firm hold of such emotion was she able to remain committed to her plan.

Readjusting the small bundle of belongings she had quickly gathered and hidden beneath her skirts, she swung Madame Fobart's skirts over her shoulder and strode from the muddy little court where she lived and worked, past Piccadilly Street and into the heart of the city. As she entered the crush of the noon hour, mill workers elbowed past, eager to use the brief respite from work to meet a comrade or get a bite to eat. Merchants hustled about as well, soliciting what business they could. Even a few masters, those who owned or ran the factories, could be seen on the street that day. Their carriages rumbled through town, pulled by fine horses and driven by liveried servants.

Hurrying west, Alexandra forced a smile at the many tired faces she passed as grimy buildings and crowded streets finally gave way to patches of green grass here and there. Small, neatly manicured gardens lay beneath patches of snow, adorning houses that grew steadily larger until Alexandra spotted Madame Fobart's.

The dressmaker's was painted in shades of pink and green and trimmed in white. A rosebush, devoid of blooms, scaled the turned posts of a wide verandah. Stairs led to a massive oak door with a heavy brass knocker. Nothing indicated that the building was anything more than the mansion of an aristocrat or merchant, except for a lace vest hanging on a brass rod outside one of its three plate-glass windows. Anything more obvious would seem vulgar to the genteel class. Madame Fobart's catered to Manchester's elite. The women of the ton came to her for their most exquisite gowns of rich silk or velvet.

And the bonnets! Madame's milliners were some of the most skilled Alexandra had ever seen.

Though Madame Fobart employed a veritable army of seamstresses, skirts were hired out. Alexandra highly doubted Madame's patrons ever faced the fact that impoverished hands stitched part of their gowns. The rich certainly paid enough for their apparel. Alexandra guessed that many of that noble class would faint if they acknowledged the truth, and she cringed at the memory of the tales that had recently circulated. One story told of the death of a great lady made ill by some poor needlewoman who had used the garments she sewed as coverings for her sick child.

Considering the circumstances of many in her profession, Alexandra believed the report. Yet she was so anxious for work, as most were, that she guiltily hoped such stories would not affect her livelihood. Especially now that she would be on her own. It was likely they would not. Hiring out was an excellent way to garner big profits and was by no means exclusive to Madame Fobart's. Skirts could be made without fitting and were easy to sew, with primarily straight seams. Production was the key to success, after all, and spring, the busiest of all seasons, was well on its way.

Alexandra knew better than to call at the front door. She hefted the heavy skirts to her other shoulder and headed to the servants' entrance in back, but today it took several knocks to rouse anyone from inside.

Finally the door opened and a willowy servant stuck her head out. "Yes?"

"I've come to make a delivery," Alexandra said, her voice sounding abnormally loud in the quiet of the afternoon. No doubt Willy would be eager to collect such a large amount once she'd delivered the skirts.

She only hoped she would be well on her way by then. "I hope I'm not too late."

The girl dried dripping hands on her apron. She appeared to be one of the kitchen help, possibly a scullery maid.

"Time doesn't matter much today," she replied. "Almost everybody's at a picnic in the country with Madame 'erself. Even most of the servants, except those of us who 'ad to stay an' prepare the evenin' meal."

"Oh." Alexandra's spirits fell as she realized that her plans to meet Aunt Pauline might be foiled from the onset. "Is there no one here to receive the order, then? I've come all this way."

The girl looked doubtful. "Mr. Calvert is 'ere, but I don't think 'e'll see you. Busy with a client, 'e is."

"But he told me to come today," she said, keeping her voice level. She dared not complain too loudly. Madame Fobart's manager was difficult to deal with on a good day.

"I'm sorry—"

"I'll come tomorrow." Alexandra could hardly stifle her disappointment as she started back through the yard. She would never have enough for the train to London now.

"Wait." Eyeing her heavy load again, the servant called her back. "I could ask 'im, but if 'e sends me packin' for interruptin' 'im, I guess we'll both know it wasn't such a good idea." She flashed an impish smile before retreating into the house.

Alexandra waited on the step for several minutes, tapping her foot. What could be taking so long? The train to London departed at three o'clock, and she knew, time constraints being what they were, she should be on it.

Just when she was about to knock again, the door opened, but it wasn't the willowy maid who poked a head out. It was Mr. Calvert, wearing his usual tight-fitting broadcloth waistcoat and dark, tapered trousers. Surprisingly, his face creased into a smile. "Miss Cobwell, isn't it? Please, do come inside."

He held the door as she passed into a large room just off the kitchen where pegs, normally draped with shawls, lined the walls.

"It's Cogsworth. Alexandra Cogsworth," she corrected, dipping into a brief curtsy.

"Of course." He lifted the skirts from her aching arms and set them on a table.

"I'm sorry to disturb you today, Mr. Calvert—"

"Don't apologize." He waved her words away, baffling her with his uncharacteristic kindness. Madame's manager was always curt, and frugal beyond belief. Alexandra didn't like him. He cared not at all that his hammer-tough negotiations resulted in human beings slaving all day for next to nothing.

"Actually, my dear, your visit is timely," he exclaimed, dabbing at the perspiration on his hairless brow. "Would you believe the daughter of the Duke of Greystone is standing in the drawing room this very minute with a nasty tear in her skirts? And alas! I have no seamstresses. They have all taken the day off. I'd almost forgotten that the skirts were due back until Sonya persisted in making me aware. Then I thought to myself, God has not left me bereft after all. Certainly any needlewoman with half a"—he cleared his throat—"I mean, after all the work we've given to your shop, certainly you could assist me rather than disappoint Lady Anne. Of course, you won't mention that you haven't formerly worked among the finer establishments."

Alexandra hesitated. She was certainly capable of fixing the gown, but time was short. And being invited into the same room as a titled lady was incredible enough, without pretending to be one of Madame Fobart's own girls. Why, every one of them paid a hefty price to apprentice, and for a good number of years before they made a salary as seamstress. Only the best ever became show women, taking measurements, helping to select fabrics and accoutrements, then passing the orders on to others who worked behind the scenes.

Still, Mr. Calvert had presented her with an opportunity. Perhaps it was the opportunity she'd been looking for.

"Actually, my stepfather asked me to collect for the skirts," she said, holding her breath as she looked into Mr. Calvert's watery eyes. "Once I've received payment, I'm sure it would be a small matter to fix the lady's dress."

His eyes narrowed, evidence that he understood her suggestion to be the demand that it was. "Willy usually takes care of such business."

"I know, but he's not well today, and we . . . I mean he . . . he needs the money, you see."

Calvert glanced over his shoulder. "I haven't time to deal with such issues now. After—"

"It shouldn't take but a moment."

He scowled. "Fine. Here." Reaching into his pocket, he shoved several notes toward Alexandra, obviously more worried about the noblewoman awaiting his return than anything else. "Here's at least half, but you'll receive no more until you've finished with my client. You are competent, are you not?"

"Of course." Alexandra's heart pounded as she took the money from Calvert's outstretched hand.

"I've sewed since I was small. But what about my clothes?" She was sure her dress constituted nothing better than a rag by Mr. Calvert's standards.

"Sonya will fetch something that's appropriate. We've a girl who looks to be about your size, though you're quite thin. Come, we mustn't keep Lady Anne waiting."

Alexandra felt gratified by her small victory over Calvert, but still she hesitated. She had never served the rich, her mother's world. The very thought made her jumpy. What if her fingers shook?

Reminded of her hands, Alexandra groaned inwardly. Her mother had been a lady, and she could act the part easily enough. But her hands were working hands. Callused and pinpricked, they were the most obvious sign of her low station.

Before Alexandra could voice her concern, Calvert moved away, obviously eager to return to his influential client. She stared at his broad back as he disappeared down the hall toward the front of the house, then swallowed hard.

Money or not, it was too late to refuse.

Spouting directions in a high, spirited voice, Sonya dropped a silk dress over Alexandra's head. As Mr. Calvert had predicted, it was a bit large. "Do ye know 'ow ter carry yerself?" she asked.

Alexandra nodded, but her answer didn't stop Sonya from offering her own advice on the matter.

"I've seen 'ow they carry on." The maid fixed a small lace cap onto Alexandra's head, one with long streamers of ribbon that fell over her shoulders down to her feet. "As ye know, the best show women are French. Monique meets with the finest clients. She glides when she walks, and smiles sweetly. Of course, she curtsies upon enterin' the room . . . but not such a 'umble curtsy," she corrected when Alexandra attempted the same. "Now, 'old still while I pin yer 'air. Let's see. She laces 'er talk with 'm'lady' this and that, an' speaks nothin' but flatterin' words, lies mostly, but they all seem to like 'er. At any rate, she's the golden calf around 'ere, an' even sups with Mr. Calvert in the evenin'." Sonya drove the last hairpin into place, muttering, "That's the best I can do. I'm no ladies' maid, any more than ye're a real show woman."

"It's fine. How do I look?" Alexandra turned on her toes so Sonya could view her from all sides.

"Beautiful. I wouldn't 'ave guessed it would be so easy, but ye look as good as any show woman I've ever seen, if ye are a mite underfed. Just remember, work quickly and don't say anythin' unless ye 'ave to."

Alexandra nodded again. Physically she stood ready for the charade, but her insides quaked. "Give me a moment to prepare my mind," she pleaded when Sonya hurried her to the door.

"That would only make it 'arder for ye. Come on"—she motioned—"I'm sure Lady Anne is not used to waitin'."

When Sonya ushered her into the vast rectangular drawing room where Mr. Calvert sat with his guest, Alexandra couldn't stop herself from staring. The furnishings were luxurious. Despite her nerves and her self-consciousness, she admired all she saw. Large gilded mirrors alternated with panels of richly textured green wallpaper; and a thick burgundy, green and beige rug stretched across the floor. Three elaborate chandeliers hung from the ceiling, their cut glass twinkling overhead, and heavy burgundy-colored draperies with gold tassels encased the windows.

Alexandra's heels tapped on the shiny wood floor, then sank into the deep pile of the rug as she walked toward the far wall, where a fire burned brightly and two women sat opposite Mr. Calvert. Engrossed in conversation as they sipped tea, they did not bother to look up until Mr. Calvert's eyes darted in her direction.

"My lady, let me introduce Miss Alexandra," he said, finally drawing their attention to her. "She is our new show woman and will mend your gown so you can be on your way. You must be eager to reach your mother. Scotland is so far, after all."

Alexandra's stomach fluttered, and she wished she had eaten. Nourishment of some kind might have steadied her nerves.

Stopping several feet in front of the small group, she curtsied as the women glanced at her before continuing their conversation with Mr. Calvert.

"Yes, poor Mother has been ill over a year and does not seem to improve," Lady Anne complained while Alexandra studied her face. She was a beautiful woman, with coloring not much different than Alexandra's own. Blond hair, coiled into two buns dripping with ringlets above each ear, framed an oval face that held wide green eyes, high cheekbones, full lips and an upturned nose. The maid was rather plain and looked at least ten years older, closer to thirty than twenty.

"I'm sorry to hear such distressing news," Calvert said. "Alexandra will be quick about her work then. She's an excellent seamstress. We just brought her from Londontown where she apprenticed at Lady

Sutherby's." He turned his small eyes upon Alexandra, looking as if he believed his own mistruth.

The falsity of Calvert's words made Alexandra want to duck her head, but she quickly realized that such poor acting on her part would surely give them away. With an effort, she forced her shoulders back and her head up.

Lady Anne's brow rose slightly as she turned to Alexandra.

Calvert nodded. "Well, I'll leave you ladies to your business." Though the words poured easily from his mouth, Alexandra understood the pointed smile that rested on his face. *Do it now and make it fast*, he urged.

Alexandra was grateful that her speech, at least, indicated her own good breeding. "It shouldn't take but a few moments," she promised.

Calvert gave Lady Anne and her maid a sweeping bow before leaving the room, then Alexandra eyed the torn gown with a discerning eye. An elegant day dress made of blue barege, it had a high, plain body that buttoned up the front to the throat. Full bishop sleeves ended in a deep cuff at the wrist, and the skirt had several flounces, each bordered with quilled ribbons.

"My lady, if you will stand before the mirror, I'll have a look at the problem," Alexandra said.

"The tear is here." Lady Anne indicated a spot that looked as though she'd caught her skirt on a nail or some such. "I was tempted to wait until I reached my mother's, but this gown was a gift from her. I'm afraid if I don't have it fixed right away, the damage will become irreparable."

"I see." Alexandra bent to examine the offending flounce. "This shouldn't be too difficult to mend. When I'm finished you won't even know it was there."

After helping the duke's daughter to remove her dress, Alexandra carried it from the room in search of a needle. She did not yet know where she was to find the color of thread she needed, but with twenty seamstresses staying under the same roof, sewing supplies could not be far off.

"How is everything?" Calvert asked. He had been hovering near the portal and nearly pounced on her when she emerged.

"So far, all is well. I need some blue thread and a needle, however, and I have no idea where to find them."

"I'll show ye." Sonya appeared from nowhere, it seemed, and led her upstairs to a large, well-equipped room.

Alexandra found thread in a rainbow of colors and chose the one that best matched Lady Anne's dress. Then the doorbell sounded, and Sonya left to answer it.

It took only a few minutes for Alexandra to stitch the tear. But when she left the sewing room and reached the landing, she stopped short. Her stepfather's voice echoed through the hall below; Willy wasn't more than ten feet away.

Panic raised the hair on Alexandra's arms. She had a good inkling what Willy would do if he found her here and learned she had already collected some of the money for the skirts. She had experienced such retribution before.

Sonya told him Mr. Calvert would be with him shortly and ushered him into a room straight off the bottom of the stair as Alexandra's thoughts flew in a thousand different directions. In a matter of minutes— as soon as Calvert saw her stepfather—Willy would learn the truth. She had to hide!

No, she had to escape! If Willy caught her now, she'd never make the train. Worse, she'd probably be unable to leave the house for several days. She'd miss Aunt Pauline for sure, and lose the opportunity to be free of her stepfather.

Feeling the weight of the money already in her pouch, Alexandra hesitated a mere fraction of a second before racing back the way she had come. She quickly donned Lady Anne's dress, praying that Willy would never recognize her so elegantly garbed, and snatched a bonnet of blue satin and dangling black lace from the workbench of some unknown milliner.

Ducking her head so the lace that cascaded down her back would fall about her face, she crept to the top of the stairs. Calvert was nowhere to be seen, but Willy hovered near the entrance to the room where Sonya had asked him to wait.

How could he have such terrible timing? Alexandra wondered, writhing in the misery of her own bad luck. She had been so close!

Her fingers curled into the palms of her hands as she started down the stairs. It was now or never. She had to escape before Calvert appeared.

Willy glanced up, his attention drawn by the swish of her skirts. His gaze passed over Alexandra like a cold breeze, but she steeled her nerves against it. Keeping her chin tucked resolutely into her chest, she allowed him a clear view only of the black tulle of her cap.

He cleared his throat as Alexandra brushed past, so close she could have reached out and touched him. The fear that seized her at that moment nearly caused her to collapse in a puddle at his feet. She knew he probably expected her to glance up, but she kept her face averted, forcing one foot to step in front of the other as she moved purposefully toward the front door.

The sound of heels clicking on the floor behind her alerted Alexandra to Calvert's approach. His voice confirmed his identity when he called out in confusion.

"My lady! Where are you going? Pray, give me a moment to bid you farewell."

Alexandra didn't so much as pause. The front door was now only a few feet away and she fled through it, nearly tripping on the hem of Lady Anne's gown as she ran down the porch steps.

The footmen waiting with the Kimbolten coach out front jumped to attention. One even moved to open the door before realizing Alexandra was not his mistress.

But before he could speak, five gruff-looking men dressed in sailor's garb rushed the liveried servants, seeming to come from nowhere, as if the shrubs in the yard had suddenly grown arms and legs.

The footmen were knocked senseless with a few bone-crunching blows, and the next thing Alexandra knew, someone was forcing a bag over her head.

She tried to scream, but managed only a squeak unworthy of a mouse as a strong hand coiled around her neck, nearly cutting off her air. Flailing in panic, she began, despite her heavy skirts, to kick at everything and anything she could reach. She hit what felt like a sturdy shin here, perhaps a knee there, but the recipient of her blows seemed impervious. He—Alexandra could tell it was most definitely a he—didn't so much as grunt or stumble, only pulled her hard against a solid chest.

"Tie her up and make it quick," he muttered, letting go of her neck.

Once the bag was in place, he crushed her face into the hollow beneath his shoulder. Alexandra caught the scent of leather, horses and soap through the cloth. Then she heard a strange whimper rise in her own throat as her hands were twisted painfully behind her back and bound with a thick, tarry rope.

"And her feet?"

"Not now."

Whoever held her hefted her easily over a broad shoulder. Then a deep, resonant voice, dripping with resentment, whispered, "Hello, dear sister. So we meet at last."

Chapter 3

Alexandra struggled against the hands that held her fast, but there was little she could do as she landed hard on the floor of Lady Anne's carriage. Her assailants climbed in around her. She could hear their urgent whispers, feel them jostle about. Then a voice said, "Let's go," and the conveyance lurched into motion.

The blackness inside the bag sparked Alexandra's memory of the trunk incident with Willy, causing the same panic to return. Once again caught in a tight, dark place, she writhed in misery. "Help! Let me out," she wailed.

"What's wrong with her?" someone asked. "She's frantic."

"Nothing. She's been pampered and petted all of her life. That's all. She'll be fine," responded the same man who had spoken to her before, calling her "sister."

Alexandra desperately wanted to believe the words spoken by that bitter voice. She *would* be fine, she told herself, over and over again. There *was* enough air to breathe. But something much deeper contradicted anything so rational, and tears began to stream down her face.

"Please. Let me out. I can't be in the dark. I can't breathe!"

Suddenly the hood was yanked off her head. "That's enough!" A man with shocking blue eyes and long black hair pulled back into a queue at his nape, a man Alexandra had never seen before, glared at her. "Tears might work with other men, but they have little effect upon me."

Alexandra gulped as she tried to stifle her tears and suck air into her lungs at the same time. "Who are you? What do you want with me?"

Her blue-eyed captor gave her a glacial smile. "I'm afraid we have never had the pleasure of being formally introduced. I am Nathaniel Kent, your older brother."

"My what?" Alexandra shook her head in confusion. "I have no brother." She struggled to right herself, but with her hands bound behind her back, she could only wiggle helplessly until one of the other men grasped her by the elbow and pulled her into an upright position. She almost thanked him before she caught herself.

Nathaniel chuckled without mirth. "Evidently our dear father has neglected to mention a few minor details regarding his past. But what's a marriage, or a child, for that matter, to a man like him? Nonetheless, I am who I say."

Alexandra studied the men surrounding her. They looked like desperate fellows. Dressed in tattered, homemade breeches and shirts, many wore thick beards and sported jagged, irregular scars on various parts of their bodies. Tattoos decorated bulging biceps: swords, dragons or hearts with the name of some ladylove.

Nathaniel, obviously their leader, was different.

Black tapered trousers revealed a lean, lithe build, and his white, blousy shirt was clean and well made. He possessed handsome, aristocratic features that could have been chiseled from stone: high cheekbones, a strong jaw, a cleft chin. Even while he sneered at her, Alexandra could see that Mr. Kent would be quite appealing to the ladies, if his lips ever curled into a sincere smile. His only physical flaw appeared to be the absence of part of one arm. A wound? A birth defect? Alexandra couldn't tell.

"You haven't answered my other question," she said, recovering her composure. Her circumstances were still forbidding, but at least she was free of the blasted hood. "What do you want with me?"

"Are you truly as oblivious as you would have me believe?" Nathaniel scoffed.

Alexandra lifted her chin and tried to shift into a more comfortable position. Lady Anne's dress was twisted about her legs, hampering what little movement she could manage, but it offered her the only clue to this surprising occurrence. Nathaniel had to have something to do with the duke's daughter. If so, Alexandra need only convince him of her identity, and perhaps he would let her go.

"What if I'm not who you think I am—" She gasped as his hand shot out and long fingers grasped her chin, turning it up toward his face.

"Don't play games with me," he said through gritted teeth. "I watched you go in, and I watched you come out. I know exactly who you are."

Alexandra tried to wrench away, but his fingers dug deeper into her flesh. "You're hurting me," she complained.

"Not half as badly as I'd like to," he replied, then released her from his bruising grip.

"What are you? Some kind of animal?"

Nathaniel grinned, an evil leer, promising in its portent. "Save your compliments for when you know me better."

"I have no intention of knowing you better. I'm not Lady Anne. I swear I'm not." She looked at the circle of faces around her as if searching for verification, but the men were obviously skeptical. "My name is Alexandra Cogsworth. I'm a needlewoman," she continued, hoping to elicit a shred of doubt. "I'm only wearing this dress to escape my stepfather. You have to let me go. I have to catch a train to London—"

"Is Trenton sure about 'er?" the mammoth of a man sitting next to her asked, interrupting the flow of her panicky chatter.

Alexandra's eyes darted to Nathaniel's face.

"Of course he's sure. Pay her no mind. What else can she be expected to say?" He cocked one eyebrow at her as if in challenge, making Alexandra clench her teeth. She wanted to rake her nails across Nathaniel's face. She had suffered enough at Willy's hands to last her a lifetime. She had no intention of allowing another man to take his place. Nor did she intend to let this band of cutthroats make her miss her train to London and Aunt Pauline—her train to freedom.

"Please. You must listen to me." She lowered her voice, keeping a tight rein on her temper. "I'm not who you think I am. Ask anyone. Stop. Let me out."

"Gag her," Nathaniel responded, and a stout, muscular man withdrew a long strip of white cloth from a satchel.

"No! Please! You must believe me. If I don't make it to London soon, I'll miss—" The gag reduced Alexandra to squeals, but she refused to fall silent.

Wild with fright and more than a little angry, she continued to grunt and kick, banging about until she slipped from her seat and landed, hard, on the floor.

"Damn hellion." Instead of moving her back to the seat, Nathaniel held her ankles while another man tied her feet together. Then he leaned back and crossed his feet on top of her, as if it were the most natural thing in the world to do, and all but the huge man followed suit.

Alexandra couldn't move anymore. The weight of their legs made her sag in exhaustion, and she lay, covered in a sheen of sweat, trying to draw enough air through the thick cloth to recover her breathing. She had indeed escaped Willy—and now she was heading straight for the fiery furnaces of hell.

Nathaniel's gaze came to rest on her face, but he said nothing to her. Instead, he rapped on the roof. "How much longer?"

A voice issued from the driver's seat: "If we continue at this clip, maybe thirty, forty minutes."

"Then go faster," Nathaniel responded. "The constabulary will be nipping at our heels at this rate."

After another four or five miles, the carriage began to slow. Alexandra wondered where they were. She was disoriented, and she couldn't see anything through the window except a round spot of blue sky. Only the smell of hay and manure and green things growing led her to believe they were in the country somewhere, far from the filthy confines of Manchester.

"Sit her up and take off the gag," Nathaniel said as he opened the door and jumped to the ground. "I think she might be willing to behave herself now."

The same man who had gagged her removed the cloth, leaving Alexandra's lips feeling swollen. She stretched her jaw to make sure it still worked and took a deep breath, grateful to fill her lungs with air again. "Where are we?" she asked.

The large burly fellow, who took up twice his share of room, began to respond. "On our way to Liv— *Oop,*" he gasped as the short, stocky man sitting next to him elbowed him in the ribs.

"Don't tell her anything, Tiny." The stocky man turned narrow eyes on Alexandra before hopping to the ground himself. Then the others, three in all, filed out after him. Tiny was the last to go.

"I know ye ain't used to bein' treated so rough and such, miss, I mean, m'lady," he explained. "An' Nathaniel ain't a bad bloke. He wouldn't 'ave bothered ye if yer father 'adn't gone an' nabbed—"

"Tiny, get out here." Nathaniel scowled at them both through the door. "She's not hurt."

"No, sir. She ain't. But she ain't used to bein' treated like this, an' I was only tryin' to explain that we didn't want to do this. 'Twas the only way."

Nathaniel rolled his eyes. "I'm sure she feels much better now. If you're finished apologizing, we're ready."

"Aye, sir." Tiny's small brown eyes, mere slits in his fleshy face, looked back at Alexandra. "Excuse me, m'lady," he said and heaved his large bulk outside.

Nathaniel waited for Tiny to clear the door before leaning in again. "Come on, Miss High and Mighty, this is where we part with your carriage." Grabbing Alexandra's ankles, he slid her across the floor toward him. Then he wrapped his arm around her waist. "I can't promise you a better seat, but I must insist you join us."

"You're making a big mistake," Alexandra told him as he brought her up against his chest.

He gave her a devilish grin. "I'm sure it wouldn't be my first."

He carried her to a less conspicuous conveyance hidden in a copse of trees, a rented vehicle that looked more like an old stagecoach, and dumped Alexandra on the floor once again.

"Trenton, let Tiny drive," he called, and the carriage swayed dramatically as Tiny hefted himself up top.

A tall, stringy man Alexandra hadn't seen before climbed inside. Fair-complexioned, with strawberry-blond hair and brown eyes, he looked almost as out of place amid the other ruffians as Nathaniel did.

"Do you think we can make it before nightfall?" Nathaniel asked him.

"Not by a long shot. These old nags aren't quite the animals your sister had pulling her around"—Trenton cast Alexandra a sideways glance—"but hers are lathered and need to rest. I'm not sure it would be wise to wait."

"They're not my horses. And that's not my carriage." Alexandra took a deep breath, hoping a simple, rational explanation might finally convince them. "I told you, my name is Alexandra Cogsworth. I'm simply a seamstress who put on this dress to escape my stepfather. And I have to make it to London in four days, or I'll miss my boat to India."

Nathaniel looked quizzically at her while Trenton stifled a laugh. "Perhaps we're doing the Indians a favor, then."

Alexandra shook her head in exasperation. "If I could, I'd show you my hands. I'll wager that you've not seen a lady born to the nobility with calluses like mine. They come from hard work, not the kind of idle stitchery performed in drawing rooms after an eight-course meal."

Nathaniel reached behind Alexandra and turned up her palms. He studied them for a moment, then looked to Trenton.

"I don't know how she got those," Trenton admitted, "but I told you, she's Anne all right."

Alexandra groaned. It didn't help that she and the duke's daughter had similar builds and coloring. "When was the last time any of you saw Lady Anne?"

"What was it, four or five years ago?" Nathaniel asked.

"It had to have been at least four. I saw her with your father in London," Trenton said. "Remember?" He turned to Alexandra. "But I'll never forget your face."

Alexandra rolled her eyes. "Do you realize what you're saying? You've kidnapped a woman based on someone you saw four years ago."

"And I suppose Greystone's carriage sitting outside that dressmaker's doesn't count for anything?" Trenton replied. "We saw you go in, remember?"

"I can explain that," Alexandra said, and she tried to do so. But they purposefully ignored her. Talking among themselves, they left her to stew in her frustration.

"Let's try and make it to Liverpool tonight," Nathaniel said. "If the horses need a break, we can stop at a posting station."

Alexandra finally fell silent and listened to every word that followed, trying to learn why she had been captured and what Nathaniel and his men had planned for her. If they wouldn't let her go, she'd have to escape somehow.

But they said little to illuminate the mystery. Besides a few references to a ship docked at Liverpool, they spoke only of cargo and auctions and supplies. Still, the farther they took her from Manchester, the more frightened she became. If she missed Aunt Pauline, she'd be on her own.

What would they do when they eventually learned her true identity? she wondered. What would they do if they didn't? Alexandra worried and fumed until, finally, the incessant rocking of the carriage made her too tired to keep up her vigil, and she slept.

Alexandra woke suddenly. She had been dreaming. Willy was beating her again. She had to get away. But as her eyes blinked open, moonlight filtering through the small window above her head illuminated the five gruff men who had abducted her. Willy was nowhere around. Only the pain was real. Her hands and feet were numb below the ropes that held them fast. They were beginning to swell, and her back ached terribly, as if she'd been sitting on the same hard floor for a week.

"Untie me."

Nathaniel glanced up at the sound of her voice. The others had nodded off. A few were even snoring. He had been sleeping, too, but came instantly awake when she spoke, making Alexandra wonder if he ever lowered his guard.

"No." He closed his eyes again.

"Please. I can't feel my hands. Or do you think I might actually overpower the five of you if given my freedom?"

"I don't fear you in any way." He didn't bother to look up.

"Then you're simply being cruel."

Blue eyes regarded her beneath half-open lids. "You've no idea of the meaning of the word, although your father is certainly a master of the discipline."

"So he's *my* father now? I don't even know the man. But a few hours ago, he was *our* father, if I remember correctly."

"Sometimes I'm loath to make the connection." Nathaniel sighed and shifted in his seat.

"If he's anything like you, that's understandable," Alexandra muttered. Struggling against her bonds, she tried to relieve the swelling in her hands. "What is it you want from me?"

"I want nothing from you. You are only a pawn."

"So you don't hate me personally. Only my father. Or rather, this duke of, what is it, Greystone?"

"You're more astute than I would have guessed."

"If you have nothing against me, then untie me."

A lazy smile told her he wasn't even tempted. "If I unloose your claws, I'd not get any sleep. I can hardly believe the hellcat we carried away from Manchester would sit, docile."

"A brougham is coming up from behind," Tiny called from the driver's seat.

Nathaniel tensed and sat up. "At this pace?"

"What is it?" Trenton asked, yawning.

"Someone is about to overtake us," Nathaniel explained. "Pull off the road on the down slope of the next hill as soon as you can find sufficient cover," he called back to Tiny. "We can't outdistance anyone with these nags."

"Who do you suppose it is?" asked a man with the shadow of two or three days' beard growth.

"I don't think it's anything to do with us. But we can't be too sure." Nathaniel leaned over and opened the door, sticking his head out to peer behind them.

A biting cold wind smelling of heather and gorse rushed into the carriage, making Alexandra shiver. While the day had been warm, the night promised to be chilly, and she had fled Madame Fobart's without so much as a cloak.

"They're too far back for me to see," Nathanial reported.

Alexandra pictured an approaching vehicle, its corner lanterns cutting through the night, and wondered who it could be. Nathaniel, no doubt, feared it was the duke, or someone who served his interests, coming after Lady Anne. But Alexandra doubted Greystone had reason to pursue them beyond retrieving his carriage. Why would he care about the abduction of a mere needlewoman?

Alexandra thought it might be Willy. While he owned no carriage, he could have rented one. Rushing to her rescue was definitely out of character, but trying to retrieve something that belonged to him was not. She had half the money for the skirts, and she made his living. He'd be loath to lose her, for all of his abuse.

Suddenly the carriage ground to a halt, and the three men sitting on Alexandra's right nearly landed on the floor on top of her. She was thrown against Nathaniel's and another man's knees. Then they were all jarred back and forth as Tiny headed off the road, presumably toward some kind of cover. When they finally stopped, everyone except Nathaniel jumped out, each pulling a knife from his boot or a pistol from his belt.

"Conceal yourselves well," Nathaniel cautioned in a low voice. "We don't want a fight unless we're forced to it."

"I'll take a fight whenever I can get one," someone whispered back with a coarse laugh.

"Not tonight. We've better things to do with our time," Nathaniel told him.

The door slammed shut as the sound of horses galloping down the road grew loud. Alexandra hated the thought of seeing Willy again, yet she prayed for some kind of rescue. The manner in which her kidnappers had drawn their weapons left little doubt that they knew how to use them, or that they would hesitate should the need arise.

Nathaniel bent down to grab Alexandra by the arm and pull her up against him. "Just in case you have any idea of screaming," he said, "I wouldn't." Producing a gleaming six- or seven-inch stiletto, he held it to her neck.

The brougham was close now. The rumbling of horses, iron wheels and creaking wood vibrated the ground. Alexandra could scarcely breathe, but she could feel the razor-sharp edge of the knife pressed to her skin, could almost taste its metallic blade.

Nathaniel thought she was Lady Anne. By his own admittance, she was a pawn he planned to use against the Duke of Greystone. Certainly, he wouldn't be foolish enough to kill her and lose his advantage. Or would he?

The glimmer of a lantern appeared outside whilst the horses beat their quick tattoo in the dirt. Whoever traveled the lonely road wasn't slowing down. In a few seconds, her only hope of rescue might be gone.

Twisting slightly, Alexandra sank her teeth deep into the hand that held the knife, then she screamed with an abandon she had never known.

Nathaniel cursed and lunged on top of her. She fully expected the blade to slice her throat. Instead, he threw it away, letting it clatter to the floor as he shifted his grip on her. Scarcely had her voice risen on the night air than Nathaniel used the only thing available to him to silence her: his mouth. The salty taste of his blood, still on her lips, filled her mind as his tongue forced its way between her teeth, stifling her cry for help.

Somehow reluctant to bite again, Alexandra writhed, attempting to free herself, to gasp for air, to scream again. But without the use of her hands or feet, she could do little. Nathaniel was too strong, too big. He stretched out, lying on top of her, until she couldn't move at all.

Spent, she listened to the receding sounds of the passing carriage until only an echo remained.

She was helpless.

Nathaniel's breath warmed Alexandra's ear. His heart thumped, almost audibly, above her own, but he didn't move for what seemed like a long time. When finally he rolled off, she gasped at the anger in his face.

"You're lucky you didn't do this to Garth," he told her, looking at her teeth marks in his hand. "Some of my men are not so long-suffering as I. Next time, you'll wear a gag and a hood." He ripped a piece of silk from the hem of her dress with his teeth, then wound it around his wound.

Alexandra swallowed hard, knowing he meant every word. She had gambled on the brougham, but her wager hadn't paid off.

And now Nathaniel held all the cards.

They reached Liverpool late in the night. Alexandra was exhausted. The ropes around her hands cut deep into her wrists, but she dared not complain, not while the bandage around Nathaniel's hand was stained red with his blood.

"Get me a room," Nathaniel told Tiny when they stopped outside an inn called the Turnbull Tavern. "I'll stay here with our fair captive while the rest of you head back to the ship. If I haven't heard anything from my father in three days, I'll meet you on board."

"An' what will ye do with 'er in that case? Turn 'er loose?" Tiny asked hopefully.

"I'll turn her loose when Greystone releases Richard, and no sooner," Nathaniel replied as the rest of them climbed out, "just like our message said."

"But—"

"Tiny, now isn't the time to develop a conscience," Trenton piped up. "None of us likes capturing defenseless females any more than you do, least of all Nathaniel. Just follow orders and everything will work out all right."

"Aye, sir." Tiny glanced at Alexandra. "But she may be nothin' like the duke."

"And she might be a lot like him." Nathaniel saluted Alexandra where she sat, still on the floor of the carriage, with his injured hand. "She's certainly not as defenseless as one might suppose."

Alexandra didn't respond. She felt as though she'd been dragged for miles, and she couldn't wait to sleep on something softer than the floor of the old carriage. The last thing she wanted right now was an argument.

She watched Tiny's broad back disappear into the inn, a Tudor-style building on one of the wider streets in town, before it occurred to her that her situation might not have improved. Where was she going to sleep? Nathaniel had told Tiny to rent only one room, and she doubted he'd be kind enough to give her the bed. The only thing in her favor was their supposed close relation. It precluded the possibility of her being raped as well as kidnapped, especially now that the others were returning to their ship.

"What if Greystone wants to exchange? Will you send for us first?" Trenton asked.

"I'll not arrange a meeting with him, if that's what you mean. It would be a trap. When I have proof that Richard is free, I'll leave Anne with money enough to get home, and we'll be far away by the time she makes it."

Alexandra sighed in despair at this revelation. She could languish as their captive for an eternity before the Duke of Greystone released Nathaniel's man. He'd surely not act on her account, not when his own daughter was safe and sound in Manchester, or Scotland, or wherever it was Lady Anne's mother lived.

"Good enough," Trenton said. "We'll be ready to sail when you arrive."

Tiny returned with a key for Nathaniel. "The steward will bring ye some food," he said. "Yer room is up the stairs, first door on the right."

Nathaniel turned to Alexandra. "Are you ready, *m'lady*?" he mocked.

"Aren't you going to cut me loose?" she asked. "You can't very well carry me in there like this."

"You've got a point." Turning to Garth, Nathaniel said, "I'll need the gag and the hood, I believe."

"No! I won't make a sound. I promise." Alexandra pressed back as far away from him as she could. "I can't bear the thought of that hood. Please, don't put it back on."

"Why does it bother you so?" Trenton asked curiously, but Alexandra didn't answer, knowing they wouldn't believe her anyway.

She kept her eyes trained on Nathaniel. "I won't so much as murmur, I swear."

"Forgive me if I tend to be doubtful of someone who would like nothing more than to bring the whole place down around me."

Climbing back inside, he took Alexandra by the shoulders. "Tie it on while I hold her, will you Trenton?"

Trenton paused. "She has such an aversion to that bag. Isn't there another way? What if I carried her up the back stairs?"

Nathaniel hesitated. "We can't risk it. We might encounter someone. Just tie it on. She'll survive."

Alexandra thrashed about, resisting them until they were grunting and breathing heavily with the effort. "She's certainly got spirit," she heard one of them exclaim when both the gag and the hood were finally in place.

"I hate to see her abused too badly," Trenton replied.

"She's just spoiled," Nathaniel scoffed. "Don't you go soft on me like Tiny."

"But look at her."

Alexandra couldn't stop the spasms that began to rack her body as soon as the hood was knotted securely about her neck. She had to breathe through the bag and the wadded strip of cloth as well, and it felt for all the world as though she'd suffocate.

"We've got to take it off," Trenton exclaimed. "She's having a fit."

"Or she'd like us to think so. Just throw my cloak over her so it will look like I'm carrying my sleeping wife up to our room. Quickly," Nathaniel demanded. "The hood will come off soon enough."

Nathaniel scooped Alexandra up while Trenton covered her with his cloak. "It'll only be a minute," he assured her. Then she felt herself being carried swiftly into the stifling hot inn. A piano played in the background, originating from what sounded like a crowded tavern, but the pungent smell of tobacco smoke was the last thing she remembered.

Nathaniel felt Anne go limp in his arms. Was this some kind of trick? His sister was more of a fighter than he ever dreamed she would be, especially after having been raised with everything she could ever want. He had expected Anne to prove herself a simpering female, duly frightened of him and his men. But this woman was strong and resourceful. Or she was used to manipulating others to achieve her own ends. He couldn't decide which.

He shook her, attempting to elicit some response.

Anne's head lolled on his shoulder.

Nathaniel began to worry that something might really be wrong. Scaling the stairs as quickly as possible, he flung back the door to their room and laid her on the bed. Then he removed the hood and the gag.

She was unconscious. Nathaniel stared down at her, feeling a twinge of guilt at having abducted a completely innocent woman. His half sister was not to blame for the way his father had treated him, but Nathaniel could figure no better way to obtain Richard's release. And his friend had to come first.

With his stiletto, Nathaniel cut the ropes that bound her wrists and ankles. Then he began to massage her hands and feet, trying to improve the blood flow. He had heard much about his sister's beauty. Looking at her now, he had to admit that the reports fell far short of reality. Silky strands of long golden hair, loosened from her coiffure, gleamed around a delicate oval face. Thick lashes rested on her cheeks. She had a small, pert nose and a full, sensual mouth. Nathaniel couldn't help but remember the feel of her soft lips beneath his own. That he'd actually enjoyed the sensation greatly bothered him.

He had to be careful, or he would become as weak willed as Trenton and Tiny. Though he had never seen Anne before, she was his half sister. She and a son had been born to the duke and his second wife after the death of Nathaniel's own mother, and anything so closely connected to Greystone was—had to be—anathema to him.

Nathaniel dropped Anne's hand when her eyes fluttered open.

"Where am I?" she asked, then groaned when she saw him. "I hoped you were just another bad dream. But dreams don't taste like blood, do they?"

"No." Nathaniel turned as a knock resounded at the door. "That's our supper. You're hungry, no doubt."

Anne rubbed her temples as though trying to relieve a headache. "Among other things," she said dryly. "Providing meals must be one of the problems associated with abducting people."

Nathaniel paused to look back at her. "Keeping them sane is another. That hood makes you a little crazy."

"I wasn't afraid of the dark before . . ."

"Before what?"

"Before Willy."

The knock came again. Nathaniel crossed the room to answer it. "Who's Willy?" he asked, his hand on the knob.

Anne sighed. "You wouldn't believe me if I told you."

Supper consisted of poached salmon, jacket potatoes, cut greens, leg of mutton and several dishes Alexandra didn't recognize. She ate ravenously. She had seldom experienced such sumptuous fare and had no intention of letting any of it go to waste, despite her circumstances.

The food seemed to appeal to Nathaniel less. He sat back and watched her, occasionally tipping a glass of wine to his lips.

"Do you always eat so voraciously?" he asked in amazement when Alexandra ladled seconds onto her plate. "Or is it your strategy to break me before your father can send for you?"

She glanced up to see a smile play at the corners of his mouth.

"I haven't had a bite to eat all day," she complained. "Besides, food takes my mind off the pain in my hands and feet. They ache terribly, you know."

His brows lifted. "Yes, you look as though you're in a great deal of pain."

"I am," Alexandra cried indignantly. "You and your men are brutes to keep me tied up all day."

"I'm holding you for ransom. Isn't that what I'm supposed to do?"

He was teasing her. Alexandra ignored him, savoring her last bite of a delicious pudding she had never tasted before and could not now identify. The hotel room wasn't large, but it was clean. Decorated in ivory and green and furnished with a tester bed, an elaborate washstand with a tiled back, a large wardrobe and a thick pile rug to cover the wood floor, it lacked only a fireplace. Had Alexandra been staying at the inn for any other reason, she might have found it quite comfortable.

"If you consume so much when you're hurt and upset, I'd hate to see what you require when you're not. I pray you don't forgive me," he chuckled, intruding upon her thoughts.

"There's not much danger in that." Alexandra tried to put some fire into her words, but it was difficult to sound angry when she was so full and sleepy. Besides, she had been right about Nathaniel. He was exceptionally handsome when he smiled. She let her gaze slide over his face, feeling a blush rise to her cheeks as she remembered the feel of his tongue parting her lips.

"I'm glad to see that you're at least as tired as I am," he commented, oblivious to the course of her thoughts. "Otherwise, it would be difficult to sleep on the floor."

She grimaced, wondering how she could have thought him appealing only a moment before. He was a black-hearted scoundrel, nothing more. "I expected as much. You'd think you'd treat your sister with at least a little kindness and respect." Alexandra knew she was foolish to play on Nathaniel's belief that she was Lady Anne, but his haughtiness goaded her. "Do I at least get a blanket or a pillow?"

"You'll get what you earn."

Alexandra set her fork on the table with a thunk. "What does that mean?"

"I could use a good massage."

"Hire a maid."

"Why should I, when I've got you? Besides, I can't exactly bind and gag you and sit you in the corner. And I can't invite anyone to my room with you on the loose."

Alexandra picked her fork back up and twirled it thoughtfully. "Only if I can earn the bed," she said at last. "An hour's massage for one night of sound sleep."

"A massage from a woman unused to giving that sort of thing—of giving anything—isn't worth the bed. My best offer is a pillow and a blanket."

"I have strong hands." Alexandra stood, rounded the table, and began to knead his shoulders.

He moaned. "Very well. You can earn the bed."

Alexandra smiled to herself. Mayhap she could cause Nathaniel to lower his guard after all.

When Nathaniel had set their dishes outside the door, he removed his shirt, exposing broad shoulders that tapered to a lean waist. A matting of dark hair covered his chest, trailing down his flat stomach to a mysterious end somewhere below his belt.

Alexandra had to fight the impulse to stare. This man was a criminal. He had abducted her. Yet she could not explain the tremor that went through her at the sight of his naked torso.

With effort, she pulled her gaze away and had him lie across the bed. She was not experienced with massage to any great extent, though sometimes her fellow needlewomen relieved the aches and pains caused from long hours of sitting by rubbing one another's backs. Alexandra felt somewhat confident she could improvise from there. Of course, Nathaniel expected her to have received many massages over her lifetime. Such luxury was a favorite pastime of the aristocracy.

Nathaniel's back was smooth and tanned to a honey brown. Though Alexandra couldn't help noticing his narrow hips, firm buttocks and long legs, it was his deformed arm that held her interest the longest. It was misshapen, to be sure, but it wasn't a hideous appendage. The same golden skin covered it as the other.

"What's wrong?" Nathaniel's eyes seemed to measure Alexandra carefully. "Are you going to give me a massage, or do you share our father's distaste for my deformity?"

Alexandra glanced away, embarrassed to have been caught gaping at him. "I was just wondering how I was going to get you off the bed should you fall asleep on it," she lied.

"You wouldn't get me off. You'd run away. That's why I won't fall asleep."

Alexandra smiled in spite of herself. He thought he had guessed her plan. Perhaps she could surprise him.

Climbing onto the bed, she positioned herself on her knees for maximum strength, then began to smooth out the corded muscles in Nathaniel's back and neck. An occasional sigh told her she was successful in her desire to relax him, and to her surprise, she soon found herself enjoying her work. Nathaniel's physical attributes were exceptional, from his thick black hair to his cleft chin. And there was something sensual about the way he smelled—all dust and sweat, leather and horses.

As Alexandra's hands glided over his warm skin, she wondered about the vendetta between Nathaniel and the Duke of Greystone. Why did Nathaniel hate his father so badly? Why would he risk a hangman's noose to capture his sister? And what would he do when he finally learned that she was not Lady Anne?

Alexandra dismissed the last question as irrelevant. She wouldn't be around to find out. She'd be well on her way to London and to the safety of her aunt.

Nathaniel's eyes closed, and Alexandra felt the tension leave his body. She doubted he was asleep, but she only needed to dull his reaction by a fraction of a second. Keeping one hand working the muscles on each side of his spine, she reached back for the stiletto he kept in his right boot.

Groaning softly when her fingers touched a particularly tender spot, Nathaniel shifted as if to make himself more comfortable. Alexandra almost had the knife. Gently lifting the leg of his pant, she quickly grasped the handle and pulled. The stiletto slid easily from its place, but Nathaniel's reflexes were quicker than her own. He had her on her back, pinned beneath him, before she could threaten him in any way.

"It would seem my massage is being cut short, so to speak." He grinned, squeezing her hand until she dropped the knife. "Too bad. It felt good while it lasted, perhaps proving that even you have a few redeeming talents. Now I shall enjoy a good night's rest while you languish on the floor."

"You had no intention of giving me the bed. You were only using it to bait me."

"Let's just say that I have now learned what I needed to know. At least I won't feel guilty while you sit on the floor, tied like a dog to the post."

Alexandra tried to free her hands from his punishing grip. She wanted to wipe that enraging smirk off his face. "I'll scream if you bring that rope near me."

"Then I'll gag you. For someone who hates a hood, you're willing to risk much."

"You're a cad."

"Which is far better than a fool, and a fool I'd be to let you get the better of me."

His eyes glittered like sun glinting off a blue sea, and Alexandra realized that Nathaniel might be many things, but a fool he was not. He had the senses of a cat, and the athletic prowess to match.

"Let me up," she said. "You're hurting me."

"Certainly." Kicking the knife far away from her reach, Nathaniel let her go. "No doubt you're ready to retire, now that sleeping arrangements have been made."

Almost before Alexandra knew her own mind, her hand lashed out and slapped Nathaniel's jeering face. They both rocked back, surprised when her palm hit its target with such force. A red welt appeared almost instantly.

"I'm glad you're so eager to deserve whatever treatment you receive," he said, grabbing her by the arm and dragging her to the foot of the bed. "I was going to leave you enough rope to lie down, but with your peculiar brand of wisdom, you'd only hang yourself with it."

"No!" Unwilling to suffer the pain and degradation of being tied up all night, Alexandra began to struggle again. But it was only a matter of minutes before her hands were bound in front of her and then tied to the bed. As Nathaniel had promised, she didn't have enough rope to lie down.

"You'd better hope I don't get free," she threatened. "You have to sleep sometime."

"I'll take my chances," he replied. "Perhaps I'm giving you too much credit, but if you do manage to get loose, it wouldn't be a good idea to bother with me. The door is that way."

"Oh . . . you! You're insufferable!" Bringing her knees up between her arms, Alexandra laid her head down and tried to block Nathaniel from her consciousness. She soon realized, however, that she would have to address him again.

"You've got to untie me. I've got to . . ." she stopped, wondering how to tell him what she needed. "A lady needs a little privacy occasionally."

He crossed the room and retrieved the chamber pot from its place behind a cloth curtain in one corner of the room.

"You're not going to untie me?" Alexandra asked in surprise.

"You don't deserve it."

"But how will I—"

"You'll figure it out."

"I deserve to take care of natural bodily functions without you watching my every move."

"Don't flatter yourself. I have no interest in watching you." He stretched out on the bed, lying on his stomach, his face buried in the crook of his arm.

Alexandra made no move until she thought Nathaniel was asleep. "Boar . . . ogre," she muttered to herself. "I hope your father catches you and hangs you from the tallest tree."

He didn't respond.

She pulled and twisted on the rope, but the knot proved tight and well made. She only managed to jerk the bed a few inches from the wall.

"Hold still," Nathaniel snapped, rolling onto his back and covering his eyes with his arm.

Alexandra glared at him. "There will come a time, when I will even the score."

"Plan your revenge tomorrow," he told her. "Get some sleep. You might need it."

With a sigh of defeat, Alexandra waited as long as she could before relieving herself. Then she eyed the screen dubiously, wondering how to return the pot to where it belonged. She certainly had no desire to sleep with it.

Suddenly a wicked thought made her lips curl into a smile. Grabbing the enamel pot around the base, she prepared to launch it right on top of Nathaniel, smelly contents and all, when a cutting voice gave her pause.

"You can't imagine the terror of what I will do to you if you don't put that thing down immediately."

So he was awake. Alexandra's smile withered. He didn't move to stop her, didn't so much as remove his arm from across his eyes, but she got the feeling he was almost daring her to incur his full wrath.

She clung to the pot for a long time, so sorely tempted that she had a difficult time letting wisdom overtake desire. When she finally set it down, she did so carefully, to ensure it wouldn't splash on her, then pushed it as far under the bed as she could. If she made Nathaniel too angry, she'd start a fight she could only lose. And she didn't want to incite his imagination as to the possibilities of what a strong man could do to a captive woman. He was a scoundrel if ever she'd met one. But he was right about one thing. Tomorrow was another day, and she'd do her best to make it as miserable for him as possible.

Chapter 4

Nathaniel feigned sleep until Anne finally nodded off. He couldn't rest while she sat on the floor without so much as a blanket. That he admired her despite himself enraged him. She was certainly unlike the women of her class, most of whom were priggish and without an enlightened thought in their heads.

Anne was quick-witted, courageous and demonstrative. Nathaniel glanced with chagrin at his bandaged hand. Not many women he knew, or men for that matter, would have risked what she did to attract the attention of that brougham. It was a smart move. She knew he couldn't harm her if he wanted to trade her for Richard. She had taken a calculated risk, and Nathaniel considered himself lucky that it hadn't panned out for her.

He frowned, glancing down at the foot of the bed where Anne's head kept nodding off its perch upon her knees. She was indeed a brave girl. Every victory he obtained at her expense was hard-won. Perhaps he could be a little easier on her.

Nathaniel untied the rope around the post, cursing himself for being a softhearted fool. Using his good arm for strength and his stump for balance, he gently lifted Anne and laid her on the other side of the bed. She stirred but didn't come fully awake. Then he fastened the rope to the post above her head and covered her with blankets.

Lying back down, Nathaniel moved carefully so he wouldn't wake her. It had been a long day. He watched his captive curl into a ball, giving the appearance of almost childlike innocence, and felt a flicker of desire at the sight of her more feminine curves.

Shocked by his body's effrontery, he quickly diverted his thoughts. Anne was his sister. Beyond that, she had been raised with everything he had been denied—the money, the power, the family. He should hate her.

And he did, Nathaniel told himself. It was just that any woman so fair of face and form would make his pulse quicken. But when he fell asleep, he dreamed of long blond hair spilling down onto his naked chest. And the woman above him was Anne.

He woke suddenly, disgusted that his subconscious would betray him with such incestuous fantasy. It had been too long since he had enjoyed the company of the fairer sex, he decided. Planning to remedy that as soon as he could and thereby put a quick end to the madness of his mind, he shifted in the bed to ease a cramped muscle and felt Anne's womanly softness pressed to his backside. She had migrated the full length of the rope toward him, instinctively searching for the warmth his body radiated.

Nathaniel swallowed hard as the flicker of desire he had experienced earlier flared again, fanned by his dream and the wonderful feel of her. Anne had no idea where she was, he knew, and he smiled to think of how she might react if she were to awaken at this moment.

No doubt she'd try to hit him again. He touched his cheek where she had slapped him earlier and decided he was glad her hands were tied.

Anne murmured something unintelligible, then snuggled more closely against him. He decided not to disturb her. Though he dared not allow himself to touch the flesh that molded so comfortably to his side, the light scent of perfume that clung to her clothes was a treat in itself.

Alexandra woke by degrees. Sun filtered into the room through a large gap in the draperies, which had been drawn across the window. For a moment she imagined herself in her own bed. She burrowed deeper into the quilts, luxuriating in their warmth, until something, or rather, someone, moved. Then the events of the previous day came back to her in a flood of remembering. Nathaniel! What was he up to now?

Her eyelids flew open, but she couldn't see him. He was behind her, his chest to her back, his legs curving beneath her buttocks. The last thing she recalled was the cold, hard floor. How did she come to be in his bed?

Lying very still, Alexandra listened as Nathaniel's slow, regular breathing tickled the hair above her ear. His body was relaxed, formed comfortably to her own. She was certain he was asleep. But he was more like a black panther than a man. Sleek, well muscled, always wary, he could pounce anytime. She'd have to be very careful.

Cautiously inching away, Alexandra wondered again how she came to be in that cozy spot. She had never been so close to a man. Willy had kept her closeted away, toiling in the house or garret. The pleasures typically associated with intimacy remained a complete mystery, but the feelings she'd experienced in those first moments of wakefulness had spoken volumes. She had felt more content, more complete, than ever before. In a way, that revelation frightened her almost as much as Nathaniel did. If all men were like her stepfather, they weren't to be trusted.

At the edge of the bed, Alexandra let her feet slide silently to the floor. A backward glance confirmed that Nathaniel's sooty lashes still rested on his cheeks. His chest, broad and golden, continued to rise and fall gently. He didn't so much as stir.

She let her breath out and began, once again, to work the rope that bound her hands. She had to escape. Nothing she said convinced him or any of the others that she wasn't who they thought she was.

Her wrists were chafed and bleeding by the time Alexandra managed to loosen the tarry bands enough to reach the knot with her fingers. Still, she was making little progress. The rope was too well tied.

Frustration threatened to bring her temper to a boil. Drawing in a deep breath, Alexandra tried to calm herself. She needed to think. There had to be some quicker way to escape. Nathaniel wouldn't sleep forever.

Glancing around the room, Alexandra's gaze lighted on the dagger he had thrown away from her the night before. If only she could reach it. She crept forward, straining as the rope became taut, but it was no use. The knife remained several feet beyond her farthest reach.

Damn Nathaniel. Damn the bloody luck that landed her in his hands on the very day she planned to escape from Willy. Would she never be free? She'd been Willy's slave, his whipping post, his convenient victim. But something inside her had received its full measure, and regardless of the consequences, she could take no more abuse.

Flouncing back to the bed, Alexandra used her feet to deliver the blows she wished her fists could land.

"You!" she accused, venting her rage at last. "I hate you!"

Nathaniel yelped in surprise. Coming instantly awake, he tried to ward Alexandra off, barely managing to save himself from a hard fall to the ground.

"So this is my reward for sharing my bed?" he asked in astonishment.

"Am I supposed to be grateful to you? When I shouldn't be here in the first place?"

She launched a heel into his muscular inner thigh, and Nathaniel sprang to his feet. He was wearing only his trousers, and his stomach looked flat and hard, nothing like Willy's rounded paunch, though Alexandra tried not to notice. Determined to land a powerful blow, she aimed for his groin, but Nathaniel whirled away, making her miss him completely.

He caught her foot with his hand, tripping her, and together they tumbled back onto the bed.

Alexandra winced in pain as he landed on top of her, then she tried to twist away from his grasp by rolling to her right. But Nathaniel had ahold of her dress. She gasped in surprise when she heard the fabric rip.

Nathaniel froze, and she went limp. His gaze dipped to the top of her décolletage, which now revealed a bounty of soft, rounded breasts bulging above her corset.

His mouth quirked into a grin. "As much as I feel rewarded for this little tussle, might I suggest that propriety would be better served by a more ladylike demeanor? I might be your half brother, but I'm no eunuch."

"Let me go," Alexandra pleaded, frightened by his look of open admiration. The blue of his eyes had deepened to inky black, and he was brazen enough not to look away.

Again, Alexandra felt grateful that Nathaniel believed her to be his sister, for it might be the only thing to keep her safe from him. At the moment, even that seemed a thin thread on which to hang her well-being.

"Let me go," she repeated. "I've never done anything to you. I don't even know you."

His smile disappeared. "This isn't between you and me."

"Then let me go."

"I can't."

Alexandra recognized determination in the set of his jaw, the rigid line of his shoulders. Nathaniel was a much more formidable foe than Willy ever was, and would not be easy to outwit. He was strong and cunning, with a fierceness that frightened her. Something told Alexandra that nothing would sway him from his purpose.

"Let me up," she said, feeling all too vulnerable. She wanted to cover what the tear revealed, stop his unwanted appraisal.

Nathaniel rolled off her slowly, as though he anticipated another sharp heel to a potentially vulnerable part of his anatomy.

Alexandra worked her way to the side of the bed, where she stood and turned away.

"Look what you're doing to yourself," Nathaniel said in a softer tone. "Come here."

Her hair had come loose from its pins and tumbled down her back in disarray. Tucking what she could behind her ear, she glanced back over her shoulder to see blood from her wounded wrists, red on the sheets. "No."

"Come here, you little fool," he insisted. "I'm going to untie you. Though you haven't earned your freedom, you're not smart enough to quit straining against the rope."

A sharp knock and Trenton's voice through the panel turned Nathaniel's attention to the door. He strode across the floor, and when he unbolted the lock, Trenton nearly fell inside.

"There's a man searching the docks for you," he explained, wiping the sweat from his brow with his sleeve. Then he caught sight of Alexandra's disheveled appearance and the bed.

"Oh hell, Nathaniel. How could you? She's your sister. The duke will never let something like this go unpunished." He began to pace the floor. "I should have stayed with you last night. I knew you wanted revenge, but I never dreamed you'd take it this way."

Nathaniel appeared puzzled until the line of his vision followed Trenton's to the sheets. Then his eyes went wide as he realized what his friend believed.

"Wait." He lifted a hand in protest. Crossing to Alexandra, he indicated her wrists. "'Tis this you see, nothing more."

Trenton raised his brows as Nathaniel threw his cloak over Alexandra's shoulders, inadvertently making the tear in her bodice more obvious as well.

"I tell you, I was more abused last night than she. I vow she bears my father's ill-humor," Nathaniel told him.

Pausing as though weighing the proof in the room against his trust, Trenton said, "She tore her own gown, I suppose?"

"It's a long story." Nathaniel waved him off. "But I'm sure you didn't come here to rescue the virtuous maid. So what is it?"

"We've got problems."

"What?"

Alexandra trained her eyes on Trenton's face, wondering if their problems were also her problems. Could things get any worse?

"There's someone visiting the taverns along the wharf asking for you. I'm not sure who he is, but he claims to carry a message from your father."

Nathaniel stroked the black stubble that had begun to grow on his chin. "Why is that a problem? That's just what we've been hoping for."

Trenton frowned, causing his brows to pucker. "I'm not so sure. If you'd seen this fellow, you might agree. He calls himself Rat, and he doesn't look like anyone your father would normally deal with. I told him you'd meet him at noon today, just in case, but I'm not sure you should go."

"Of course I'll go. The duke wouldn't be stupid enough to kill me before he secures the safety of his daughter. As long as you're here to watch Anne, I'll retrieve Fury from the stables and see what this messenger has to say."

Trenton grunted, obviously unconvinced that Nathaniel's decision was a wise one.

Though her reasons differed, Alexandra had to agree. If the Duke of Greystone was anything like the man her captors thought he was, he would have no compunction about killing Nathaniel, knowing Anne to be safe with her mother. Should that happen, Nathaniel's mates could very well try to avenge his death with her own.

Nathaniel Kent strode through the crowded streets of Liverpool with Fury, his giant black stallion, prancing at his heels. His mood was darker than reason would suggest. They had managed to kidnap Anne without any significant problems. By rights he should be feeling differently. But holding his half sister against her will didn't sit right on his conscience, despite Richard. He had thought it would be easy to hate her. Now he knew he was wrong. He wasn't sure what he felt—grudging respect, perhaps, a small amount of admiration—but certainly not hate.

As he walked toward the docks, ridge-capped waves rose and fell as a restless sea bucked against the ships at harbor like a horse resisting its rider. Nathaniel reflected upon the fickle nature of the sea. How deceptively gentle she could be. How enraged and unforgiving. Still, she was his first love and had been a part of his life for almost fourteen years.

Rubbing his temples to relieve the sudden pounding of a headache, he scanned the docks for the man he was to meet. The salty air smelled of fish, and the throaty coo of pigeons resounded as the gray-and-white birds made a nuisance of themselves, flapping and hopping among the crates being loaded into the bellies of various ships.

Finally Nathaniel spotted a small, slender figure who appeared uncertain amid the sailors, merchants, clerks and bawdy women. He glanced at the sun. Good, the man was on time.

From a distance, the stranger appeared no older than twenty, but closer inspection revealed the shadow of two or three days' beard growth and lines that creased a leatherlike face. Nathaniel guessed he was at least forty.

"Are you Rat?" he asked, checking to make sure no one seemed to be taking particular notice of either of them.

"That's what they call me." Shabbily dressed in drab breeches and gaiters, a ragged, oversize coat and a top hat smashed accordion-style, Rat looked as though he hadn't bathed in weeks. And he smelled no better.

"What do you want?" Nathaniel came quickly to the point. Meeting a stranger, especially one associated with his father, made him nervous, even on such a busy quay.

"Don't worry, I'm a friend."

"I trust friends less than anyone. At least my enemies never surprise me."

Rat's whisker-peppered cheeks broke into a smile. "Ye'll change yer mind when ye 'ear what I've got to say. What I know might save yer bacon."

"I'm waiting." A burly sailor hefted the crate closest to them, and Rat hesitated, making Nathaniel scowl. "Pray, make your point. My patience wears thin!"

"Not so fast." Rat picked something green from his teeth with a long, dirty fingernail. "I'm wonderin' what it's worth to ye."

"So you're after money. Now we're getting somewhere—"

"That's not all. I want ye to take me to sea with ye." He rubbed his hands together before continuing. "I got myself in a bit of trouble, an' I got nowhere else to go."

Nathaniel studied the other man's muddy boots and the tears in his baggy clothes. There was something about Rat he didn't like, but the bloke had definitely raised Nathaniel's curiosity.

"What kind of trouble?"

Rat scratched his greasy head, smiling. "'Is Grace is lookin' for me. I worked in the stables at Bridlewood for a time, until a pair of fancy candelabras went missin' from the 'ouse. Unfortunately, the 'ousekeeper claimed I took 'em."

Nathaniel winced as sunlight glared off the mirrorlike sea, making his head feel as if it would explode. "*Did* you take them?"

Rat revealed his diseased gums with a grin. "Why would I do a thing like that? I could go to gaol, ye know."

Nathaniel shook his head, irritation making his nerves raw. This man was a common thief and didn't even have the good sense to hide it. "I'm in no mood for games," he bit out. "I'll pay you what your information is worth, but our association ends there."

A look of surprise claimed Rat's features. "Yer not cross about the candelabras, are ye? A man's got to eat. Kimbolten 'as the money of a king, but 'e's bloody mean. 'E feeds 'is servants nothin' but 'ardtack biscuits an' gruel. I was starvin', that I was."

Nathaniel let the contempt he felt show in his face, and Rat's voice trailed off. "You expect me to believe that you lived in a household as rich as my father's and had to resort to stealing in order to get full? Any servant worth his salt can manage enough to eat in a household such as Greystone's, from the family's table scraps if nowhere else."

Rat sighed. "Yer awful uppity for bein' a glorified thief yerself," he grumbled under his breath, but his eyes nearly bulged out of their sockets when Nathaniel gripped him by the lapels of his jacket and lifted him several inches into the air.

"I am nothing like you or any other thief," he ground out, his face so close to Rat's that he could smell the stench of alcohol on the man's breath. "I take only what should be mine by rights."

"Aye." The smaller man tried to shrink away. "I didn't mean nothin' by it. I know ye claim to be the duke's son an' all, an' of course that makes us different. The truth of it is, I took the silver to sell for a bit of grog. But there never was a bigger miser of food than Greystone's 'ouse-keeper. I wasn't lyin' about that."

Nathaniel set the man back on his feet, none too gently. "As I thought. What do you have to tell me?"

"Ye 'ave to take me with ye." Rat's voice took on a pleading quality. "'Is Grace will kill me if 'e finds out I've met with ye, whether I tell ye anythin' or not. Ye've got 'im actin' like a mad dog, ye do, what with troublin' 'is ships an' all."

Nathaniel ran his fingers through the hair that had worked itself free of the black ribbon holding the rest back. His small band was a loyal, well-trusted group, only a few of them true criminals. But what Rat said was true. He had risked his life in coming to Nathaniel. "You don't look like a sailor. Do you know the sea?"

"A bit."

"Do you have any idea what you're getting into? What could happen if we're caught?"

Rat shrugged. "I'm already a wanted man. I'd go to Newgate regard-less. An' a man's got to eat—"

"Save your breath." Nathaniel frowned. "What can you tell me about my father? Is he going to trade Richard for Lady Anne?"

"Lady Anne?" Rat squinted up at him.

"Aye. Is he going to let Richard go?"

"Nay. Mary wanted me to tell ye that 'e's on to 'er. She 'ad to tell him where ye were. 'E's on 'is way 'ere."

Nathaniel's heart began to pound in his ears, keeping rhythm with his headache. "How did the duke catch her?"

Rat shook his head. "That I can't say. But she told me to find ye and warn ye."

"What about Lady Anne?"

The small man looked puzzled. "I don't know about 'er. But Mary told me to tell ye somethin' else. She 'eard the duke's controller tellin' someone that three ships are leavin' Bristol a week from Wednesday, the *Frederica*, the *Honest George* and the *Eastern Horizon*. The *Frederica* an' *Honest George* are 'eadin' to China by the regular route, but the other is 'eadin' to Russia."

Nathaniel stiffened in surprise. To send a ship into the Black Sea given the current political climate in that area was unusual indeed. England was nearly at war with Russia. What did it mean?

Rat grinned, a greedy glint entering his eye. "Mary said that bit of news should be worth a fair amount of coin."

Nathaniel pulled a wad of notes from his pocket, not even bothering to count the amount he handed over. That the duke was coming after him meant his father had no plans to trade Richard for Lady Anne. What would Nathaniel do with his half sister now? And how would he rescue Richard when he had to flee himself?

"Mary wanted me to tell ye one other thing, but as far as I can figure, it's of no account. She said she wouldn't 'ave 'elped ye if ye weren't so bloody 'andsome." Rat spat at the ground, barely missing his own foot. "Women."

Nathaniel ignored the remark. Whatever the reason Mary had risked herself to warn him, he was grateful. "We have to leave today. I'll meet you here tonight, late. But be forewarned. Working for me is not easy. Gaol is the least of your fears. A man could get himself killed. Understand?"

"Ye provide three meals a day an' a bit of grog, don't ye?"

Nathaniel nodded.

"I'll be 'ere, Cap'n."

"Then get yourself a bath as well," Nathaniel added, tossing the man another coin.

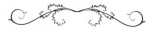

Alexandra sat still while Trenton bandaged her chafed wrists. Nathaniel had been gone for over an hour, and in the strained silence of their waiting, Trenton had applied ointment to Alexandra's wounds. Though she wasn't sure what the unguent was, by its smell she suspected it was intended for animals, not humans. Still, she wasn't about to complain. At least Trenton had cut her loose, and the pain in her hands and feet had finally ebbed.

"What happens if Nathaniel doesn't come back?" she asked when the minutes began to drag like days. Though both Trenton and Tiny seemed like decent men compared to the dangerous Nathaniel, they were all pirates, plain and simple. Alexandra had overheard enough about their business to know that much. And the man called Garth was less kind. The others could be even worse.

Nathaniel was obviously their leader. Should something happen to him, she had no idea who would gain control. Or what they might do with her. After all, they thought her to be the daughter of their nemesis.

Trenton shrugged. "He'll come back," he said, but Alexandra could feel his anxiety as he turned about the room like a caged animal.

"If he doesn't, will you let me go?" Her voice sounded small and frightened, even to her own ears. She cleared her throat and spoke more surely. "I mean, if Greystone kidnaps Nathaniel, or . . . or something, what will happen to me?"

"Nathaniel will be back," Trenton nearly shouted, making Alexandra cringe. "You're the duke's daughter, for heaven's sake. Surely you mean enough to him that he wouldn't be so foolish."

"But you can't be sure what Greystone will do," she said, taking a line of reasoning he would understand.

Trenton ran his fingers through his hair and sighed. "I'm sorry. I know you're scared. I just don't have any answers right now. We wait. That's all. We just wait."

Alexandra stood and walked to the window. One story below, the street was jumbled with women selling flowers, gypsies recaning chairs, peddlers plying their wares. Horses and carriages plowed through the melee amid singsong voices—"Who'll buy my sweet lavender?"—and she longed to walk freely among them.

"Why does Nathaniel hate the duke so badly?" she asked.

Trenton spoke from behind her. "When Nathaniel's mother bore your father a deformed son, he—"

"Deformed?" Alexandra glanced over her shoulder. In her mind, Nathaniel was anything but deformed.

"His arm, of course. Greystone refused to have an imperfect heir. He tried to smother him, and would have succeeded if his housekeeper hadn't stopped him. Martha Haverson rescued Nathaniel and ran away with him, raised him as her own."

"The duke tried to kill Nathaniel?"

Trenton nodded. "Aye. Your father's a dark man."

Alexandra didn't reply. She couldn't imagine a man attempting to murder an innocent newborn, much less one of his own flesh. But then, she didn't know Greystone.

Still, Nathaniel's past didn't justify his actions now. She was as innocent as he had been as a baby, and she could be in just as much danger. "How did you meet Nathaniel?"

"We served in the same frigate during the Opium War. Nathaniel was only eleven then." Trenton's voice softened as he warmed to the tale, no doubt as eager as she to keep their minds off their present anxiety. "He was a powder monkey, and the quickest one I've ever seen. At first, the other men teased him about his arm. They liked to rile his temper, and Nathaniel's got a good one." He chuckled. "But through the years he stood toe-to-toe with every last one of them until no one dared say anything about his arm or anything else, especially as he became stronger and quicker with only one than they were with two. He certainly earned my respect. I was a bit older than he when we met, closer to seventeen or eighteen—"

"You don't know?"

Trenton shook his head. "I grew up as an orphan. My mother abandoned me when I was young, and I was raised in a workhouse. That place was hell," he murmured, his words holding no self-pity. "I ran away to join the navy early on, and believe me, I've never looked back. Nathaniel's all the family I've got."

Alexandra couldn't help but feel a twinge of empathy for the tall, brown-eyed man in front of her. When he fell silent, she tried to draw him into conversation again. "How long did you serve together?"

"Nearly five years, until our ship was decommissioned. Then we struck out on our own. We worked for a Swedish merchant for a while who took quite a liking to Nathaniel. Said he was the son he never had. When Sven died, he left his ship to us."

"So why would you risk your lives and your ship, stealing other people's cargo?"

Alexandra's words caused Trenton to glower. "I don't expect you to understand. You were raised with all the money you could ever dream of, with finery and plenty to eat. Nathaniel and I had nothing, some days less than nothing." He paced in front of the door, brooding. "Even still, for Nathaniel, it's not the money."

"What about the housekeeper who rescued Nathaniel? You said she raised him as her own. Certainly he knew love."

"Martha did her best, but servants don't make much, and she had to live with her employers. Nathaniel stayed with her sister, Beatrice, and Beatrice's eight children. I guess Bee was none too kind . . . or generous."

"I see." Alexandra tucked a loose strand of hair behind her ear, understanding to a small degree what might have formed Nathaniel into the bitter man he was. "Is Martha still alive?"

"No." Trenton spat into the empty chamber pot and arched a brow at her. "Your father staged an accident. Nathaniel was nearly killed, too. It happened just after Martha took him to meet the duke—"

"Meet him?" Alexandra repeated in surprise.

"Aye. He was only seven or so, and she thought Greystone might change his mind when he saw how capable and clever Nathaniel was. Evidently he didn't."

Alexandra shivered. "How did the, er, accident happen?"

"They were traveling post. Someone ran their carriage off the road, and it overturned. Martha was pinned beneath it. Another fellow was killed, too. A stranger. But Nathaniel managed to crawl out."

"Did he go back to Martha's sister's then?"

"For a while. But without Martha's income, times got even harder, and Beatrice became more resentful of his presence. He ran away several times. Lived on the streets for almost a year. Then he joined the navy."

"By the law, Nathaniel is the duke's rightful heir. There is nothing Greystone can do about that," she pointed out.

"There is if no one can prove the duke is lying." Trenton gave her an aggravated look that told Alexandra he didn't believe she hadn't heard any of this before, but he continued with the story anyway. "Your father claims the son his first wife bore him died the day of its birth, only minutes after his mother. Martha was the only person who knew otherwise, besides the midwife, who was old at the time and died shortly after."

"But why didn't Martha try to establish the truth while Nathaniel was still a baby? It would have been far simpler back then."

"I don't know. She was probably afraid of the duke at first, afraid for Nathaniel. And she wanted him as her own. She went to London and lived in hiding for several years. Then she heard about your birth and decided, since you were a girl, that the duke might welcome Nathaniel back after all, especially when he saw that the boy's arm was no handicap. She knew she could never give Nathaniel all the duke could, so she risked her life to take him home—and she paid the price."

"Could the duke be so evil?"

Trenton's eyes became as hard as flint. "You have no idea."

"Listen," she said, hoping an honest appeal to Trenton might help her case. He seemed like a decent man. "I've not heard any of this before.

I'm not Lady Anne. I don't even know her or the duke. Can't you see that? If you don't let me go, I'll miss my boat to India and then—"

Frantic banging at the door made them both jump as Nathaniel's voice came through the panel.

"Trenton! Let me in."

Trenton appeared relieved by the sound of his captain's voice, but Alexandra suspected he was equally glad to be saved from having to respond to her entreaty. He crossed the room and threw back the bolt, and the pirate captain pushed inside.

"We must go. Now," Nathaniel told him, a determined look on his face.

"What happened?" Trenton followed his friend around the room as Nathaniel stuffed into a bag what few belongings he had brought with him the night before.

"Mary's been found out. My father's on his way here."

"But what about Richard? And her?" Trenton indicated Alexandra with a nod of his head.

Nathaniel lowered his voice, but Alexandra could still hear his words and the anger that infused them. "He's coming after us, so he must have no plans to release Richard, even for her."

"What do we do now?"

"She goes with us."

"Why? What good would that do?"

"What other choice do we have?"

"She's no good to us if the duke won't trade for her. I say we let her go."

"Not on your life."

"But the *Royal Vengeance* is no place for a woman!"

"That's the way things are for now." Nathaniel held his bag next to his body so he could tie it shut with his hand. "We'll simply have to do the best we can."

"It's too dangerous. Even if we could keep our own men from molesting her, the *Vengeance* could take a ball and sink, or we could lose our lives in the middle of a boarding. Then what would happen to her?"

Alexandra held her breath as she awaited Nathaniel's response. Besides the dangers Trenton had already enumerated, she knew Aunt Pauline would be long gone if she didn't get away from Nathaniel and his men soon. *Please listen to him*, she prayed. *Let me go. Let me go.*

"Then her life shall rest on my father's conscience. He had the chance to rescue her, and he didn't take it," Nathaniel responded.

Alexandra felt her heart plunge to her knees.

"Nathaniel—" Trenton began.

"Look," the pirate captain interrupted, "when my father's played his ace and comes here only to find us gone, maybe he'll see that we're serious and agree to the trade. If we let Anne go, there's no telling what he might do to Richard. Things are too precarious to go after our own right now. My father's been counting upon our taking the bait all along."

Trenton nodded, and Alexandra could have guessed his next words before he spoke them. Concession, pure and simple.

"Then we have no choice."

"None."

"But how can we go?" Trenton asked. "We don't have much by way of supplies. We weren't planning on leaving for another three days."

"Get what you can," Nathaniel told him. "Regardless, we sail tonight."

Trenton crossed to the door, then turned back, his hand still on the knob. "Where to?"

"To the Black Sea. One of my father's ships is heading there, and I want to intercept her."

"To Russia?" Trenton's brows drew together.

"I'll explain later." Nathaniel motioned him away. "There's no time now. I've got to take care of a few details before we go. I'll meet you at the dock at midnight. And one more thing. That man I met today, Rat, will be joining us."

"Why—"

"Later. For now, get back and stock the ship. We're going to need all the provisions we can get if we're sailing to the Crimea."

Trenton nodded. Glancing almost apologetically back at Alexandra, he saluted his captain and was gone. And with him went every hope Alexandra had of being released.

Chapter 5

"Don't say a word." Nathaniel spoke from behind her. Alexandra could feel him, tall and rigid, his hand on her arm like a vise. She wanted to jerk away or cry out for help, but she dared not. He had been in a vile mood the entire day. After Trenton had left, he had gagged her again and tied her to the bed while he went out.

When he returned a few hours later, he had stalked the room, silent and brooding, his rage worrying Alexandra. The Duke of Greystone was no easy mark. What did His Grace have in store for these pirates? Would she be able to escape before calamity fell?

Alexandra walked through the inn, not daring to turn her head to the right or to the left. She had promised Nathaniel she wouldn't scream or try to get away if only he would forgo the hood and his blasted ropes, and his dire threats should she break her word echoed in her head.

Still, she was tempted to bolt. It wasn't too late to head to London, if she could only get away.

Voices clamored about her, but the people behind them remained a blur. They ate, drank, laughed and toasted the queen, all in complete oblivion to her plight.

"Did you enjoy your stay, sir?"

The hotel steward intercepted them, and Alexandra gave the man a pleading look. He nodded and turned a solicitous smile on Nathaniel, no doubt intent on the vails he expected to receive.

"Everything was satisfactory." Nathaniel tossed the man a coin and prodded Alexandra on, but the steward was not so easily put off.

"And the fare, sir? Did you find that to your liking as well?"

"Indeed." Nathaniel flipped him another coin, his quick movements evidence of his impatience.

The steward beamed. "Thank you, sir. Come again, sir."

The pirate captain didn't bother to answer. He shouldered the door open while guiding Alexandra out into the dark night.

Once they were clear of the inn, he picked up his pace, all but dragging her behind him.

"I can't go that fast," Alexandra complained when she tripped on the hem of Lady Anne's gown for the fifth time. "Slow down."

Nathaniel whirled and glared at her but didn't speak. Grabbing a handful of her skirt, he lifted it to her knees and insisted she take hold of it. "There," he said. "Let's go."

Alexandra's own temper began to simmer like a teakettle on the hob. She had just finished mending the tear he had made in her bodice. Now an immodest display of ankles and calves showed as she hurried along behind him.

"How far is it?" she managed breathlessly when he didn't slacken his pace.

"We're almost there."

He was true to his word. Upon rounding the next block, Alexandra saw hundreds of tall, needlelike masts stabbing the black velvet belly of the sky. Another few minutes and she could hear the creaking of the hulls that rocked in the harbor and the slip-slap of the waves. While the port was full of ships, the docks seemed deserted except for the crowded taverns. A loud din poured from these establishments each time a door opened, luring everyone within miles to the welcome of their fire and their flowing ale.

Distracted by some small movement on a clipper anchored between a couple of larger packets, Alexandra realized that men were aboard the ship. Their shadowy figures took on more definite shape, moving silently, almost phantomlike, as she and Nathaniel reached the water's edge.

"There ye be."

Alexandra jumped as a man separated himself from the side of a wooden shed and stepped into the moonlight.

"I see you spent my money on something other than a bath," Nathaniel remarked without so much as a greeting.

"I 'ad a bit of bad luck at the tables. There was a cheat in the group, I swear." He scratched his crotch. "'Tis just as well, though. I'd 'ate to catch me death."

This must be Rat, Alexandra realized, the man Nathaniel had told Trenton to expect. She wrinkled her nose. The alcohol on his breath was only slightly stronger than his body odor.

"Who's the lady?" he asked.

"You don't know the duke's daughter?" Nathaniel's gaze darted from Rat to Alexandra, and a flicker of hope made Alexandra's heart beat faster.

"You see?" she said. "He doesn't know me because I'm not Lady Anne. I'm a seamstress from Manchester. And I have to get to London without further delay—"

Nathaniel's fingers tightened painfully on her arm.

"I've never seen Lady Anne," Rat said. "Spends most 'er time in London at the family town 'ouse. But I've 'eard she's a beauty, an' I'd 'ave to agree." He whistled as he looked Alexandra over. "She's a fancy piece, eh?"

A lighter had been lowered from the clipper, and two men rowed toward them. Alexandra knew in a matter of minutes she'd be taken aboard Nathaniel's ship, where she'd be unable to escape.

"Listen to me." She laid her hand on Nathaniel's arm.

He rounded on her. "No, you listen to me. One moment you don't know my father, the next you admit to being his daughter, depending upon your whims. But I'll tell you something. For better or for worse, it no longer matters. I can't risk letting you go. The life of my friend might depend upon it. So whether or not your outlandish story is true, you're along for the voyage. Do you understand?"

Alexandra glared at him as the boat drew up at the water's edge and two men climbed out. "I hope my father destroys you," she said at last, knowing that, whether she liked it or not, being Lady Anne was now the safest alternative available to her. As long as Nathaniel believed he had something to gain by taking care of her and protecting her from the others, not to mention the perils of life at sea, she would be relatively safe on the ship. But the moment her captor discovered her true identity, she had no guarantee.

"Our father may do just that, little sister. But mark my words, I'll topple him from his lofty perch before I go, so you'd do well to accustom yourself to wearing that dress. It might be the last fancy gown you own."

Alexandra jerked away and headed toward the boat on her own.

Rat, chuckling, followed behind her. "Greystone and 'is family are a spirited bunch," she heard him tell Nathaniel. "I'd not turn my back on 'er if I was ye."

Nathaniel didn't respond. He caught up with her easily enough, then waved the rowers back into the boat. Wrapping his arm around Alexandra's waist, he lifted her in, and once Rat had climbed aboard, they set out for the ship.

Alexandra turned to watch the near-empty dock as they moved away. It was too late now, she realized in despair. She'd miss her aunt for sure.

Trenton was waiting for them when they arrived. He helped Alexandra into a ship with the words *Royal Vengeance* painted on its side.

Nathaniel began barking orders to the crew, most of whom appeared to be mesmerized by the appearance of a woman on their ship. "Trenton, take her to my cabin so that I can get something done up here," he told his friend, and Trenton took Alexandra by the elbow.

"I'll not spend another night with *him*." She looked pointedly at Nathaniel.

"Perhaps you'd rather spend the night with them." Nathaniel indicated the rest of the crew. "There's plenty of room below. I'm sure

Trenton can locate a hammock for you, though I doubt you'll need one of your own."

Alexandra shivered as her eyes scanned the eager faces of the pirates. "N-n-no," she stammered. "Your cabin will be fine."

"As I thought." Nathaniel gave her a mocking bow, then turned to his work.

Trenton took her to a large cabin that reflected the masculine tastes of the ship's owner. An outsize bed was flush against one wall with a large sea chest at its foot. A desk, strewn with maps and other documents, sat below a round window; a small washstand stood opposite it; and a table and four chairs rested on a rug in the middle of the floor.

"Make yourself comfortable," Trenton said. "I shan't tie you up, but for your own sake, stay put. No one will dare bother you here."

"But you don't think—"

"There are thirty men aboard this ship, my lady. I can't give you any guarantees. Just stay close to Nathaniel, and you'll be all right."

The door slammed, and Trenton was gone, but his words still rang in her ears. *For your own sake . . . stay close to Nathaniel.*

The last thing Alexandra wanted was to stay close to Nathaniel. He was to blame for everything.

But some fates were far worse than others.

Alexandra woke abruptly as the cabin door banged against the inside wall and Nathaniel strode in, looking exhausted. The sun's rays bathed the cabin in a mellow light, testifying to the passage of many hours. The rocking of the ship indicated that they were well on their way.

Alexandra sat up, still tired, but suddenly wary.

"Sleep well, little sister?" he asked, crossing to the desk and lowering his tall frame into the chair.

"I wish you wouldn't call me that," Alexandra responded.

"You loathe our familial connection as much as our father does, eh?"

"More so, if that's possible. You're a pirate, a thief and a brigand. No longer a mere babe."

He laughed. "At least your reasons are more valid than his." He dug through the papers on his desk, pulling a creased map from the stack and spreading it out before him.

"What happens if—"

Nathaniel raised a hand to silence her, his attention on his work. "No questions."

Alexandra watched him from beneath her lashes. Despite his arrogance and his frightening temper, Nathaniel was handsome; she had to give him that. She wondered what the duke looked like. Surely he was attractive if Nathaniel resembled him in the least.

"Is there a reason for such intense scrutiny?" he asked, leaning back in his chair and crossing his long legs out in front of him. "Perhaps I can be of some help. Should you manage to gain possession of my dagger again, it would best be placed here, between these two ribs. Otherwise, you might only wound me." He gave her a sudden disarming smile, proving that his mood had finally improved now that they were safely away.

Alexandra couldn't help but wonder what she would have thought of Nathaniel Kent had she met him under different circumstances. As it was, his frightening intensity and criminal activities kept her from admiring him too greatly.

"What do you expect the duke, er, my father will do?" she asked.

He quirked an eyebrow at her. "I said, no questions. As long as you stay here with me, you'll be safe."

"That's rather like telling the rabbit not to worry about the wolf," Alexandra muttered, and Nathaniel laughed out loud.

"Perhaps." Standing, he pulled the queue from the back of his neck, letting the full thickness of his hair fall to his shoulders. Alexandra thought of the pale-faced nobles she had seen about the streets of Manchester. Nathaniel looked nothing like them. His skin was too dark, the planes of his face too hard. He might wish to take his place among the aristocracy, but he didn't belong where a plethora of rules and other minutiae would govern his behavior. Somehow the role of pirate suited him better.

"I need some rest," he said. "Mind you don't bother me while I sleep."

Alexandra paced around the room, keeping her distance as he stretched out facedown on the bed. "I'm hungry," she told him, wondering how long she'd have to wait to be fed if she let him settle in for a good long nap.

"I'd forgotten about the size of your appetite." His voice was muffled by the bedding. "The galley is below. Help yourself."

"Dare I leave here? Trenton made running about the ship sound unsafe."

"It is."

"But you just told me to go to the galley if I wanted to."

No response.

"Should I go or not? Surely you don't expect me to wait until you've had your rest."

Nothing.

"Ohhhh, you're contemptible!" Alexandra grabbed a brass-rimmed compass and hurled it across the room, narrowly missing Nathaniel's head. She reached for something else to throw, anything that would make a good projectile, but when Nathaniel sprang to his feet, she backed away.

"I-I-I'm sorry," she managed, forcing her eyes to meet his icy blue stare.

"I'll not be threatened in my own cabin." He loomed above her, advancing until he stood less than an arm's length away.

Alexandra felt the wall at her back and realized she could retreat no farther. She shook her head. "No, of course not."

"Right now, my need for sleep is greater than your need for food." She could feel his breath on her face, smelling faintly of citrus.

"Of course it is."

"I'm glad we finally agree." Taking her by her upper arm, he dragged her across the room.

"What are you doing?" Alexandra tried to free herself, but his grip was like iron. "I'm not tired."

Tossing her on the bed, Nathaniel lay down beside her and wrapped his legs and arm around her to hold her still. "Now you can't get into any trouble."

Alexandra writhed and squirmed until he held her so tightly she could scarcely breathe.

"Go to sleep," he commanded. "Or I'll tie you up and take your clothes from you."

"You wouldn't." Her gaze lifted to Nathaniel's face, only inches away from her own, and what she saw there convinced her that he would. She immediately stopped fighting.

"That's better," he said, and though he was too close to tell for sure, Alexandra could have sworn a grin tugged at the corners of his mouth.

She lay stiff as a board in his arms as his breath brushed her temple. His heart thumped beneath her arm, and his sinewy leg rested heavily upon her while the smell of the sea, which clung to him, filled her nostrils. She hated him, she thought vehemently. Yet her skin tingled beneath his touch long after his body relaxed. She would have escaped him then, except the warmth and comfort of being where she was somehow overcame her, and she slept.

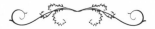

When Alexandra opened her eyes again, Nathaniel was gone. She was relieved to find herself alone, yet strangely disappointed as well. She climbed off the bed and crossed to the porthole. The sun was high in the sky. Nathaniel couldn't have slept more than a few hours.

Turning back, she allowed herself a small sigh. What was she to do throughout the day? The cabin was barely twelve feet wide and only slightly deeper, and contained few items with which to amuse oneself.

She went to the washstand where she spied a hairbrush. Next to it lay tooth powder and a new toothbrush. Evidently Nathaniel had anticipated her needs.

Using the small, diamond-shaped mirror hanging above, Alexandra tarried over her hair, brushing the long tresses until they shone. After she washed her face and hands and cleaned her teeth, she felt enormously better, except that the rest of the afternoon yawned before her with absolutely nothing in store. And she was hungry.

She moved restlessly about, examining the maps and papers on Nathaniel's desk, straightening the covers on the bed. It was her first day at sea, and she was already bored. She wished she could go topside and see, firsthand, a sailor's world. But the thought of the unsavory men who worked for Nathaniel made her reject that possibility, just as it made her reluctant to search out the galley, as Nathaniel had suggested earlier.

Alexandra's eyes lighted on Nathaniel's trunk. What would a man such as he treasure? Gold or silver? Objects stolen from the duke? She crossed the room and knelt down next to his chest.

Surprised to find it unlocked, Alexandra sent a glance toward the door. There was no lock to bar Nathaniel's entry. She would have little warning if he returned. Still, the pirate captain was so different from other men that she wondered what drove him—beyond an unhealthy hatred for his father.

Despite a prick of conscience, she lifted the lid. It was Nathaniel, after all, who had brought her here, he who was to blame for her boredom. The least he could do was to share what little entertainment the cabin afforded.

A beautiful sword, possibly an antique, rested atop a suit of clothes any man could wear to court and not be found wanting. Alexandra fingered the rich fabric, noting the precise stitches. Whoever had constructed the expensive clothing was a talented seamstress. But then, Nathaniel would look good in anything. He was a tailor's dream, with a physique that easily lent itself to rich garb.

If only his character were as flawless.

Below the formal clothing, Alexandra was delighted to find several books ranging in subject matter from the philosophy of Marcus Aurelius to herbal medicine. She scanned the titles, hoping for something to interest her, and was pleased to discover a compilation of Lord Byron's poems. She thumbed through the well-worn pages, then set the volume on the bed.

Digging deeper, Alexandra pulled out other articles of men's clothing similar to those she had seen Nathaniel wear, along with a length of white cotton fabric. Her fingers itched to sew, something she never dreamed they'd do after the long hours she'd put in since her mother's death. Still, there had been a time when she had loved her needle.

She pulled the fabric out to ascertain its size, and as she did so, a small miniature of a woman fell to the floor.

Who is this? Alexandra wondered as she retrieved the picture. *Nathaniel's sweetheart?* The woman's thick, long hair began at a widow's peak and was pulled back and piled on top of her head. Her wide eyes gazed unblinkingly back at Alexandra, holding a touch of . . . what? Sorrow? Tenderness? Alexandra couldn't say. But she had to admit that the woman was exceptionally beautiful.

A knock at the door startled Alexandra. Dropping the miniature back into the chest, she quickly folded the fabric on top of it and replaced the other articles, including the poetry.

"Who is it?" she called when all appeared as it should.

"M'lady? Don't be frightened. 'Tis only me, Tiny."

Alexandra breathed a sigh of relief. Of all the pirates, Tiny seemed the most kind.

"I brought ye somethin' to eat," he said.

Alexandra opened the door. "I'm starving. Thank you."

He ducked into the room. The low ceiling made it impossible for him, like Nathaniel, to stand at his full height. "The cap'n sent me."

"I see. I thank you anyway." Alexandra took the tray from Tiny's huge hands.

"Is there anythin' else ye be needin'?"

She shook her head, eager to start on the meal, then called the big man back when he turned to go. "Tiny, do you think it's safe for me to go topside?"

He appeared surprised. "'Course it is, m'lady. Ain't a man 'ere that wouldn't rather die than find 'imself on the cap'n's bad side. No one will 'arm ye. If they even look like they might, I'll give 'em a good thump myself."

Alexandra couldn't resist a smile. "Thank you, Tiny. You're very kind."

"'Tis the least I can do." He looked uncomfortable as he added, "Under the circumstances."

After Tiny left, Alexandra ate with relish, surprised that the meal, which consisted of boiled mutton, suet pudding and steamed rice and vegetables, was as tasty as it was. Evidently Nathaniel didn't lack for much now, she thought bitterly, remembering the expensive clothes and the sword in his trunk—not to mention the cost of his books.

Setting her dishes aside, Alexandra retrieved the volume of poetry and settled herself to read. But it wasn't long before she was bored again, and the lure of the upper deck finally overcame any hesitancy she felt about going there. She had never been on a ship, though she had heard much about sailing from some of the old tars with whom Willy drank. Even they waxed eloquent when speaking of the beauty of the open sea, and she longed to view it for herself.

Banking on Tiny's words and the loyalty of Nathaniel's crew to their captain, Alexandra left the cabin and made her way forward until she stood beneath the open hatch. A patch of clear blue sky could be seen beyond, nothing more, though Alexandra could hear the movement of men above her, their voices rising and falling with the wind.

She gathered her nerve and climbed the ladder, unprepared for the boisterous gale that hit her full in the face as she emerged. It snatched her breath away and nearly blew her back down the hatch.

Alexandra gasped and steadied herself with one of the cables that moored the mainmast to the deck. The ship was a world of rope and canvas and wood. Rope raised and lowered the sails, created ladders and footholds for the men, even caulked between the planks to keep the ship watertight. The white of the sails was the only relief from the brown of everything else, except for the small spot of color at the stern where the British flag waved.

The air was colder than Alexandra had expected, but her heart thrilled to the feel of the ship heaving beneath her feet. Saltwater sprayed her face as they plowed through the waves, the sails above cracking as loudly as guns.

"M'lady, ye should 'ave a cloak or somethin'." Tiny had spotted her and lumbered toward her as he spoke. "'Ere, take my coat."

Shrugging out of his massive, well-worn coat, Tiny generously offered it, and Alexandra gratefully accepted. She wanted to spend more time above decks and knew she'd be chilled through within minutes if she didn't put something on.

"Thank you," she called above the wind, smiling. "What a spectacular view."

Tiny grunted, glancing around him. Then something, or someone, caught his eye, and he turned to go, mumbling, "Best get back to work—"

Alexandra stopped him with a hand on his arm. "Your tailor isn't quite as gifted as your fierce captain's, I'm afraid." She indicated a tear in his sleeve that had been hastily mended, most likely by Tiny himself. "Why don't you bring your shirt to me tonight and let me do that justice? I'm rather handy with a needle."

Tiny flushed, looking as embarrassed as he was surprised. "I wouldn't want to trouble ye none."

"It will only take a moment. Surely your captain wouldn't mind if I put myself to some good task."

Alexandra turned to look behind her, searching for Nathaniel. He wasn't hard to find. He stood at the wheel, the wind flowing through his hair, his legs planted firmly apart on the rolling deck. He watched the two of them with a speculative eye, and Alexandra guessed it was he who caused Tiny's discomfiture.

"I'd better get back," the big man said, and hurried away.

Alexandra smiled as she watched him go. She'd told Nathaniel that she was a seamstress by trade, but there was hardly a lady in England who couldn't sew. Mending Tiny's shirt certainly wouldn't give her away. And she could use a few friends in her strange new world.

She turned to make her way over to the side, but Rat intercepted her before she reached it.

"Ye look fresh an' lovely, m'lady. Even a bit flushed." His foul breath washed over Alexandra, making her take a step back. "Seems last night agreed with ye."

"I slept well," Alexandra replied, unable to miss his more subtle meaning. "Too bad your daring captain didn't rest as easily. The floor of his cabin makes a rather unsatisfactory bed, I'm afraid."

Rat snickered. "If 'e spent the night on the floor, than 'e's a bigger fool than most men."

"Or you are." Alexandra stood ramrod straight. "Regardless of where Mr. Kent and I stand in each other's esteem, we are related. If I remember the sharpness of your captain's sword with any degree of accuracy, you'd be wise to remember that."

"What? Ye think 'e'd test the point of 'is sword for ye?" Rat scoffed. "'E 'as no love nor loyalty in 'im. An' you can remember this: when 'e's done with ye, I'll be waitin'—"

Unwilling to hear more, Alexandra whirled and stalked over to the railing. Below, the waves fanned out in neat furrows, but she barely noticed. Her hands were shaking, her knees weak. How could she protect herself from Rat? If—*when*, Alexandra corrected herself—the pirates found out she wasn't Lady Anne, Nathaniel might no longer provide the buffer between herself and his men that he did now.

Nathaniel's voice at her elbow made her turn. "What's wrong?" he asked. "The smell of a servant too repulsive for your refined senses?"

Alexandra gave him as scornful a look as she could muster under the circumstances. "Indeed. And it seems the air is not about to clear.

I think I shall go below." With that, she stumbled back to the hatch, feeling more than ever that she must find some way to escape.

Nathaniel watched Anne go, wondering what Rat said to upset her. She'd looked happy, almost exuberant one minute, and the next, her entire countenance had changed. But he was in no mood to coax anything out of a spoiled young woman. She had provided them little protection from the duke thus far, and he feared for Richard. Was Anne enough to keep his friend safe? How could he swing the odds back into his favor?

His half sister had finally quit denying her identity, but Nathaniel could only wonder at her story. The calluses on her hands were a mystery. Though Trenton adamantly denied the possibility, if Anne was indeed Alexandra, a seamstress, then Richard was as good as dead. The duke was the kind of man to mete out his own justice quickly and efficiently. Nathaniel doubted Greystone would bother to give him a fair trial first.

"Captain?"

Nathaniel glanced up to see Trenton standing beside him.

"How's our little charge?"

"She's not the docile lady I expected her to be."

Trenton chuckled. "No. The duke is probably grateful we've taken her off his hands."

Nathaniel scowled, succumbing to the foulness of his mood. "I don't know what he's up to."

"You want to tell me why we're going to the Crimea?"

"Rat says that three ships will be leaving Bristol on Wednesday. Two are headed for China, no doubt opium runs, but the *Eastern Horizon* will be sailing for Russia."

Trenton rubbed his chin. "Haven't we intercepted the *Eastern Horizon* once already?"

"She was the second ship we took."

"Why Russia?"

"That's what I want to know. Maybe it's a decoy, the message a plant, and my father's trying to protect the other two. Or he's hoping we'll get ourselves killed over there." Nathaniel chuckled without mirth. "It could even be something else."

Trenton's eyebrows shot up. "Such as?"

Nathaniel shook his head. "I don't know. But it can't bode well that a ship of my father's would be sailing to a port he's never sailed to before—"

"We don't know that for sure," Trenton interrupted.

"Well, he hasn't sailed there in recent years, anyway. So why now? I'm sure you've heard about the Ultimatissimum. England has officially given Russia until April thirtieth to vacate the Baltic states, or we go to war. You don't really expect the czar to lose face with his own people by complying with our demands, do you? War is inevitable."

"But the crown is giving great latitude to merchants. The queen is intent upon keeping the effects of the coming war at a minimum. Maybe your father has decided to trade in timber or hemp."

"I can't imagine that. My father has specialized in opium, textiles, sugar and tobacco for so long, trading with either the United States or China, that it seems out of character."

"So we're going to intercept the *Eastern Horizon* and find out what's going on?"

"Exactly."

Trenton spat over the railing. "The *Horizon*'s captain's not going to like a second go-round. He was furious the last time."

"Frenchmen are always passionate about something."

"What about the ships destined for China?"

"They won't be carrying much until they stop at Calcutta. Which reminds me, what about the opium from last week's take? Did you make sure that every last crate was dumped into the sea?"

Trenton nodded. "Aye, but I hated to do it. Opium is worth quadruple the value of any other cargo we've taken."

"Just remember the war, my friend. You agreed with me then."

"I still do. The opium habit is a cursed thing. I'm just getting greedy in my old age." He waved a hand. "It all seems so futile. Even if we dump it, there's tons more reaching the shores of China every day."

"I don't want any part of it, regardless," Nathaniel insisted. "England may have won the right through brute strength to import opium into China, and I may have helped her do it. But I'm out of service now, and I refuse to make money from the trade." He grinned. "Raiding my father's ships is definitely more to my liking. That way, only he gets hurt, not thousands who live each day for another pipe."

"We might not think it's so much to our liking if we ever get caught," Trenton muttered. "This last escape was a little too narrow for my comfort. What if Mary hadn't sent Rat to warn us? Newgate isn't a pleasant place to spend the rest of one's life, you know."

Nathaniel measured Trenton with his eyes. "My father is an impatient man. I don't think he would bother with Newgate."

Alexandra glanced up as Nathaniel walked into the cabin, then finished biting off the thread she had used to mend Tiny's shirt. She had been relaxed, almost enjoying the solitude of her work, until the pirate captain appeared. His presence always unnerved her.

She tried to ignore him as she leaned toward the candle to better examine her handiwork.

"What are you doing?" he asked.

"Tiny needed some help." Alexandra neatly folded in her lap the shirt she had mended. "You don't expect me to sit idle the entire voyage, do you?"

Nathaniel watched her dubiously. "Forgive my skepticism, but such selfless service on behalf of a poor sailor hardly seems compatible with your station and upbringing. Not to mention your character. I feel it only fair to warn you that he wouldn't betray me or his mates. Not for all the shirts in Bond Street. Or even a beautiful woman."

Alexandra's spine stiffened. "A pirate counsels me on character?"

"Hardly a pirate." Nathaniel crossed to the bed and shrugged out of his shirt. "But since you've taken it upon yourself to do some mending, perhaps you'll see to this. I just tore the seam." He tossed his shirt into her lap.

Alexandra tried to hold her gaze away from Nathaniel's tanned chest, but it seemed to wander there almost of its own volition. He stood facing her, his shoulders square, the muscles of his arm chiseled as if hewn in stone. A blush rose to her cheeks as the memory of that chest, solid against her back, flashed unbidden in her mind.

"No." She stood and placed the garment on the desk. The shirt was still warm and smelled of Nathaniel, heating her blood in a way she had never experienced before. She dared not touch it.

She turned away so she would no longer be tempted to stare at the handsome spectacle he made. What was there about this man that titillated her every nerve? "I'll sew when and for whom I want. I'm not one of your men. You'll not command me."

Alexandra heard his tread on the floor behind her, but she held her ground until Nathaniel reached over her shoulder to run a thumb lightly over her jawline and slowly down her neck. Then she couldn't restrain a shiver.

"What's wrong?" he murmured. "Must you list to ensnare Tiny's humble heart? I am the only one who can set you free. Am I too much of a beast?"

"I have no desire to ensnare your heart or any other. Tiny was simply kind, and I-I—" Alexandra forgot what she was about to say as Nathaniel's lips replaced his thumb at her nape.

"I'm your sister," she gasped, trying to whirl away. But her words sounded unconvincing, even to herself, and he easily restrained her.

Turning her to face him, he asked, "Are you?" His eyes glimmered with a light Alexandra had never seen there before as he moved closer, so close that his sweet-smelling breath fanned her cheek. "Would my sister let me touch her like a lover? Kiss the slim column of her throat?"

His head bent to follow the suggestion of his words, and for Alexandra, the world stopped revolving. Swaying toward him, she could think of little besides the yearning to feel his mouth on hers.

She hated this man. Why was she doing this? she wondered, as his arm curved behind her back, pulling her against him. His mouth was only a fraction of an inch away when her befuddled brain finally produced the answer that had momentarily eluded her: *He's testing me. He wants to know if I'm Anne or the seamstress I claim to be.*

Suddenly the terrifying picture of Rat's leering face conjured in Alexandra's mind, and she remembered how essential it was that Nathaniel believe her to be his sister. Rat was waiting for when she was no longer valuable to Nathaniel, for when he discarded her, as he would if he learned the truth.

Denying herself the very sweetness she longed to taste, she shoved Nathaniel away with a strength born of panic. "How dare you?" She attempted to put as much loathing into her words as she could muster. "I'm your sister."

Nathaniel's breathing was ragged as he continued to stare into her eyes. He wet his lips, as if he would kiss her still; then with a heavy sigh, pulled back.

"Aye. You're a heartless wench," he said, and with that he turned on his heel and left.

Chapter 6

It was dusk and difficult to see very far, even with a glass. After patrolling the Mediterranean Sea for more than a week, Nathaniel was ready to give up. No Greystone ships were to be found. The message Rat had delivered must have been garbled, or the schedule of shipments altered. Either scenario was entirely possible.

Nathaniel strode to the wheel. "Tack to the east and make another pass. If we don't find anything, we'll head back come morning," he told the ship's navigator.

The boat shifted as his instructions were carried out, and the *Vengeance's* course was set for another sweeping circle. They moved at a moderate speed, sails billowing like huge pillows in the sky, while Nathaniel watched the sun melt into the water.

The color of the ocean darkened to inky black, mirroring the stars that began to shine overhead, and he thought he would never leave the sea. It was the mother he never knew, his teacher, his healer, his friend.

"Are we going to head back?" Trenton came to stand beside his captain, and Nathaniel's eyes shifted to his friend's face.

"Aye. I thought it strange that a ship of my father's would put in at a Russian port. Although England has yet to declare war, it is only a matter of time. Soon English ships will no longer be allowed in Russian ports like those of neutrals."

"Ever since the Russians destroyed the Turkish squadron at Sinope last November, war has been inevitable," Trenton agreed, propping himself against the railing. "England can hardly allow her ally to sustain such aggression without some kind of support. If Czar Nicholas takes Constantinople, he'll control the overland route to India."

"Regardless of our allies, England could never stand for that." Nathaniel sighed, watching the dim shadow of Garth climb about the rigging, trimming and adjusting the sails. "My father has eluded us, this time. But there will be other opportunities."

"Do you think he purposely leaked faulty information?"

"Perhaps."

"Is Rat in league with Greystone?"

"No, he wouldn't have placed his life in our hands if he were. I think the schedule was altered after we received our information. If my father was wise, he would make more last-minute changes."

Trenton grunted, then moved away as Nathaniel looked heavenward.

If only life could be so peaceful, Nathaniel thought, his mind once again returning to his half sister. After the day he had almost kissed her, he had ordered a hammock strung in his cabin. He slept there himself, giving Anne the bed. He'd offered no explanation, nor could he think of a good one. Nathaniel only knew that he avoided any contact with her because the test he had given her had backfired. He had meant to finally put his mind to rest concerning her identity. But that was hardly the outcome of their brief encounter. Now touching her was what he craved most.

He pictured her long blond tresses curling down around her face, her large green eyes gazing up at him with their thick, sooty lashes, and couldn't help but smile. She was beautiful. And stubborn. And courageous. And so damn tempting that sometimes he couldn't sleep for listening to her every movement in the bed.

Nathaniel swore. How could a man desire his own sister? It wasn't natural. But there were times when he wanted to caress her tenderly, to protect her from the world, and to his utter mortification, feel her soft flesh beneath him.

He had to think of a way to rescue Richard, he decided, and rid himself of Anne at the earliest opportunity.

At dawn Alexandra braved the sailors and the chill air to visit the deck. She stood near the bulwarks, gazing out to sea, enjoying a rare moment of tranquility.

Though the sun peeked over the horizon, the water was still dark and glassy, with occasional white foaming waves that splashed high into the air. The sight captivated her. She had not seen its equal for beauty. But even the prospect of such a spectacular view had not been the reason Alexandra had left the cabin and risked running into Rat again. Nathaniel was. He had washed, shaved and brushed his teeth before leaving their cabin only moments before, and she had followed him.

What was it about him, she thought irritably, that made her listen for his step at the door, hear his voice amid the hum of many others? He was a blackguard.

He looked dangerous, stealthy, full of grace and power. Yet he was not like the usual ruffian. No common slang marred his speech, and an air of authority, even magnetism, flowed from him. Alexandra could hardly keep her eyes on the splendor before her, knowing that he stood nearby.

". . . we'll stop there next trip . . ."

She enjoyed the rich timbre of his voice as she listened to him talk to Garth somewhere behind her, and she thought about the fabric she had found in his trunk. She longed to create something with it, but the garment that kept coming to mind was none other than a full dress shirt for the pirate captain himself, which made no sense at all. Why would she want to please him? Or was it simply that his physique so easily lent itself to the creation of beauty?

Alexandra allowed herself a sidelong glance at Nathaniel, then felt the blood rise in her cheeks when she found him watching her. She looked quickly back to the east, trying to ignore him, but a moment later he came to stand beside her.

"Have you ever seen anything more beautiful?" she asked, growing uncomfortable when he didn't speak.

"Only you," he said.

Startled, Alexandra looked up into his face. She expected him to turn his words into some kind of a taunt, but he looked in earnest.

"I've done everything I can do to improve this dress with my needle," she said, unsure how to respond to the compliment. "Washing it in seawater has all but ruined it and makes me itch like mad."

"I could lend you something else, but I doubt my clothes would do justice to your form."

Alexandra raised an eyebrow, remembering her part as Lady Anne. "Wear men's clothing? Never."

"Perhaps I shouldn't give you a choice. It's foolish to be so uncomfortable."

John interrupted them then, and Nathaniel excused himself. Striding off to settle some issue between the cook and the purser, he left Alexandra to puzzle over his unpredictable behavior. She never knew what to expect from him.

She lingered on the deck until the sun grew bright and full, then went below to find a hip bath sitting in the middle of the floor.

"Oh!" she exclaimed, rushing over to feel the water. It was fresh, and warm as well. She longed to rid her body of the salt that made her skin miserably dry, but a knock interrupted her before she could remove her clothes.

"Come in," Alexandra called, afraid to turn her head away from the bath for fear it would disappear.

Charlie, the ship's cook, entered. He carried a pail of water, his frown so deep it reminded Alexandra of the lines on the face of a wooden puppet.

"As if the captain doesn't bathe enough already," he grumbled, eyeing her resentfully. "Now we got to be haulin' water for the enemy's kin. But I ain't never 'ad to heat it before."

The buxom woman tattooed on Charlie's arm danced as he poured the water out of his pail, and Alexandra suppressed a giggle of delight, unaffected by the cook's displeasure. She couldn't imagine what had motivated Nathaniel to provide her with such a rare treat, but at that moment she could have kissed his feet.

"That's the last of it," Charlie muttered as he left.

"Thank you." Alexandra twirled in circles once the door closed behind him. She'd had nothing but sponge baths for a week and was anxious to enjoy the real thing—until she remembered that the cabin door had no lock. Nathaniel had had it removed before she ever boarded the *Vengeance,* refusing her the option of locking it against him. Now Alexandra feared he, or someone else, might interrupt her.

Letting her fingers dangle, she felt the water quickly losing its precious heat.

She couldn't waste such a luxury, she reasoned. Charlie had gone to a great deal of trouble, and fresh water was too precious aboard a ship.

Retrieving the cake of soap from the washstand and setting it within easy reach of the bath, she undid the myriad tiny buttons that descended from her collar to her waist. The gown fell past her hips to the floor. She laid it across the bed, then hurriedly removed her undergarments and stepped in.

"Ohhhh," she groaned, hunching down until the water rose up to her neck. Sinking beneath it, she scrubbed her head, then lathered her body.

Once clean, Alexandra lingered, unwilling to get out until the water's heat had completely dissipated—or she turned into a prune, which happened sooner than she would have liked. Rising, she felt the chill of the drafty cabin as she began to dry off.

No sooner had she wrapped the towel around herself than Nathaniel opened the door.

"I'm sorry. I thought I had given you ample time—" He stopped as his gaze traveled from the top of Alexandra's wet head to her cleavage, over the round curve of her hips and down to her bare calves and feet. Instead of turning away with a mumbled apology as a gentleman surely would have, he stared at her with such hunger that she wondered if she might be his next meal.

Instinctively she raised her hands to shield her breasts from his view, then realized they were covered already.

"I-I—" Her words died at the passion in his eyes. Tearing her own gaze from Nathaniel's face, she turned away, and when she looked back over her shoulder, he was gone.

That night Nathaniel came in late. Alexandra heard him strip in the dark and get into the cold bath and scrub his hair. Silently she rolled over in the bed to see if she could catch a glimpse of his muscular torso, but the moonlight filtering in through the porthole was too dim. She could only hear his movements and smell the soap he lathered over his body.

In her imagination, it was her fingers that moved over his skin, not his own. She felt every ripple of muscle, the thickness of his hair, the straightness of his back, the broadness of his shoulders . . .

Alexandra squeezed her eyes shut and swallowed hard. What was wrong with her? Dreaming of Nathaniel was madness. He was a criminal. She was his captive. Yet the moment he stepped from the bath, she pictured the water running off his wide chest and down over his long legs.

She knew when he finally dressed and got into his hammock. And she continued to hear every move he made for hours afterward.

At dawn, when the first rays of the sun streaked across the sky like long, purple fingers, Nathaniel was already on deck. He had left Anne sleeping, curled into a tight ball. She had stirred often in the night, and once had even whimpered. He knew because he hadn't slept himself. He'd tossed and turned, unable to get the vision of her wrapped in that towel out of his mind, especially considering she was little more than an arm's distance away. She was going to drive him mad if he didn't get rid of her soon.

Charlie gave him a mug of tea. Nathaniel wrapped his hand around the warm cup, then called to his navigator to see how they were progressing on their return to London. Some of his crew moved sluggishly about the rigging, adjusting the sails and checking the rope as he took a sip of the hot brew.

"Ahoy, Captain," John called. He had the early watch and sat on the fore-topgallant yard, looking out. "Vessel on the windward side."

Nathaniel handed his unfinished tea back to Charlie. "Can you see the flag?"

Charlie took the cup as a toothless grin split his face. "You think that be the one?"

Nathaniel didn't answer. He had expected to find his father's ship closer to the Crimea, but perhaps it had been delayed. He began shouting orders, getting the crew ready just in case.

"The flag! Can you make out the flag?" Nathaniel prompted as John continued to squint through the glass without responding.

"Aye. She's English all right."

"And?"

Those crew members who had been lingering in their bunks now flooded the deck.

"'Tis the *Eastern Horizon*."

A chorus of approval broke from the men as Nathaniel sought out his first mate. Trenton stood on the quarterdeck, where he had been testing the wind and searching the skies for any sign of a storm.

"We're in luck," Trenton called, making his way toward Nathaniel. "If the weather holds. But Captain Montague was no pushover when we met him last. I wonder how he'll react in a second go-round."

Nathaniel shrugged. "You'd think that with as many ships as my father owns, we wouldn't have to take the same one twice, at least not so soon. But Montague won't put up much of a fight, not with Anne on board."

"Do you think your father realizes that we've taken her to sea with us?"

"Where else would we take her? Besides, doubt alone should be enough to forestall him, and if not, Montague understands the rules of the game. He knows we won't harm his crew. Maybe he'll be more cooperative this time."

"I wouldn't bet my life on it," Trenton retorted.

Facing the black speck he now knew to be one of his father's ships, Nathaniel shouted, "Full press sail. Chase her down. But be careful," he added. "There's no telling what new defense they might manage. We will come as no surprise to Montague."

When the *Eastern Horizon* spotted the pirate ship, her captain turned her around and tried to run. It was not a wise decision, Nathaniel thought. She was so laden with cargo that she moved like a tugboat in the choppy water while his sleek, fast-cutting clipper fairly flew toward her. By the time the merchant brig was positioned for a fight, the *Vengeance* was little more than half a mile away.

Taking his own glass, Nathaniel climbed the mast. He was amazed to see almost forty men crawling about the deck of the *Horizon*, preparing shot for the ship's four short carronades, a smaller and lighter version of regular cannons. "Take cover!" he barked. "They mean to fight."

Seconds later the sound of cannon fire erupted, followed by the splash of shot plunging into the sea less than five feet off their bow. The *Vengeance* keeled slightly to leeward as it rode the resulting swell before answering with a burst of her own guns. Then both ships tried to position and reload for another round.

"Quickly, quickly," Nathaniel prodded, sliding down to the deck. If they could get off a round before the *Horizon*, it might intimidate the brig's crew, he thought. By no means did he want a prolonged fight.

"And . . . fire!" Nathaniel yelled the words only seconds before a second blast told him the *Horizon* had done the same. He braced for possible impact, knowing the small size of his ship was in his favor. He hoped it would be enough. No heavy cargo impaired the *Vengeance*'s movements, but Nathaniel was fighting four guns with only three—one long, thirty-two-pound swivel cannon amidships, and two brass guns.

"What's happening?" Anne stumbled out onto the deck, struggling to keep her feet amid the violent rocking of the ship. Her eyes grew wide when she saw the *Eastern Horizon* and its guns, still smoking from its last volley. "They're going to sink us!"

"Not if we get them first," Garth grumbled from where he worked to clean a cannon muzzle of any remaining powder so he could reload.

"Go back to the cabin," Nathaniel called, intercepting her before she could stray too far from the hatch. "It's not safe up here."

"Is it any safer below?"

Nathaniel could tell Anne was terrified. She glanced around as though in disbelief, but he had no time to calm her. "Go! Hurry!"

Another blast of shot sent the ship reeling, and Anne nearly fell back through the hatch. Only Nathaniel's sure legs and quick reaction saved her. He reached out, holding her upright until she regained her balance. "Now go," he insisted, "before you get hurt."

Anne coughed on the acrid smoke that now concealed most of the deck, and turned back. To reassure himself of her safety, Nathaniel watched her go, wondering about the captain of the *Eastern Horizon*. The son of a passionate Frenchman and a cool English mother, Montague had fought better than expected the first time they had met. But he was proving more stubborn now, despite Anne's presence.

What could possibly be so valuable that Greystone would risk her life to save it? Pride sometimes made a man do foolish things, but Nathaniel couldn't fathom the duke firing upon his own daughter. For any reason. By all accounts, he doted on the offspring of his second marriage.

The same doubt that had flickered in Nathaniel's mind since he had seen the calluses on Anne's hands made him scowl. What if they had the wrong girl? What if Trenton were mistaken, the story Anne told them about being a needlewoman, true? Too many things didn't make sense. The duke never responded to their offer to trade for Richard. Of course, his father had thought he had them regardless. But now one of Greystone's ships fired upon them with seemingly no regard for Anne's safety.

Fresh anger boiled within Nathaniel, making him more determined than ever to win the private war that raged between him and his father. If it was Anne with whom he'd shared his cabin these ten days past, his father was more despicable than Nathaniel had ever dreamed. And if it wasn't, if Anne had somehow escaped unscathed, Nathaniel vowed that the *Eastern Horizon* would not be so lucky. He would take her for Richard.

Trenton approached, shaking his head. "They're digging in, Captain. I think we can win the fight eventually, but we might end up sinking her in the process. How badly do you want this ship? It could get bloody."

Staring at the *Horizon*, Nathaniel mulled over Trenton's statement. He wanted the ship, more to discover his father's purpose in sailing her than for any other reason. But he had no desire to kill innocent men or to sink a perfectly good brig.

"There's no need to waste lives." He squinted across the distance. "We'll make as though we're hit and pull away. Then we'll follow at a safe distance and surprise Montague and his crew again before dark."

Trenton whistled. "That kind of thinking is why you're captain and I'm not."

"Trenton?"

Nathaniel's first mate turned back.

"How sure are you about Anne?"

Trenton shook his head, then spat. "If you would have asked me yesterday, I would have bet my life that we had our girl. I still think she could be none other. She looks like the woman I saw four years ago. And we all watched her go into Madame Fobart's."

"Still, I have a feeling—"

"Are you sure it's not just wishful thinking?" Trenton cocked an eyebrow at his captain. "I've seen the way your gaze trails after her, and I don't mind telling you that it's got me a little nervous. She can be nothing but trouble for you, Nathaniel."

"You've no need to warn me. I'm not some love-smitten boy, unfamiliar with the realities of life."

Trenton stared at him for a moment. "Whatever you say," he replied, and went to deliver the necessary orders.

Alexandra paced Nathaniel's cabin, out of her mind with fear long after the explosions had ceased. The duke would stop at nothing to kill Nathaniel and his men. As pirates, their fate would not be undeserved. But what about her? Nathaniel assumed she brought them some kind of insurance she did not. And he was risking their lives based on that assumption. She had to convince him of the truth, for his own sake as well as hers.

Nathaniel's step outside the cabin made Alexandra bite her lip. He was coming. Now was her chance. She rushed to the portal and flung the door wide, but it was not Nathaniel who approached. It was Rat.

"There's the fair maiden," he mocked, putting up a hand to block the door when she tried to shut it. "I guess yer father cares more for the money in 'is pocket than 'e does about protectin' ye. Mayhap the cap'n will let us 'ave a crack at ye now. Yer not worth much to 'im anymore." He forced his way into the room, closing the door behind him.

Alexandra backed away, stopping only when she bumped into Nathaniel's desk. "He's still my half brother and your captain," she pointed out.

"'E won't mind if I 'ave a little kiss."

"He'll not stand for you handling me like some common doxy."

"I don't see 'im 'ere to protect ye." Rat bit off one long, jagged nail and spat it at the wall. "Besides, what can 'e do after it's all over? 'E's not goin' to kill a man simply for sampling the sweetness of those virgin curves. Ye'll be no worse for the wear."

"Don't come near me." Alexandra's heart raced in panic as dread filled her soul. The others were preoccupied with the ship they fought; she doubted anyone would hear her scream. And the cabin contained nothing she could use as a weapon. Nathaniel had seen to that the day they set sail.

Her eyes flicked to the door as her only hope. Perhaps she could make it into the passage before Rat set upon her.

"If yer father cares naught about ye, there's no need to keep ye so safe anymore. Perhaps even the cap'n will take 'is turn. Or is that where it lies? 'As all yer seemin' disdain been a cover for the two of ye keepin' each other busy at night?"

The lustful gleam in Rat's eyes nearly turned Alexandra's stomach, and his words frightened her more than a little. She darted toward the door, feeling the air near her arm stir as Rat's hand shot out to stop her.

He missed. She grasped the knob and started to turn it, then screamed as she felt his arms snake about her waist, pulling her back.

Alexandra twisted as they fell and used her nails to claw at Rat's face, hoping to gouge his eyes or any other vulnerable part of his anatomy. But he kept his face turned away. She felt only the rough stubble of his beard beneath her hands. Still, a loud curse indicated a small victory as her nails raked his cheek.

"Ye little bitch," he swore. "Ye think ye can stop me?"

He grunted as they rolled together. Alexandra kicked and flailed, but her blows only seemed to prolong the inevitable. Finally, panting with exertion, she lay immobile beneath the weight of Rat's body while he undid his pants.

"Ye like it rough, eh?" he cackled, slapping Alexandra hard across the face.

Alexandra's ears rang from the blow that left her face numb, but she revived to some degree and began to fight again, this time more desperately than before as Rat tried to wrench up her skirts.

Then the door swung open. Nathaniel filled the portal, a look of stunned surprise claiming his features right before rage descended and his fist sent Rat flying across the room.

"How dare you?" he snarled, crossing to pick the smaller man up by his disheveled clothes.

Rat cowered in the corner, the pallor of his skin white beneath the dark stubble that covered his cheeks, his lip bleeding. "It's not what ye think, Cap'n. I was just givin' 'er a good scare, is all. I didn't mean nothin' by it. Look. She's not 'urt."

Nathaniel threw a glance over his shoulder, surprising Alexandra with the murderous intent etched into the lines of his face. "I'll hang you from the yardarm if I so much as see you look at her again. This is my cabin, and what's inside belongs to me. Do you understand?"

The biceps of Nathaniel's good arm bulged as he slammed Rat against the wall again to punctuate his words.

The small man nodded, swallowing audibly. "Aye, sir."

"You deserve a good flogging. Fortunately for you, as well as her, I got here in time. Still, you'll be confined below with nothing but bread and water for five days." Nathaniel dragged him across the floor and threw him out into the hall with the promise that he would deal with him later.

Alexandra was still shaking when Nathaniel turned to help her up. "Are you all right?"

"Yes," she replied, but she felt far from fine. Her heart still hammered against her ribs, and her legs were too rubbery to stand.

Bending, Nathaniel picked her up, bearing the brunt of her weight with his good arm. He carried her to the bed where he laid her down and smoothed the hair out of her eyes. "I'm sorry," he said. "Rat's not one of my men. I can't trust him like I can the others."

Alexandra nodded, afraid her voice might crack if she tried to speak.

Nathaniel knelt next to the bed and lightly caressed the welt on her cheek. "I need to know something," he said when silence stretched between them. "Are you the duke's daughter?"

Alexandra stared back, willing herself not to glance away from the intense blue eyes that probed her face. Only moments before, she had felt it paramount that Nathaniel know the truth. But Rat had changed that. The memory of him attempting to force his sweaty body upon her made her shudder. Nothing was worse than leaving herself vulnerable to animals like him—nothing.

"Yes," she whispered.

Nathaniel's fingers tightened almost painfully on her chin. "Are you my sister?" he asked again, anger flashing across his face.

Alexandra licked her lips and swallowed. She could lose herself in his eyes, forget any earlier existence, forget everything beyond the moment. Rat's attack had left her frightened and confused, yet Nathaniel provided an anchor with which to ground herself. He was so confident, so capable. She couldn't lie to him any longer. The mere force of his will brought the truth to her lips.

"No," she admitted. "I'm not."

Alexandra wasn't sure what she expected at that moment. She felt as though she hung suspended, waiting to fall.

"Alexandra." She heard him use her name for the first time as his arm circled beneath her, half lifting her to him. He crushed her mouth with his lips, and she drank passion from his kiss until it filled all her senses. The rocking of the ship fell away, the cabin's four walls fell away. There was only Nathaniel.

His tongue gently parted her lips, and she opened herself to him like a flower yawning before the sun. The heat of his body warmed her skin, yet burned within her. The thickness of his hair filled her hands.

Soon she began to crave something she could not identify. She wanted to press her body to him, to unite with him in some ancient yet indescribable way, as natural as when the snow melts on the mountains to run down into the sea.

Nathaniel's breathing was rapid as he moved away from her lips to trail kisses down her throat. She pulled the tail of his shirt from his trousers and reached beneath to feel the muscles of his back, as she had longed to do. They rippled smoothly beneath her touch, thickening as her hands climbed to the full width of his shoulders.

"Alexandra. Beautiful Alexandra," he murmured, making her shiver at the butterfly touch of his mouth on her skin. "How I have wanted to hold you."

Alexandra closed her eyes at the sound of his voice. It was thick with desire, deep, throaty. She felt his mouth upon the swell of her cleavage, the heat of his breath. Then his hand closed around one breast, gently teasing the nipple through the fabric of her dress, until she pulled away.

His eyes were the color of the sea after sunset. He didn't speak, but his gaze fastened to her face like that of a hungry wolf who watches the movements of a darting hare.

"I must not do this." She shook her head, trying to rein in her emotions. She felt giddy, eager, deprived all in the same moment.

"Why? You want me as badly as I do you. Do you think I am so naive that I can't recognize a woman's desire?"

"What I want has nothing to do with it."

"Desire has everything to do with it." His brows lowered darkly, and he looked as though he would reach out and pull her to him despite her objections.

"Not if you'd known the sadness my mother carried with her all her days; the life she was forced to live." Alexandra kept her distance, scooting across the bed as that part of her brain responsible for rational thought rallied from the blow her dazed senses had dealt it. "I'll not make the same mistake. I won't settle for anything less than a husband, a home and children. And you can't give me that."

She saw Nathaniel's Adam's apple bob as he swallowed. He stared at her for a long time as though trying to master his own emotions. Slowly, he stood. "No," he said. "I can't give you that." Then he turned and left.

It was midafternoon when Nathaniel ordered his crew to open fire once again on the *Eastern Horizon*. The brig turned to fight with seemingly more determination than before, but she was no match for the *Vengeance*. Obviously unprepared for further hostilities, the *Horizon*'s carronades managed only two shots for their every five. Still, she lasted longer than Nathaniel had expected, and he was relieved when a white flag finally ascended her mainmast.

"What do you think?" Trenton came to stand beside him.

"I think we might be in trouble," Nathaniel admitted.

His friend looked up at him in surprise. "You think it's a trap?"

Nathaniel shrugged. "It doesn't smell right. Something's wrong."

"What do you mean? Ships are like women. If they give up too easily, you'd be a fool to trust them." Trenton grinned, then sobered. "Although I'll be the first to admit that it's strange the duke would fire upon his own daughter."

"She's not his daughter," Nathaniel said.

"What?" Trenton rounded on him in alarm.

"She's a seamstress from Manchester, like she said."

"But how could she be?"

Nathaniel shook his head, then ran a hand through his hair. "I don't know. But she isn't Lady Anne."

Trenton looked sheepish. "I'm responsible for the mistake. Perhaps if we'd detected it sooner . . . I just couldn't imagine another woman emerging from that dress shop wearing the same clothes, with the same height and build. It's uncanny."

Nathaniel nodded. He didn't blame Trenton. How could he, when he'd suspected their mistake for some time? Maybe, on some level, even from the beginning.

"You stay here," he said, staring across the water toward the *Eastern Horizon*. Regardless of Alexandra and the poignant emotions any thought of her evoked, it was time to find out why his father had sent a ship to the Black Sea. "If I don't come back, blow that damned boat out of the water."

Trenton nodded. "That's a bloody promise."

Nathaniel's long legs carried him quickly to the side, where his men lowered a boat. He checked the seven-inch knife he kept in his boot and primed the pistol at his belt, then climbed down, dropping into the lighter.

Tiny did likewise, nearly making the small boat keel over.

"Take it easy," Nathaniel muttered crossly.

"Sorry, Cap'n."

"Garth, you too," Nathaniel directed.

Garth was smart in a fight and loyal to a fault. Nathaniel watched as he lowered his short, muscular frame into the boat, then the rowers hopped in behind him.

The boat moved across the chasm between the two ships in short, jerky strokes until the vast hull of the *Eastern Horizon* loomed before them, straight up. A rope ladder dangled to the water.

Nathaniel paused for a moment to listen. He had to be ready for anything. He had no idea what he might find, but there was only one way to find out.

Hoisting himself up, he climbed aboard.

The men of the *Eastern Horizon* stepped back, their weapons still in their belts. They remained docile but speculative as they cleared an open path to their captain.

"So we meet again." Nathaniel bowed after crossing the deck to Montague. "I'll not take much of your time. My demands have not changed since the last time we met."

"You obviously care little for your own neck," Montague ground out, his black mustache twitching as he spoke. "Eventually His Grace will win this little war you have started, and then I wouldn't give three pence for your hide."

"It is I who have won this day," Nathaniel returned, eyeing the short, dark Frenchman. "And I have no desire to spar with you. If you and your crew will kindly step aside, we'll take what we want and leave your ship intact. Otherwise, I'm afraid my jittery first mate will fear for my safety and begin firing at will."

"Then let him fire." A short, stocky man fought his way to the forefront, a boy who was barely a man, judging by his lack of facial hair. "If we go down, you go with us."

The boy had removed his shirt, revealing a hairless, muscular chest. He clasped a knife tightly in his right hand. "I'll not let you take this ship while I'm alive to protect it."

Nathaniel laughed with calculated insult. "It would seem a bit late for that."

The crew began to gather into an expectant circle, murmuring among themselves.

"'E's got but one arm," Nathaniel heard a gruff voice announce as they began to place wagers. "An' Jake's the best among us," someone else agreed.

"Jake is young and reckless. Ignore his childish bravado," Montague said, waving for the men to quiet down.

"And you are a fool," Jake hissed. "You are playing right into the hands of these thieves."

"You, young man, are a danger to all those present," Nathaniel told him, letting his voice drop to a menacing level. "You would do well to take lessons from an older and wiser sort, like your good captain, before you lose something you value. Like your life."

"He is a coward! And you are a pig!" Jake made a lightning jab for the heart. His blade grazed Nathaniel's shirt, leaving a tear that exposed the skin over his ribs as he whirled away.

Dropping to one knee, Nathaniel retrieved the knife from his boot, and the men who surrounded them hooted in gratification as the fight erupted.

Jake lunged again, and Nathaniel sprang to his feet. The boy was not so inexperienced as Nathaniel had expected. He fought with practiced skill, but he was overly aggressive. Nathaniel had seen eagerness cause a man's downfall too many times. He dodged and jabbed and dodged again, but remained mostly on the defensive, patiently conserving his energy until Jake began to tire.

The cool wind reached inside Nathaniel's shirt like fingers, pulling the fabric away from his perspiring torso as he began his own series of thrusts and jabs. His knife caught Jake's forearm, opening a small cut that spurted blood, but Jake's eyes barely glanced at the nick. Red-faced with fury, the boy lost all discipline and began a feverish onslaught, repeatedly aiming at Nathaniel's heart.

Nathaniel managed to avoid the point of Jake's knife, pressing his advantage when the momentum of the boy's own blows knocked him off-balance. Making a stab at Jake's chest, he quickly changed direction, aiming instead for the hand that held the weapon.

A split second later, Nathaniel's blade sliced deep into his opponent's wrist.

The crew hissed as Jake's knife clattered to the deck when he could no longer grasp it. The boy's fingers dangled limply, the tendons in his wrist severed, as blood washed over his hand and dripped onto the wood planking.

Nathaniel lowered his knife, but the noise and motion of those around them acted like a douse of cold water to Jake. With a wild growl, he launched himself at Nathaniel's feet.

Taken by surprise, Nathaniel felt himself hefted into the air, then slammed into the deck. The jolt forced the air from his lungs as Jake's good hand landed a blow to his stomach.

Twisting away and gasping for breath, Nathaniel pushed Jake off. His own knife skittered across the deck toward Garth as he tossed it away, then sprang to his feet to deliver a punishing blow to Jake's nose.

The boy's head snapped back as blood spattered those closest to the fight, but Jake only shook his head as if to clear his vision. Then, with a curse, he threw a swift kick to Nathaniel's groin.

Nathaniel intercepted the blow with his hand, toppling Jake to the ground. "Bloody hell, Montague, call this cockfighter off. Are you trying to get him killed?" he shouted.

The crew had been silent for several seconds. They were no doubt waiting for someone, likely Montague, to intercede. It was obvious that Nathaniel had won the fight. But the captain of the *Horizon* said nothing, only watched with hooded eyes as Jake staggered to his feet.

The boy tried to land a blow with his injured right hand, then looked about himself in obvious confusion, and finally Captain Montague stepped in. Turning to two men hovering just on the edge of the circle, he said, "Take him below and clean him up. And see about that hand."

Nathaniel watched Jake struggle against those who would help him, and came to a decision. "Wait, I'll take the boy Jake with me."

Silence fell over those who heard his words. Even Tiny and Garth gaped at him.

Montague's eyes nearly bulged from their sockets. "*Mon Dieu!* I could never allow it. It is simply out of the question."

"Nothing is out of the question," Nathaniel replied. "You are hardly in a position to refuse."

Captain Montague stubbornly protested, but Nathaniel was in no mood to mince words. He turned to Garth, who handed him his knife, and the circle around them instantly widened.

"Would a taste of my blade convince you more readily? You were eager enough for Jake to try it."

The Frenchman paused, his tongue continually wetting his lips. "No. I am no fighter. He is yours."

Nathaniel bowed stiffly, his blood still pounding in his ears. "I am glad you are a man of reason," he said, forcing back the desire to challenge the cocky Frenchman anyway.

A few minutes later, several men hoisted a bound but struggling Jake over the side. They lowered him into the boat beside Garth, who immediately began pulling for the *Vengeance*. Nathaniel and Tiny stayed to oversee the exchange of cargo.

As the first crates appeared on deck, brought up from the hold below, Nathaniel halted the procession, too eager to discover what had drawn his father's attention to the Black Sea to wait any longer. The boxes were long and flat, yet curiously heavy—certainly not sugar or tobacco. Neither were they typical of opium.

Using his knife to pry one of the boards away, Nathaniel dug through the packing to reveal six clean, shiny rifles—the newly invented Minie rifle currently being issued to the English infantry.

"Bloody hell!" he exclaimed. "Why on earth would my father be shipping rifles to Russia?" His eyes sought Montague's, but even as he asked, he knew, and the answer turned his stomach. In war, what commanded a better price than arms?

"It's treason," Nathaniel said, disgust sticking like tar to his voice. "And you are as guilty as he."

"I had no idea what we carried. His Grace chose not to reveal that to me." Montague's voice was strained. He glanced worriedly toward his crew. "None of us knew."

"Guns!" The word rippled through the men like a wave. They appeared as startled as Nathaniel. More than a few became angry. "We were told we carried provisions for the poor Turks," they shouted.

Instinct told Nathaniel that the *Horizon*'s captain, at the very least, knew exactly what lay inside the boxes of his hold, which was why he had fought so tenaciously to keep them. "If I were you, I'd be worried about my own hide," Nathaniel told Montague. "Treason can play havoc with one's neck."

"You will test the rope long before I do," Montague hissed. "You are making a big mistake taking that boy. You have enemies in very high places."

"It is you who has cause to worry—because you consider them your friends." Though Nathaniel affected a calm demeanor, the discovery of his father's treachery had sent him reeling. Why would the duke betray his own country? Why would he risk his life, his good name, his fortune and his title? It didn't make sense. But then, there was much about his father that Nathaniel had never understood. He was only grateful that he had something, at last, that would make the Duke of Greystone sit up and take notice. And if it wasn't too late, release Richard.

Turning his back on Montague, Nathaniel said, "Tiny, you oversee the transfer of the rest of the cargo. I'm going back."

Chapter 7

"Who is he? What's wrong with him?" Alexandra stood at Nathaniel's elbow, watching as Garth and Trenton entered the cabin carrying a wounded young man.

"Lay him on the bed," Nathaniel instructed, ignoring her. "Get Nanchu."

Alexandra couldn't miss the blood that ran from the stranger's wrist down his flat stomach like sheets of rain against glass. The sight made her own blood curdle in her veins. "He's bleeding," she gasped.

Nathaniel stared down at the man, his face a mask. "'Twould seem that way."

"But why?"

"I had to convince him to give up the cargo he carried."

"You did this?" The morning's battle had frightened Alexandra, but the uneasiness she had felt since the pirate captain and his small party had departed for the conquered *Horizon* had been worse. The silence had seemed unnatural, as though the ears of the entire crew strained to catch the slightest sound.

"I asked him nicely first."

The sarcasm in Nathaniel's voice made Alexandra's stomach knot with renewed anxiety. How could he injure a man so badly—and that man an innocent, like herself, a mere sailor on one of his father's ships? She shrank from Rat, but who was to say which man was more dangerous, he or Nathaniel?

She crossed numbly to the bed. The long days at sea had somehow dulled Alexandra's fear of the pirate captain. He had treated her decently, if not kindly. But now she witnessed, firsthand, the fate of anyone who stood in his way, and it was a rude awakening.

The injured man writhed in pain. He looked young, not much older than her own nineteen years. With blood smeared across one cheek and a small trickle still running from a rather large Roman nose, he shook with reaction. Perspiration rolled off his wide forehead into sandy-colored hair, wetting his temples as he hugged a wounded wrist close to his chest.

A commotion behind Alexandra made her turn. Garth, Trenton and the small Oriental doctor she had seen once or twice about the ship hurried into the room.

"Nanchu, this is Jake. I'm afraid he needs your expertise," Nathaniel said as the doctor crossed to the bed. The pirate captain moved back to allow him space, and Alexandra did likewise.

An old but wise-looking man with a flat face and silver hair, Nanchu inspected the pupils of the boy's eyes while Trenton tied a strip of fabric just below Jake's elbow to slow the bleeding.

"Is he going to be all right?" Nathaniel asked.

The doctor turned his attention to the wound. "Don't look good—"

"Get yer filthy hands away. I don't want no yellow bastard pokin' at me," Jake cried, but he was in too much pain to put any fire into his words.

Trenton and Garth moved to restrain him.

"What are the chances of saving his hand?" Nathaniel asked.

"Hard to say," Nanchu replied. "If rot stay away, there is chance."

The pirate captain sighed. "Do what you can. You've worked miracles before."

"I need more blankets, must keep him warm. And please, move boy to my quarters," the doctor suggested. "I stitch hand."

Nathaniel nodded as Nanchu secured Jake's arm to his body with some clean linen. Then Garth and Trenton moved the boy out of the cabin, followed closely by the doctor.

An awkward silence ensued as Nathaniel strode to the window and peered out, leaving Alexandra to study his back while she tried to find some sense in what had just happened. Who was Nathaniel? A man sorely wronged, his actions justified, or a vengeful, bloodthirsty pirate?

Trenton returned only minutes later. "So? Are we any wiser about your father than we were before?" he asked, ignoring Alexandra's presence altogether.

"Indeed." Nathaniel spoke without turning. "My father is selling guns to the Russians."

"What?" Trenton was obviously surprised, but not half so much as Alexandra. She almost fell from her perch on the edge of Nathaniel's trunk. England was at war with Russia, or very nearly.

"You've seen the new Minie rifle," Nathaniel continued. "The *Eastern Horizon*'s hold was full of them."

"Bloody hell! That explains everything: why Montague risked his life, his crew, the duke's ship." Trenton shook his head in disbelief. Then his long face broke into a smile. "But that's good. Perhaps now the duke will release Richard. He could hang for what we know. His title and all his lands could be confiscated. We have the proof."

Nathaniel didn't return his first mate's smile. Alexandra could see his somber profile from where she sat.

"Aye. It bodes well for Richard as long as my father didn't do anything rash when he thought he had us back in Liverpool."

"He's going to be awfully sorry if he's hurt Richard," Trenton exclaimed. "Except that we wouldn't want him to force our hand. If the crown takes his title and lands, you'll be as poor as the rest of us, and rightfully so."

A look of determination crossed Nathaniel's features. "He's already forced our hand by shipping the guns in the first place."

Trenton's brows rose. "But even if you manage to establish your identity, there'll be nothing left to inherit."

Nathaniel leveled his gaze at Trenton, and Alexandra felt the full weight of his commitment. "That doesn't matter. I'll not let him get away with treason."

Trenton didn't speak for several minutes. "Your father must be mad to risk so much," he said at last. "But what could you possibly be thinking, taking that boy from the *Horizon*?"

Before Nathaniel could answer, quick footfalls thudded down the hall outside and a frantic voice called through the door.

"Captain, come quick. There's someone chasing us."

"What?" Nathaniel darted across the room as Trenton opened the door.

Garth's alarmed face appeared in the dim rectangle of light that spilled through the portal. "It came out of nowhere, sir, at a full press sail. Looks like a schooner of some sort, but we can't make out the flag."

Nathaniel's gaze locked with Trenton's. "Bloody hell," he swore. Then they dashed topside, leaving Alexandra alone in the cabin with the door swinging ajar.

The ship that pursued them was indeed a schooner. Nathaniel could tell from his perch in the rigging as soon as he lifted the glass to his eye. With only two masts instead of three, it was smaller than a brig, more maneuverable—and faster. It cut the water cleanly as it swooped toward them, closing the distance at an alarming rate.

Who was it? Nathaniel's heart hammered as he tried to see the colors of the flag that rippled from its stern. But it was almost dusk. Wisps of fog rose from the sea to meet low-lying clouds, shrouding the schooner as if in smoke and making the details of the ship too difficult to discern. As much as Nathaniel wanted to know his pursuer, he was grateful that he had some time, however little, to try to effect an escape. He had no friends at sea, of that he was certain. And with a cargo hold full of stolen merchandise, he had no desire to meet anyone who might be set on capturing him.

Shimmying down to the deck, he crossed to Trenton, who had taken the wheel. "She's about five miles off our weather quarter, standing on the wind on the same tack as we are," he told his first mate.

"Could you make her out?" Trenton squinted in the direction Nathaniel indicated, though with so much ocean curving between them, Nathaniel knew he wouldn't see anything but water.

"No. I can't even guess who she might be. But the timing of her visit is highly suspect. She likely came upon the *Horizon* and has taken it upon herself to pursue us."

"If that's the case, we're in trouble. With so much in our hold, we're too heavy to outrun her."

"Our only hope is to lose her in this fog. All sail," Nathaniel shouted, watching one of his men loose the main-royal and sit on the yard while the others hoisted him up so he could get a better look.

"She's gaining," the man called down. "I think she has a drag out."

"Hell." Nathaniel ordered the *Vengeance* to tack to the west, keeping a little off from the wind to make good way through the water. Somehow he had to get clear of her.

The schooner seemed to skim over the waves as it devoured the distance between them. Though Nathaniel tried every trick he knew to escape, she gained steadily until she was less than half a mile to the windward.

Nathaniel could see her clearly despite the sinking sun. She was a long, low, straight topsail schooner, a Baltimore clipper painted black with a narrow white streak, and looked to be about one hundred and fifty tons burthen. Her masts were raked aft with a large main topsail, and she carried a long thirty-two-pound swivel cannon amidships as well as smaller guns on each side.

She raised British colors as Nathaniel did the same, then fired a shot for the *Vengeance* to heave to.

"The guns are ready," Trenton told Nathaniel. "Looks like we're going to have to use them."

"If it comes to that," Nathaniel replied as a hail came in English from the schooner.

"Where are ye from an' where ye bound?"

Nathaniel peered across the water, trying to make out the man whose voice he heard. What motivated him? Outrage? Honor? Was he experienced? Wise? Overzealous? He could only hope his opponent was not so smart as his dogged pursuit had been determined.

"My arm marks me," he whispered to Trenton. "If they came upon the *Eastern Horizon*, they're probably looking for the one-armed pirate. Chances are, they haven't been able to see us with any more clarity than we've seen them, so if we can convince this Captain Do-Good that he's got the wrong ship, perhaps we've got a chance to avoid a broadside from his cannons."

Trenton nodded. "Shall I act as captain then?"

"Aye." Nathaniel moved subtly back among his men as the question came again.

"I'm Captain Errington of the *Voyager*. Who are ye an' where do ye hail from?"

"I'm Captain Taylor," Trenton yelled. A few snickers resounded from the crew at his creative title, but Trenton ignored them. "What purpose do you have in chasing us? There are pirates in the area, and as the captain of this vessel, I'll not be catering to the whims of such as those."

A pause followed as Trenton's words seemed to hover over the sea.

"Aye. I'll not be blamin' ye, that I'll not," Captain Errington called back. "We came upon the *Eastern Horizon* some three 'ours ago, an' she a victim of the pirate bastards who beset 'er. We thought ye might be the very scoundrels."

Trenton squinted across the distance. "On that you're mistaken, sir. Another vessel, the *Westwind Riser*, was likewise attacked not more than two days ago. Her captain decried a cunning, bloodthirsty group of cut-throats."

"Indeed." Another interminable pause. "Just the same, I'll ask ye to lower a boat an' come alongside. An' bring yer papers."

Trenton cursed under his breath. "What now?" he whispered, glancing back at Nathaniel.

"Tell him no. You don't know who he is any more than he does you."

"I'm sorry, friend," Trenton called back. "I'll go to my guns before I'll leave my crew or my ship vulnerable to a hostile boarding. I've nothing but your word that you're not the very ones you claim to be looking for. We're not pirates, but we stand ready to fight if need be."

Nathaniel's muscles began to ache with the prolonged anxiety. Would Captain Errington resort to his guns? And if he did, could the *Royal Vengeance* best him?

"I'll see yer papers," Captain Errington yelled, "or 'ear a satisfactory explanation for the strange signal comin' from yer ship. If a message it be, it makes no sense whatever."

Signal? Nathaniel blinked in surprise. What signal? He glanced around at his men. All were accounted for, even Rat, who still languished in a small cubical below.

Then his blood ran cold. Alexandra! It could only be her. Jake was with Tiny and Nanchu, and in his condition, he could scarce overpower the both of them.

"What do I say?" Trenton asked.

"Tell him we've a man sick with yellow fever who's not in his right mind—that it must be him. The possibility of disease should make them less motivated to try and board us. I'll go throttle the culprit now."

Nathaniel heard Trenton repeat his words as he disappeared down the hatch. But he knew if Captain Errington didn't believe them, Alexandra might prove their undoing at last.

Alexandra heard footsteps pounding down the hall and nearly dropped the mirror she was using to signal the other ship. Only rigid self-control enabled her to keep her tenuous grasp on its hard, slippery surface. This could be her only opportunity to escape Nathaniel and the others, adrift as she was and completely at their mercy.

Gritting her teeth, she continued to reflect what little sunlight remained, watching the flashes streak across the water. But they were random and probably meaningless. She had no knowledge of any official system of signals and could only hope that her cry for help would be interpreted as such—or cause enough of a stir to make the other ship take a closer look.

Alexandra heard the door to Nathaniel's cabin bang open at the other end of the corridor, and repressed a shiver. She had taken Nathaniel's diamond-shaped mirror to the purser's small quarters, just in case. Now she thanked whatever providence had guided her to do so. Whoever searched for her would have no trouble finding her eventually, but her new location would buy her a few more seconds at least. And that might be all she needed.

"Please respond, please respond," she whispered without really knowing what she expected the schooner to do. Would they signal back? Try to board? At that particular moment, Alexandra didn't care, just so long as they helped her.

"Where are you, dammit?"

Alexandra heard Nathaniel's voice as he moved closer, doors crashing open as he made his way forward. So it was the pirate captain himself who came after her, she realized with mild surprise, wondering what was happening on deck without him. She wished the voices that called above were more than a low rumble, but they were barely audible above the creaking of the berths and the slapping of the waves against the ship.

She stared across the water. *Do they see me? Will they help?*

The door to the purser's quarters banged against the inside wall, and Alexandra screamed and dropped the mirror.

Nathaniel filled the portal, his face thunderous. "There you are," he growled. "What are you trying to do, kill the entire lot of us, yourself included? Or would you have *us* kill *them*?"

Alexandra threw a glance toward the schooner she had been trying to signal. There was no visible evidence that they had seen her. They kept the same position they had from the beginning, though the voices from above continued.

"I'm not trying to kill anybody." She pressed her back against the wall as two long strides brought Nathaniel so close she could reach out and touch him. "I'm trying to save myself, and possibly that boy you injured, before anyone else gets hurt."

"The best chance that boy's got at saving his hand is with Nanchu. The *Horizon*'s own surgeon would have hacked it off directly. And that's what will happen to him still, if he returns now. Why do you think I brought him here in the first place?"

Alexandra shook her head. "I have no idea, but perhaps you'll forgive me if I didn't see it as an act of charity." She let sarcasm enter her own voice, using it to conceal her fear as Nathaniel's face twisted into an angry grimace.

"Don't make judgments on matters you know nothing about," he snapped. "That boy asked for everything he got. And as for you and your safety, I'm taking you home directly."

"You're what?" Alexandra dropped her shield of outrage as surprise took its place.

"You heard me."

"So what now?" She stared at the shards of glass at her feet. They reflected Nathaniel's dark image, contorting his handsome face into something more akin to a monster.

"That depends on what the *Voyager* makes of your little mirror trick." He grabbed her by the wrist and pulled her from the room. "If they open fire, there's no telling."

Alexandra shivered, remembering the morning's battle against the *Eastern Horizon*. The *Vengeance* had rocked violently, making her stomach churn with seasickness. Smoke had burned her throat and brought tears to her eyes, and her ears still rang with the blast of cannons. The worst of it was the fear: not knowing whether they'd take a ball and sink into a watery grave, or be captured, or come off victorious, which, for Alexandra, might prove just as bad.

If they open fire . . . She heard Nathaniel's words again in her mind. The schooner had seemed like a lifeline. She was desperate to get away from Nathaniel before . . . before what? Before he refused to shield her from Rat? Before she witnessed any more proof that he was the blackguard she had originally thought he was?

She remembered the powerful response his touch evoked in her, and felt a deep-seated panic nearly overwhelm her. She craved the kiss of a criminal, a thief, a pirate. Somehow she had to protect herself from that alone.

But the *Vengeance* couldn't surrender. Nathaniel and his crew had to fight, or they would probably hang. And how many might be killed in the process?

Nathaniel retrieved a bit of rope when they reached his cabin, but Alexandra raised a hand to forestall him.

"That won't be necessary," she said in resignation. "I'll stay put."

The pirate captain quirked an eyebrow at her, obviously skeptical, but shrugged. "It's probably too late anyway," he said, throwing the rope back into the corner. "The damage has already been done. Besides, if something should happen to me, I wouldn't want you trapped below."

He moved to go, but Alexandra reached out, catching him by the arm. "I'm sorry," she said when he turned back. "I-I suppose I panicked."

Cupping her chin in his hand, Nathaniel tilted her face up. He studied her for a moment as she gazed into his eyes, blue eyes of almost unfathomable depth. Then he dropped his hand and disappeared down the corridor without another word.

Alexandra almost screamed when the sound of cannon fire shattered the still night air. Peering through the porthole, she saw a series of small orange flashes in the vicinity of the other ship, and nearly swooned. It was happening. The schooner was attacking.

The *Royal Vengeance* shuddered as Nathaniel and his crew returned fire, causing Alexandra's stomach to turn queasy again. The ship already swayed drunkenly against a strong breeze, rising and falling on great troughs of water like a horse jumping hedges, and the weather promised only to make matters worse. Dark clouds obscured the stars, revealing only a faint slice of moon, and the wind whistled through the rigging above. Its keening wail, though barely audible in the cabin, sent a chill of foreboding down Alexandra's spine all the same.

A second round of shot barked from the big guns, and Alexandra threw herself on the bed. What fate would befall her? What fate would befall them all? How could she have been so thoughtless? She had wanted only to escape and to save the injured Jake before matters grew even worse, but she had probably signed the boy's death warrant along with her own.

Somehow, the thought of Nathaniel floating in the briny water gave her little solace. She might have practiced a thousand forms of revenge upon the pirate captain in her dreams, but his slow, sardonic smile always taunted her in the end.

She groaned aloud and covered her ears, attempting to block out the din of battle. Grabbing one of the pillows, she buried her head beneath it until the sound of feet running down the companionway made her sit up and take notice. What was happening?

Crossing to the portal, Alexandra poked her head out just as a thin young man she didn't know came charging down the hallway.

"What is it?" she asked in alarm.

"Just goin' for more powder, miss. Can't store powder near the big guns, ye know. Might explode the whole ship. With the storm it'd only get wet anyway."

He hurried on as Alexandra closed the door. So they were preparing for a serious fight. Returning to the window, she clung to the bedpost for support, straining her eyes to see beyond the darkness.

Lanterns dimly lit the opponent's ship between the brief, fiery flashes of cannon fire. The schooner wasn't more than a quarter of a mile away.

Vaguely Alexandra wondered about the *Vengeance*'s chance of survival. How many men vied for their destruction? What kind of firepower did the schooner have? She knew next to nothing about cannons or gunfire or sailing, but the danger of battle after nightfall and in the middle of a storm seemed obvious enough.

The ship lurched to one side, and Alexandra yelped as she landed hard on her backside. She could scarcely rise for the ship's movements, but when water began to creep beneath the door, covering the floor like a thin layer of ice, she sprang to her feet.

They were sinking! Why else would water be rising so quickly?

Alexandra's fear of closed places once again reared its head, and she sloshed toward the door. The water reached her ankles now, making the polished wood slick. But she wasn't about to be caught in the cabin, buried by water, pressed somewhere to the ceiling.

The door opened easily against the pressure of the water coming down the corridor, but Alexandra had to fight that same current as she made her way forward. Were they taking on water from above because of the storm, or below due to a ball, or both?

A man came up from behind, startling Alexandra as she waded through the icy coldness. He shoved her aside in his haste, carrying more powder, no doubt. The sound of cannons still reverberated above all else, despite the water, despite the storm, despite everything.

This time Nathaniel was not at the wheel when Alexandra emerged on deck. She was almost completely drenched, doused by the water pouring down upon her head as she climbed up the slippery ladder, but it didn't matter because the storm finished the job, quickly wetting her to the skin. Rain slanted into her face, stinging droplets that pelted them all, though the men, who yelled and cursed and rushed about cleaning cannon muzzles and trimming sails, seemed oblivious.

Alexandra instinctively searched for Nathaniel. She had to see that he was in control to give herself some small scrap of hope and perhaps relieve her fear. But she couldn't identify one man from another. A palpable urgency ran like a current through all on board as they ducked against the elements and fought to control the ship while getting off another round of shot.

Alexandra hugged the mast to help keep her balance. Then she saw him. Nathaniel stood near the binnacle, muscles taut as he kept his footing on the rollicking deck. His shirt gaped open to the waist and billowed in the wind as spray from the frothy ocean mingled with rain to course down his bare torso in rivulets. His black hair dripped water onto his chiseled face; his teeth gleamed as he shouted instructions to his crew.

"Nathaniel," she cried, shoving away from the mast to force her way toward him. Her voice was drowned out by pistols that popped like toy guns as the crews of both ships drew firearms and began to pick men off from the opposing deck.

Alexandra took a deep breath and called Nathaniel again. She didn't know what she wanted to tell the pirate captain. No doubt he already knew about the water filling the ship; his men slogged through it to retrieve the gunpowder stored below. But Nathaniel was always so self-assured. Surely his confidence would comfort her now.

"There's water down below. Are we sinking?" she cried above the cacophony of storm and bullets when she reached him.

He turned, apparently noticing her for the first time, and scowled. "What are you doing up here?"

"I can't stay below."

Lightning flashed across the sky, momentarily illuminating the entire scene and freezing it in Alexandra's mind's eye like the painting of some famous naval battle. The other ship approached just off the bow, so close she could nearly jump from one deck to the other. It looked for all the world as though they would collide.

In the same moment she saw a man high in the schooner's rigging. He held a pistol trained on Nathaniel. She knew its ball was meant for the captain just as she could feel its owner's concentration, sense his struggle to keep his aim steady despite the wildly bobbing ship. And she knew the instant he pulled the trigger.

Nathaniel motioned her to go back, distracted by her presence and obviously preoccupied by the menace of collision. He yelled something to Trenton at the wheel that Alexandra neither heard nor understood. Time seemed to stand still as the crack of the pistol resounded, singularly loud in Alexandra's ears but probably negligible amid the general tumult.

"No." Alexandra mouthed the word and launched her body toward the pirate captain. She noticed the look of stunned surprise that claimed his features right before something hit her shoulder, knocking her down with such force that she wondered if he had struck her. Certainly a bullet didn't feel this way. There was no sting.

In the next instant her shoulder was on fire, sending white-hot, searing pain radiating throughout her chest and back.

Her hand rose to examine the wound. Something warm and sticky burned her fingers like hot water tingling frosty toes. She found a hole, how big she had no idea, nor did she trouble herself to feel further as she lay on her back, staring into the black expanse of sky overhead.

"She's been shot." Nathaniel's anxious voice came to her as though from a distance. She understood his words; she knew by then, too, that she had taken the bullet intended for him. But strangely enough, she didn't regret her actions. His well-sculpted features appeared above her, worry etched into the crease of his brow, just as the *Vengeance* suddenly keeled and nearly upended in the mountainous waves.

Alexandra felt herself slide across the deck, carried by the icy cold tongue of the ocean, and began to flail in panic, despite the pain in her shoulder. She was being swept overboard. She felt Nathaniel try to grab her, felt her arm tear away from his fingers, then screamed as her body plunged into the freezing water.

Chapter 8

Nathaniel slid across the deck, struggling to reach Alexandra, until he smacked into something rock hard. He reached out, instinctively grasping the mizzenmast with his good arm as the same hungry waves that had swept her overboard licked at his feet.

"Alexandra!" Fear born of something worse than battle shocked Nathaniel's system. Where was she? She had disappeared into the churning, angry sea. He knew it would not be easy to spot her amid the wind and the waves and the darkness.

The ship righted itself, and Nathaniel staggered to his feet. He dashed to the bulwarks, frantically searching the white-foaming waves.

"Alexandra!" he cried again, praying for a glimpse of her blond head. Deep down he knew the chances of rescuing her, of rescuing anyone under the circumstances, were remote. Alexandra would die. The cold would seep into her muscles and slow her movements until she simply went to sleep. If she couldn't swim, water was probably already filling her lungs.

"Nathaniel, no! It's too dangerous," Trenton called from behind him, but Nathaniel ignored him. Alexandra had saved his life. Though he couldn't begin to understand why she would risk herself on his behalf, the fact remained that she had taken a bullet meant for him. And she could survive in the water only a few minutes at most.

The thought of her death wrapped itself around his heart and squeezed until he thought he'd die himself. The battle ceased to exist.

The storm ceased to exist. There were only the two of them and the greatest of all enemies in such situations—time.

Trenton's hand clamped down on his shoulder. "Let me. I've got two good arms."

Nathaniel shook his head, singularly intent as his eyes caught sight of something in the water.

It was her! Alexandra bobbed up and down in the swirling blackness like a piece of driftwood.

"Hang on," Nathaniel murmured. He quickly tied a length of rope around his waist, secured the other end to the mast, and dived overboard.

The jolt of the cold water stole Nathaniel's breath away. He struggled to fill his lungs with air as he fought the turbulent waves and swam with all his strength toward the place he had last seen Alexandra.

Trying to remain calm, he counted his strokes to provide some measure of time and distance, but the churning water pushed him back again and again, making progress difficult. He would never reach her in time. Maybe he would never find her. Some nether region of his brain wondered if he would be able to fight their way back even if he did.

Nathaniel's chest soon felt as though it would burst. His lungs burned; he tasted blood at the back of his throat. Still he pressed on. Alexandra had to be close now. He lifted his head to try to catch a glimpse of her, and instantly swallowed a mouthful of water as a wave crashed down on his head.

When Nathaniel finally surfaced, he turned back toward the *Vengeance*, hoping for some direction. The cold was sapping his strength, and he could no longer see Alexandra. Nothing but great mountains of water rose before him, churning and plunging and plunging again.

On deck, Garth yelled, waved and pointed, but Nathaniel could barely make him out. *Just a little farther*, he thought, *just a little farther.* Making one last Herculean effort, he lunged forward and his hand thumped against something solid. Alexandra!

Her struggle to save herself had thrown her into a frenzy, and she was stronger than Nathaniel had anticipated. She almost drowned them both before he managed to encircle her waist with his rope and begin the long haul back.

Seconds later Nathaniel felt the rope become taut as Trenton and the others tried to reel them in. He helped by continuing to swim, though his muscles screamed with the effort and his body was numb with cold. Alexandra wasn't struggling anymore, but with his one arm, towing her behind him was awkward and difficult.

At least he had her. At least she wasn't going to drown. Those thoughts alone gave him the strength to continue. But when Trenton and Tiny and several other members of the crew succeeded in hauling them back aboard, Alexandra lay white-faced and still, her eyes closed.

Nathaniel wanted to pound the deck and scream at the injustice of it all—except that he couldn't get enough air in his lungs or enough strength in his limbs. His own body shook almost as violently as the storm-battered ship, and darkness fringed his mind, threatening to overcome him. "Is she alive?" he croaked.

The chalky whiteness of Alexandra's skin gleamed in the pale moonlight as Nathaniel waited for Tiny to press two fingers to her slim throat. The wind whipped at her wet hair and clothing. He wanted to shelter her from that icy blast, alive or not. But he couldn't move.

Without speaking, Tiny pulled Nathaniel's hand across Alexandra's body and held it to the indentation above her collarbone. An almost imperceptible heartbeat drummed softly beneath his touch.

She was alive.

Nathaniel began to laugh as relief surged through his body, causing a type of euphoria. "Get Nanchu," he coughed. Only then did the silence of the guns register in his mind. What had happened to the schooner?

Straining to lift his head, Nathaniel peered toward the bow just as Garth arrived with blankets. Trenton, still trying to recover from hoisting the two of them back onto the ship, gasped for enough air to speak.

"They've turned away," he said, answering Nathaniel's unspoken question. "I guess the storm was more than they bargained for. When we nearly collided, I think Captain Errington realized that he risked more for our capture than he was willing to lose. If the storm passes soon, we should be all right, though we've taken on a good deal of water."

"The pumps?"

"Still going." Trenton fell silent as Nanchu approached.

Nathaniel nodded, then looked to the Chinese doctor. "She's alive," he said.

Nanchu's face was somber as he examined the gunshot wound in Alexandra's shoulder. "Perhaps not for long."

The pain in her shoulder brought dreams of Willy. Fragments floated piecemeal through Alexandra's consciousness, memories mostly, none of which were very pleasant: her stepfather's drunken voice bellowing from the doorway, his clothes reeking with alcohol and tobacco smoke, his shoulders shaking as he vomited into a chamber pot.

Alexandra flinched, causing the dream to shatter, and blinked. Her eyes felt gritty and would not focus, as though they resented the intrusion of light into their quiet, dark domain. And her body seemed unnaturally heavy. She was tired and sore in a way she had never experienced. What had happened?

Her gaze traveled around the room, taking in her surroundings. She was relieved to find Willy nowhere in sight. Instead of the neglected wattle-and-daub cottage where she had grown up, Nathaniel's cabin materialized. The pirate captain himself sat on a chair next to her bed, his head falling forward in sleep.

She studied him, her eyes beginning to work more smoothly, like two squeaky wheels after getting a bit of grease. His hair was disheveled, his face covered with dark whiskers. Tiny lines around his eyes and mouth made him look tired, or worried. His sleeves were rolled up and his shirt only half buttoned, as though he'd scrubbed his face and hand but hadn't bothered to straighten his clothes.

Was she going to die? Evidently the ship and Nathaniel had survived the storm. All was quiet now. But if the pirate captain's ragged condition served as any indication, she was not so well off.

She reached up to touch the shoulder that pained her. A linen bandage covered the wound, thwarting any real investigation, but her movement made Nathaniel's head snap up. His blue eyes regarded her searchingly.

"Thank God," he said. "How do you feel?"

"Like I've been shot." Alexandra tried to smile, but even that small expense of energy exceeded her strength. "I hope I look better than you do," she managed weakly.

A ghost of a grin flickered on Nathaniel's face, deepening the cleft in his chin. "You still look good enough to eat. Isn't that what you accused me of once? Of being a wolf?"

Alexandra felt a blush rise to her cheeks. "Aye, and it appears you haven't had a good meal for some time."

"Shall we remedy that, then?" He licked his lips as he moved closer, and Alexandra's breath caught in her throat. She thought he might kiss her. Though her head cried out for her to spurn such an advance, her heart raced with anticipation.

He hovered only inches away. "I only want to know one thing," he murmured. "Why? Why did you step in front of that bullet?"

"I don't know." Alexandra forced the words out, knowing that, even if she were strong and well, she could never explain the emotions that had converged upon her senses when she had spotted that sniper. Admiration was perhaps most dominant. Despite the illegal methods Nathaniel used to obtain his ends, he was a born leader. He was strong, resourceful and courageous. His men respected him. Her own opinion of him had changed drastically since their first encounter outside Madame Fobart's. Watching him die would have been like witnessing someone shoot a wild black stallion, like seeing something of great strength and beauty brought low.

Nathaniel took her hand, and she realized that just the vibrancy of his touch was enough to lend her strength.

"Go ahead and rest," he said. "I won't let anything happen to you."

Alexandra gave him a tired smile and let herself drift away, knowing, for the first time in a long while, that she was completely safe.

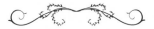

The next morning Nathaniel nearly bumped into Trenton as he entered the companionway. "How are the repairs coming?" he asked.

"The repairs aren't as much of a problem as that boy you brought from the *Horizon*. I moved him below with the rest of the men like you said, but he still won't let Nanchu treat his wrist. He's raising hell down there."

Nathaniel ran a hand through his hair. For the most part, he had turned the running of the ship over to Trenton, too concerned about Alexandra to perform his usual duties as captain. But his absence from command was beginning to show. He knew Trenton disagreed with his bringing Jake on board, and most of the crew thought likewise. Still, Nathaniel felt obligated to do what he could to save the young man's hand. Jake was a fool, but he was barely nineteen if he was a day. "What's he doing?"

"He's constantly trying to pick a fight. I'm having a hard time keeping the men focused on their work. Most of them would give a week's pay for only one shot at the little bastard, injured or no. And I'm tempted myself. He's caused nothing but problems since the day he set foot on deck."

"We'll be rid of him soon enough. How much longer before we can head home?"

"Another day, maybe two. But we're running low on supplies. You've eaten so little that you probably haven't noticed the fare, but the rest of us have not been so preoccupied."

"We'll make it," Nathaniel said, feeling the weight of responsibility settle back onto his shoulders. "We always do."

"I only hope our luck doesn't run out."

Nathaniel gave his friend a tired smile. "Will you tell Nanchu that Alexandra's awake? Have him come take another look at her while I have a talk with our friend Jake."

Trenton nodded, and Nathaniel moved to go.

"Nathaniel?"

"Aye?"

"Whatever possessed you to bring Jake along in the first place?"

Nathaniel shook his head. "I don't know. I guess I'm just hoping Nanchu can save his hand."

Trenton scowled. "He was eager enough to shed your blood. From what Garth says, he wanted to kill you."

"Of course he wanted to kill me. We were in the process of raiding his ship, remember?"

"Still, he's not as helpless and innocent as you seem to think. You were capable enough at his age."

Nathaniel paused, unsure how to answer. He'd been in more knife fights by the time he was nineteen than he could remember, but not everyone grew up as quickly as he had. "There's no need to let him lose his hand if Nanchu can save it," he responded simply.

"And what if he can't? What then?"

"Then there's nothing more we can do. We'll cross that bridge when we come to it."

"But what are we going to do even if Nanchu does save it? Let him go back to England with a list of all our names?"

Nathaniel scowled as irritation welled up inside him. Only because Trenton was a lifelong friend did he steel himself against it. "Once his wrist has had a chance to heal, we'll drop him at the nearest port and be done with him. He knows nothing that can threaten us. We'll just have to keep it that way."

Before Trenton could respond, Nathaniel turned on his heel and strode down the corridor. His mind was relieved about Alexandra, but he was still tired and certainly in no mood for an argument. Trenton, on the other hand, seemed eager to vent the frustrations of taking over the captain's post.

His friend was right about one thing, though, Nathaniel realized as his stomach began to complain of its neglect. He'd eaten little over the past twenty-four hours, and now he was starved. As he descended to where most of his men slept, he wondered what Charlie might be able to whip together from their dwindling stores.

Negotiating row upon row of hammocks slung from the ceiling like giant cocoons, Nathaniel passed Tiny. The big man must have had the night watch to be sleeping at this time of day, but the hand that suddenly reached out, impeding his progress, told Nathaniel Tiny was wide awake.

"Can I 'ave a word with ye, Cap'n?"

Nathaniel paused. "What is it?"

"That lad ye brought from the *Eastern 'Orizon* . . ."

"What about him?" The same feeling of annoyance he had experienced with Trenton swelled in Nathaniel again.

"There's something unusual about the bloke. 'E—"

"I know," Nathaniel interrupted. "I'm going to take care of everything right now."

He strode past Tiny to where Jake lay glowering at him. "I hear you're a pleasant sort to live with."

Jake leaned up on his elbows. "You haven't seen anything yet."

"I suggest that you behave yourself while aboard my ship. Otherwise, I might be persuaded by one of many offers to rid us of your presence *before* we reach port. A swim in the sea might not improve your health, but your absence would do wonders for my peace of mind."

"How do you expect me to behave when you closet me away with filthy men crawling with vermin?" Jake snarled. "The stench of unwashed bodies nearly suffocates me, and the itching is sending me mad."

"Sounds as though you've finally found something that enjoys your company."

"'Tis you who brought me here."

"I must have had a mental lapse."

"Which you will live to regret, I assure you."

Jake certainly had spirit, but Nathaniel was not amused. "Let's forgo the threats for the time being. I had no idea that we have a problem with lice. It is a rule aboard this ship that my men keep themselves bathed, for the comfort of all. If they are neglecting that duty, it is well you brought it to my attention."

"Are you daft, man? How do you miss thirty men itching like dogs?"

By keeping vigil over a beautiful woman who has lingered just this side of death for nearly two days, Nathaniel thought. He could have missed the Second Coming, immersed as he was in watching Alexandra whimper and moan and turn in his bed.

"If things are as bad as you say, there's one way to solve the problem quickly enough," Nathaniel said. "I'll see that you and my men have your heads shaved and a good bath. Immediately."

"You bloody won't touch a hair on my head," Jake shouted as Nathaniel returned to the ladder.

Ignoring the colorful epithets the boy hurled at his back, Nathaniel chuckled. Jake could outdo them all for swearing.

"I couldn't 'elp but over'ear, Cap'n," Tiny said before Nathaniel could ascend the ladder. "Surely ye don't truly intend to—"

"Yes, I do." Nathaniel spoke with conviction. "Any man found with lice will be shaved. I'll not have vermin aboard this ship. All the hammocks will be washed as well."

"But those critters are aboard every ship," Tiny complained, twisting his thick, stubby fingers through a full beard. "The men will not be 'appy—"

"Then they should have followed my instructions from the beginning. They've been warned before."

By midafternoon, nearly half of the crew milled about the deck, temporarily bald. Acting as self-conscious as shorn dogs, they slunk back into the corners of the ship whenever they could, grumbling to themselves about feeling naked.

Jake was the only one to put up a fight. But Nathaniel was on hand to see that his orders were carried through to the letter.

"The itching can't be too bad if you're not willing to be rid of the cause," he told Jake as Tiny tried to hold the young man still for Garth, who was acting as barber. "Could it be that you're the one who brought lice aboard in the first place?"

Jake tore away from Tiny's grip and charged Nathaniel, his good arm swinging, but three other men interceded in time to haul him back. "I'll not suffer this," he yelled as the first thatch of sandy-colored hair hit the deck.

"And I'll not tolerate the spread of lice," Nathaniel returned calmly. "I hope everyone understands that now."

"Aye, Cap'n," the men murmured, and Nathaniel doubted they would soon forget.

"I'll make you pay for this." Jake twisted and turned to avoid the razor, but with his injured hand still bandaged and hanging in a sling, he was easily overpowered. "You don't know who you're dealing with."

Forgetting their own humiliation long enough to enjoy Jake's misery, a ripple of laughter went through the men.

"Look! The high and mighty first mate of the *Eastern Horizon* is as bald as a baby's butt," someone chortled as the locks fell away.

Trenton laughed. "I'm just counting my lucky stars that I don't bunk with the lot of them," he told Nathaniel. "I have no doubt you'd do the same to me."

"I'd have my own head shaved if I had lice—" Nathaniel's words suddenly fell away. Jake was now as hairless as those who had undergone the blade before him, but a purplish birthmark, shaped like a boot, marked the top of his head.

The sight of it made Nathaniel sick. Tiny was right. This boy was no ordinary sailor.

Jake opened his mouth as if to shout yet another curse, but no sound came out. Something akin to fear entered his eyes as his gaze met and locked with Nathaniel's, and a sudden awareness passed between them as surely as though they had spoken the words aloud.

"Take him back to his bunk," Nathaniel ordered, feeling as though the wind had been knocked out of his lungs. "Everyone back to your posts."

Trenton watched Nathaniel curiously. "Do you feel all right?"

Nathaniel didn't answer. He'd never felt worse. He motioned for his first mate to follow him as he pivoted on the heel of one boot, then headed below.

Chapter 9

Alexandra was still recuperating in Nathaniel's cabin, so Nathaniel led the way to Trenton's, where they could afford themselves some privacy.

"What is it?" Trenton asked as soon as he closed the door behind them. "What just happened up there?"

Nathaniel didn't speak. He paced the short expanse of floor while Trenton leaned against the wall, arms folded, waiting.

"Does the name Albert Jacob Kimbolten mean anything to you?" he asked at length. He stopped moving to stare out the porthole, where a meager amount of afternoon sunlight streamed in.

"The Kimbolten name always means something to me," Trenton replied. "It's the duke's name. Why do you ask?"

"Because Jake is Albert Jacob Kimbolten, the duke's son."

A look of stunned surprise struck Trenton like a thunderbolt. "He can't be."

"He can, and he is. Think about it." Nathaniel watched his friend's face as Trenton tried to reconcile the boy Jake to his image of Nathaniel's half brother.

Nathaniel knew it was hard to imagine. He could scarcely believe it himself.

"He's the duke's son? The Marquess of Clifton? Jake talks like a sailor, not some high-born aristocrat."

"Aye, and under the circumstances, he'd be an idiot not to."

"He's a belligerent fool—"

"But who could my father trust to oversee the delivery of the guns more than his own son?"

"Still . . ." Trenton shook his head.

"He has a birthmark. Maybe you saw it. It's in the shape of Italy."

His first mate nodded.

"You remember when I was young, and Martha took me to see my father?"

"Aye. He called her a liar and insisted that his first child died at birth."

Nathaniel nodded. "He also had the nursemaid bring his new son in to show us his heir. It was his moment of triumph. The baby had the same birthmark."

Trenton rubbed his chin. "That was eighteen years ago."

"Aye, and I'll never forget it if I live to be a hundred. Do you think the day Martha died could ever fade from my memory?" Nathaniel flinched at the bitterness in his own voice.

"Nathaniel, you were only seven. Martha made the decision to go back to Bridlewood, not you. How could anyone have expected the duke to send his men after the two of you—"

"But I wanted to go," Nathaniel replied softly, closing his eyes. "I was so hopeful that my father would—" Afraid his voice might crack, he fell silent.

"You hoped what every other young boy would have hoped in your situation. That your father would finally accept you. I'm not sure that's the kind of thing a child ever outgrows."

"Well, I'm not a child anymore, and I'm not a powerless woman, either, a mere servant who loved a deformed boy to distraction. I can fight back. Greystone killed Martha. I know that as surely as I'm standing here."

Nathaniel pictured Martha's broken body trapped beneath the carriage, remembered tugging on her arm with all the strength his seven-year-old body could muster. The agony that had gripped him as the one person who loved him, had always loved him, slowly died was the worst hell he could ever endure. He'd been careful not to love so deeply since, for fear of suffering the same kind of loss again. He owed the ugly scar that experience had left on his heart, as well as all the years of loneliness afterward, to his father. "How I long to punish him for that," he whispered.

Trenton shifted away from the wall and crossed to sit at his small desk. "Did Martha really plan to go to a barrister and fight for your birthright?"

Nathaniel shrugged. "I can't be certain. She talked about it a great deal. She knew by law I would inherit everything if she could prove who I was. But she was the only person who could testify to what happened on the day I was born."

"That Greystone tried to kill you."

"Aye, but fate doesn't always follow a man's will, even a duke's."

"It takes a great deal of money to run an empire like your father's," Trenton mused. "So he starts smuggling rifles to Russia, and here we are."

Nathaniel closed his eyes, kneading his forehead with his fingertips. "Aye, here we are, with a beautiful, innocent woman lying in my bed, fighting for her life. And a bitter, injured half brother." So many thoughts assailed his brain that he could scarcely sort them out, let alone deal with the emotions they provoked.

"What happened to Alexandra is my fault, not yours," Trenton said, as though reading his mind. "I was certain she was the woman I had seen four years ago."

Nathaniel shook his head. "It's been my plan from the start. I'm responsible for Richard's capture, for Alexandra and now Jake, or rather, Lord Clifton."

"But your father deserves—"

"Therein lies the problem," Nathaniel interrupted. Damn if he didn't want to shout. "I know what my father deserves, and I bloody well want nothing more than to give it to him. But shouldn't the lives of others— of innocents—mean more to me than destroying him? The marquess is young. He's bitter and misguided perhaps, but he's not to blame for

Greystone's actions any more than Alexandra deserves what has happened to her." He sighed. "I know what I *should* do. I should salvage what I can of my future, forget my father and move on."

Trenton paused, as if trying to put sufficient thought into his next words. "Nathaniel, a couple of years spent picking the pockets of the unwary just to get a bite to eat numbed my conscience years ago. I have felt no guilt about stealing from the duke. And I'm not overly worried about Newgate or whatever our final punishment will be if we're caught. I figure I'll deserve it by then; I've always expected such an end anyway. What I'm trying to say is that I don't know if I'm the best person to offer advice, but if living a pirate's life is troubling you, there's no reason you can't change."

"Aye. I wish it were so easy." Nathaniel stared into space. "I can't explain it or even understand it, but there's a part of me that has ahold of this thing, and I can't let it go."

"What does that say for Alexandra?"

Nathaniel steeled himself against the pang of sadness that the thought of life without Alexandra provoked. "It says nothing. I'm taking her back, just like I planned."

Nanchu was spooning clear broth into Alexandra's mouth when Nathaniel entered. She glanced up as he shut the door, her eyes like saucers in her pale face, and Nathaniel felt a twinge of guilt. Despite Nanchu's assurances that the bullet had passed cleanly through her shoulder without causing any major damage, Nathaniel worried that the wound would not heal well.

And he knew it should be he convalescing in that bed from a bullet wound, not some poor girl.

"This patient know what good for her," Nanchu said as Alexandra continued to obediently sip soup from the spoon he held out to her. "Unlike young man."

"The marquess still won't allow the poultices?" Nathaniel asked in surprise.

Nanchu shook his head. "I cannot force a fool from his foolishness."

Nathaniel frowned. He'd moved his half brother into the purser's cabin where the boy could be more closely watched, but the knowledge of who Jake was didn't help his popularity among the crew. The boy had as much pride and arrogance as their father, but very little wisdom. "Then there's nothing we can do. Perhaps mettle alone will save his hand. It's saved me on occasion."

Nanchu gave a snort that let Nathaniel know he disagreed about the Marquess of Clifton possessing any such redeeming trait. "Come." He motioned Nathaniel toward the bed. "If you please, finish here? Henry waiting in sick bay. Need to check arm before his watch."

Henry was a member of the crew who had fallen from the rigging several days earlier and broken his arm. Nathaniel didn't doubt that the man needed attention, but he hesitated to perform the task of feeding Alexandra. It was easier to keep up a shield of indifference when he wasn't so close to her.

He glanced toward the bed, frowned, considered making some excuse, then chided himself for being weak-willed. Taking the bowl Nanchu held out to him, he moved irritably into the doctor's place.

"See she eats to last drop." Nanchu clasped his hands in a prayerlike attitude and bowed his head in Alexandra's direction.

Alexandra gave the doctor a smile, and Nathaniel noticed how it made her face light up. The dark rings around her eyes became less conspicuous. Her cheeks bloomed with a bit of their usual color, and her hair, cascading onto the pillows in wild disarray, looked as soft as silk and more tempting to his hand than spun gold.

Nathaniel wondered what it would feel like to entwine his fingers in those golden tresses and pull, forcing her head back to receive his kiss. Then he wished he could pass the bowl back to Nanchu and head to the deck or to Trenton's cabin—anywhere his heart was safe from melting. But the little doctor had already left the room.

Alexandra glanced up at him expectantly, long dark lashes making a perfect frame for her big green eyes.

Nathaniel let his scowl darken, hoping to discourage her from smiling again, or looking at him, or doing anything else that might make him want to touch her. She had complicated his life enough already. The revelations of the day had burdened him alternately with guilt, anger and chagrin.

He filled the spoon and held it to her lips, but it was difficult to concentrate on the soup. She wore one of his own shirts, her dress no longer serviceable after the rigors it had been through, and the swell of her breasts beneath the cloth lured him to distraction. The thought of her naked beneath his clothes made the blood pound in his ears until suddenly he laughed, his voice ringing loudly in the silence.

"What is it?" Alexandra asked.

Nathaniel didn't answer; he just grinned, remembering how he had thought himself a pervert, a deviant, to be so attracted to his sister. Now he reveled in the knowledge that he was completely normal after all—and decided to seek a little revenge for the sleepless nights her impersonation of Anne had put him through.

"What is it?" Alexandra repeated, smiling with the contagion of his mirth.

"I was only thinking that you must feel very strongly about me, to have taken that bullet the way that you did."

"I must?" Alexandra laughed herself. "I don't know why I was foolish enough to jump in front of you, but I doubt it stemmed from anything more than impulse."

Her color deepened, contradicting her words, and Nathaniel warmed to his game. Placing the soup on the table, he sat on the edge of the bed and took her hand in his. "You wouldn't have saved my life if you didn't care for me."

Alexandra snatched her hand away, looking uncomfortable, as though she didn't know what to do at this odd turn in his behavior.

"What I feel doesn't matter." She glanced at the bowl of soup. "Aren't you going to feed me any more? Nanchu said I should eat it all—"

"You can try to change the subject," Nathaniel replied, gently caressing her arm with his knuckles, "but I have a way of learning the truth."

He admired the delicate arch of her brows as she raised them. "I think you must be well into your cups."

Nathaniel had enjoyed more than his usual mug of rum for dinner. Everyone had. There was precious little to eat, and drink filled the belly. But he doubted the alcohol had half as much effect upon him as the softness of Alexandra's skin. "I'm drunk only on desire," he admitted.

Alexandra's eyes flew wide, like those of a startled child, as he retrieved her hand and kissed the tip of each finger.

"What are you doing? I'm not well," she said breathlessly.

Nathaniel smiled, enjoying her discomfiture. He let her go, but only to shift his position on the bed so he could hover over her.

"You're beautiful." He let his hand delve into her thick curls as he had longed to do. Twisting the shining tresses around each finger, he pulled gently until Alexandra's head tilted back and her breath fanned his face.

Nathaniel expected her to object, but she didn't. She merely closed her eyes, like someone savoring the feel of the sun on her cheeks.

He bowed closer. Alexandra wore no cologne—she had none—but her skin smelled slightly of soap. After the heavy perfumes many women wore to camouflage the reek of everyday perspiration and dirt, the mere absence of such appealed to him. He nuzzled her neck and ear, taking in the clean, sweet scent of her.

"I want you," he said, longing to kiss her.

Alexandra's lids fluttered opened. "Don't," she whispered, but the word held no conviction, and she didn't resist or pull away. She waited, her mouth slightly parted, watching him beneath her lashes.

Nathaniel bent his head until his lips lightly touched hers. Velvety soft, full and promising, her mouth moved beneath his own until he could control himself no longer. His grip tightened on her hair as he parted her lips, then he groaned in pleasure when she allowed his tongue access to her own.

Alexandra's hand climbed up his arm to circle his neck, and Nathaniel had to struggle to keep his passion in check. She was injured; he didn't want to hurt her. Forcing himself to use some restraint, he left her lips to travel kisses across her cheek and nibble at her earlobe with his teeth.

"Wait . . ." She gasped as his tongue darted into her ear. He blew gently on the wetness it left behind, feeling a degree of satisfaction when her body quivered against him.

"Alexandra, sweet Alexandra, how you have plagued my dreams," he whispered, alternating between sucking her earlobe and slipping his tongue into her ear again.

"Nathaniel—" Her hands reached for his hair and tugged him back for another kiss. As he drank from the wetness of her mouth, he feared he'd lose himself and simply drown. His body was making commitments his mind could not keep, yet he felt as powerless to resist as a leaf tossed against the wind.

It took all of his focus to pull away. When he did, Alexandra's face was flushed, and he could hear the soft pant of her breathing.

Suddenly Nathaniel was angry—angry with Alexandra for complicating his life when he least needed it, angry with his father for filling his heart with hatred until he had no chance at love, but mostly angry with himself for walking too close to the flame of his attraction. He wanted Alexandra, so much that it rankled to deny himself. Yet he couldn't take advantage of her innocence, especially after all she'd been through because of him. She wanted things he could not give her: a husband and a family. There was no place in his life for a woman. There was room only in his bed.

Quickly putting the distance of several feet between them, he moved away. "You're a witch, fair maiden," he murmured, admiring Alexandra's stormy eyes and her hair, tousled by his own hand. Then, afraid her beauty would weaken his resolve, he turned and left.

Slamming the door behind him, Nathaniel strode briskly down the companionway, heading up on deck. He needed the chill night air to cool his body and his mind, but movement in the hall behind him made him turn. Rat approached, carrying a lantern and singing some bawdy song about a sailor and his woman as he hurried toward the hatch, no doubt intent upon gathering with some of the others to do more drinking.

The little man froze when he recognized Nathaniel. "Cap'n? Is somethin' wrong?"

Even from several feet away, Nathaniel could smell alcohol on Rat's breath and guessed he'd already had a great deal more than his daily share of rum. "Where are you coming from?"

"I just took my turn standin' watch over the marquess. This voyage 'as certainly turned into a family affair, eh?" Rat's grin led Nathaniel to believe he knew, or at least suspected, Alexandra was not Anne. It looked more like a leer in the shifting light of the lantern.

Instantly alarmed, Nathaniel asked, "Who put you on the schedule?" He wanted to keep Rat as far away from Jake—from Clifton—as possible, and he'd thought he'd made that sufficiently clear to Trenton already.

"Daniel took sick, so I told 'im I'd take 'is watch."

"He took sick, or he drank himself into a stupor?" Nathaniel asked.

Rat laughed. "Well, 'tis not far from the same thing, aye?"

The knowledge that his orders had been undermined stoked Nathaniel's wrath like a fresh log on a roaring fire. "Why didn't you get Trenton's approval first?"

"I was only doin' the bloke a favor. Didn't think it'd be necessary."

"You were wrong. It's very necessary. If someone can't take their turn, I want you to come find me. Do you understand?"

"Aye, but—"

"Just follow orders," Nathaniel ground out. "You got that?" Unable to abide Rat ever since the incident with Alexandra in his cabin, Nathaniel pounded his finger into the smaller man's chest.

"What'd I say? What'd I do?" Rat cried in alarm, stepping back.

When he heard the defensiveness in Rat's voice, Nathaniel dropped his hand. He was overwrought and probably just looking for a target, but it goaded him that Rat had been left in charge of his half brother. Nathaniel didn't trust the little thief. Trenton and the others had to be more careful.

"Go below and get some sleep," he admonished, and Rat fled.

Chapter 10

"Sorry, Captain, there is nothing more to do. Hand must come off or boy will lose more of arm," Nanchu said quietly.

Alexandra was sitting in Nathaniel's bed, propped up by pillows. She was feeling stronger, the wound in her shoulder healing without any hint of infection, but the doctor's news made her look worriedly to the pirate captain. Naked to the waist, he'd just left his hammock and was standing at the washbasin, using a cloth to bathe before starting his day. The doctor stood at the door.

"It's beginning to rot?" Nathaniel's face was inscrutable as he set the rag on the edge of the bowl and turned toward the Chinese man.

"I'm afraid so. Boy has been so . . . uncooperative." Only because Alexandra had come to know Nanchu over the days of her convalescence was she able to detect his dislike for Jake, or rather, Lord Clifton. "Otherwise, maybe outcome different."

Nathaniel sighed and looked at Alexandra, then turned and finished tying his hair back. Finally his eyes found the doctor in the mirror. "Do what you must for his ultimate well-being. I'll be there momentarily."

Nanchu bowed and backed out of the room while Alexandra sat, picturing the face of the man she had seen carried aboard the *Vengeance*. The tragedy of losing a limb while fighting for some noble cause, as in war, was bad enough. But this was infinitely worse. The marquess would lose his hand because of Nathaniel—and he'd be lucky if the stump didn't fester and cause him to lose his life.

Nathaniel brushed his teeth and drew on his shirt while Alexandra watched.

"Do you have something to say, or have you taken new interest in my attire?" He turned his back to her as he strapped on his pistol and put his knife in his boot, a ritual he performed every day.

"Trenton told me who Jake is," she said, ignoring the sarcasm in his voice. "Surely you know the duke will hate you more after this. He'll probably kill you for it."

"I think you need to decide which role you mean to play"—he turned and raised a mocking brow—"my sister Anne, or an unconcerned needle-woman from Manchester. Adviser and confidante are not among your options."

Alexandra winced beneath the sting of his words. She hadn't seen Nathaniel for more than a brief moment over the past two days since he'd kissed her. It seemed that he was as eager as she to keep plenty of distance between them. "I didn't ask to be here," she retorted. "Besides, someone needs to talk some sense into you. Not all of life's problems can be handled with a knife or a gun."

"Now you're a philosopher?"

"I've done my share of living by my wits."

"Then perhaps you know when to keep your opinions to yourself."

Alexandra swallowed hard, once again at the receiving end of Nathaniel's angry glare. Unwilling to let him have the last word, she lifted her chin. "Now that I know you don't have the good sense to appreciate my wisdom, I will."

"Next time I'm lost in indecision, I'll remember to ask for your help."

"I won't be around. You promised to take me home, remember?"

Nathaniel gave her a slight bow. "Indeed. And it won't be long now. Soon you'll be back in your safe existence, just as if nothing had ever changed."

With that he stalked from the room, leaving Alexandra to wonder why she cared if the duke killed him or not. She should have let the sniper have a clean shot and saved them all a great deal of trouble.

Judging from his behavior, he felt worse about his half brother's hand than she did, but he couldn't open up and say so. Nothing about Nathaniel was simple. She hated his autocratic manner, his cynicism, his sharp temper and . . . Alexandra thought for a moment. What else did she hate about the pirate captain? She couldn't put her finger on everything just then, but when her temper began to cool, she knew. She hated the risks he took, the enemies he made, the hurt he had suffered as a child. Worse than anything, she hated the fact that soon she might never see him again.

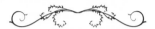

Nathaniel cringed as his eye caught sight of the doctor's instruments: two sharp knives for slicing through skin, muscle and tendons; a bone saw; a piece of rope to clamp between Clifton's teeth; and a bucket of boiling pitch to sear the flesh and stop the bleeding.

For all Nanchu's advancement in the field of medicine, cutting off a limb was still cutting off a limb. He did it the same way any other doctor would—with a little bit of rum and a saw, and in less than a minute. Much longer, and the patient would bleed to death, if the shock and pain didn't kill him first.

"Are you sure we have to do this?" Nathaniel asked as Tiny, Trenton, Garth and John used ropes to strap the frantic Clifton to the table.

Nanchu didn't answer. He removed the bandage from the marquess's wrist and let the putrid smell and grayish-green flesh speak for themselves.

"No! Don't! Please!" Lord Clifton thrashed wildly as they tried to tie him down. Managing to free a leg, he kicked John and sent him sprawling, but Nathaniel stepped in.

"You did this," the marquess snarled, his eyes glassy. "You want me to be no more whole than you are."

Nathaniel stared down at his half brother while Nanchu applied a tourniquet just below Clifton's elbow. He thought he'd feel hate, maybe even the morbid sense of satisfaction that his half brother accused him of feeling, but he was wholly unprepared for the poignant remorse that flooded his heart. The boy thought he had done this on purpose? Regardless of who Lord Clifton was, at that moment he was simply a man about to lose his hand, and after struggling to live a normal life with such a handicap, Nathaniel would have given anything to save it.

"Nanchu, is there any chance? Any chance at all?" he asked. The marquess's body quivered as everyone looked hopefully at the Chinese doctor.

"So sorry. Too late." The ropes were secure, the tourniquet in place. Waving them all back, he asked Tiny to hold Clifton's arm still, but Nathaniel volunteered for the odious task himself.

"I'll do it," he said. "The four of you can go."

Tiny, Garth and John glanced at each other in obvious relief, then beat a quick retreat.

"Let me do that, Nathaniel," Trenton said, staying on.

Nathaniel shook his head, unable to explain why he had to see the amputation through. For him, escape at that moment seemed a cowardly thing. Holding tightly to the marquess's arm, he forced his mind away from what was taking place and pictured Alexandra the way she had looked when he had kissed her, imagined her caressing him softly, saw her smile invitingly . . .

Clifton let out a gut-wrenching scream and the vision instantly dissipated. The doctor had made his first cut several inches above the original wound. Blood splattered everywhere as he continued to slice through the muscles and tendons. Then he began to saw through the bone.

Nathaniel turned his face away, feeling sick. His half brother's arm twisted back and forth with the friction, then there was a soft thud as the cankerous hand fell to the floor.

Silence. The marquess had fainted, but no such oblivion eased Nathaniel's pain. When he closed his eyes, he could still hear Clifton's screams echoing in his head.

"Are you all right?" Trenton watched Nathaniel with a look of concern.

"I'm fine. I think Nanchu can finish now. Let's get out of here."

The putrid smell of burning flesh combined with hot tar followed them all the way to the galley.

"Charlie, give me that bottle of Blue Ruin I had you tuck away," Nathaniel said.

Charlie raised his tufted eyebrows. "That bad, eh?"

"That bad," Trenton breathed, but it was Nathaniel who grabbed the bottle from the cook's hand when Charlie retrieved it, and together they headed to Trenton's cabin.

Alexandra knew something was wrong the moment Nathaniel opened the door. Normally quiet and as sure-footed as a cat's, his step was loud and uneven, and he groaned as he clipped the wall with his shoulder.

She tried not to smile at his clumsiness. He'd obviously had too much to drink. The headache he'd own in the morning would be a just revenge.

"Bloody hell!"

Hearing the mumbled curse, Alexandra wondered what other mishap Nathaniel had managed. It was too dark to see anything except the soft glow of his teeth and the whites of his eyes, but she thought he'd hit his shin on the chair as he stumbled to the window.

He was close enough for her to smell the alcohol on him, and she wrinkled her nose in distaste. She hated that smell. She associated it with everything she had suffered at her stepfather's hands. But she'd seen little evidence that Nathaniel drank much. His men downed rum like water—the slimy ship water tasted so bad that half the time she didn't blame them—but rarely had she smelled an excess of alcohol on Nathaniel.

So he has one redeeming feature, she thought grudgingly.

Evidently he still had a bottle in his hand. Alexandra heard the soft pop as he tipped it up and took a long drink. Then he sank down onto the floor in the small circle of light made by the moon and gazed up through the porthole.

What's he thinking? Alexandra wondered, noticing how much softer the hard planes of his face looked in the mellow light. His hair, loose from its tie, fell tousled about his shoulders; his clothes were uncharacteristically disheveled. He looked like a forlorn lad sitting there, like the lonely little boy he must once have been.

Alexandra wrestled with herself, trying to remain indifferent. After a few moments, she rose and padded over to him.

He didn't so much as turn at the muted sound of her movements. He just continued to stare out the window at the stars.

"Let's get you to bed." She tugged gently on his arm, and he stood, letting her pull the tails of his shirt from his trousers and undo its buttons. As she slipped the garment over his shoulders, she tried not to notice how her hands burned when they brushed his skin.

"That's good," she said. "Now sit."

"You don't know what good is." He remained standing, just inches away from her, and she could feel his eyes cutting through the darkness. "But I could teach you."

His gentle invitation made Alexandra giddy. How many nights had she watched him disrobe for bed, heard the sounds he made as he settled himself and wished he'd come to her? But did she want him like this? He was only searching for a way to stop the pain. He wanted to lose himself in her arms for the same reason he had tried to drown himself in the bottle.

"You're not up to teaching anyone anything tonight," she chided.

She saw the glint of his teeth as his mouth stretched into a lascivious grin. "Try me," he said, pulling her hand to the physical proof.

Alexandra let her fingers linger as the most delicious sensation assailed her. She could spend this one night with him and hold the memory of it forever, except that her terms demanded more than one brief encounter. She couldn't give her body without giving her heart. Pulling away, she pressed him back, and he sank onto the bed.

She knelt between his legs to take off his boots. He was in shadow now; she could no longer see the silhouette of his face, but she could feel his gaze on the top of her head. She nearly changed her mind about joining him—until one moment's imagination showed her what it would be like tomorrow, knowing she could never have him for good. Willy had shown her pain enough; she wasn't going to ask for more, especially of such an exquisite type.

Rising, Alexandra tried to press Nathaniel back so she could cover him with blankets, but he resisted her attempt. He sat rigid for a moment, then his arm went slowly around her waist. Pulling her to him, he laid his head on her breast.

Alexandra's hands lifted instinctively to caress him as she would a hurt child. Running her fingers through his hair, she used her nails to gently scratch his scalp until his breathing slowed, and he relaxed against her, falling asleep.

Still weak from her injury, Alexandra couldn't hold him long. Smiling, she kissed the top of his head, then laid him back, and this time he relaxed into the covers.

Marveling at the many facets of the pirate captain, Alexandra climbed into his hammock, her bare legs chilly beneath his long shirt. He could have the bed for the night, she decided. But her arms felt cold and empty without him, and it was a long time before she slept.

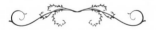

Alexandra woke to find the sun streaming in at the porthole and Nathaniel staring at her from the bed.

"Tell me about your stepfather," he said softly.

Alexandra blinked in surprise. To convince Nathaniel of her true identity when he thought she was Lady Anne, she had told the pirate captain as much as she wanted him to know about Willy. It wasn't a subject she enjoyed talking about. "Why do you ask?"

"I know you wanted to leave him badly enough to steal a dress and flee. There had to be a reason."

Alexandra lowered her gaze to the scarred wooden floor, avoiding the intensity in Nathaniel's eyes. She wished she could just as easily avoid a recounting of the miserable years with Willy. "Willy turned to gin when my mother died nearly five years ago, and drinking makes him . . . violent."

Nathaniel flinched, but whether in response to her words or what had to be a terrible headache after last night, Alexandra didn't know. "He hurt you?"

She nodded.

"Often?"

"Whenever he got drunk, which was often enough. Only, I learned to avoid him when he was like that . . . most of the time." She forced a smile to her lips to cover the ache in her heart. Willy was the only father she had ever known. His betrayal was not an easy thing to understand or accept. Neither was the fact that his actions had forced her to break the promise she had given her mother that she would look after him.

Shoving the pillows behind his back, Nathaniel sat up. He still wore the pants she'd left on him the night before, but as he moved, the blankets slid down to his waist, revealing his powerful torso.

Alexandra hoped her face did not show the longing she felt to touch him. Now that he had broached the subject of her background, she found she wanted to talk about it after all. She needed someone to hold her and to tell her that she wasn't to blame for Willy's hatred. That she hadn't earned his derision. That under the circumstances, she couldn't be expected to make good on her promise to stay and care for him.

As if reading her mind, Nathaniel motioned her to him.

Alexandra paused only a moment before moving closer, her need for solace overriding her usual wariness.

He held back the covers, welcoming her into the warmth of the bed and sharing the heat of his body by wrapping his arm around her and holding her close. "What now, sweet Alexandra?" he murmured against the hair at her temple.

She breathed in the scent that was uniquely his own. "Now I find work in London," she said, finding his embrace and the slight motion as he rocked her comforting in a very basic way. She'd had no one to ease her fears or calm her troubled thoughts for so long. She felt like a starving man sitting down to a sumptuous feast, though she thought it strange that it would be the insolent pirate captain who knew what she needed—and just how much of it to give.

"Why London?" he asked.

"Why not?" She pressed her cheek to his chest and tried to absorb every texture that was Nathaniel Kent. Never had she imagined a man so virile and appealing to the senses.

"Because you said your aunt is on her way to India. Do you know anyone else there?"

She shook her head, wishing he wouldn't talk, wanting him to simply hold her forever.

For several minutes, she had her wish. Then he broke the silence. "We'll reach Bristol today. I have to make arrangements to trade Lord Clifton for Richard, but then I'll take you wherever you want to go."

Alexandra opened her mouth to argue. The tenderness she felt for Nathaniel at that moment, and the night before, had destroyed a good measure of her reserve, and she thought it best if they parted sooner rather than later. But she didn't say so. Her words might cause him to let go of her and get out of bed, and she wasn't ready for that. Not yet.

Part of her wondered if she ever would be.

Nanchu had just finished taking a final look at the marquess's arm when Nathaniel entered the sick bay.

"I want to send a message to your father," he told his half brother, keeping his eyes carefully averted from the boy's right arm, which now ended in a white bandage where his hand should have been.

"My arrival in this condition will be message enough." Clifton sent him a scornful glance. "You will pay for this. Mark my words."

Nathaniel ignored the threat. The boy had brought the injury on himself through his own stupidity. "There will be no arrival unless your father releases Richard," he replied. "So you'll only help yourself by cooperating. Where do you think we can find the duke? At Bridlewood or at Greystone House in London?"

"He's not at Bridlewood."

"So he's in London. Buying another shipment of rifles to send to Russia, perhaps?"

"You don't know what you're talking about."

Lord Clifton's voice grew passionate. "My father would never do anything to hurt England."

"Treason is by its very nature injurious. But he will pay the price. You see, I'm a bit of a patriot at heart."

"My father is a powerful man with friends in very high places. You can do nothing to hurt him."

Nathaniel gave a sardonic laugh. "Then you have nothing to worry about."

When the *Vengeance* finally arrived in Bristol, Alexandra was eager to stretch her legs on land and to eat some decent food. And she couldn't wait to wear something more attractive than the baggy men's garb she'd had on since the storm. She decided to visit a bakery on her way to buy fabric—and then she frowned. A dress was no small expense. She certainly hadn't anticipated such a need when she planned to strike out on her own from Madame Fobart's.

She quickly plaited her hair into one long braid that fell down her back, and cinched up Nathaniel's belt for what she hoped was the last time. She was just about to head up on deck when Nathaniel entered the cabin.

"I'm ready," she announced, overcompensating for the twinge of shyness that the memory of their time together in his bed, though completely innocent, evoked. In a way, his kindness had forged a bond between them as strong or stronger than if they had become physically intimate, and she no longer knew how to treat the pirate captain. "I can already taste a fresh bun. And oh, for some butter and clear water—"

Nathaniel scowled. "How soon are you expecting such fare?"

"As soon as possible." She smiled at him. "Can I take the first lighter to the dock?"

Shrugging out of a damp coat, he threw back the lid to his sea chest and withdrew a fresh one. "I'm afraid not. You'll need to stay here with Trenton."

She blinked at him in surprise. "But why?"

"I have to take care of some things."

"Which has nothing to do with me. I'm not your prisoner anymore. You've said so yourself, remember? You said you were going to release me."

"I didn't say when."

Despite his answer, Alexandra had to struggle to keep her gaze from drifting over the cotton shirt that stretched taut as he moved. How well she remembered the feel of his muscles moving beneath her hands when he'd held her earlier.

"You're just being difficult," she said. "Surely there is some way to convince you . . ." She stepped closer and offered him a sultry smile. She felt a little deprived that he hadn't tried to kiss her while she was in his bed. He had never been indifferent to her before. Had his interest waned while her desire for him only grew stronger?

He cocked a dark eyebrow at her and dropped the coat on the bed. "That depends on what you're offering."

Alexandra felt her pulse quicken. She'd caught his attention all right, but wasn't it foolish to tempt fate? "What is it you want?"

His gaze roved over her, leaving little doubt as to his answer, but at last his eyes focused on her lips. "I'll settle for a kiss."

"For a kiss you'll take me to shore?" she asked, his ready acceptance of her offer making her suspicious.

"Not such a hard bargain, eh?" He spread out his arm, the planes of his face softening with a smile. "I'm waiting."

Alexandra twisted her hands, suddenly wishing she hadn't started this bold little game. "Could you at least close your eyes and pucker up or something?"

He laughed softly and closed his eyes. "Your wish is my command."

Butterflies fluttered in Alexandra's stomach as she gazed at his handsome face. He had the look of a rogue, with his long hair falling from the thong in back and a small scar near the cleft in his chin. And he could play the role of a rogue better than any man she had ever met, which only made her more nervous. "This is ridiculous—"

"Don't you want that bun you mentioned?" The corner of his mouth quirked up, but his eyes remained shut. "And some clear water?"

"Fine. Just kiss me," she said, stepping closer.

"No, you set the price yourself. You're going to do the kissing."

Alexandra took a deep breath. It was only a kiss. How difficult could it be? Placing her hands on his chest, she stood on tiptoe and pressed her lips to his. Planning to deliver a quick, pristine peck, just enough to satisfy her end of the bargain, she gasped when his arm pulled her roughly against his hard frame.

He parted her lips with his tongue, kissing her thoroughly, until her lips burned from the warmth and the movement, then set her away from him. "That's one of the better bargains I've made," he said, looking as though he'd kiss her again if she so much as leaned toward him. "Consider me convinced—"

"Wonderful!"

"—to take you to town in the morning."

"In the morning?" Alexandra's mouth gaped open as his words sank in. He didn't plan to take her ashore now any more than he had when he'd told her no in the first place. "You deceived me," she accused.

He winked. "Aye, and it was well worth the damage to my character." Smiling as smugly as the cat who swallowed the canary, he turned to rummage through his desk and retrieved a roll of bills from a drawer where they'd been cast inside as carelessly as trash. "This is a quick stop," he explained, counting the money. "I can't afford any complications."

Alexandra's hands clenched into fists. Truth be told, she had enjoyed the kiss as much as Nathaniel, but a bargain was a bargain, and getting cheated did not sit well with her. Especially when it meant another night of drinking slimy, brackish water. "Do you think I would turn you in?"

He pulled on his fresh coat and shoved the money into his pocket. "How do I know what you might try in some misguided attempt to help the marquess? You nearly got us all killed with that schooner. My father is a very powerful man. In most regards, he owns this town, and I've done little to endear myself to you." He grinned. "One kiss hardly guarantees your loyalty. But I'm willing to let you try again, if you think you can convince me otherwise." He closed his eyes and puckered up.

Ignoring the mocking gesture, Alexandra crossed her arms over her chest. "I want to get off this boat," she said. "And only if you refuse me will you have reason to worry."

He opened his eyes to consider her threat, then infuriated her further by giving her a careless shrug. "I'm capable of providing my own insurance, thank you." He dipped his head in parting.

"Why are you being so stubborn?" she asked, her voice rising with her temper. "Are you doing something with Lord Clifton I might not agree with?"

Nathaniel paused at the door. "I'm taking him to London with us. We'll go by carriage while Trenton gets the *Vengeance* ready to sail again. So now you know. Are you satisfied?"

"No, what are you going to do with him in London?"

"Eat him for supper—right after I finish with you." Laughing, he walked out.

"I hope you get caught," Alexandra shouted after him, but the closing of the door was her only response.

By midnight the guns were safely deposited in a warehouse not too far from shore. Nathaniel thought it a perfect location, given the constraints of time.

After Tiny and the rest of the small party he had brought from the ship had left, he sat on the last of the crates, exhausted, thinking about Alexandra. The vision of her face made him long to return to his cabin and kiss away her anger, to take her to his bed and become one with her before he lost her forever. Part of him argued that a single night wouldn't matter. But deep down he knew if he went that far, he would never be able to let her go. He was already feeling protective and too possessive for his own good.

"Cap'n?"

Nathaniel turned to find Tiny standing just inside the door of the vast, hollow-sounding building. The moon silhouetted his large bulk. "What are you doing back here, my friend? I thought you'd be enjoying a good booze up by now."

Tiny ran a hand over the prickly new growth on his head, which was now barely a quarter of an inch long. "I was 'opin' to catch ye before ye went back to the ship. I 'eard somethin' at the Yard's Arm I thought ye might want to know about."

The tone of Tiny's words caused Nathaniel's stomach to tense. "What's that?"

"England's gone to war. The infantry embarked to Malta March twenty-eighth, but the first shots weren't fired until April twenty-second, when our warships attacked the port of Odessa. Everyone's talkin' about it."

That England and France had finally, or rather, officially, backed Turkey in the fight against Russia came as a shock, even though Nathaniel had been expecting it for some time. Now that English blood was being spilled, his father's intentions to sell arms to the enemy became that much more distasteful to him, especially because the Minie rifle was more accurate and far-carrying than the smooth-bore firelock, which was still the regulation weapon in line regiments.

Fleetingly, Nathaniel wondered why a man with so much would commit treason, but then, he had never understood his father. His desire to do so had been the bane of his existence.

"That raises the stakes a bit, doesn't it?" Nathaniel asked.

Tiny nodded. "Aye."

Allowing himself no more time to rest, Nathaniel got to his feet. He had to stop his father from shipping any more guns to Russia, which meant he had to get back to the *Vengeance* so they could leave for London at dawn.

Chapter 11

The carriage Nathaniel rented was an ordinary black conveyance that seated eight people. Alexandra was squished between Tiny and the pirate captain himself; Garth was on the other side of Tiny. Samuel, an average-looking fellow with a thick head of hair; Shorty, a tall, heavyset man with a tattoo on the bald pate of his head; and John sat with the marquess on the other side.

They started out shortly after dawn, traveling in silence as they passed the elegant squares and graceful crescents of Bristol. Alexandra had never visited the city before. She loved the Georgian architecture, complete with its colonnades and terraces.

"That's Royal York Crescent, the longest crescent in Europe," Nathaniel pointed out as they passed a long building of flats that curved like a half-moon. "It was started before the turn of the century, but wasn't finished until 1820 or so."

"Isn't Blaise Castle around here somewhere?" Alexandra asked. "My mother once mentioned having seen it."

"It's in Clifton," the marquess said, speaking for the first time. "So is Bridlewood, my father's home."

Nathaniel glanced at his half brother without responding.

"Then you're familiar with this area," Alexandra said.

"The air and the water of Clifton are unsurpassed."

"So I've heard. So are the beautiful hills and dales." Alexandra smiled, wondering what the marquess was really like. He was not unhandsome with his short, sandy-colored hair and green eyes. His nose was rather wide, and his stocky build was enough to suggest a preponderance of weight as he grew older, but he had sensual lips and straight, nice teeth. She marveled that, other than the lips, there was so little resemblance between Nathaniel and his younger brother.

"Is the Clifton Suspension Bridge as spectacular as they say?" she asked.

"Yes, though it's not finished yet. The Severn is one of the most beautiful rivers in the world."

Nathaniel had brought Alexandra a basket of fresh buns that morning, together with a small crock of butter, and she took two out now, offering one to Lord Clifton. She was sure the marquess had eaten nothing but hardtack biscuits and salt pork since coming aboard the *Vengeance*. They'd had nothing else.

Clifton smiled and accepted the bread from her outstretched hand. "I can see why these miscreants mistook you for my sister. You're not only beautiful, but generous as well."

Alexandra gave him a dimpled smile. The last thing she expected was a compliment as she sat there in Nathaniel's clothes. But she would have felt even more self-conscious wearing the now ruined, expensive blue dress she had taken from Lady Anne.

"Sometimes it's wise for prisoners to pull together." Just as the marquess had emphasized *miscreants*, she emphasized the word *prisoners* for Nathaniel's benefit, still goaded by his refusal to trust her enough to take her into Bristol the night before.

Nathaniel ignored them, but as Alexandra's conversation with Lord Clifton warmed, touching a variety of subjects from the Royal Strand Theater in London to the hot wells of Bath, his gaze repeatedly flicked her way. Evidently her friendliness with his half brother struck a nerve, so she remembered to laugh gaily at whatever Clifton said.

Suddenly a large crack resounded, like the snap of a whip, and the carriage tilted dramatically. Nathaniel's hard body slammed into Alexandra, but the reassuring strength of his arm instantly encircled her waist and held her steady.

"What happened?" she asked as their carriage skidded to a halt. Dust rose all around, clogging her nostrils and making her cough.

"We've probably lost a wheel," Nathaniel said. "Are you all right?"

Alexandra nodded, and he disappeared through the door into the cloud of dust.

A moment later he poked his head inside the carriage and spoke to Tiny. "It's a wheel, all right. Damned if this won't cost us a day."

Tiny heaved himself toward the door. "Can we fix it ourselves?"

Nathaniel stepped back to let the big man out. "No." He squinted against the sun. "Someone will have to ride to the next town and get a blacksmith."

"What about Clifton? If someone stops to see if they can help, it might not bode well to find a captive," Samuel interjected.

"Don't worry about the marquess," Nathaniel said, helping Alexandra down. "I'm sure the point of my knife will convince him to act like one of us." He grinned at his half brother. "He's so close to home, he'd be stupid to raise an alarm now, anyway."

"I'll go for the blacksmith," Garth volunteered, seemingly eager to accept the task at hand rather than sit in the heat and wait.

"No. You stay here with me. Sam can handle it," Nathaniel told him.

Garth frowned but nodded, then moved with the captain and the other men to the shade of a large oak tree, leaving the marquess to get out on his own and hover about the carriage as Samuel rode away.

Alexandra climbed a small hill not far from the road and sat at the top to survey the countryside. She'd never been away from Manchester, but the verdant grass and purple and yellow wildflowers around her couldn't hold her attention. Her gaze was drawn back to Nathaniel again and again. Now that she was finally on her way to London, her anger at him had softened, despite her best efforts to shore it up. And though she had flirted with the marquess, Lord Clifton held no attraction for her. Only the pirate captain could make her heart pound with the simplest look or gesture.

She sighed heavily. Fate had dealt her an unlucky hand. Perhaps she would never know another who drew her as Nathaniel did, another who was so strong and cunning and virile.

But it wouldn't be hard to find a man who wasn't a criminal, she reminded herself. Even if she and Nathaniel had a chance together, the duke would never let them live in peace. She'd be forced to watch Nathaniel die or go to prison, and she couldn't endure that.

Neither had he asked her to remain with him, in any capacity.

She lowered her lashes when Nathaniel's glance flicked her way. There was something between them. She could feel it even from a distance. But whatever the seed that had been sown, neither she nor Nathaniel would give it room to grow. They couldn't afford to.

Samuel brought back a rotund man who set himself immediately to the task of fixing the carriage.

Alexandra watched him work from her perch at the top of the hill, enjoying the slow-moving day. The time when she would be separated from Nathaniel was looming too close already. She liked listening to his deep voice as he spoke to Tiny, and she tried to catch every syllable that floated to her on the wind.

He seemed equally aware of her. Every few moments his eyes lingered on her almost like a caress, as if he needed to reassure himself of her presence. Once he smiled, and Alexandra's heart swelled to see the uncharacteristic abandon on his face. She wanted to make him smile like that more often.

But she wouldn't be around to do it. Some other woman would have to soothe his hurts. And it was for the best, she told herself as she watched Lord Clifton make his way toward her.

Before speaking, Nathaniel's half brother jammed his good hand into the pocket of the sailor's breeches he wore. He commented on the weather and the countryside, then cleared his throat and lowered his voice.

"Nathaniel's guard cannot be raised against us both all of the time. Perhaps if one of us were to create a diversion, the other could gain access to a weapon, or escape and bring help."

Alexandra didn't have to ask which role the marquess expected her to play. No doubt she was to be the diversion. But she couldn't do anything that would get Nathaniel hurt, or worse, killed.

"He has the senses of a cat," she replied honestly. "I doubt it would be wise to try and thwart him now. Besides, there's no point in it. He's already agreed to release the both of us."

"When it suits him," Lord Clifton responded bitterly. "I'll not have him hold me as ransom for that thief Richard."

Alexandra studied Lord Clifton's injured arm. The marquess was brave, she had to admit, but pride seemed to motivate most of his actions. "You could be harmed if you don't cooperate. Haven't you paid too heavy a price already?"

Hate contorted Clifton's features. "I'll have that blackguard's head mounted on the gate at Bridlewood someday," he vowed.

Alexandra's stomach clenched at the thought. "I don't doubt that you will." *Or rather, that your father will,* she added silently. "But today is not the day. We're too close to freedom to risk further loss of life or limb. We'd be foolish not to go along with him until he releases us."

She noticed Nathaniel scowling at them and stood, brushing bits of twig and dirt from the trousers she wore. "I think it's time to go. It looks as though the wheel is fixed."

Fortunately, the marquess seemed to take her advice. The journey to the next small town was uneventful. Lord Clifton didn't speak again, to her or anyone else. He stared out the window, his face an emotionless mask.

Nathaniel, on the other hand, studied her every move. Alexandra felt his gaze upon her like the sun beating through a window and wondered if he, too, dreaded the moment when they would part. Had the desire for revenge captured the whole of his heart, or had she managed to achieve some small purchase there?

They rolled into Farringdon long after dark. Alexandra had expected to continue through the night, so she was surprised when Nathaniel called to Garth, whose turn it was to drive, to stop at the first inn.

"Why are we stoppin'?" Tiny posed the question, but the rest of Nathaniel's men stretched and looked to him for the answer as well.

"I'm going to send a message to Greystone. We'll arrive in London tomorrow afternoon, several hours after our message has been delivered."

Tiny shrugged. "Whether we wait in London or 'ere is all the same to me. But I am longin' for a bed, that I am."

"Aye," a tired, dusty Garth agreed.

Alexandra didn't say anything, but she was glad for the delay. They'd arrive in London soon enough. She took a deep breath as the stranglehold of emotion that had squeezed her heart all day lessened just a bit. *A few more hours,* she thought. A few more hours were better than nothing.

The inn was on the outskirts of town, just beyond a series of small farms. A string of squat buildings with thatch roofs, it was old, but the proprietor and his wife kept the place clean and in good repair.

Nathaniel rented several rooms for the eight of them, and made Garth guard the marquess. He knew Garth was tired, but Clifton was easier to control when Nathaniel wasn't near him. Nathaniel didn't want to end up killing the boy during the night, which was, at times, no small temptation.

Besides, he had enough to worry about. The closer he came to freeing Alexandra, the more reluctant he was to do so.

Using one of the keys the steward had given him, he opened a door at the end of a dimly lit corridor and motioned Alexandra inside. "You'll sleep here tonight," he said. He was tempted to follow her in, but forced his feet to continue on to the next room.

She stepped back into the hall long enough to watch him open his own door. "You're going to trust me?" she asked.

"You have no reason to go anywhere. I'm already taking you to London."

"Don't you think I'll implement some desperate plot to save the marquess? Isn't that what you were afraid I'd do in Bristol?"

"My father doesn't live in this town," he countered. "Besides, I don't think you're foolish enough to risk Lord Clifton's life. Garth is tired and bad-tempered. A stupid move would only get my half brother shot, and possibly yourself as well."

Nathaniel knew that he was the one who sounded tired and bad-tempered, but it provided a safe facade behind which to hide his true feelings. "Good night."

Alexandra smiled and nodded before entering her own room. She closed the door, and he wondered if she was pleased with her newfound privacy. His own room seemed cold and empty without her. After spending the past few weeks in such close proximity, he'd become accustomed to Alexandra's presence—the small sounds she made in her sleep, the way she arranged his few personal belongings on the wash-stand, the womanly smell of her.

But he dared not place temptation in his path tonight. He was too close to releasing her. Besides the fact that he had made her miss her aunt's ship, she wasn't much worse off than she'd been when he'd snatched her, now that her injury was almost healed. If he allowed the desire that curled around his heart and tightened his groin to take con-trol, however . . .

Nathaniel tried to direct his thoughts away from Alexandra. Dwell-ing on her would only undermine his resolve, which felt amazingly weak already. Stripping off his clothes, he crossed to the washstand and busied himself washing up. As he did so, his mind's eye presented him with a picture of Alexandra doing the same, and he felt the familiar pull that threatened to be his undoing.

Plunging his head beneath the water, he scrubbed his hair. After toweling off, he forced himself to lie down, even though he could hear Alexandra moving about next door, and knew he'd never be able to sleep.

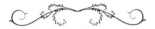

Alexandra paced the floor of her room. She was grateful for the reprieve from the bone-jarring carriage ride, but the large featherbed shoved against one wall held no appeal for her. She could think only of Nathaniel.

The memory of their last kiss played in her mind, causing something deep inside her to stir. She longed to feel his touch again, if only for a brief moment.

She poured herself a glass of water from the pitcher on the washstand. He couldn't burn for her the way she burned for him if he could set her free so easily, she thought, irritated at her own foolish craving. No doubt she had misinterpreted the many times his hand had brushed her arm throughout the day, the looks he'd given her. He felt responsible for her current precarious situation, nothing more, and he was doing what he could to make it right.

A soft knock at the door interrupted Alexandra's musings. Casting a quick glance in the mirror, she hurried across the floor. Her brushed and gleaming hair fell to her waist, framing a flushed face, and she wore what she had worn throughout her convalescence—Nathaniel's shirt.

At the door she paused, knowing better than to open it. It could be anyone, though deep down, she knew it was him. "Who is it?"

"Nathaniel."

Alexandra unbolted the door and opened it a crack to see the pirate captain standing in the hall, wearing only his trousers and boots. His broad chest gleamed in the light of the lamps that lit the hallway, though his eyes were as dark as pits. She couldn't see what emotion smoldered inside them. She could only feel the current that ran between them like a physical force, pulling them together.

She resisted whatever compelled her to rush into his arms, knowing that to succumb to such desire would be foolhardy. Her heart was already in jeopardy; she didn't want Nathaniel to own her soul as well. Still, to her own mortification, she stepped back so he could enter.

Nathaniel's hair was wet, and Alexandra could smell the scent of freshly washed skin as he stepped across the threshold. She wanted to reach out and touch him, to knead his thick muscles, but she knew the slightest contact would ignite a flame so intense it would be difficult to extinguish.

Perhaps he had come for a reason. Perhaps he needed to tell her something.

When Nathaniel turned to face her, Alexandra knew he hadn't come to talk. He reached out and captured one of her hands with his own, then kissed each fingertip.

Before his touch left her completely senseless, she pulled away, eager to have the advantage over him, since she so rarely possessed it.

"Is there a problem with your room?" she asked, trying to sound flippant.

His eyes narrowed and his voice lowered almost to a growl. "Don't tease me tonight, Alexandra. Your lips may say one thing, but your eyes tell an entirely different story."

"Which is better than my lying to you outright, like you did to me at Bristol."

"I had good reason for leaving you on the *Vengeance*."

"And you're not to be questioned, is that it?"

"You can ask, but I might not answer." He smiled and moved toward her, his eyes smoldering as he again took her hand and kissed her palm. "Besides, you had your revenge in the carriage today, and you know it."

Alexandra couldn't help but smile. She'd been right about her interest in the marquess bothering the pirate captain. "Still, you made a bargain you didn't keep," she reminded him.

"If it's honesty you want, I'm ready to tell you anything you want to hear."

Alexandra easily detected the mirth in his words as his lips started moving up her arm. "Isn't there something contradictory about that statement?"

He chuckled. "Everything about us is contradictory, except this." He nuzzled the curve of her neck below her left ear as his fingers found the baby hairs at her nape.

"And this is honest?" she asked, scarcely able to breathe as his mouth moved toward her lips.

"Can you think of anything more so?"

Alexandra had no answer for that. Her mind might prevaricate and insist she had no interest in him, but her body refused to lie.

She groaned and swayed toward him as his mouth found hers. His tongue parted her lips and flicked against her teeth before making deep thrusts that mimicked the complete possession to come.

Alexandra wondered if Nathaniel did indeed mean to extract her very soul. She felt the strength of the arm that encircled her, the rapid but sure beat of his heart beneath her hand on his chest, and her own resistance began to slip away.

But scarcely had her hands found their way up Nathaniel's back and into the thickness of his hair than a loud thud came from Garth's room next door.

Clifton!

Nathaniel pulled back, a look of panic seizing his features as he darted back into the hall.

Nathaniel crashed through the door to see the marquess grappling with Garth on the ground. The two were fighting for control of Garth's pistol, and first one then the other gained advantage. Grabbing the knife from his boot, Nathaniel leaped over the bed to reach them just as Clifton managed to roll on top. His half brother had got ahold of the gun, but Nathaniel wrapped his arm around Clifton's neck and lay the blade against his throat.

"That's enough," Nathaniel said through gritted teeth.

Lord Clifton froze.

"Drop the gun."

Sensing the marquess's hesitancy, Nathaniel pressed the knife deeper into his skin, until a drop of blood rolled down over his thumb. "I'm not playing games."

The marquess dropped the gun as Samuel, John and the others congregated just inside the open doorway.

"What happened?" John asked.

Garth was breathing heavily as Clifton got off him. "I don't know. I tied him up, then turned around to close the shutters. The next thing I knew, he attacked me." He sat up and swiped at a small stream of blood that trickled from his mouth. "I don't know how he managed to get out of the ropes, but he hit me with something, then went for my gun."

Nathaniel cursed. It had already been a long journey, and it wasn't getting any easier. "Tie him up again," he told Samuel.

"I'll do it," John volunteered. "He might not be able to feel the hand he's got left, or his feet, but he'll not get free again."

When Alexandra knew that Nathaniel was safe and all was once again in order, she left her vigil in the hall and went back into her room, closing the door behind her. She knew Nathaniel would not be back. Together they had stood at the edge of a yawning emotional precipice and nearly tossed themselves over the side. But she wasn't willing to risk so much again. She had no future with Nathaniel. She couldn't give her heart to a criminal, not if she wanted a house, and a family, and some degree of assurance that her husband would come safely home each night. And she knew the pirate captain's plans didn't include her, either.

Alexandra listened as footsteps approached the door and paused on the other side. Leaning against the panel, she squeezed her eyes shut and held her breath, hoping all in the same moment that Nathaniel wouldn't knock again—and that he would.

An eternity passed, it seemed, but finally she heard the floor creak as he moved away. She had been right. He would not return.

Feeling empty and deprived, Alexandra moved to the bed and lay down. Her lips tingled from his kiss, and her arms ached with the need to hold him again, but she wasn't a fool. He could never marry her, and she knew it.

She only wished she could stop her traitorous heart from wanting him.

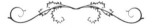

Nathaniel and Alexandra spoke little when they started out again at dawn. Lord Clifton's swollen lip and a bruise showing just below one eye told her Nathaniel's men had exacted their revenge for his attempted escape. But they seemed in no better humor for having beat him.

The marquess was sullen as well, and the ride passed almost in complete silence. The few attempts Tiny made to draw Nathaniel out were met with terse responses, until the big man gave up and lapsed into watching the countryside pass by his window.

By the time their coach reached the fields of strawberries outside London, darkness had fallen. A paper moon hung low in the sky, cloaked in the same mist that encompassed the sprawling metropolis ahead.

Alexandra felt a measure of relief as they passed fresh gravel pits and new brick kilns, knowing the tiresome journey would soon be over. Her right shoulder was beginning to pain her again, and she longed to rest.

Evidently she had not recovered from the gunshot wound as well as she had thought.

"Are you all right?" Nathaniel asked when she allowed herself to sag against him.

She nodded. Lord Clifton had fallen asleep, but Nathaniel remained watchful and pensive.

"London is a big place," she murmured. Despite all she had heard, Alexandra was surprised to see how crowded the city was. Buildings appeared to be stacked one on top of the other, creating tall brick walls that turned the avenues into canyons.

The streets were rivers of filth. A combination of rotting garbage, horse excrement and urine ran in the gutters, creating a terrible stench, but the homeless men, women and children huddled in doorways or crouched on the ground held Alexandra's attention the longest. Whether old, new, rich, poor, pleasant or vile, everything seemed more extreme in London.

"Where are we going?" she asked. Now that she knew her aunt had left the city, the capital no longer seemed a haven, though it was certainly big enough to get lost in. With any luck, Willy would never find her here. But she would be alone in a strange place. Would she find work? A place to live? Friends?

"It's not much farther." Nathaniel shifted as if making himself more comfortable, but Alexandra couldn't help noticing the brace his body gave hers when he settled back again. She was grateful, for it softened the jarring of the carriage.

"Do you think the duke will trade Richard for Lord Clifton?" she whispered, eyeing the sleeping marquess.

Nathaniel cocked an eyebrow at her. "I'm sure he'll be more motivated to trade for his son than some impostor from Manchester." Alexandra caught the gleam of Nathaniel's teeth as he flashed her a grin.

"Still, I'm . . . I'm afraid of what might happen," she admitted, focusing the brunt of her worries on Nathaniel and his situation instead of her own. "How can you keep yourself and your men safe? Even if

Greystone releases Richard, he'll hunt you to the ends of the earth once he sees Lord Clifton's stump."

"I know."

"But what will you do?"

"Whatever seems expedient at the time."

Alexandra let the subject drop, too tired to push at the moment.

"Does your shoulder trouble you a great deal?" he asked when she didn't speak again.

She nodded. "I'll be glad when we get there."

Nathaniel tipped her head onto his shoulder. "Perhaps you should try to rest. I'm afraid the ride has been too much for you." He gently stroked her cheek, then paused in mid-motion, his gaze cutting through the darkness.

The marquess was awake and was watching them, Alexandra realized.

"Do all your captives receive such tender treatment?" he asked.

Nathaniel gave him a scornful glare, but dropped his hand and turned to the window.

After a few minutes more, the carriage came to a stop. Alexandra felt the conveyance sway as Samuel descended from the driver's box and opened the door. "Broad Street," he announced as she sat up.

Nathaniel helped Alexandra down. A sign hung off the road a few feet in front of them. Alexandra squinted to see through the fog that curled around it, expecting the name of some small inn. She was surprised to read the words DR. WATTS'S SURGERY AND REMEDIES.

Glancing over her shoulder, she realized that the others weren't getting out. "Aren't they coming?" she asked.

"No. You need a doctor. I'm going to leave you here."

The impact of Nathaniel's words hit Alexandra like a fist. She hadn't prepared herself to be left quite so soon. To be separated from him. How could he drop her off so casually?

Pride came to Alexandra's rescue, imbuing her with the strength to pull away and stand on her own power. "I see."

The pirate captain stared at her with an inscrutable expression on his face. "Staying with us is too dangerous," he explained.

"Of course. I thank you for bringing me." Alexandra couldn't help slipping into a more formal tone. Whirling around, she poked her head inside the carriage and said good-bye to the others before preceding Nathaniel through a wrought-iron gate that swung inward to a small yard.

A brick path led to a three-story building that was obviously part business and part residence. A dim light escaped from beneath the door and gleamed around the windows, indicating someone was still awake despite the late hour.

"You'd better kiss me good-bye here," he told her when they reached the door.

Alexandra swallowed the lump that had swelled in her throat. "And why would I want to do that?" she asked, standing stiffly at his side.

"Because I don't plan on giving you a choice." Pulling her into his arm, he kissed her almost as thoroughly as he had at the inn, despite her efforts to escape his hold.

"Aren't you in a hurry?" she asked when he finally let her go.

Nathaniel laughed. "Aye, but knowing how much you like me, I couldn't leave without a token of your esteem."

She glared up at him, and he sobered.

"This is for your own good," he said, speaking softly. "Just remember that."

When Alexandra didn't answer, Nathaniel sounded the brass knocker. Moments later a short woman with plump arms opened the door.

"Is Dr. Watts available?" he asked.

"Yes, sir. The doctor's just now returned from a house call. Is there an emergency?"

"Not an emergency, but I think a doctor is in order."

"Come inside and have a seat. I'll get him directly." She showed the two of them into a comfortable-looking parlor where a large leather chair and cloth settee sat opposite a coal fire. Alexandra sat down, but Nathaniel remained standing.

When Dr. Watts appeared, Alexandra thought he looked like the male counterpart of the woman who had answered the door. Short, with a halo of white hair circling his otherwise bald head, he had a ruddy face and a jovial voice.

"Caught me, you did," he exclaimed. "And this time before I donned my nightclothes."

"Then our timing is good after all. My name is Nathaniel Kent and this is my sister Alexandra, er, Kent. We appreciate your willingness to see patients at this hour."

"Mr. Kent, I see patients at any hour. It's all part of the territory, you know. What seems to be the problem?"

Alexandra tried to memorize Nathaniel's face as he explained her injury to the doctor. The square jaw, the cleft chin—the blue eyes she could never forget—the hollows of his cheeks, the broad brow. She felt an inexplicable sense of panic at the thought of his leaving her, and wanted to be able to conjure up his face at any moment. She would go on and meet and marry another, she told herself, but she would never forget Nathaniel.

She heard the pirate captain say that he would cover all expenses. He negotiated a price with the doctor, and Alexandra watched the money change hands. Then Nathaniel hunkered down and pressed a roll of notes into her own palm.

"This will buy you some new dresses and other necessities." He spoke briskly, as though eager to be on his way.

"And what shall I do with your clothes?" Alexandra asked numbly. Nathaniel had told Dr. Watts that he'd check back with him in a few days, but she knew it wasn't true. Worse, she had told Nathaniel that this was what she wanted.

It *was* what she wanted, wasn't it?

"It doesn't matter." He glanced over his shoulder through the window. "I'd better get going."

"Of course." Alexandra managed a brave smile, wondering what Dr. Watts thought of the two of them and their strange, unemotional parting. No doubt he wondered about her wearing men's clothing and having a gunshot wound besides.

"Good-bye." Nathaniel bent and kissed the top of her head, then strode briskly to the door.

"Nathaniel?" Alexandra now wished she hadn't wasted her opportunity at the door to give him a proper good-bye.

He turned back, his dark hair shining in the glow from the kerosene lamp on the table beside him.

"Be careful," she said.

He nodded as he stepped out, and the housekeeper closed the door behind him.

Chapter 12

Nathaniel refused to look back. He climbed into the carriage, hurrying to leave before he changed his mind. This was what Alexandra had asked him to do—to take her to London—and it was for the best. She'd nearly died once because of him. He wasn't about to risk her again. He wouldn't lose her as he had Martha.

But if their parting were predestined, if it were for the best, why did he feel as though his heart were being torn from his chest?

"Take us to the Golden Crown," he called out to Samuel.

Clifton's gaze immediately fastened to him, and Nathaniel resisted the urge to punch his half brother in the face. The marquess had talked and flirted with Alexandra the whole of the previous day, just to goad him. And it had worked far better than Nathaniel wanted to admit.

The carriage stopped again a few minutes later, and Samuel announced Charing Cross. Nathaniel motioned the others out, then drew his knife and waved Clifton to the door. "Don't make a sound in the lobby," he breathed, "or the spectacle that others see will be your murder."

Nathaniel didn't have to force the sincerity that rang in his voice. At that moment he was looking for an opportunity, and he hoped Clifton knew it.

Garth rented several rooms in the large coaching inn, where one could get lost in a crowd.

Nathaniel followed behind the marquess as Garth led the way past a plethora of pictures, porcelains and knickknacks arranged on polished mahogany tables. Heavy wood settees and chairs were clustered in groups on a thick pile rug, and blue silk draperies puddled on the floor.

The halls were long and dimly lit, with a water closet at the end of each one. Garth stopped at a room that corresponded to the number on his key and opened the door as Nathaniel motioned Clifton inside.

"Keep a close eye on him," Nathaniel said, his eyes burning with the need for sleep. "If there's another incident like last night, he won't survive to tell about it."

The marquess jerked his arm away from Nathaniel's hand and entered the room with Garth. "Sleep well while you can, Dragonslayer," he taunted over his shoulder. "It won't be long before our roles are reversed."

Garth gave Nathaniel a pointed look. "Are you sure he's safe with me?"

"After the beating you gave him last night, I'm not," Nathaniel responded. "But at this point, I'd just as soon put him out of his misery." He tossed Tiny a key. "Tiny, you tie him up. You'll stay across the hall with John."

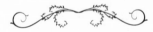

"But the doctor said you're not strong enough to go anywhere," the doctor's housekeeper protested when Alexandra tried to get up. "You need to rest."

"I need to purchase some fabric so I can make a dress, and I need to find work," Alexandra argued from one of four beds that lined the wall of the dormitory-style room.

The housekeeper, whose name was Mrs. Tuttle, clucked her tongue. "What if I brought you some cloth? Then you could work right here. The doctor is gone, and I don't know when he'll return, but I'm sure Mr. Kent has already paid for you to stay for several days yet."

Alexandra fell back on the pillows. She'd been up most of the night trying to understand why she felt so despondent. She was finally in

London, and though she wasn't with her aunt as she had planned, she was still away from Willy. Nathaniel had kept his word and let her go. She had enough money to get a start. Yet she had never felt so abandoned and alone in her life.

She was just overly concerned about the future, she decided. Anyone would be frightened when faced with the prospect of suddenly earning one's keep as a stranger in such a big city. Alexandra knew she wouldn't be able to relax until she had a few basics settled in her life, such as a more permanent place to stay and employment.

Thinking about the seamstresses who were most likely sewing in the garret of her old home at that very moment, Alexandra felt a sharp sense of loss. But she dared not dwell on her friends for fear the temptation to cry would overwhelm her.

Forcing her attention back to the concerned Mrs. Tuttle, she decided the housekeeper was right. She was in no shape to venture forth today. Tomorrow would be soon enough. "If you could bring me a large piece of broadcloth, then," she said, "I'll work from my bed."

The woman's ruddy face broke into a smile.

"That's a good lass. I'll get you a cup of good strong tea first. That'll help you get your strength back. Then I'll pick up the fabric when I go to market." She smoothed her white apron with her hands. "The tea will take just a moment, dear."

Tutty, as Alexandra had heard the doctor call her, shuttled between the doctor's office and his residence upstairs with amazing agility for a woman of her age and weight. Only minutes later, Alexandra heard her banging around the kitchen in an effort to produce the promised tea.

The doctor returned just as Tutty descended the stairs, tray in hand. He joined his housekeeper at Alexandra's bedside, a kind smile on his bespectacled face.

"Feeling any better?" he asked.

Alexandra nodded. She didn't, but she knew they would never let her leave if she told them the truth.

"Tutty said you wanted to do some sewing today. I think that should be fine, providing you don't overdo. You need several days of bed rest, you know."

Alexandra sipped her tea, thinking she'd go mad staying in bed that long. Memories of Nathaniel haunted her constantly. She had to occupy her time more completely to make herself forget the tall, dark pirate, and she had to get her life in order. The doctor and his housekeeper were kind, but she couldn't stay forever in the freshly painted room with its three other wrinkle-free beds. The fear of the unknown would quickly undermine her determination to get a start.

But might Nathaniel come back?

Alexandra tried to bury the hope that wiggled at the back of her mind. He wasn't coming back. His good-bye the night he left was final, and she needed it to stay that way. She didn't want to be around when the duke finally caught up with him—and she had no doubt Greystone eventually would.

The doctor was speaking to her. Alexandra looked up, attempting to catch enough of his words to provide a coherent answer.

". . . is not common I treat a woman for a gunshot wound. How did it happen?"

Alexandra remembered the eyes of the sharpshooter aiming for Nathaniel as vividly as she'd seen them the day of the battle with the *Voyager*. "My brother was cleaning his gun," she said, "and it went off."

"Did you find a messenger?" Nathaniel asked. He, Garth and the others were waiting at the hotel with Lord Clifton. Tiny had just returned.

"Aye. I gave 'im the letter, an' 'e's on 'is way to deliver it to the duke now."

Nathaniel stroked his chin. He hadn't shaved yet and could feel the prickly growth of his beard beneath his fingertips. "Now all we have to do is wait," he told Garth. "If Richard shows up at the Tower, we let Lord Clifton go."

Garth nodded, and Nathaniel leaned back in his chair. The hotel steward had brought them a breakfast of fried eggs, bacon, a cold joint of meat and rolls with preserves, but he had eaten little. Too preoccupied to enjoy the food, he sipped a cup of tea instead, watching his men devour everything in a matter of minutes.

From that point, time passed on lead feet. Nathaniel paced in front of the window, staring out at the day; the others played cards. Still bound, the marquess remained on the floor where he had spent the night.

Rain drizzled out of a gray sky, lacking any real commitment. Nathaniel wished it would pour. Frequent rains were the only thing that kept London habitable during the hot summer months, and it was already a warm spring. The water cleaned the air and the streets, helping to relieve the terrible stench that rose from the gutters.

"Untie me, I can't stand lying here any longer," Clifton said.

Nathaniel ignored him. He had no plans to wrestle with the marquess again today, nor was he willing to endure any of his half brother's verbal abuse. He inclined his head toward the table where he had put a strip of cloth, just in case they needed a gag, and Clifton got the message.

At noon Nathaniel sent John and Garth to the Tower of London for Richard.

They returned nearly two hours later. Nathaniel could hear their voices as they came down the hall. At first he thought he heard Richard's as well, but when they burst into the room, they were without him.

"He wasn't there," Garth announced. "We waited almost an hour, but there was no sign of him."

The marquess closed his eyes and dropped his head in disappointment. Nathaniel wanted to do the same, except his men were watching him, waiting.

"What should we do?" Garth asked.

"We wait until tomorrow and send the same message," Nathaniel replied. "Maybe Greystone didn't get word in time."

John stiffened in his chair. His eyes locked with Nathaniel's, then turned to stare his hatred at the marquess. "If the duke has killed my brother, I'm going to kill his son."

"And I wouldn't blame you," Nathaniel admitted, watching his half brother shrink away from John's intense regard.

The next morning Nathaniel sent another messenger to Greystone House on Berkeley Square, and the wait began anew. Only, this time, they untied young Lord Clifton. He sat in a corner, silent and morose, while the rest of them talked among themselves or gambled.

At noon John and Garth went back to the Tower. When they returned this time, Richard was with them. He had a number of bruises, a black eye and possibly a broken nose, but he laughed and threw his arms around Nathaniel the moment he saw him.

"You did it. I'm free from the bloody bastard," he exclaimed.

Nathaniel pounded his friend on the back. "We're just glad you're alive."

Richard shook his head. "The duke was furious. He had his men beat me one last time, just for good measure, but you had him by the bollocks, and he knew it."

Richard's carrot-colored hair was matted with blood from a cut just above his temple, and he favored his left side, but otherwise, he seemed to be the same boisterous soul he'd always been.

"What did he do to you?" Nathaniel asked.

"Nothing more than what I'd get in a good brawl at the corner tavern." Richard laughed, but Nathaniel suspected he'd received a great deal more than that. "Your father wanted me to tell him where he could find you, and when I wouldn't say, he let his men rough me up a bit. Damn near broke a few ribs, I think." He gingerly pressed the offended side. "But I'll heal."

Nathaniel glanced at Clifton. His half brother watched them with obvious relief, knowing Richard to be his ticket home.

"Tiny, you go rent a carriage and two extra horses. Bring them down the alley in back, then come get me," Nathaniel told him. "Garth, help me tie Lord Clifton up again."

"Wait," the marquess cried. "What are you doing? You told my father you'd let me go."

Nathaniel laughed. "Did you think I was going to let you walk out of here and go straight to the constabulary?"

"But you said—"

"I said I'd trade you. I didn't say when or how."

By the time Tiny returned, Clifton was bound and gagged and lying in his place on the floor.

"The rest of you be ready to leave as soon as I get back," Nathaniel admonished, motioning for Tiny to help him. Together they lifted the marquess and carried him out the back way, where they put him in the carriage.

"You drive," Nathaniel said. "Take us out toward Bristol, beyond the city."

"Aye, Cap'n." Tiny hefted himself up to the driver's box, and Nathaniel climbed inside with Clifton. It had not stopped drizzling since the day before, but Nathaniel gave it no heed. He was relieved on two accounts: a portion of his plan had fallen into place, and he would soon be rid of his half brother.

The ride took a little over an hour. Finally Tiny pulled to the side of the road and stopped in the shade of an elm tree. "This good enough?" he called.

Nathaniel jumped to the ground. "Perfect. Untie the horses." Turning back to the marquess, he said, "This is where we say good-bye. I hope forever."

Lord Clifton squirmed and groaned, but the gag in his mouth prevented him from formulating his various grunts into words.

"I'll take that as a fond farewell." Nathaniel laughed and slammed the door. Then he and Tiny climbed astride the horses and headed back into town.

"Are you goin' to let the duke know where the marquess is at?" Tiny asked at length.

"No. I'm going to let the stables know where they can retrieve their carriage. They'll notify the duke when they find Clifton."

"That's a good idea." Tiny sounded genuinely impressed.

"We need to rent some horses from another stable first," Nathaniel explained.

"We're leaving town?"

"Of course."

"What about the guns?"

"They can be handled at a much safer distance, for the time being."

They rode in silence the rest of the way. By the time they rented more horses and reached the Golden Crown, Garth and the others were waiting in the alley. They each took a mount and climbed on.

"Is it done?" Richard asked.

"Greenwalt Stables is on their way to retrieve their property," Nathaniel informed him. "It'll happen soon enough."

"Then let's get the hell out of here," he whooped. "I hope Trenton's got the *Vengeance* ready, because that duke's hopping mad. I'd say we should head to America, but I'm not sure it's far enough away."

"Trenton will pick us up in Newcastle," Nathaniel said. "We'll deal with the rifles there, before my father sends any more guns to Russia."

He nudged his horse into a gallop and the others followed suit. They cleared the cart- and vendor-laden streets of the capital and emerged on the rolling green hills of the surrounding countryside.

Suddenly Nathaniel reined in.

"What is it?" Garth asked, slowing along with him.

Nathaniel paused in indecision. "Nothing. Never mind. Let's go." He shook the reins and started out again, but it wasn't five minutes before he wheeled around a second time.

"Is something wrong, Captain?" Garth's face revealed his puzzlement.

"There's something I need to do." Nathaniel squinted back the way they had come, knowing in that moment that he couldn't leave Alexandra. She drew him back as surely as a river flowed to the sea.

The entire group slowed to a stop and came back to meet him. "What's going on?" Richard called.

"I'm going back."

"But why?" Alarm rang through Richard's Scottish lilt.

"There's something I have to do. I'll catch up with you tomorrow."

"You don't want to go back there," Richard insisted. "Believe me, Nathaniel, Greystone will be turning that town upside down to find you as soon as he gets Clifton back."

"If it has anything to do with a beautiful blonde with big green eyes, now is not the time, my friend," John added.

Then when was the time? Nathaniel wondered. Once Alexandra recovered enough to leave Dr. Watts's, he might never find her again. "I'll catch up with you tomorrow. If not, go on to Newcastle without me."

"I don't think we should leave you." Richard trotted after him. "We'll come, too."

Nathaniel scrutinized his friend's battered face—the swollen lip, the black eye, the congealed blood from the cut at his temple. He was grateful to have Richard back in one piece, knew he was extremely lucky, in fact, and wanted him and the others well away from the city. "No. You stay with John. I'll catch up."

Richard lowered his voice. "You're foolish to take any more chances, Nathaniel. Being a one-armed man makes you an easy mark."

"I've always managed to look out for myself before," Nathaniel told him, but he didn't say what was equally true: though he feared the duke, somehow the thought of never seeing Alexandra again was worse.

"Nathaniel, don't." Tiny added his voice to those of the others, but Nathaniel waved them all off as he kicked his horse into a gallop.

"I have to," Nathaniel told them, but he didn't know what he was going to say or do once he reached Dr. Watts's. Nothing had changed. He couldn't take Alexandra away with him, because it wasn't safe. He had nothing to offer her, but he had to see her one last time. Surely he could allow his heart that one small concession.

The Duke of Greystone paced angrily behind the huge mahogany desk, inlaid with ebony and ivory, that stood in the center of his study. The man from Greenwalt Stables, who had found Jake and brought him home, had left only a few hours before. But Nathaniel and his men were already long gone from the Golden Crown, just as Jake had said they would be.

"On my own life I will avenge you," the duke swore, crossing to the window that overlooked the fenced gardens and the street below, his emotions too powerful for him to remain in one place for long.

Jake sat on the other side of the desk. He was unshaven, his eyes bloodshot, and the sight of the white bandage that covered the end of his right arm made Greystone want to slaughter the world.

"I should never have sent you to the Crimea. But I thought you'd be safe with Captain Montague."

"There was little Montague could do, or anyone else for that matter," Jake said. "Dragonslayer—"

"His name is Nathaniel," the duke broke in. "I will not have him called by that ludicrous name."

"Nathaniel, then. He tricked us. We managed to hold him off in the morning, but he followed us and attacked again when we least expected it. Though we fought as best we could, most of the men were drunk by then and there was nothing to do but surrender. And he took full advantage of the situation, as you can see."

Greystone faced the window, turning away from the sight of Jake's stump. On the grounds below, a formal garden bloomed in the gentle sunshine—sweet peas, heliotrope, phlox, larkspur and love-in-the-mist.

He watched as his gardeners worked among the plants, trimming and clipping. The serenity of the view mocked his inner turmoil. Red roses, yellow roses and green shrubbery, all perfectly manicured, blurred before his vision.

It was time he put an end to Nathaniel once and for all. If not for his firstborn, Jake would still have his hand. The marquess would be whole and healthy, and there would be no threat to Greystone Shipping, an asset the duke loved almost as much as he loved his second son.

"He wanted to get to you through me," Jake said. "I'm your heir. He wanted to leave me no more whole than he is himself."

The marquess's words acted like kerosene on the flames of the duke's fury. Nathaniel mocked him? "I'll rot in hell before I let him escape me now," he swore.

"He'll pay for his crimes, Father. I have all the information we need to put an end to Dragonslayer—that is, Nathaniel."

The duke whirled around. "What information?"

"I met a man who is willing to help us." Jake leaned forward, his eyes alive for the first time since he'd returned. "He's a member of Nathaniel's crew, and for a price, he's promised to provide all the information we need to capture Nathaniel. He said he will send us word as soon as he can meet with us. It shouldn't be more than a few days at the most."

Greystone felt a tremor of anticipation run through him. "Excellent," he said. "Then it is only a matter of time after all."

Nathaniel's horse was lathered by the time he let it slow to a walk. As he listened to its labored breathing, he called himself a fool for returning to London. Alexandra would be better off if he left things as they stood, but he couldn't help himself. His feelings for her had grown too strong. Had circumstances been different . . .

No, he chided himself. It wasn't wise to think like that. Love was too dangerous an emotion.

Fog flowed in from the Thames, settling over the streets like some biblical plague, as he headed to Oxford and then on to Broad. It was getting late, probably too late to make a social call, but Nathaniel tied his horse to the ring outside Dr. Watts's small garden anyway. He dared not delay his visit till morning. Trenton and the others would be waiting for him in Newcastle as it was.

Nathaniel knocked at the door, wondering what he was going to say to Alexandra when he saw her. He couldn't make any promises. Neither could he let her disappear from his life.

The housekeeper answered his knock, but before he could so much as greet her, she beckoned him in. "Oh, Mr. Kent. Thank goodness you're here. We've never been properly introduced, but my name is Mrs. Tuttle."

Stepping inside the cozy house, Nathaniel let the housekeeper take his frock coat as dread turned the blood in his veins to ice. "It's a pleasure to know you, Mrs. Tuttle. Is something wrong? Has Alexandra taken a turn for the worse?"

Dr. Watts descended the stairs. "Tutty, did I hear Mr. Kent arrive? Ah yes, it is you. What a relief. We were getting quite beside ourselves, really."

Nathaniel turned to the doctor. "What is it?"

"Can't say for sure—"

"Where's Alexandra?" Nathaniel glanced through the door that led to the adjoining examination room and the dormitory beyond, but all was quiet. They seemed quite alone in the house.

"That's the problem, my good fellow," Dr. Watts explained. "She's gone. She left this morning with a picnic lunch and a list of dressmakers she intended to visit. And she's not come back."

"*What?*"

Dr. Watts sighed. "She's a stubborn lass, your sister. I told her she wasn't well enough to be up and about, but she kept insisting she felt fine. She was so eager to search for gainful employment, you know."

"She promised to be gone only a few hours at most, just long enough to make a few inquiries," Tutty cut in. "But she hasn't returned, and we don't know what to make of it."

Nathaniel stood looking at the pair in astonishment. He had expected Alexandra to move on eventually. She needed to establish a new life in

London. But he never dreamed she'd disappear so soon. "She didn't arrange for other lodgings?"

"None we know of," the doctor replied. "She made herself a dress, managed it in a single day, mind you. And she's got the fabric to begin another still here—"

"I know she planned to return," Tutty interrupted, wringing her hands. "She took only enough food for one small meal."

Chapter 13

The burned-out warehouse was cold and drafty. Great gusts of wind whistled through the broken windows along the top, blowing rain inside until the wet nearly reached the circle of seamstresses pressed against the back wall.

Alexandra sat in a dim corner, bent over her work, struggling to see the tiny stitches in the wavering light of several candles. Her gaze flicked toward the windows as she acknowledged the storm gathering outside, but her mind was preoccupied with thoughts of Dr. Watts and Mrs. Tuttle.

"What's the problem, missy?" asked the woman next to her. Her long dark hair, streaked with gray, was pulled severely off her face. "Are ye too cold?"

Though her fingers and toes were nearly frozen, Alexandra shook her head. "No. Someone's expecting me tonight, is all, and I'm far from being finished." She jammed her needle back into the wool of the livery she sewed.

"Ye'd best stay till morning now anyway. The streets aren't safe along the docks after dark, an' ye won't last long around 'ere if ye miss yer deadline."

Alexandra nodded. She'd walked a long way from the doctor's residence, deep into the rabbit warrens of London, and was reluctant to start back so late. But she wished she could notify the doctor and Tutty somehow. She knew the pair would be worried about her.

Allowing herself a small sigh, she tried to concentrate on her work despite an audible growling in her stomach. Tutty had packed her a few slices of cold meat and a biscuit, but she'd eaten it long ago while she was still visiting dressmakers on the housekeeper's list.

"I'm Mariah," the woman volunteered. "How did ye come to be 'ere? I mean, forgive my boldness, but ye seem, well, different from the rest of us."

Alexandra glanced around the circle of drawn, pinched faces. The others were obviously tired, and judging from their clothes, poor. But then, the same thing could be said for most needlewomen.

"Another shop I visited, looking for work, told me Mr. Gunther is always hiring."

Mariah nodded. "That's true enough. Are ye new to London, then?"

"Yes."

"Ah . . . that explains it."

"Explains what?"

Mariah's eyes darted across the room. She fell silent as Gunther, a short man with heavy whiskers who was almost as wide as he was tall, came to stand beside the circle of working women.

"I need to get these orders out of here," he barked. "Come on, ladies, we've got deadlines."

Mariah muttered something under her breath, making Alexandra glance up at her.

"What did you say?"

"I 'ate Gunther," she whispered. "An' Gould is almost as bad."

Gunther had hired her, but Alexandra could only assume Gould to be the stringy, fair-complexioned man who stood at her boss's side.

"Are we all working, ladies?" Gunther's words acted like the crack of a whip, making the seamstresses bow closer to their needles.

One, more bold than the rest, said, "Whippin' a dead 'orse won't make 'im run any faster."

"If a horse don't run as fast as I like, I get me another horse," he bellowed back. "Anyone who goes home before they get their order done shouldn't bother to come back."

Alexandra frowned, wondering how she'd make it through the night. When she'd taken the job, she'd planned to return to Dr. Watts's and begin the following morning. But Gunther had pressed her to start immediately, saying he had an order that needed filling right away. Now she realized just how ill-prepared she was to meet his demands. She was hungry and cold, with only a thin shawl to warm her, and she wasn't as strong as she should be.

Silence reigned as the hour grew late. Even Mariah grew reticent, and Alexandra was glad. She scarcely had the energy to continue sewing, let alone provide any kind of interesting conversation. She was tempted to give up and leave, but the discouragement she had faced earlier in the day, when dress shop after dress shop had turned her away, had frightened her. What if she couldn't find anything better?

Thunder cracked in the sky, louder than any cannon. A boisterous wind began to fling the rain ever farther into the room, blowing out several candles, and those women along the outer edge of the circle began to complain about the wet.

The other seamstresses seemed reluctant to move, but they could hardly continue to work without light. They rose, grumbling beneath their breath. Some held the remaining candles while others shoved the tables and chairs back even closer to the far wall. This done, they sat wordlessly and went back to work.

Eventually some of the seamstresses made pillows out of their aprons or shawls and found an empty place on the floor to grab a few minutes' rest. Alexandra longed to do the same. Her tired, sore body ached for a bed, but she was determined to continue. She needed a job to provide some sort of stability in her life, and she welcomed anything with the potential to divert her thoughts from the one person who remained center stage: Nathaniel. Frustrating though it was, his face forever appeared in her mind's eye. Even with work to distract her, she caught herself remembering him, the things he'd said, his smile, his touch, his pain.

"'Ave ye 'ad anythin' to eat?" Mariah asked.

Alexandra shook her head.

"Then 'ere." Cold hands pressed a portion of a roll into her lap. It was a hard, crusty remnant of an earlier supper, but Alexandra was hungry enough to eat anything.

"Take a few ticks to rest," the woman suggested.

"Thank you, but if I do, I'll never get done." Alexandra stuffed the entire roll into her mouth so her hands could remain free.

"Listen. I just finished my own work. I'll stitch for ye if ye'll take fifteen minutes or so an' sleep."

Surprised by the kindness of Mariah's offer, Alexandra looked questioningly into her face. "But you could go home now."

"I don't mind 'elpin' ye for a while. Now pop along an' do as I say."

Carefully avoiding the small puddles caused by the rain, Alexandra lay down, wondering if she'd ever be able to get up again. Her back and arms ached, her head throbbed, and the cold, unyielding cement provided little comfort.

Still, she drifted into a dreamless sleep almost as soon as she lay down.

In what seemed like seconds, a gentle hand woke her. "I 'ave to go now," Mariah said. "Ye've been sleepin' for an 'our. That ought to 'elp. I'm sorry I can't do more."

"An hour!" Alexandra scrambled to her feet even though her body still felt like she'd been thrown from a horse. "You let me sleep an hour? And you've been working that entire time?"

"Aye, but I 'ave to go now. I'll be back in the mornin'."

"Wait." Alexandra clutched the other woman's arm. "I'll do the same for you sometime. I promise."

"I'm sure ye will." Mariah studied her, then lowered her voice. "Ye know, ye seem like a good lass. I 'ate to see ye get into trouble, so let me give ye a piece of advice. Stay away from Gunther if ye can."

"Why?" she asked in surprise. But Mariah pulled away, leaving Alexandra to stare after her as she walked out onto the rain-spattered docks.

A man with a wet newspaper under his arm hurried down the street several blocks from Dr. Watts's residence. The hour was so late and the weather so poor that he was the only person Nathaniel had seen in two hours of searching for Alexandra.

"Excuse me, sir." Nathaniel nudged his horse forward.

The man turned, obviously surprised at being stopped in the middle of a downpour.

"Have you seen a lone young woman with blond hair and green eyes around these parts tonight?"

The man scowled as the wind blew rain into his face. "No," he shouted above the inclement weather, then ducked his head and rushed away.

Nathaniel sighed. He was wasting his time. He'd never find Alexandra by rambling about without some clue to tell him where to look. Unfortunately, the dress shops on Tutty's list were long closed, and he had no way of determining the identities of the owner or manager of each one, though he wouldn't have hesitated to raise them from their beds if he could.

He sat in the downpour, blinking rain out of his eyes, a solitary figure. As much as he hated to give up, there was nothing he could do except return to the doctor's and pray for better luck in the morning.

Alexandra was exhausted. She'd worked for nearly thirty-six hours with little sleep, and now she could only lay her head back on the cushioned seat of the pony-chaise as a chill wind whipped at the strands of hair straying from her bonnet. Occasionally drops of rain fell onto her cheeks from the black night overhead, but she didn't bother to wipe them away. She was oblivious to the weather, and almost everything else, until a coughing spell seized her. Then she sat up, her eyes blinking in bewilderment. It was so cold, and she'd had nothing to eat but the spot of tea Gunther had pressed on her earlier.

"Where are we?" she asked.

Her new boss sat at her side, driving. "You're not well," he told her. "I'm taking you home, where there is someone to care for you. Don't worry, it's only another street or two."

It seemed as though they'd been traveling for hours. "But you said you'd take me back to Dr. Watts's," Alexandra protested, pulling her shawl more tightly about herself. She shivered. Her fingers were like ice, yet her face felt flushed.

"A hot bowl of soup, and you'll be good as new. Believe me, I've got just the thing," he said.

The rain began to fall more heavily, disturbing Alexandra's sleep. Soaked to the skin, she wished for a heavy wool cloak to replace Mrs. Tuttle's knitted shawl. Then she realized that the chaise was no longer moving. Where was she?

Raising her head to look about, she saw that she was alone in a filthy street outside a tall, rickety building made of wood. It leaned sadly to one side as tattered drapes escaped from an open window on the second story to slap against the pane overhead. A light silhouetted the figures of a man and a woman in the same room. The male form clasped the woman from behind and tossed her onto a bed, and their laughter rippled down with the rain.

Climbing unsteadily to the ground, Alexandra clung to the side of the pony-chaise, feeling as though she might faint. All the strength was gone from her legs, but she forced herself to move. She had to find her way to Dr. Watts's.

"Wait!"

Before she'd traveled more than three steps, the door to the teetering house opened. A girl came bounding down the front steps, despite wearing a full skirt, and skidded to a halt in front of her. "Going somewhere?" she asked, her eyes gleaming.

The most remarkable thing about this stranger, besides a broken front tooth, was a lovely feather boa that rested above a revealing bodice.

"I'm afraid I'm lost," Alexandra admitted, wondering just what kind of woman dressed as this girl did. "Could you perhaps direct me to a constable?"

The girl whistled through her teeth, proving that she could put the broken one to good use. "I doubt there's a constable who dares to walk these parts. I've never seen one, anyhow."

Gunther came out of the house and descended the steps, his face dark with the shadow of night and his usual thick black whiskers. "Maggie, go inside. Her room is ready now. I'll handle it from here."

"Can't I help her settle in?" Maggie pleaded. "We're friends already."

Gunther scowled but acquiesced. "Very well. You can take her up." He turned to Alexandra. "I'm going to see a friend of mine while you get some sleep. We'll talk later."

"I'm afraid there's been some kind of misunderstanding," Alexandra said. "I can't stay here. My friends are expecting me." She glanced from Gunther to the girl he had called Maggie. "I don't know what you were thinking, but—"

"Nonsense." Gunther took her by the elbow and began to pull her toward the house. "You're only exhausted. I know the place don't look like much, but Maggie's happy here. Right, Mag?"

Medium brown curls bounced as Maggie nodded.

"You just need some rest. There's a lot to be done come morning. I have a big order to get out, and I need you to be ready."

Something told Alexandra that Gunther was lying about the order, but she was too ill to figure out why. She felt her legs give way and saw the ground rushing up to meet her only seconds before Gunther caught her in an iron grip.

"Watch out," she heard him say to Maggie. "I'll have to carry her in."

She felt him swing her up into his arms, then heard him grunt while climbing the stairs. His breath came in heavy gasps by the time they entered the decrepit house.

Alexandra opened her eyes just long enough to see several female faces gaping at her. She heard the creak of a stair, smelled rotten food and sweat and bodies, and soon found herself lying on a large, rumpled bed in the middle of a room containing a washbasin and an overstuffed bureau. The walls, covered with purple lilac paper, were smudged with dirt and dulled by the years. A heavy shade covered one small window.

Time seemed to pass in an erratic fashion. Alexandra didn't know if it had been minutes since the ride in the pony-chaise or hours, but she was grateful for the fire that raged at one end of the room.

Managing to climb off the bed, she crawled toward its warmth, anxious to dispel the terrible chill in her bones. She was so cold, not just on the outside, but deep within as well.

Glancing back, she cringed to see the bed she had been sleeping in and guessed it had been months since the linens were changed. Even in the flickering firelight she could see the brown stains of God knew what.

But she couldn't worry about that. Not now. She stretched her fingers toward the flames.

"There's our new lass." A large woman with carrot-colored hair burst into the room, carrying a lamp. Freckles covered her face and arms and the good deal of bosom revealed by her low décolletage.

"I'm Caroline," she announced. "I'm sorry I wasn't here to welcome you sooner, but I was rather . . . indisposed." She laughed gaily as she set the lamp on the dresser. "I suppose Maggie took care of you all right. But now we must get those wet clothes off before you catch a chill."

Alexandra wanted to tell her that it was far too late for that; she was already freezing. But her tongue was too thick and heavy to obey her will.

Caroline rummaged through the chest, withdrew a flimsy red night-dress and wrapper, and began to dress Alexandra as though she were a doll.

"You don't look well, love," she commented, chafing Alexandra's hands to warm them as a nanny might do for her ward. "We'd better get something hot down you. Gunther tells me you've had nothing but a cup of tea all day, and that will certainly never do. You'll lose what precious few curves you have in no time."

Alexandra was too weary to understand why Caroline, or whatever her name was, should be talking about curves. The woman's voice was gentle, and at that moment, kindness was all that mattered. Alexandra needed a friend, someone to care for her, as she felt so incapable of caring for herself.

"Perhaps Drake will have to wait until morning to take a look at you," she commented. "You couldn't cross the channel like this."

"What?"

"Just get in bed. I'll bring you something to eat."

The feel of the place was all wrong, the smells revolting. Gunther had led her to believe he was doing her a favor, but she was beginning to suspect him of putting something in the tea he had given her earlier. She had to leave, find her way back, except that she didn't have the strength to stand, let alone propel herself to the door. Her eyelids soon grew so heavy, she couldn't lift them any longer, and she let them close, welcoming the oblivion of sleep.

"Wake up. There's someone who wants to see you."

An insistent hand jiggled Alexandra awake. She blinked several times before a face came into focus. It was Caroline, the woman she had met before.

"Alexandra, lass, can you hear me? You've got your first bite."

"Bite?" She had dyspepsia, maybe. She didn't know anything about a bite. "I don't know what you're talking about," she said, her words sounding as slurred and unnatural as she felt.

"You don't want Gunther to come after you. Come on, we have to get you ready."

Slowly Alexandra's faculties began to return. She still felt terribly ill-equipped to do anything difficult, like stand or walk, but she could think two coherent thoughts in a row. And she had recognized Caroline.

"Caroline?"

The woman smiled. "Aye, it's me."

"What is it I'm supposed to do?"

Caroline turned away and began to ransack the drawers of the bureau. She tossed a burgundy corset on the floor, mumbling to herself, "I've never seen a man who could refuse that."

"What are you talking about?" With no more strength to hold herself up, Alexandra slumped back onto the floor where she'd been lying in a heap. She wouldn't have gotten back in the bed, even if she could have dragged herself across the room. "It's still dark yet. Gunther said I could sleep here until morning. Surely any sewing can wait that long."

Caroline chuckled and turned to face her, hands on her hips. "Sewing! My, you are an innocent. No one sleeps here at night, my precious, or any other time they have a paying customer. And you just got your first."

Lifting her head off her arms, Alexandra gazed at the sheer lacy corset Caroline shoved toward her. "My first what?"

"Paying customer. Put this on. There's a gentleman downstairs who's had too much to drink, and he grows impatient. Believe me, things will go much smoother if you simply hurry and be done with it. The drunk ones can get violent."

The things Alexandra had heard and seen since coming to Gunther's house had swirled in her mind like dreams, weaving themselves in and out of her consciousness. She hadn't known what was real and what imagined, but finally they coalesced into something that made some sense—only, the picture they painted was frightening indeed.

"You expect me to sell myself?" she gasped, shoving herself back into a sitting position. The question was more of an accusation, but instead of getting defensive, Caroline rolled her eyes.

"I don't expect nothing. I'm just telling you how to survive here. It's Gunther who does the expecting—and the collecting. Now, unless you want him to give you a few bruises and maybe a split lip to go with the coming sting to your bottom, I suggest you get dressed. I don't know how to tell you any plainer."

"You're saying he'll beat me if I refuse? But I never agreed to come here in the first place!"

Caroline shrugged. "He doesn't always ask permission. And you're here now, aren't you? Drake's coming to take you across the channel in the morning. You'll never escape once that happens. You won't even want to. For all the rough riding, a brothel is still better than the gutter, which is where you end up if you leave."

She paused long enough to study Alexandra's face, and softened, "Maybe if you act eager to earn a few coins on your back, Gunther will let you stay in England. He only sells the ones he nabs. If he can make a good profit off you here, there'll be no reason to sell you. That's your only chance of avoiding France, but that's the best advice I can give."

"How can you help him do this?" Alexandra felt panic surge through her veins, weakening limbs that were already too weak to perform their usual functions. "You know I'm ill. He drugged me, didn't he? That has to be what happened. And I was weak already."

Caroline shrugged again. "It's a living. Like I said, a woman will do a lot of things before she lets herself be tossed in the gutter. And I'm not young anymore. We all do what we can."

Caroline swallowed, as though trying to rid herself of her guilt as easily as she did the spittle in her mouth. "Now, I'm going to change your clothes, and you're going to let me because I don't want a beating, even if you do."

Alexandra tried to fight, but she was far too ill to make any impact on the sturdy Caroline. Soon Caroline had Alexandra dressed in the lacy corset she'd taken from the bureau.

The redhead went out, briefly, and came back again with some sheer silk stockings that looked as though they'd seen better days. After sliding them up Alexandra's legs, Caroline combed Alexandra's hair until it shone in the lamplight. When she finished, she stood Alexandra in front of the mirror.

"You have to admit, you look a fetching sight," she breathed, obviously impressed. "There ain't a man alive who wouldn't pay a fortune for a girl like you."

Alexandra stared at herself, now a stranger, as Caroline dabbed perfume below her ears. "This can't be happening," she murmured, feeling tears prick the back of her eyes. She could never allow a strange man to grope and fondle her, to . . .

She turned beseeching eyes on Caroline. "Please. Please let me go. Give me a few moments to sneak out the back. Lead me to the door. Tell them I was gone when you came up. Anything!"

Pity flickered in Caroline's eyes, but only momentarily. "Nay, I'm sorry, love. I hate to force you into this kind of life, but Gunther's my bread and butter. For all his wicked ways, it's my place to do what he tells me."

"But I have no chance of defending myself!"

Caroline sighed. "It will hurt the first time. If you need something to bite so you don't cry out, there's this." She reached into the top drawer of the bureau and pulled out a foot of rope, knotted at both ends.

My God, what were they going to do to her that she'd need something like that?

Caroline pulled a chair across the floor and positioned it in front of the fire, then motioned Alexandra into it.

Alexandra obeyed because her head was spinning, and she feared she'd fall if she didn't sit soon.

"You don't have to worry about smiling or acting like you're enjoying yourself, at least," Caroline said, heading to the door. "This gent knows you're untouched. A virgin is exactly what he's asked for, so give him his money's worth, and maybe I can talk Gunther into keeping you." With that, she left, locking the door behind her.

Alexandra felt faint. Squeezing her eyes shut, she bowed her head and shoved the blackness away. She had to remain lucid. She had to think, since she could never strong-arm her way out of what was coming.

After a moment she lifted her head, determined to view her surroundings with fresh purpose. Was there anything she could use as a weapon?

Her eyes scanned the dilapidated furniture, the rumpled bed, the trinkets on the dresser. She found a hatpin holder, but no pins, a single boot, cosmetics, a dirty toothbrush. She even got down on her hands and knees to look under the bed, but found nothing more dangerous than dust and cobwebs and dirty pantaloons.

Coughing, she forced herself to her feet, pausing when she swayed and nearly lost her balance. Then she made her way to the dresser and delved into its drawers.

Feather boas, bits of lace, wrinkled gowns, a single glove and a wadded up sheet. Nothing there, either. She managed to don a thin wrapper to cover the vulgar apparel Caroline had put on her, but soon found herself at the limit of her strength. With sweat beading on her upper lip, her hand closed around the brush Caroline had left on top of the dresser.

It was all Alexandra had. It would never be enough.

Chapter 14

Booted feet sounded in the hall, drawing closer. Whoever her customer was, he sounded large and every bit as drunk as Caroline had said. Gunther was with him. Alexandra heard the whoremaster curse and tell his companion to watch his step. Then the key turned in the lock.

Instinctively Alexandra drew the wrapper tightly closed. Setting the brush on the dresser, she pulled the chair within easy reach of it and sat, trying to conserve her energy. She felt every bit as though a hungry lion paced beyond the door, fangs bared. How would she live through the coming nightmare?

No, how would she stop it? Saying a silent prayer, she forced her arms to remain at her sides instead of hugging herself as she was tempted to do. She had to convince Gunther she was compliant so he would leave. Never could she take on two men. Not in her current condition. One would be difficult enough, but Alexandra had already decided she'd die before she'd be a victim again.

The door creaked on its hinges and Gunther appeared, wearing a grin on his swarthy face. The tall bulk of a man moved behind him, but Alexandra refused to look at him. She kept her eyes on the floor, where the reflection of the fire leaped and danced.

"You have company, lassee," Gunther said. "Now stand up and show this gent what you've got for him tonight."

Alexandra couldn't stop the tremors that shook her from head to foot. Closing her eyes, she used the chair to stand, then slipped her wrapper off and slowly turned full circle.

Gunther whistled. "What sweet promise. I've half a mind to take you for myself, but this man's determined to have first crack. And if I'm right about the lust in his eye and the bulge in his pants, he's ready for you. He'll make a woman of you, all right, and there'll be plenty left over for me later, eh?"

An animallike grunt told Alexandra that Gunther's client admired her as much as Gunther said. The sound left her sick with dread.

"Fair enough?" Gunther said to the man, who hung back in the shadows behind him.

Alexandra sank into her seat while the money changed hands, trying to will herself the strength she lacked. She could hardly stand. What good would her feeble weapon do her? She had no power to strike with the brush. What she needed was a gun.

"Ride her easy, she's worth a lot to me," Gunther said, "and just knock when you're finished. Caroline will let you out."

The door shut, a key rattled the lock, and Alexandra forced herself to finally look at the man who had come to prey on her flesh. Primed to defend herself against the threat he posed, it took a moment for her to realize that there was something familiar about him. And not until he stepped out of the shadows and doffed his hat did she recognize who he was.

"Nathaniel!"

He came forward and dropped to one knee, taking in the sight of her with one long, hungry perusal. "Aye, it's me, but don't give me that look of relief. I'm more than half tempted to take what I've paid for."

Nathaniel's eyes devoured her, making Alexandra wonder if she'd mind if he did. She had already shared her body with him in her dreams. Just the thought of making those fantasies a reality was enough to warm her as the fire never could. "How much did you pay?" she asked, giving him a temptress's smile.

"Gunther was a fool to sell you so cheaply. I'd have given him everything I own."

Alexandra fought the weakness that weighted her limbs and even her smile. "An unnecessary sacrifice, considering I wouldn't charge you a farthing."

His mouth descended on hers, claiming it in a passionate kiss that spoke of desire long suppressed. Alexandra wanted to respond, to abandon herself to the joy of seeing him again. She knew he'd make her safe. She wanted him to teach her pleasure. But she was too weak even to clasp her hands around his neck.

"You're ill," he said, worry entering his voice as he pressed a hand to her flushed cheeks. "Has this to do with your gunshot wound?"

She shook her head. "Gunther . . . drugged me, but I can't seem to recover." She let her head loll on the back of the chair because it was too much effort to hold it up.

"I'm going to get you out of here," he said, his voice fading in her ears. "Where are your clothes?"

Alexandra heard the question. Her mind struggled to communicate that Caroline had taken them, but her mouth refused to form the words, and finally she slipped into the void.

After depositing Alexandra on the bed, Nathaniel crossed to the dresser. He moved it against the door, and then pulled the flimsy garments from its drawers. None of them looked like something he'd want Alexandra to be seen wearing in public, so he settled on the thin wrapper she had used herself. He put it on her over the revealing corset that nearly drove him mad with longing, and strode to the window to try and jimmy it open. He had to get Alexandra out, and he had to do it now. God had granted him the small miracle of finding her; he was going to make the most of the opportunity.

The window gave way after a moment, and he looked out. It was a long drop, but short of breaking down the door and fighting his way through Gunther and who knew who else, it was the only way.

As if to confirm this, voices rose in the hall outside.

"I tell you, a man with one arm came to the Purple Cow asking about you and the girl not more than two hours ago. Ed would not lie."

"You'd better be right, Gould. I'll have your hide if you're not," Gunther swore.

Nathaniel scowled. He'd visited the seedy tavern called the Purple Cow in his search for Alexandra. The bartender had evidently given him up.

Gunther tried to open the door, and cursed when he could not. "He's blocked the entrance."

The sound of something smashing against the panel reverberated as Gunther made several attempts to break the door open. After the third hit, the dresser began to slide away.

Nathaniel crossed to the bed. "Alexandra." He added a gentle shake to rouse her.

She blinked up at him, but he could tell by her eyes that she was still dazed. "Alexandra, listen to me. I need your help. I need you to keep yourself from getting scratched and bruised on the way down."

"The way down?" She gripped his hand in her small, cold ones. "I'm not going anywhere without you."

Nathaniel raised her fingers to his mouth, giving them a brief kiss. "Don't worry. I'll follow you."

She nodded hesitantly and maneuvered her weight so Nathaniel could strip the sheets from the bed. He tied them together and then around her waist, but she could offer him little help as he carried her to the window and lowered her to the street.

Her feet had scarcely touched the ground when Gunther forced his way into the room. Nathaniel threw the sheet-rope down after her, hoping Alexandra had the strength to make it away from the house where someone might help her. But he couldn't wait to see. Gunther and the man he had called Gould entered the room, and they both had knives.

Nathaniel pulled the stiletto from his boot and turned to defend himself.

"She's gone," Gunther shouted. "Caroline, find the girl!"

Movement in the hall outside told Nathaniel that Caroline was heading down the stairs. He had to move quickly.

Dodging a jab from the gangly Gould, Nathaniel made Gunther his goal, but the shorter man blocked the thrust of his knife. Nathaniel felt a sharp sting as Gunther cut his chest. Fortunately, it was little more than a scratch, because he was immediately forced to fend off Gould for a second time.

Ignoring the pain, Nathaniel spun back around and slashed at his attackers, trying to keep them both off-balance. At times he came dangerously close to his targets, causing them to rally and circle around him. Though Gunther was slow and ponderous in his movements, he was powerful. Gould, on the other hand, was less skilled, but in Nathaniel's opinion, more dangerous. It was difficult to anticipate the action of his knife.

They eyed each other, looking for a vulnerable moment, then Nathaniel dodged left and made a lightning jab at Gunther, who was too slow to escape. Plunging his knife deep into the shorter man's shoulder, Nathaniel pulled it out again, expecting to defend himself against Gould. But the tall man did not advance. He stood, staring in horror, as blood poured from Gunther's wound.

Gunther collapsed to his knees, covering the hole in his shoulder with his hands. "He's killed me. The bloody devil's killed me!"

"He'll live," Nathaniel told Gould, "but only if you spend your time fetching a surgeon instead of troubling me further. Otherwise, you'll soon find yourself similarly afflicted."

"Get a doctor," Gunther groaned.

Gould dropped his blade and ran out of the room while Nathaniel retrieved his money from Gunther's pockets, along with a tidy sum he considered the whoremaster owed Alexandra.

Nathaniel wiped his knife on Gunther's trousers, and slid it back into his boot before heading through the hall and down the stairs. Caroline had ahold of Alexandra out front, but she let her go when she realized Gunther had been hurt.

Scooping Alexandra up, Nathaniel placed her on the saddle of his horse and climbed up behind her. She settled against him, stirring a pleasant sensation in his loins, especially when he remembered what little she wore under the wrapper.

What was it about this girl that made her different from all others? he wondered. She was beautiful, but he'd known beautiful women before, none of whom had held his interest for more than a short while. Alexandra was impetuous, stubborn, high-spirited and so incredibly innocent. Was that what beguiled him? He wasn't sure. He only knew that he was drawn to her by something he couldn't identify. He wanted to protect her, caress her, feel her lips beneath his own—and he wanted to possess her body. But what about her heart?

Nothing has changed, he reminded himself firmly. *There's no room in my life for a woman, especially now. Newcastle awaits.*

The room was hot and stuffy. Flushed faces hovered over mugs, talking incessantly, and loud guffaws rang out from a group of men seated in the corner. Normally, Rat would have felt quite at home in the small, cheerful pub. Tonight, nervous tension kept him from enjoying the atmosphere or his ale. He expected the Duke of Greystone at any moment.

Swirling the amber liquid in his cup, Rat tried to concentrate on what he would say when the duke arrived. He decided upon the amount he planned to demand for his information, then quickly tossed it out as too low. He could deliver Dragonslayer on a silver platter. That had to be worth a great deal, and Greystone was as rich as a king.

A fresh gust of air made Rat's eyes flick toward the narrow portal that separated the cool, soggy outdoors from the smoke and confusion within. It was only a sailor reeling drunkenly into the street. The door jingled shut and the room became as stifling as it had been before.

Checking the pocket watch he had managed to lift from an unwary gentleman as they passed in the street, Rat frowned. The duke was late. Would he show?

Rat tapped his foot, wondering if perhaps he was at the wrong place. But the sign above the door read GREENTREE TAVERN, just like Lord Clifton's note had said. Rat had asked three different gentlemen, just to be sure.

Just when he was about to give up, the door opened again, and the duke stepped in. Greystone's dark hair was tinged with gray at the temples, and he was elegantly garbed in a greatcoat of the finest wool. One bejeweled hand clenched the ivory crook of a cane. A footman, dressed in livery, stood at his heels.

Rat let his breath go in relief. The next few minutes would make him a very rich man.

He waved to get the duke's attention.

Greystone nodded to his servant, who immediately turned and headed back outside, evidently to wait with the coach. Then he made his way toward the table.

"Yer Grace." Rat stood and offered the duke a deep bow. "'Ow good of ye to come."

Greystone's eyes narrowed. "Let's dispense with the formalities, shall we? You have something I want."

"Aye, Yer Grace. But, please, won't ye sit down?"

Rat motioned to one side of the tall booth, realizing that the power he had felt earlier must have been an illusion. This man paid homage to no one, for any reason.

"Please," Rat said again when a serving maid hurried to their table to ask the duke his pleasure.

The nobleman grudgingly relinquished his coat and cane to the maid, but refused refreshment. "Do you have the information I need or not?" he asked as soon as the girl left.

"Aye, Yer Grace. There is the small matter of price—"

"Considering you're the thief my housekeeper ran off, and were among the pirates who have raided my ships, you're hardly in a position to dictate terms," he interrupted.

Sweat beaded on Rat's upper lip. "But Yer Grace! 'Twas never proved that I took those candelabras, an' I was only the ship's servant. I took no part in the plunderin'. I offered my assistance to yer son, certainly that proves my intentions were honorable from the start."

"Honorable?" the duke scoffed. "I'm no fool. You're motivated only by greed." His fingers drummed on the table. "What is your price? Perhaps the knowledge that I am aware of your past will keep you honest."

A pretty young woman with a low décolletage sidled up to the table and smiled at the duke. When Greystone glanced up, she curtsied. "I've been worried, Yer Grace. I 'eard ye was ill."

"As you can see, I have recovered," he told her.

"And it's glad I am. It's been a long time." She lowered her lashes. "Too long."

"Later," the duke replied tersely. "Wait for me." He waved his hand, and the woman moved away to hover in a corner.

Rat was too preoccupied with the large emerald glittering from one of Greystone's many rings to be distracted for long. He quickly forgot the woman as he wrestled with his greed, lost his nerve somewhat, and backed off the five-thousand-pound figure he had hoped to achieve. "One thousand pounds," he ventured.

"I'll give you ten pounds," the duke replied. "*And* I won't report you to the authorities."

"But Yer Grace, I came 'ere to be of service to ye at great risk to myself—"

"You look whole enough to me. Make no mistake. I will capture Nathaniel Kent with or without your help. It is only a matter of sooner or later."

Rat felt the blood rise to his face. "Twenty pounds or I tell ye nothin'," he said, seething. His information had to be worth at least that much. The marquess had been far too eager to receive it.

"Perhaps you misunderstood me." The fire raging in the pub's hearth reflected in the duke's eyes. "My terms are not negotiable, and trust me, you do not wish to have me as your enemy." He raised a hand to summon the proprietor.

The maid who had taken his coat came immediately to the table and dipped into a deep curtsy. "Can I get ye somethin', Yer Grace?"

"Yes. You can contact a constable—"

"All right!" Rat almost choked on his words. "Certainly there's no need for that."

"Indeed." A grin curled Greystone's lips as he waved the girl away, mumbling something about changing his mind. "Now then, where is the troublesome one who calls himself Dragonslayer?"

Rat hated to sell his information so cheaply, but he could figure no way to wheedle any more money out of the duke. He remembered the days he'd spent locked up in the ship's hold. At least Nathaniel deserved it. "Right 'ere in London," he said.

Greystone's eyebrows shot up. "Here? Where?"

"I'm not sure exactly. 'Is men returned from London only 'ours before I slipped away, but I over'eard one of 'em say 'e's seein' a woman who's stayin' with a doctor. I think the man's name is Dr. Watts. Lives somewhere on Broad Street, just off Oxford Road."

"Yes. That makes sense." The duke rubbed his chin. "The Golden Crown isn't far from Broad Street. And his ship?"

"'Is ship, Yer Grace?"

"His ship! Where is his ship?"

"In Newcastle. The crew is awaitin' its captain there."

"Excellent." Greystone smiled, then shot a glance at the young woman who was waiting for him.

Rat followed his gaze, more than a little disgruntled by the nagging feeling that he was losing the duke's interest. "An' my money, Yer Grace?"

"Not so quickly. Once a thief, always a thief—and a liar. That's God's own truth. If you would betray Nathaniel, you would betray me.

Dogs like you will do anything for money. What proof do I have that what you have told me is the truth?"

"I 'ave no reason to lie—"

"You have ten pounds as reason and had a hope of one thousand. I'll not pay the likes of you ten pence. Now get out of here before I call the authorities. You're lucky to escape with your skin."

The woman across the room blew the duke a kiss, and Greystone stood up.

"But Yer Grace. We 'ad a bargain. Ten pounds is nothin' to ye," Rat cried.

"Not turning you in was part of that bargain. That is the part I will keep if you leave immediately. I'll not have the likes of you dunning me for money."

Rat wanted to call the duke a thief and a liar, but he was now convinced that the nobleman was more dangerous than he had ever imagined.

"Be gone." Greystone waved Rat off with obvious distaste.

Knowing it would be futile to plead, Rat left his ale and hurried out into the rainy night. He glanced back just in time to see the duke signal the young woman to approach him.

"Where did you find her?" Dr. Watts whispered so he wouldn't wake Alexandra.

"St. Giles Street." Nathaniel ran his fingers along Alexandra's arm. "A man she sewed for was planning to sell her into prostitution. Fortunately, I got there first."

Tutty's eyes grew round. "Poor child. I shudder to think what might have happened."

"I tried to tell her London was no place for a young girl to gallivant around in." Dr. Watts peered over glasses that rested halfway down his nose. "Perhaps now she will listen."

Nathaniel grunted. Such sentiments came easily to someone with a comfortable home and the means to survive. Alexandra didn't possess those luxuries. He knew she'd done only what she felt she had to.

He sighed. Now he had to do the same. As dangerous as the city could be, Alexandra was better off in London than accompanying him. He was out of time. He had to leave for Newcastle—without her.

"If you'll excuse me for a moment," the doctor said. "I've a colleague coming in just a few minutes. When the laudanum wears off, your sister will be good as new, thanks to you."

"Don't let me keep you." Nathaniel stood, but couldn't relinquish his contact with Alexandra so soon. "I was just leaving myself."

Dr. Watts turned back. "Leaving, you say?"

"Aye." Nathaniel reluctantly pulled away from Alexandra and followed him to the door. "I'd like to keep our arrangement as before, if possible. I have pressing business."

"That's fine, if that's what you want. And don't worry about your sister. We won't let her out of our sight again, at least not until she has secured a position with a reputable shop."

"I can't tell you how much that relieves my mind." Nathaniel hated to manipulate Dr. Watts and Tutty, but if anyone needed someone to keep her out of trouble, Alexandra did, whether she acknowledged it or not. Or perhaps he needed their reassurances to make a difficult parting easier.

He was just about to pass outside when a backward glance told him Alexandra was awake.

"Nathaniel?"

"I'm here," he said, moving back to her bed.

"Are you well?"

"I'm faring better than you are."

She tried to laugh. "I thought I'd found employment."

"You got more than you bargained for."

She cringed. "How did you find me?"

"I traced your steps from dress shop to dress shop, but there were several times your trail went cold. If it hadn't been for Mariah, I probably never would have found you."

"She told you where I was?"

"She told me what she thought had happened to you. She didn't know exactly where Gunther's brothel was, but between her help and a bit of money in other places, I extracted the information I needed. I'm just glad I found you in time." He smoothed the hair back out of her face, and their eyes met and held for a moment. Nathaniel was tempted to kiss her, but he doubted he could temper his desire into an expression of affection appropriate to brother and sister. Tutty was still in the room, fussing about. He put his hand on Alexandra's cheek instead and rubbed her bottom lip with his thumb.

"Richard is back," he told her.

She smiled. "Good. Tell him he owes me. If it weren't for him I'd never have"—she glanced at Tutty's back—"gone to sea."

He nodded. "The two of you will have to meet someday."

"Will we?" Alexandra studied him.

"I hope so."

"Is Jake home?" she asked, using Clifton's given name so Tutty wouldn't know who she was talking about.

"He should be by now."

"Have you heard anything from . . . his father?"

"No news is good news, as they say." He gave her a weak grin.

"Or it's the calm before the storm." Alexandra's hand found his.

"I have to go."

"I'm coming with you this time." She tried to get up, but Nathaniel pressed her back.

"You know I can't take you."

"Then why did you return?"

Her eyes challenged him, and Nathaniel felt a moment of helplessness. Why indeed? It had been a foolish concession to his heart, but he wasn't willing to explain that. "I don't know. I'm just glad I did."

"But I'm feeling better already." With a glint of determination sparkling in her eye, she spoke louder, causing Tutty to turn toward them. "And you promised Mother you'd never leave me."

Nathaniel dropped his voice to a threatening level. "Alexandra, don't play games. There is no better place for you right now."

A sympathetic look crossed Tutty's face as the housekeeper went about her business.

"I can't take her, Tutty," Nathaniel explained, stepping away from the bed. "I wish I could, but I can't."

"Of course, Mr. Kent," she said, but her expression held a hint of accusation.

Nathaniel turned back to Alexandra. "If things were different, perhaps . . ." He shook his head. "Never mind. I'll not make empty promises. I have to go."

Alexandra's lids lowered in defeat, then fluttered open again. "Be careful," she whispered.

He nodded, wishing he'd left before she'd awakened. It was more difficult this way. Bending, he dropped a kiss on her forehead. "Leave word with the good doctor as to your whereabouts, will you?"

She nodded.

After saying good-bye to Mrs. Tuttle, Nathaniel headed out the door. The rain was gone but the fog persisted, making him damp within minutes. He frowned at the bothersome weather as he mounted his horse, then tried to turn his mind to what lay ahead instead of the lovely woman he was leaving behind.

Soon he would be on the sea again, where the heavens were clearly visible, stretching forever above him; where the stars were so bright they looked as though he could pluck them from the sky. Closing his eyes, he pictured the serenity of a calm night on the ocean. He could even feel the gentle rocking of the ship—until his head exploded in pain as something hit him from behind, and the ground rushed up to meet him.

Chapter 15

When Nathaniel awoke, he could barely open his eyes for the pounding in his head. He squinted at first, trying to take in his surroundings.

"I think he's waking up."

The voice, though muted, had a quality Nathaniel recognized.

"He's beginning to stir. Go get my father."

Where was he? The blurry images surrounding Nathaniel were unfamiliar. Everything was strange except for that voice.

"Where am I?" he croaked, tasting dried blood. He tried to lift himself from the bed on which he lay, but fell back as a wave of nausea overcame him.

"You're where you've always wanted to be, big *brother*," Lord Clifton responded. "With your family. Do you find it to your liking?"

A flood of memory engulfed Nathaniel, and he closed his eyes against it. His half brother had been there, as well as the duke. He had been surrounded, attacked from all sides. Though he had fought as best he could without a weapon—and had taken down more than a few men—he had been too befuddled from their initial blow to last very long, or to escape. There had been too many of them.

Nathaniel opened his eyes again to survey the room. While expensively decorated, it was too lavish for his tastes and rather impersonal. A hotel perhaps?

"Back with us, eh?" The voice had changed. This time Nathaniel was sure of the speaker: it was his father.

"For now," he managed, licking his swollen upper lip.

"We were beginning to wonder if perhaps we had been a little overzealous in apprehending the thief who has plagued my ships these past months."

"*Zealous* is a good word." Nathaniel blinked as the man leaning above him came more clearly into focus. It was indeed Greystone, his handsome face twisted in a sneer.

"You gave us little choice, Mr. Kent. Believe me, a few of my men are not as well-off as you seem to be."

Nathaniel struggled to voice some response, but his eyes closed of their own accord, causing the duke to speak sharply to someone who stood at the periphery of the room.

"Fetch a glass of water. I don't want him lapsing into unconsciousness again."

It seemed as though an eternity passed before someone raised Nathaniel's head and pressed a glass of water to his lips.

"Drink." The word came as a command, but it did not need to be repeated. Nathaniel was parched. He greedily gulped the cool water while trying to determine how many men were in the room. At some point, he had to get away.

He counted at least five, including his father and Clifton. Unfortunately, he was in too much pain to handle even one.

"How did you find me?" he asked, becoming lucid again.

The duke laughed. "A little money in the right places usually provides what I want. Your crew is not so loyal as you may think."

Nathaniel knew differently. He'd trust any one of his men with his life—any one except . . . He groaned. "Rat."

"There's always a weak link." Greystone gave him a dramatic sigh. "Unfortunately, you found one in my world, as well. Mary. Wasn't that her name?"

"What have you done with her?"

"Thanks to your man, Richard, she escaped. But I believe he received his just due for that one."

Nathaniel nodded, remembering Richard's bruised face. So that was the crux of it. Leave it to him to make light of his bravery.

"Where is my cargo?" the duke asked.

The marquess's hate-contorted face came into view as the two of them waited anxiously for Nathaniel's answer.

"I don't know," Nathaniel said with a smile.

"Come now. I'll find out eventually, you know. You're in no condition to refuse me."

"You'll rot in hell before I tell you anything."

Nathaniel was unprepared for the vicious blow Clifton struck him from the other side of the bed. His head swam. He groaned and struggled against the darkness that threatened to overtake him again.

"Jake!" the duke bellowed. "I'll not have you knock him senseless before I find out what I want to know. Are you as big a fool as he?"

"But father—" Clifton protested.

"Leave!"

The marquess shuffled reluctantly from the room.

When the door closed behind him, Greystone turned back to Nathaniel.

"You are a stubborn man," he said, "but then, so am I. Perhaps you don't understand the depth of my power. I am a peer, a cousin to royalty. I help to control the electoral system, fill the benches in both houses of Parliament, command the militia and monopolize the magistracy."

"Who gives a damn? You don't control me." Nathaniel's words were soft, but he had never meant anything more in his life.

The duke's jaw clenched. "My servants would say you have a good deal of *pluck*, but do you truly think you can withhold anything from me?"

"If you don't release me, my first mate will send a message to Chief Commissioner Mayne informing him about the rifles you tried to sell to the czar. I think we both know the punishment for treason."

"You're joking, of course." The duke stared daggers at Nathaniel. "You have no idea what you're talking about. How dare you threaten me with such nonsense."

"Call it what you will. I've seen the guns with my own eyes, and so will Commissioner Mayne."

"There is nothing you can do to hurt me, you arrogant bastard," Greystone bellowed, his nostrils flaring. "I can crush you, put you away until you rot, until you beg for a morsel of worm-eaten bread. Who do you think you are?"

"I'm your son." Nathaniel said it through clenched teeth, struggling to sit up despite the two burly fellows who came forward to shove him back. "You deny it to the world, but we two know the truth."

Greystone's face flushed red. "You have no idea what I have in store for you."

"Another carriage accident perhaps?"

"Nothing so short and sweet. You'll pay for your insolence. I'll see to that." The veins in the duke's neck throbbed for a pregnant moment, then he whirled and left the room.

A hand covered Alexandra's mouth. Coming out of the depths of sleep, she struggled against it, trying to pry it away so she could scream.

"Alexandra!" Her name came as a harsh whisper, but she stopped fighting as soon as she recognized the voice. It was Trenton. He stood above her, his face shrouded in darkness.

Tentatively pulling away, he said, "It's only me."

"What's wrong?"

"Where's Nathaniel?"

Fear tightened Alexandra's chest. Nathaniel had left the day before to meet Trenton and the others. Why wasn't he with them?

She started to answer, then froze as she heard shuffling from above. Tutty's voice called down the stairs. "Alexandra, dear? Are you all right?"

"I'm fine, Mrs. Tuttle. Just a little restless. I hope I'm not disturbing you."

"No, no, don't worry." Alexandra could hear the sleep in her voice. "Just checking."

The ceiling creaked as Mrs. Tuttle made her way back to her bed. Trenton and Alexandra didn't speak again until the house fell silent.

"He left yesterday to find you," she whispered at last.

"He never arrived." Trenton moved away from the side of her bed and crossed to the window. Moonlight poured into the room as he pulled the drapes back to gaze outside.

"Where could he be?" Alexandra heard the tremor in her own voice, and swallowed.

"Rat disappeared a few days ago as well," Trenton explained. "He must have gone to see the duke."

Alexandra gasped as her mind briefly conjured Rat's face. She remembered Nathaniel's anger when the dirty little man had attacked her, and the punishment that had followed. "What does that mean?"

Trenton glanced back at her, his profile outlined in silver. "If Nathaniel's father has captured him, there's no telling."

"Why didn't Nathaniel stay with you in the first place?" she asked. "You would all be at sea by now."

Trenton didn't reply, but Alexandra could feel the accusation in his stance.

"He came back here to see me," she said, answering her own question. "And when he arrived, I was gone." Alexandra shuddered to think what might have happened to her had Nathaniel not come back for her. But she also realized that the time he spent searching for her might very well have cost him his life.

"We must go to Bow Street," she exclaimed. "We have to take a constable to see the duke—" She started to get out of bed, but Trenton's bitter laugh robbed her of the energy.

"The constabulary won't believe us. They'd never question a man like Greystone on our word alone. The guns are our only hope, and we have to deal with them the right way, or the authorities will think we stole them from somewhere else in order to entrap a powerful peer of the realm." He jammed his hands into his pockets. "Nathaniel said he was going to write to the Lord High Admiral at Doctor's Commons. I think we should do the same."

"But that will take time."

"I know. Meanwhile, we've got to figure out where the duke is keeping Nathaniel and see if we can help him." Trenton didn't add, "If he's still alive," but he didn't have to. The words hung in the air between them, too heavy to be spoken and too real to be ignored.

"There must be some way of finding out what Greystone has done with him," Alexandra whispered. She had to believe Nathaniel was alive. She couldn't bear the alternative. "The duke might have attempted to smother an infant on the day of his birth, and he might have hired some men to run a carriage off the road. But even Greystone couldn't get away with capturing a man and having him killed, could he?"

Trenton shrugged. "The question isn't what His Grace could get away with. It's what he *thinks* he could get away with that matters."

Nathaniel stared into the somber face of his father's friend and political ally, Sir John Ballard. The duke had called the magistrate from his bed, and now, despite the late hour, Nathaniel, Greystone, Clifton and two of the duke's men stood in Ballard's study while Sir John sat behind his oversize desk and rubbed the sleep from his eyes.

"What are the charges?" Sir John asked the duke. Evidently, the judge hadn't taken the time to put in his teeth. A distinctive lisp slurred his words, and his mouth looked oddly sunken.

"Piracy."

The magistrate's brows raised beneath the gray stubble of his hair that had probably been covered by a white-powdered wig earlier in the day. "A serious charge," he commented. Taking up his quill, he began to scratch something on the papers before him. "Do you have any evidence against him?"

"Just sign it, John," Greystone insisted. "The details don't matter."

"I've got my own arse to consider," the magistrate cried.

"Then invent whatever is necessary. Just sign the order and let's be done here."

Sir John's frown deepened. "I'll take care of the details in the morning," he relented. "Now, what is it you want done with Mr. Kent? I doubt we could get away with having him executed on my signature alone, if that's what you're hoping."

"Why not?" the duke asked.

"Because it will incite a great deal of interest—"

"We can't kill him yet," Clifton interrupted. "He's got an entire shipload of our cargo, and it's worth several thousand pounds. Send him to the hulks. Perhaps a good long stay in such a place will make him more cooperative."

Nathaniel threw a smoldering glance at his younger brother, but couldn't move for the two thugs who held him fast on either side. He pictured the decaying line-of-battle ships moored on the banks of the Thames near the royal arsenal at Woolwich. Essentially prison barges, notorious for their poor living conditions, the hulks housed hundreds of hardened criminals and were probably the place most like hell on earth.

"He'll be secure enough there, for the time being," Greystone added, sounding amused.

Sir John snickered. "Capital idea! We've had few escapes from Woolwich." His quill went back to work on the documents before him. "Most of the men there are too sick to attempt any such thing, and the shackles are a convincing deterrent." He paused. "The only problem is that most of the convicts aboard those rotting ships are awaiting deportation. Where do you want Mr. Kent to go? Australia? Tasmania?"

"Nowhere," the duke returned coolly. "He might someday find his way back, and such a surprise would be unfortunate. Sentence him to remain forever in England, yet laying foot on English soil only to work in a heavily guarded gang."

Nathaniel began to struggle, even though he felt barely strong enough to stand. He could not allow his father to send him to the hulks. Such a sentence was far worse than spending the rest of his life at Newgate. Prison barges were even more rife with disease, violence and corruption; it was a miracle anyone survived them.

Greystone scoffed at Nathaniel's feeble efforts. "I'm afraid you're in no condition to object."

Sir John rose from his chair. "Take him over to the gaol. I know the gaoler. There will be no questions asked."

"Excellent." The duke smiled. "I won't forget this little favor."

"What are friends for?" Sir John clapped Greystone on the back as the duke's men dragged Nathaniel out of the room.

When they reached the main entry hall, Nathaniel began to shout. He hoped to rouse a servant or a family member who might help him, but a meaty fist thudded against his skull, and once again he saw only darkness.

At dawn Alexandra stood outside the ornate iron gate that circled Greystone House, dressed as a maid and carrying a tin box that contained everything she owned in the world. She couldn't see anything beyond the plethora of windows that winked at her in the early sunshine, reflecting the trees in the yard, the small lawn in front and the fashionable square across the street with its flowers and cherry trees, but she hoped to find something that would lead her to Nathaniel.

After taking a moment to gather her nerve, she lifted the latch and forced her feet to move along the flagstone path that approached the house, then veered off to circle behind. Not knowing whether the marquess would deem her friend or foe, should he see her, left her frightened and more than a little nervous. He knew she had been captured against her will. Had he discerned the softening of her heart toward the pirate captain?

At the back door, she met two tradesmen carrying daily supplies. The butcher drove a high dogcart and was busily engaged with a woman Alexandra assumed, from her dress and manner, to be Greystone's housekeeper. The baker was just leaving. Carrying bread in a large basket covered with a white cloth, he called, "See you Monday week, Mrs. Wright."

Alexandra remained silent until they had concluded their business, then stepped forward when the butcher drove away.

"Who are you?" A hardy woman with shoulders the width of a man's and hands that were almost as callused, the housekeeper regarded her with frank appraisal.

"I've come to see Lady Anne," Alexandra told her. "Has she returned from Scotland?"

The housekeeper's brows rose as shrewd eyes swept over Alexandra's plain dress and apron. "Aye, she's back. But what business would she have with the likes of you?"

Alexandra cleared her throat. "It's personal," she said, trying to ignore the anxiety churning in her stomach. Afraid the housekeeper would dismiss her if she didn't explain, she added, "I've come to replace something I took. Tell your mistress I'm the seamstress who was supposed to fix the dress her mother gave her. We met in Manchester. I'll wait here until she wakes."

Alexandra set her tin box on the ground and sat on top of it.

The look of skepticism didn't change on Mrs. Wright's face, but she said, "It'll only be a minute. Lady Anne's up already."

She went inside, leaving Alexandra to chew her lip in agitation. How would Nathaniel's half sister receive her? In light of their last meeting, Lady Anne could just as easily have her thrown into gaol as hire her as a maid. But Alexandra knew of no better way to find Nathaniel. She could only hope her and Trenton's plan would work.

A moment later, Mrs. Wright poked her head through the door. "Come inside. Lady Anne will see you in the sitting room."

Alexandra followed the housekeeper through the anteroom of a large kitchen and into the kitchen itself. A stove sat in one corner, flanked by a huge brick hearth. Utensils hung from pegs along the wall. Copper pots dangled above a large deal table. Several baskets littered the floor. One was filled with fresh eggs, another with carrots just out of the ground.

A green baize door separated the kitchen from the rest of the house. Mrs. Wright charged through it, and Alexandra hurried behind, amazed at the opulence that suddenly surrounded her: drawing rooms, parlors, sitting rooms, music rooms and libraries furnished with silk and cashmere draperies that puddled on the floor; doors carved from exotic hardwoods; carpets from Smyrna and Madras. An impressive wide stairway wound its way up to the second floor, where several Aubusson tapestries hung on the wall.

They stopped at a set of double doors off a large, vaulted entry. Mrs. Wright knocked, then motioned for Alexandra to follow her inside.

Lady Anne sat at a desk, wearing a pale blue Louis XV–style dress with a jacket bodice and tabbed skirt. A Bible was open in front of her. She looked up as they entered—and frowned.

"There you are," she said, her voice indignant. "Where is my gown?"

Alexandra stared at her shoes. "I'm sorry, my lady. The dress is ruined."

"Ruined! I should have guessed as much. Is that why you're here? To tell me you ruined the gown my mother gave me?"

"No." Alexandra glanced up. "I came to see if I could make up for its loss. You see, I never meant to steal it—"

Lady Anne waved her words away, the look on her face softening. "The fact that you're here tells me that. Besides, I heard the fuss your stepfather made after you ran off. I can hardly blame you for leaving. Sometimes I wish I had as much nerve." She glanced pensively back at the fire before a hesitant smile claimed her lips. "You caused quite an uproar. Mr. Calvert was beside himself. Really, between him and that father of yours, the entertainment was almost worth the loss of my dress."

Alexandra nearly chuckled at the picture Lady Anne's words created in her mind—a flustered Mr. Calvert, a duke's daughter standing in her shift, her dress gone, and Willy raging about his money—only she feared Lady Anne might interpret her mirth as insincerity. "I'd like to repay you, my lady. I have no money, but I'll work off whatever figure you deem fair."

"As a housemaid?" Lady Anne's voice rose in surprise as her eyes marked Alexandra's attire. "But you're a seamstress."

"I realize I have no experience as a servant, but I'd like the chance to learn." Alexandra swallowed, feeling a twinge of guilt at her duplicity. She had chosen the role of maid only because, should Lady Anne take her on, it would allow her access to the house and its staff, and bring her into frequent contact with the duke.

"How difficult can it be?" Lady Anne shrugged, glancing at Mrs. Wright. "Surely you can teach her."

The housekeeper nodded. "If you'd like, m'lady."

Nathaniel's half sister glanced back at her Bible. "Yes, I'd like that. A woman with so much pluck would be an asset to any house, and the Good Book says we're to forgive, doesn't it? You'd have to work several years to pay for such a dress on a maid's wages, but I'll be content with one. Are you agreeable?"

Alexandra curtsied. "Yes, my lady."

"Good." She turned to the housekeeper. "Make room for her in the attic."

Mrs. Wright led Alexandra back to the kitchen and from there up a tall, narrow staircase to a small attic.

"You'll sleep here," the housekeeper informed her. "Put your trunk on that bed. You'll have to unpack later."

Alexandra deposited her box on a worn quilt thrown over the top of an iron bedstead. Hers was one of three beds that lined the wall; a fourth was next to the only window on the opposite side. A spotted mirror hung above each cot, and a chest of drawers sat between them on bare floorboards. A chipped washbasin occupied the end of the room; next to it sat a chamber pot.

"The position of housemaid normally pays eighteen pounds a year," Mrs. Wright said as she turned back to the stairs and motioned for Alexandra to follow her. "Time off will consist of one full day each month and one afternoon a week, beginning at three p.m. You might be working for nothing, but at least you'll have a roof over your head and food in your stomach."

Alexandra nodded as Mrs. Wright glanced her way before continuing, "You'll rise at five o'clock every morning and begin by lighting the fires. Then you'll carry water up for the family's baths. After your breakfast, you'll sweep the carpets downstairs and dust the main entry hall."

Mrs. Wright spoke quickly, sounding as though she were attempting to fit an hour's worth of instruction into the time it took to reach the kitchen, and she seemed to remember more and more things as they went along.

Alexandra struggled to absorb the onslaught of information, listening to every word with rapt attention. Now that she had established herself in the duke's household, the last thing she wanted was to lose her position before she found out what she had come to learn. Trenton and the others were counting on her. And no one wanted to find Nathaniel more than she did.

As they reached the bottom of the stairs, another servant approached, looking more than a little distraught. "Mrs. Wright, the tweenie has run off. I guess Cook had a few harsh words for her yesterday, and she popped off in the middle of the night."

The housekeeper groaned. "The girl was so homesick, she was no good to us anyway. Very well, Janet. Alexandra is here now. She can help out in the kitchen until we find someone to replace Ruth."

"The stove has yet to be lit," Janet complained. "And it needs to be black-leaded. At this rate, we won't have hot water by the time Cook wakes."

"Then get it done. Alexandra will help you in a moment."

Janet frowned but went to work, and Mrs. Wright turned to face Alexandra. "His Grace demands a great deal from his servants," she warned, lowering her voice, "so until you're properly trained, try to remain as inconspicuous as possible. Lower your eyes and step out of the way if he should come upon you while you're performing your duties."

She raised her brows, as if questioning whether or not Alexandra understood her, and Alexandra nodded. "Your cleaning is to be done by noon each day," she went on. "The afternoons are spent darning socks, mending clothes, or helping Cook. Now get along. Janet needs you. A good French cook is hard to come by, and Madame Plume is a fussy individual. I'd rather avoid a tirade this morning."

So would I, Alexandra thought. The last thing she wanted was to have someone in authority angry with her on her first day.

"Come to my quarters at bedtime for further instructions. Any of the other maids can tell you where to find me," the housekeeper said as she moved away.

The kitchen was already a beehive of activity. Everyone had a purpose and knew exactly what it was and how to do it, except Alexandra. She looked for the girl Mrs. Wright had instructed her to join, and found Janet kneeling in front of a coal-fired range, busily polishing its steel bars with emery paper.

A pail of cinders at her feet indicated she had already swept out the inside.

Alexandra knelt next to her, overwhelmed by the myriad instructions Mrs. Wright had rattled off. She remembered well enough that the duke was someone to be feared, but she didn't need the housekeeper to tell her that—she thought him dangerous already.

The morning meal was a brief affair of bread and milk, shared only with the other maids. They gathered around the large table in the kitchen shortly after eight o'clock and ate in silence, then scurried off to finish their work by noon.

The rest of the day revolved around work, work and more work, interspersed with meals. Dinner lasted a mere twenty minutes, after which Alexandra spent the afternoon mending shirts and socks. Supper consisted of cold meat, bread and cheese. Beer was served all around, and for the first time that day, Alexandra saw the other maids, fifteen of them total, talk and laugh.

At bedtime Alexandra visited Mrs. Wright's room just off the large kitchen, as she had been told. It was after nine o'clock, but some emergency with Cook, over pan drippings no less, had kept the housekeeper late. When Mrs. Wright finally arrived, she sent Alexandra off to bed with the promise that they would talk the following evening.

Carrying a single tallow candle, Alexandra stumbled up the long flight of stairs to the attic. Fortunately, the girl with whom she shared a bed was already asleep and didn't stir when Alexandra unpacked her box. She put her belongings in the two drawers allotted for her use in the chest next to the bed, and snuffed out the candle.

Six other girls shared the same small attic, but Alexandra gave them no mind. She slid into bed in her clothes and lay tense and expectant and too preoccupied to worry about the lumps in the thin mattress or the chill of the unheated room.

For she was only biding her time, waiting until the entire house fell quiet.

Chapter 16

The boat jerked along as the oarsmen guided it toward a dozen mastless vessels sitting like huge ducks with heads buried in the shallow water. The hulks loomed before Nathaniel as he glanced wistfully back at the docks, envying the men who were busily engaged there, free to do as they wished.

A lavish carriage drew to a halt at the edge of the wharf, causing Nathaniel to clench his jaw. He had no doubt as to the owner of that conveyance. Though he could not make out the golden crest emblazoned on each door, he knew that the duke and Clifton had come to watch the final nail being driven into the coffin they had prepared for him.

"Is this yer first time in such a place?" asked another prisoner, a man with a black patch over one eye. Five convicts crowded the small boat, along with an armed guard and two oarsmen. The prisoners could overpower the three guards easily enough, Nathaniel knew, except they were double-ironed and unlikely to do anything to cause their own drowning.

When Nathaniel nodded, the stranger laughed. "If yer like most newcomers, ye'll fall sick inside a year."

Nathaniel was not impressed. He shrugged, but offered no retort.

"See this eye? I lost it in a fight aboard the *Warrior*. That's 'er, five hulls down. The fightin' gets pretty rough." He grinned. "A one-armed man would 'ave reason ter fear."

"Not if you were me." Nathaniel gave him a scorching stare, refusing to be intimidated, and eventually the man turned to the prisoner on his other side.

"Ye 'ave reason to fear, too. Ye look no older than a lad. Once it's dark, the big men who've been around awhile prefer lads like you with fair 'air and blue eyes."

Nathaniel nearly laughed aloud at One-Eye's bully tactics, except that they weren't funny. He was entering a whole new world, one less than a mile from the life he knew, yet oceans apart. No one escaped from the hulks, except through death. Whether that was because of the chains they wore, or the despair that weakened both mind and body, Nathaniel did not know.

He'd have to reserve his strength and be alert for any opportunity. Greystone and Clifton had not seen the last of him. Somehow he would survive.

Squinting up at the prison barges, Nathaniel grimaced. The place smelled worse than a common lodging house. The tide was out, leaving the hulks sitting in mud for ten hours out of every twenty-four. With the marshes nearby and a pond the tide reached only during winter, there was no flux to carry away the stagnant water. The smell of dead animals combined with the stench of the waste dumped off the ships to create a cesspool that reeked for miles around.

The ships were rotting, that much he could tell, but what really concerned him was that the prisoners inside them probably fared no better.

Swatting at a fly buzzing near his neck, Nathaniel watched one of the rowers jam his oar into the muddy water to steer the boat toward one of three large vessels clustered together.

The name *Retribution* was painted in faded red letters on the side of the first hull. Nathaniel knew the moment he saw it that he had arrived at his new home.

The men with the oars laid them down, and together with the guard, steadied a rope ladder that dangled before them. Then the shackled prisoners climbed slowly aboard.

The *Retribution* had originally been a thirty-two-gun ship captured from the Spanish, Nathaniel heard One-Eye boast. But it was a hellish place now. Only splintered stubs remained where masts had towered into the sky. The wheel was gone, and the deck, once polished and clean, lay beneath grime at least an inch thick. Vermin droppings filled every nook and cranny, evidence that the prisoners had ample company.

Instinctively Nathaniel raised his eyes to the sky. Thick clouds covered the descending sun, but gold, purple and magenta hues shimmered through. He was relieved to see the horizon. That, at least, remained unchanged.

A man who referred to himself as the overseer, and another named Sampson, who held the designation of clerk, met the new prisoners. The overseer was obviously the man with supreme authority; Nathaniel soon learned he did not live on the ship, but came at sunrise and left at sunset each day. The clerk appeared to be a fellow prisoner who enjoyed a certain measure of power and greater freedom on the ship than his companions.

While the prisoners were temporarily unshackled, Sampson demanded they strip and bathe in a tub, which had been delivered by other convicts. By the time it was Nathaniel's turn to step into the cold water, it was black from the grease and dirt of the previous four bathers. He desperately longed to scrub the grime from his body, but he could hardly force himself to step into the filthy water.

Except that he knew he had no choice.

Once Nathaniel had bathed, no matter how profitless the ritual, the clerk provided him with a coarse gray jacket and breeches. Fortunately, they were clean. Two other prisoners were given used garments that looked as though they hadn't been washed since their last wearing. When one man dared to object, Sampson grabbed a pistol from the nearest guard and shoved it in his mouth.

"Dead men don't know if their clothes are clean or dirty," he warned. "Given a day or two, they'll look no different anyhow."

The glitter in the clerk's eyes betrayed his eagerness to enforce his words. The prisoner pulled on the garments without another word while Nathaniel wondered who or what gave Sampson his power.

When leg irons were once again fastened about their ankles, the overseer spoke. "If you obey without question, work hard and keep to yourselves, you will be left alone. Anyone who attempts to escape, or cause insurrection, will be eliminated immediately. Life here is just that simple." Turning to Sampson, he added, "Have them join the others. I'll be in my cabin. I'm starving."

Though Nathaniel had expected the worst, he was still surprised by the appearance of the three hundred and fifty men who already lived aboard the *Retribution*. They were a lean, sickly lot, with scraggly beards itching with lice, and many wore only rags. Some had no shirt, shoes or stockings.

They stood at attention for a brief ceremony, which consisted of Sampson reading the rules and the punishment affixed to each infraction. The rules were long and varied, but the punishment was always the same: flogging, flogging and more flogging. Then the prisoners filed below for their evening meal.

The dining room contained nothing but wooden tables and benches. No cleaner than the deck, it was dank and smelled strongly of mildew. Four portholes shed just enough light to lend a hazy glow to the room, much like smoke in a tavern. The lanterns that hung overhead cast dim circles on the floor that moved as the hull rocked.

With only ten tables, the men had to eat in shifts. The bulk of the prisoners were herded beyond the dining room into the sleeping areas. Nathaniel and the other new convicts were allowed to join the first shift.

Nathaniel was famished and more than eager to receive his meal— until he saw what it was. A detestable souplike substance called smiggings, it was made from boiled beef thickened with barley and was served in a tine bowl. The smell alone nauseated him. The others ate ravenously, but Nathaniel's soup went untouched, and again he felt the clerk's eyes upon him.

"If you got any brains, you'll eat," Sampson said, moving closer to Nathaniel from where he had stood along the periphery with the guards.

"There's nothing else coming till morning. As you can see, the others have figured it out. They're bloody smart, eh?"

While Nathaniel was momentarily distracted from his rancid dinner, the prisoner next to him grabbed for his bowl and slurped up his soup, letting the juice dribble down his chin.

Watching him made Nathaniel's skin crawl. He was locked up with animals, no longer of a sound state of mind.

Before his lump of bread could be stolen as well, he closed his mind to the taste of mold and forced himself to both chew and swallow. Sampson was right about one thing: he had to eat to keep up his strength, or he would end up no different than the rest of them.

From dark until ten, the men were left to pass the time as they would. Split between three decks and six wards, they were allowed free range only in their own small areas, and many loitered about, visiting or causing trouble.

Nathaniel stretched out on the hammock that had been assigned to him, struggling to block out the constant rattle of chains and hum of voices. What now? Had the duke captured Trenton and the *Vengeance* as well? Or was his first mate free to collect the guns and take them to the Lord High Admiral?

If only he knew. If only he could communicate with Trenton.

"My son."

Nathaniel raised his eyes at the soft-spoken voice to see a chaplain standing above him.

"I am Reverend Hartman. I offer classes each night that might provide you with some solace. It would please me to have you join us. It could make the transition here easier for you."

Shaking his head, Nathaniel almost rejected the invitation, then thought better of it. Here was someone who was neither prisoner nor guard. Clergymen were privy to a wealth of information, and it could only help him to understand how things were run in this strange new world—and by whom. Coming to his feet, Nathaniel said, "Anything is better than sitting here, Father."

Pleased at recruiting another member to his flock, the Reverend Hartman led Nathaniel to a corner of the ward where a handful of men waited with open Bibles. Though most couldn't read, the reverend performed that service aloud, and Nathaniel was glad he had joined the group if for no other reason than to enjoy the peace it provided against the bawdy songs and activities of the others.

When the chaplain finally closed his book and the group dissipated, Nathaniel took the opportunity to strike up a conversation with him. "I was hoping you could enlighten me on a few subjects."

The chaplain started stacking the Bibles on a corner shelf. "Of course. What would you like to know?"

"The clerk is dressed like a prisoner, but he doesn't act like one. Who is he?"

Reverend Hartman's manner changed instantly. He glanced about before answering, "It's best to steer clear of him. He's a prisoner, but he works for the overseer."

"Why is it he has no chains, and fares so much better than the rest of us?"

"He is a cruel and dangerous man. I suggest you stay well away." The reverend changed the subject: "You don't speak like a prisoner; I would guess you are an educated man."

"Self-educated, mostly."

"What did you do to arrive here?"

"I'm not sure what the final charge was." Nathaniel shrugged off the question. He wasn't here to talk about himself.

"I'd be curious to learn the details sometime," the reverend answered. "But they're setting the watch now. You'd better get back to your bunk."

The watch consisted of several seasoned prisoners who sat up through the night with a light burning. They relieved each other every two hours and were supposed to ensure that no one spoke or moved about, but bribes and favors rendered the watch ineffective. And Nathaniel heard many suspicious moans and groans and other things that kept him on his guard, making sleep impossible.

Like some mythical dragon that snorts and shifts as it descends into a comfortable sleep, the Greystone residence took some time to settle in for the night. Alexandra waited, listening to the movements of those servants who still worked in the nether regions of the house, banking fires, polishing silver or putting away the plate. Tomorrow morning would come all too soon, and with it her tiresome responsibilities as maid. She had to take advantage of every opportunity to seek information on Nathaniel.

As those around her snored softly, she climbed from her bed and tiptoed to the stairs, grateful when no one stirred, not even her bedmate. The stairs creaked as she made her way down though, and Alexandra was certain the racket could be heard all over the house. She feared Mrs. Wright would be waiting for her by the time she reached the bottom, but when she entered the kitchen, it was dark save for the moonlight streaming in at the windows.

The duke and his two children were out for the evening. Alexandra knew Lady Anne had gone to a dinner party somewhere—the other servants had mentioned it—but she had no idea what had called Lord Clifton and his father away, or when they'd come home. She only hoped it wouldn't be now.

Heading through the green baize door that separated the servants' domain from that of Greystone's family, she checked to make sure the front of the house was equally quiet.

Evidently Lady Anne had already returned and retired, as no one waited up for her. Perhaps the duke and Lord Clifton had returned as well. A footman sat in a room off the entry playing solitaire, but Alexandra knew he'd be there all night, just as he was every night, to guard against thieves and the like.

The glow from the footman's candle spilled out of the room he occupied, giving her just enough light to slip by without banging into anything.

As she started up the winding staircase, the plush carpet muffled her movements, allowing her to make quick progress. But when she reached the second floor, she had to travel more slowly. The darkness in the long halls on either side was now complete, and she feared she'd bump into a table or a whatnot shelf and knock some priceless porcelain to the ground.

Greystone's study overlooked the front gardens, but the heavy draperies blocked most of the moon's light. As soon as Alexandra entered, she shut the door and began to fumble through the room, looking for a candleholder.

A moment later she found a lamp on the desk. Sulfur matches sat beside it in a cold, smooth container.

The match Alexandra struck flared with a blue light, then faded to yellow as she held it to the wick of the lamp before replacing the cover.

The duke's study held a large mahogany desk, a high-backed leather chair, a card table and several smaller chairs. A picture hung on the wall above the desk. A man astride a horse. Likely the duke in his younger years, Alexandra decided. She recognized the slight flare to his nostrils, the chiseled planes of his face. These features were very much like Nathaniel's, but the resemblance ended there. Greystone's eyes were more green than blue, and his hair was brown, not the ebony color of his firstborn son's.

Various documents cluttered the duke's desk. Alexandra rounded it to stand between desk and chair as she dug through the pile, examining every item. Most of what she saw related to business: bills of lading, bills for household expenses, letters from associates or friends, a few legal documents—nothing that had any obvious connection to Nathaniel.

She sighed and glanced about the room again. How could she find out what had happened to him? There had to be some way, short of visiting every gaol and—Alexandra shivered—undertaker.

The sound of a cough coming from the hall outside made Alexandra freeze. Someone was coming. Quickly raising the glass of the lamp, she blew out the light. Her mind searched frantically for what she should do, but there was no time to do anything. The floor creaked and the doorknob turned as she ducked beneath the duke's desk.

The light of a candle flame glowed in the darkness as footsteps crossed the room toward her.

Alexandra squeezed her eyes shut, praying she wouldn't be discovered, and pressed back as far as she could against the smooth underside of her wooden haven.

The footsteps stopped on the other side of the desk. She heard the rattle of paper above her, then a loud belch.

"Damn cook."

It was the duke. It had to be. Alexandra would have recognized Clifton's voice immediately.

More rummaging, and a bit of cursing. Then Greystone seemed to discover whatever it was he was looking for and fell silent for a while, as though reading.

"Good," he mumbled, grunting in satisfaction, and the steps and the light began to recede.

Alexandra held her breath until the duke was gone. She hadn't realized she was shaking, but she could hardly stand as the acrid scent of Greystone's candle lingered, covering the smell of her own lamp and reminding her of just how close she'd come to making herself his new target.

Waiting until her eyes adjusted to the meager moonlight, Alexandra looked around the study a final time. She sorted more carefully through the duke's correspondence, squinting to make out who had written him, then rifled through his drawers until she encountered a locked metal box.

Judging from its weight, the box held nothing more valuable than a few legal documents, but the fact that it was locked intrigued her. She padded quietly to the door, which the duke had left standing wide, and closed it. Then she returned to the desk and picked up a marble paperweight to smash the lock.

She stood close to the window to afford herself what light she could, and glanced through what appeared to be love letters. Fierce protestations of undying devotion and lewd invitations written in torrents of misspelled words and incorrect grammar covered sheet after sheet of cheap foolscap. Only one was written on expensive stationery by a woman who appeared to be educated. It came all the way from Scotland and was signed "Ellyne." Alexandra soon realized she was reading the words of Lord Clifton and Lady Anne's mother.

My children beg me to come back to England and yet I have never received a single letter from you. Not even the apology I so deserve or a thank-you for holding my tongue. In my more generous moments, I think guilt keeps you so remote. But that must be the beginning of my dementia speaking. I have lost all of my hair and too much weight, but the sores have gone for now. When I am strong enough to be honest with myself I know you do not care that you brought such a fate home to me. You had to have your doxies, and they had to be of the most common variety, didn't they?

Yet I gave you the son you wanted and, for my children's sake, say nothing of your trips to the Greentree Tavern and others like it. I bet you thought I didn't know where you went at night. More's the pity . . . I didn't know until it was too late. Still, I want to tell you this: my revenge is knowing that you will soon follow me. We can't live forever, Your Grace, and so I hope someday to see you burning in the fiery furnaces of hell. Just as you deserve.

Alexandra blinked as she absorbed the meaning of the flowing script. Was it syphilis? Had the duke given his wife syphilis? Anger and pity nearly brought tears to her eyes for the women who had been destroyed by Nathaniel's father, and for Lady Anne and Lord Clifton, and much more poignantly, for Nathaniel.

Daring to light the lamp again, Alexandra used a sheet of the duke's own stationary to pen a letter to Trenton. Perhaps it was time Greystone received a measure of his own medicine.

The guards woke Nathaniel at dawn for a breakfast of boiled barley. Though the meal would not have been considered edible anywhere else, Nathaniel hungrily swallowed the tasteless gruel, noting as he did the absence of so much as a crust of bread. Evidently rations aboard the hulks were scantier than he had anticipated. He wondered at the possibility of receiving a second serving, but as he glanced at the empty bowls of the other men, he saw that no one asked.

"Can we have more?" he asked the prisoner seated next to him.

Small-boned, with a gray, wispy beard and sunken eyes, the man looked almost like a sage, except for the long scar that disfigured his cheek. He studied Nathaniel dubiously. "You can ask, if you want to go without for the rest of the day. Bloody Sampson spends the government's money on pig slop—and gives us less than a child's ration at that—so he can pocket the difference."

"Now, that's a serious charge," the clerk interrupted, suddenly bearing down on them. "Haven't you learned to control your tongue yet, Joseph? After five years in this stinkin' place?"

Joseph cowered in Sampson's presence. "I didn't mean nothin' by it! I swear."

"Perhaps it's time to show our one-armed man what happens to those who make trouble. Come on, Old Joe. You first."

"But you know me, sir," Joseph cried. "I'm harmless enough. Just an old man, minding his business."

"Didn't sound as though you were minding your business to me." Sampson motioned to a guard, who grabbed Joseph by the shirt front and hauled him up. "It's time for a flogging, boys!"

Everyone poured out of the mess hall behind Nathaniel, Joseph and those who pulled them both along. Unable to keep up with the quick pace of the guards because of the shackles on his feet, Joseph fell and received a kick in the ribs for his folly.

"Get up, coward!" Sampson raged, drawing back for a blow to the head.

Nathaniel grasped Sampson's fist in his hand. "Give him a minute."

The other prisoners stared at them, mouths agape, as silence fell over the room like a blanket.

"Touch me again and you're a dead man," Sampson threatened, spittle wetting his lips.

Nathaniel's eyes met those of the clerk, and he refused to look away. Finally Sampson pulled his hand back and turned to the guards. "Give Joseph double the usual for this man's interference. And give One-Arm double as well. He'll soon learn what I will tolerate and what I won't."

The flogging triangle was connected to what used to be the mainmast. Though not particularly large or threatening in looks, it waited ominously while the other prisoners formed a tight circle around Nathaniel, Joseph, Sampson and a single guard.

The guard removed Joseph's shirt and tied his hands and feet to the triangle, then made ready with the cat-o'-nine.

"No, please!" Joseph jerked as the first lash struck his bare skin, causing several welts to appear.

Nathaniel cringed at the sight, trying to block the other man's cries from his mind, but they seemed to echo off the sky.

Most of the prisoners watched with disinterest, as though a flogging were such a common occurrence as to warrant little or no attention, but others seemed to enjoy the spectacle. Some even encouraged the guard to continue when he finally stopped.

Only the chaplain showed any empathy for Joseph's suffering. He stood with a pained expression on his face throughout the ordeal.

When it was over, Sampson took hold of the whip to administer Nathaniel's blows himself. "This will teach you some respect, cripple," he said. "You think I haven't noticed your haughty attitude? It certainly won't last long around here."

A guard began to remove Nathaniel's shirt, but Nathaniel jerked away and took it off himself. A bewhiskered man tied his arm and both feet to the triangle as Sampson shook out the nine thongs of the whip.

Pain exploded across Nathaniel's back as the clerk dealt him a hearty blow. But he was ready. He gritted his teeth and focused his thoughts on other things, imagining Alexandra standing beside him, looking on. He would not want her to see them break him. For her, he would not cry out . . . or beg for mercy. He would endure his punishment like a man, and when it was all over, she would comfort him by kissing his eyelids closed and pressing her small, cool hands to his burning cheeks. Alexandra could ease the pain. *Oh God, where was she?*

Soon something trickled down Nathaniel's back, and he knew it must be blood. Only the thought of Alexandra watching gave him the strength to stand, the will to endure until silence replaced the roar of the crowd. Finally Sampson stopped and threw down the whip, and Nathaniel slumped, letting himself dangle, at last, from the ropes that held him.

"It's time for work," Sampson announced. "Get these animals ashore and stacking shot at the arsenal before they think this man's some kind of hero. And put One-Arm here in solitary confinement."

The clerk stomped away, and Nathaniel felt a small sense of victory. Alexandra would have been proud of him. The flogging hadn't given Sampson the satisfaction he'd been looking for—and he and the clerk both knew it.

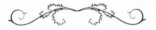

On the surface, Alexandra's second day went very much the same as her first, except that the duke was about the house. Fear that he would soon discover the broken lock on his metal box left Alexandra edgy. So did her apprehension that the milkman would not deliver her message to Trenton, as he had agreed. What if Mr. Donaldson read her words, or didn't bother to keep his bargain? Worse, what if he betrayed her to the duke?

She hauled water, beat rugs, blackened the stove and cut vegetables for Cook before sitting down to a light dinner, but her thoughts were always on Greystone—and Nathaniel. She remembered the pirate captain standing on the deck of his ship, the wind whipping his hair, the smell of his clothes, the warmth of him sleeping beside her, the rich sound of his voice . . . and feared she'd go mad with worry and longing if she didn't find him soon. She'd had to break the lock, and she'd had to trust the milkman. For Nathaniel, she'd take the same risks again.

After dinner Alexandra began to scrub the kitchen floor, only to be interrupted by the robust form of Mrs. Wright.

"His Grace and Lord Clifton would like to see you," the housekeeper said, a slight frown on her face. "They're in the study."

Alexandra's heart felt as though it came to a sudden, skidding stop. The box! Had he discovered her tampering? "Lady Anne mentioned me to them?" she asked hopefully.

"Must have. A new hire doesn't warrant much of their attention. They usually leave that sort of thing to me."

Alexandra rushed up to the attic to improve her appearance as best she could, then headed to the second floor. The memory of snooping in the duke's study made her cheeks burn, but she paused to collect herself before knocking timidly at the door.

"Come in." The voice belonged to the duke, but it was Lord Clifton who stood and came toward her when she entered.

"Alexandra." He gave her a congenial smile.

"You're looking fit, my lord," she replied.

Greystone sat at his desk, scratching something into a thick black book. He looked up at their exchange, put his pen in its well and leaned back in his chair. His eyes traveled slowly from her feet to her white mobcap.

"What are you doing here?" he asked.

Alexandra blinked in surprise. "You sent for me, Your Grace."

"I mean, what are you doing in my house?"

"I-I'm working off the dress I took from your daughter, Your Grace."

His eyes narrowed. "My son tells me you have some connection to Nathaniel."

"No connection, Your Grace. I was abducted against my will. The pirate mistook me for your daughter, Lady Anne."

Now that they were face-to-face, the duke's gaze proved more unsettling than Alexandra had anticipated. His eyes were shaped like Nathaniel's, but where the pirate captain's were vibrant, filled with unspeakable passion, Greystone's were devoid of any warmth. Still, the flesh-and-blood version of the man resembled Nathaniel much more than his picture had. The square cut of his chin, the high cheekbones, even the arch of his brows were all familiar, except that the duke was a much smaller man.

Alexandra shivered. Greystone had tried to murder his own son. He had succeeded in killing the housekeeper who had saved Nathaniel. And he'd brought syphilis home to his wife. Alexandra's intuition backed everything she had ever heard about him, and she knew then that the duke's heart had to be as hard as the flinty look in his eyes.

He pressed his fingertips together. "What brought you here?"

"Once Nathaniel released me, I tried to find work as a seamstress. But I had no luck. I had nowhere else to go, and I thought"—she paused and glanced at Lord Clifton—"I thought perhaps I could work off the dress I took from Lady Anne. At least I'd have a roof over my head."

The duke stood and positioned his hands on the desk as he leaned forward. "I see. And, of course, you have no contact with Nathaniel Kent or his cohorts now."

Alexandra had the uncanny feeling that Greystone could see right through her. "No. But I know where they are," she said, hoping to improve her credibility.

Lord Clifton spoke impetuously. "We already have Nath—"

"Jake!" The duke slammed his fist on the desk and gave his son a silencing glare. Then he turned his attention back to her. "Where?"

"I overheard them talking. They were going to Newcastle."

"See, Father? After everything he did to her, why would she sympathize with him? Though I daresay, I think he was a bit taken with her."

"A mere needlewoman? How quaint." Greystone sat back in his chair and picked up a clean quill, twirling the nib in his mouth. "You can go back to your work," he told her, "but remember one thing: you'll be sorry if you're lying. I shall be watching every move you make. And you do not want to make an enemy of me."

Chapter 17

Trenton patted the pocket that contained Alexandra's message as he waited for the duke outside the Greentree Tavern. The note had indicated that the duke might come to the tavern alone. After Trenton had spent three nights in the shadow of the pub, only to be disappointed, his luck had finally improved. Tonight the duke had arrived without so much as a valet or a footman to interfere. And Trenton had already made quick work of the coachman. The poor man lay in his underwear, bound and gagged, behind bushes not more than ten feet away.

It was a cool night for late May, with fog as thin as a watery gruel swirling in the streets. Trenton would have preferred the fog to be thicker, but one couldn't have everything. At least Greystone was alone.

As the hour grew late, the tavern began to empty, but there was no sign of the duke. Uncomfortably clad in the ill-fitting blue livery of the duke's driver, Trenton grew impatient. Now that Greystone had actually come to the tavern, Trenton was eager to put an end to the waiting.

When the duke finally stepped outside, he was no longer alone. A young woman, dressed like a prostitute, hung on his arm.

Trenton coughed to hide his surprise, but Greystone and his companion paid him no attention. The woman played with the fur on the collar of the duke's cloak and giggled when he whispered something in her ear.

Stepping up to the driver's box, Trenton pulled the team to the curb, keeping his head averted. Greystone gave the woman's behind a meaningful grab as he handed her up, then laughed and climbed in.

"Hurry," the duke ordered, rapping on the roof.

Trenton merged the carriage into the street, heading north, away from the city's lights and people. Silence reigned inside the conveyance, making him wonder what was happening, but he was grateful for whatever kept Nathaniel's father from noticing where they were going.

By the time Greystone finally realized they were heading in the wrong direction, only cattle and a few lonely farmhouses dotted the countryside.

"Bloody idiot!" he cursed, rapping on the roof. "Where are you taking us?"

Trenton pulled to the side of the road. They'd come far enough. "Get out," he cried.

The command proved unnecessary. The duke barreled through the door, still bellowing at Trenton, who he assumed to be his coachman.

Trenton pulled his knife from his sleeve and jumped to the ground.

"What's this?" Greystone's rage-reddened face gaped in astonishment. "Who are you? What do you think you're doing?"

"Never mind me. It's what you do that counts, if you want to come out of this alive," Trenton said.

"See here, if this is some sort of robbery attempt, I carry very little on my person—"

"I'm not after your money, just a bit of information."

The sun's rays were just creeping over the horizon, and Trenton let the light reflect off the blade of his knife.

"What do you want?" the duke repeated.

"I'm going to ask you a few simple questions, and you're going to answer them. Understood? Now, where's Nathaniel Kent?"

Greystone's face hardened. "I don't know."

Trenton stepped forward, the point of his knife less than a foot away from the older man's midsection, which was still leaner than most men of his years. "I'll ask you once more. Where is Nathaniel?"

The woman poked her head out of the coach and gave a startled cry, but Greystone waved her back inside and she quickly complied.

The duke's gaze flicked to the knife, then back to Trenton's face. "He's in Liverpool. I had him taken out of London because I have a friend, a magistrate, who agreed to put him in a gaol there for a while."

"So Nathaniel is alive." Trenton tried not to show his relief. His friend was in gaol, but he was alive. "That's all I needed to know. Now, move over to that tree."

Suspicion entered Greystone's eyes. "What are you going to do now?"

"Less than you deserve, to be sure. Now move!"

The duke backed up to the tree and Trenton tied him to it.

"I'll take the carriage for now," Trenton said, "and drop your lady friend near the edge of town. I'm sure she'll bring help, though it might take a day or two to find you."

He gave Nathaniel's father a mocking salute, then stowed his knife and climbed into the driver's seat, laughing as he drove away.

Alexandra groaned silently as she dusted yet another small table in the drawing room near the main entrance of Greystone House, a room she hated for its excessive conglomeration of furniture and bric-a-brac. It had been several days since she had sent her message to Trenton, but she'd received no response. Had the milkman not delivered her letter as he had agreed?

"There you are." Lord Clifton filled the doorway.

"Good morning, my lord." She smiled congenially, pushing her fears for Trenton and Nathaniel to the back of her mind. "Are you finished with breakfast so soon?"

"Yes. Breakfast was a brief affair. We've had some unfortunate business to attend to this morning."

Alexandra kept her voice as neutral as possible. "I'm sorry to hear that, my lord. Everything is going to be all right, I hope?"

He nodded, studying her. "You'll never believe what happened, though."

She finished wiping off the whatnot shelf in the corner and began to replace the extensive collection of porcelain thimbles and birds she had removed. "What's that?"

"Evidently Nathaniel has disappeared, and his men are looking for him. They held my father at knifepoint at dawn." He picked up an ivory elephant that graced the table next to the window and examined it thoughtfully.

Alexandra paused from her work. "Nathaniel has disappeared? From Newcastle, you mean?"

"From everywhere. Like I said, his men are looking for him. You wouldn't happen to know anything about it, would you?" He set the elephant back where he had found it and turned to look at her with such intensity that Alexandra almost dropped the vase she cradled in her lap.

"How would I?"

"I was just wondering how they knew where to find my father."

Alexandra set the vase down. "I'm sure I don't know. Perhaps they followed him."

The marquess smiled and crossed the floor, coming to stand behind her. "You're probably right. I've always liked you, you know. You have a certain . . . appeal."

He touched the nape of her neck, but Alexandra didn't move. She felt the pressure of his hand on her shoulder, turning her toward him, and risked a glance at his face. The look in Lord Clifton's eyes reminded her of Rat and the way he had looked at her in Nathaniel's cabin.

The marquess's hand traveled over her shoulder and traced her collarbone, then started down toward her breast. His gaze followed his hand as it moved inexorably lower until Alexandra could stand his touch no longer. She pulled away, attempting to hide her distaste by averting her face.

"What's wrong?" he asked. "You didn't react that way when Nathaniel touched you."

She remembered how her pulse had raced at the slightest contact with the pirate captain. Clifton's fondling brought nothing but revulsion. "I had no choice when Nathaniel touched me."

"I can give you much. I have never taken a mistress before, but I would be generous. I could get you out of here"—he glanced around them—"and into a place of your own. You would have clothes and jewelry, nearly everything you want."

Alexandra shook her head. "You have no idea of what I want."

"I know what every woman wants. Are you so different?"

"I want a family of my own," she countered.

"I didn't say children were out of the question."

Alexandra moved back, putting a few feet between them. "I didn't say I want children. I said I want a family—and that means a husband."

A look of irritation descended on Clifton's face, and his next words sounded incredulous. "Certainly you're not so naive. You can't expect me to marry you. Someday I'll bear the title in my father's place. The son of a duke can't marry a maid."

"No, of course not." Alexandra let bitterness ooze through her voice. By demanding the one thing Lord Clifton could never give her, she hoped to keep him at arm's distance until she was able to help Nathaniel. Depending on what Trenton had learned at the Greentree Tavern, that could be sooner rather than later.

"I've got to finish my work," she said. "If you will excuse me." Setting the porcelain birds back on their shelf with a clink, she skirted past the marquess and darted through the door.

That night Alexandra found a small gift lying on her pillow. She worked later than the other maids, so they were usually asleep by the time she climbed to the attic. Tonight was no different. She glanced around the room, wishing she could ask one of them where the package had come from, then contented herself with opening it.

Soon the answer was obvious. A pair of diamond earbobs sparkled in the mellow light of her candle, simple yet elegant, and obviously expensive. A note fluttered to the ground from the open box. She retrieved it, then bent toward the light so she could read the sloppy writing of Lord Clifton's left hand.

> *Dear Alexandra,*
> *Please accept these as a token of my esteem.*
> *There are many good things in life besides marriage.*
>
> *Fondest wishes,*
> *Jake*

Stunned, Alexandra sat numbly on her cot, staring at the teardrop earrings. Her refusal of Clifton was producing the opposite effect to what she had hoped. Instead of keeping him at bay, it created a challenge, causing him to pursue her, evidently without compunction.

Abbey stirred, prompting Alexandra to replace the lid. The marquess could give her many things, anything money could buy, but she wanted only one, and that was to know what had happened to Nathaniel.

Rising, she decided to return Lord Clifton's gift immediately. She didn't want her fellow maids to learn of his interest, nor did she want him to think a pair of earrings could change her mind.

She quickly descended the back stairs and used the servants' door to enter the second floor. The marquess's bedroom was just down the hall. If he was at home and the door was closed, she'd leave the small box on the ground, where he'd nearly step on it come morning. If he happened to be away, she'd put the earrings on his bed so he couldn't miss them when he returned.

Before she'd gone halfway down the hall, however, she heard voices coming from the library. Someone was still up. Who? The duke? Lord Clifton? Lady Anne?

Alexandra paused to listen.

"Why would you buy such a costly gift for a maid?"

Recognizing Lady Anne's voice, Alexandra crept closer.

"She probably would have been just as happy with a shawl or other trinket. She's lucky a man of your status has decided to take an interest in her."

"Not this maid. Alexandra is different."

The marquess's sister laughed. "Are you sure Nathaniel didn't do something to that head of yours as well as your hand? I just took your bishop."

Alexandra heard the clink of crystal.

"Pour me one, too," Clifton said.

There was a moment of silence, and Alexandra pictured the two of them puzzling over a chessboard.

"Nathaniel's getting his just due for what he's done to me," the marquess said.

"Holding Father at knifepoint is scarcely getting one's just due."

"That wasn't Nathaniel. It was one of his men. Nathaniel is languishing in prison. He'll never get out."

"He's at Newgate?"

Alexandra could barely hear the surprise in Lady Anne's voice above the beating of her own heart. *Nathaniel is alive,* it thumped. *Nathaniel is alive!* She closed her eyes in relief and strained to hear Clifton's next words.

"No, he's in the hulks at Woolwich. Not a pleasant place, I assure you. It's your move."

In the hulks? Alexandra's eyes flew open. That place was a living hell. Did Trenton already know? Was that why she hadn't heard from him?

Or had Greystone captured Trenton as well? Her heart raced at this last thought. She didn't want to be alone in her efforts to help them both.

"Do you ever wonder if Nathaniel is telling the truth?" Lady Anne surprised Alexandra with the sudden sincerity in her voice. "I mean, if he is our older brother, then he has been sorely wronged."

"I am the one who has been sorely wronged. Nathaniel's nothing but a liar and a thief," the marquess retorted. "Besides, Father has chosen between us. Otherwise, Nathaniel would inherit everything, and you and I would find ourselves dependent upon that scoundrel's charity. Is that what you want?"

"Of course not. I was just—"

"Don't."

"But I was only asking."

"It doesn't matter. Some things are better left alone."

Alexandra didn't hear Lady Anne's response. The sound of footsteps came from the hall below, and she fled, seized by a mixture of emotions. Relief that Nathaniel was alive surged through her, along with a certain satisfaction in knowing, at long last, his situation. But the hulks . . . She covered her mouth, remembering the bits and pieces she had heard about the prison barges.

At least he was in London—and still alive. Her mind returned to that one small ray of hope as she made her way to the attic. Only when she reached her bed did she realize that she'd forgotten to return Lord Clifton's earrings.

Alexandra received word from Trenton the following day, but his message said that Nathaniel was in gaol at Liverpool. Confused, she wondered how that could be. If Nathaniel was in Liverpool, why had Lord Clifton said he was imprisoned at Woolwich?

Biting her lip in consternation, Alexandra considered sending Trenton another message. She had to let him know what she had learned, but she hesitated to trust the milkman with yet another letter. He delivered their correspondence only while traveling his normal route, so it would be delayed another day. She was certain Trenton would be on his way to Liverpool by then.

Instead, she approached Mrs. Wright in the kitchen, arranging her face into a worried frown. "Mrs. Wright?"

The busy housekeeper looked up. She was going over something with Cook, but Alexandra's tone succeeded in gaining her attention.

"I'm afraid I've had some bad news." Alexandra clutched Trenton's letter to her breast. "It's my mother."

"What's wrong?"

"She's very ill. My sister says she's on her last breath. I was wondering if I might have the afternoon off to visit her—just this once."

"Oh dear, child. I didn't know you had family close by. Of course we can manage here. Do you need some money for a cab?"

Alexandra squirmed at having to lie. "No. I'll walk or beg a ride with someone who's going that way."

Cook, who stood next to Mrs. Wright, clucked her tongue in sympathy. "I hope your maman pulls through, mademoiselle."

"I'll use this as my afternoon off and won't take another," Alexandra offered, to appease her own conscience.

"Don't worry about that now." Mrs. Wright waved her away. "You'd best hurry along."

Alexandra grabbed her shawl and headed out the door. At least her eagerness to escape the house was a reality. She fumbled in the pouch tied beneath her dress for the coin she would need to hire a cab, then ran around front. Woolwich was much too far to walk.

It took Alexandra well over an hour to get to Woolwich, and her palms sweated the entire way.

When she saw the outline of the prison barges in the distance, her breath caught in her throat. Could she do this? She had heard awful things about the hulks, but she had to know if Nathaniel was there or not.

The cab finally stopped near the royal arsenal, and Alexandra bade the driver to wait. She would only be a minute, just long enough to catch a glimpse of him.

It was a hot, dreary day, the onset of summer. Alexandra left her shawl in the carriage before descending.

A quick glance at the darkening sky told her a storm was on its way. She'd spent most of her time indoors and had all but missed spring. Now she felt deprived. The summer months were hot and miserable. And they had to be doubly so for the inmates, she thought, watching a gang of men stacking shot.

Unmistakably prisoners, they were sixteen to a group with a club-carrying guard to keep them in line. Most were shackled; those who were not seemed too weak to move, let alone work, but work they did.

Alexandra scanned the group, trying to see the face of each convict. Six prisoners were being led through the throng toward the water, evidently heading back to the ships, but Nathaniel was not among them.

She turned her gaze to those who were stacking shot. *Please, just let me know where he is and that he's alive,* she prayed, her eyes frantically searching among the filthy, emaciated bodies.

When Alexandra finally saw Nathaniel, she wondered how she had ever missed him. He stood, working with the others, not more than thirty feet away. Dirt and sweat streaked his face. He wore rags like the other prisoners, but his arm gave him away—that, and an undeniably confident air.

Nathaniel seemed to feel her stare, as if it were something physical that spanned the distance between them. He paused from his work and rose to his full height, gazing back at her as though she were some sort of vision.

Alexandra gasped, and her nails curled into her palms. She wanted to acknowledge him in some way, but the ache in her heart made it difficult to move.

She forced her hand open to wave. "Nathaniel," she whispered as her throat constricted with unshed tears.

Nathaniel's face looked hewn from stone. He did not react, but Alexandra was positive that he recognized her.

Then a guard appeared next to him. "Ogling the ladies, are we, cripple? Get back to work."

Nathaniel glared at the guard, then looked back at Alexandra. She could almost see the clarity of his blue eyes—until the guard struck him with a large, ponderous stick.

"I said, back to work," the guard shouted, hitting him again.

"No!" Alexandra cried, clinging to the fence. "Please, let him be!"

The blows continued as another guard approached her. "Miss! Miss! Who are you, miss?" he asked, and Alexandra knew she had to get away from the pitiful scene before she caused Nathaniel any more harm.

Turning, she stumbled blindly toward the carriage, tears streaming down her face. She tripped on her hem and fell once, then scrambled to her feet, biting her lip to hold back the sobs that racked her frame. Finally she climbed inside the waiting conveyance, and the driver pulled away.

Chapter 18

Something snapped inside Nathaniel as Alexandra disappeared from the wharf. He had bided his time and paced himself for ultimate endurance, but the sight of her horrified expression broke the tenuous grip he had on his patience. He exploded with a ferocity that stunned the guard who beat him. Wrapping his arm around the stick, he jerked it away in one fluid motion that left those around him gaping in surprise. Then he used it to knock the guard to the ground.

The chaos that erupted after that seemed to last forever, but Nathaniel knew it could have been no more than a few seconds. He fought with the energy of a wild man while the shouts and cries of the other prisoners and guards rang in his ears. Some of the prisoners took his lead and began to fight as well, while others cowered in fright.

Ultimately the prisoners didn't stand a chance. Nathaniel had known it before he landed his first blow. The chains were too much of a hindrance, the clubs too devastating with so many guards to wield them.

After some initial fear and confusion, the guards rallied with a vengeance. Nathaniel felt the pain of their attack, but he didn't care. He kept going when most men would have stopped. Nothing mattered except his need to fight back, to answer their cruelty. But he knew he would pay. Even as the blow that knocked him senseless landed on the back of his head, he knew.

Alexandra had the cab driver drop her at the end of Berkeley Street. She wasn't quite ready to face Mrs. Wright and the others. She was still shaking despite the long ride back, and needed a few minutes more to compose herself after the horrifying sight of watching Nathaniel being beaten like a dog.

She had to let Trenton know. The duke had misled him, had sent him off to Liverpool when Nathaniel was right here all the time, in London. Worse was the thought that Trenton might not be able to help Nathaniel. How could they, or anyone else, get him out of that terrible place?

Perhaps she should head to Liverpool in search of Trenton, she thought, anxious to do something. But she instantly knew the folly of that idea. How would they find each other? Besides, her sudden disappearance would arouse the duke's suspicion, and until they had Nathaniel safely away from the hulks, she didn't dare provoke Greystone.

If they *could* get him safely away . . .

The wrought-iron gate of Greystone House loomed before her, and Alexandra took a deep breath. She didn't want to go back, but she had to face the other servants and Lord Clifton and the duke and pretend she mourned for an ill mother. Otherwise, Trenton wouldn't know where to find her. For caution's sake, she knew he couldn't return to the inn where he had stayed before.

"Where have you been?"

Alexandra jumped as the marquess stepped out from beneath an elm tree. "You frightened me," she said, pressing a hand to her chest as if she could stop the racing of her heart.

"You haven't answered my question. Where have you been?"

"If you needed me, you had only to ask Mrs. Wright, and she would have sent another maid." Alexandra kept her voice calm, trying not to reveal how much his attitude irritated her.

"Mrs. Wright said you went to see your ailing mother. You told me when we were with Nathaniel that you have no family."

Alexandra's knees went weak as her mind groped for something that Lord Clifton might believe. "Actually, I-I wanted to show the earrings you gave me to a friend," she said.

The marquess smiled, making Alexandra grateful that his vanity was sufficient for him to accept the lie. "Of course. Do you like them?" He took her hand and drew her back under the tree with him.

"Not every maid receives such a gift from the son of a duke," she said, playing her part.

"You're not every maid. I've never seen another so lovely." Taking her by the chin, Clifton tilted Alexandra's head back so he could kiss her. She knew what was coming, and for Nathaniel's sake, she steeled her nerves to accept it. But when the marquess's ardor mounted and his hand moved down over her hip, she pulled away.

"Perhaps I misunderstood," she said. "I thought the earrings were a gift, not a form of payment." And she ran back inside the house.

Alexandra sat in Greystone's study, her ears trained for the slightest sound. It was late in the night. The grandfather clock down the hall chimed the hour of three as she hurried to finish.

Dipping the duke's quill back into his ink pot, she signed her name, then quickly read over her letter. She had no idea if Nathaniel would ever receive it, but word from her was the only thing she could give him at the moment.

The milkman came before dawn every morning and left a can of milk by the back door. Alexandra met him outside today, her letter in hand.

She stepped from the shadows as Mr. Donaldson pulled his wagon to a stop. He got down, and with work-roughened hands lugged a huge can of milk to the ground, its thump as familiar as the rooster's crow in the morning. Then he turned to Alexandra and silently accepted the letter. She pressed a few shillings in his palm besides, and he nodded his head in acknowledgment.

Alexandra started back through the door, but he caught her by the elbow. She watched as he reached into his other pocket and withdrew a wrinkled piece of paper that had been folded several times.

She smiled her thanks and waited until he left to read Trenton's words:

> *Alexandra,*
> *Nathaniel must not be in Liverpool. I would think perhaps he was transferred to Newgate, but I can find no record of it. I'm back in London now and hope you have better news. Meet me beyond the stables at midnight Wednesday next.*
>
> *Trenton*

Tucking his letter into the folds of her skirt, Alexandra hurried inside lest the new tweenie, who rose earlier than everyone else, find her. Wednesday next, Trenton had said. Why, tomorrow was Wednesday.

Tomorrow night, then, she thought, and prayed the hope of Trenton's impending visit would be enough to block from her mind the recurring vision of Nathaniel being struck by the guard.

The following night Alexandra sat in the kitchen, sewing. She had volunteered to make fresh aprons for some of the maids. Servants bore the cost of their own uniforms, and their low salaries often made such purchases a hardship, so she had agreed to do the work for free. Mrs. Wright was grateful for her help, and it gave Alexandra something to occupy her mind and to calm her nerves while she waited for Trenton.

"You've put in a long day, lass. Why don't you go off to bed?" Mrs. Wright asked as she carried jars of fresh preserves to the pantry.

"I'll go up soon. I'm not tired yet." In truth, Alexandra was exhausted, but she didn't dare lie down for fear she'd fall asleep and miss Trenton.

"You're a hard worker. I'm glad Lady Anne knew enough to hire you, though your story had me worried at first."

The housekeeper disappeared into the pantry and returned for another load. "You wouldn't mind retrieving the tray I took up to His Grace in the study, would you? He's up late tonight."

Alexandra hesitated, wishing she could beg off. She avoided the duke at every turn, afraid her hatred of him would be too difficult to hide. She also feared his discovery of the broken lock on his metal box, knowing her connection to Nathaniel could easily make him suspicious of her. But Alexandra could think of no good excuse to avoid the task Mrs. Wright requested.

"Is Lord Clifton with his father?" She hoped the answer would be no. She'd made several attempts to return the marquess's earrings, but he had refused them outright. And instead of losing interest in her as she hoped he would, he seemed to be more and more obsessed with winning her affection, or at least her acquiescence.

Mrs. Wright headed back for another load. "I'm not sure."

Alexandra set her work on the table and left the kitchen to climb the back stairs. The other servants were asleep in their quarters, so she ran into no one on her way. Much to her chagrin, however, Clifton was in the study with his father.

Alexandra entered as unobtrusively as possible, but the two still glanced up. As she removed the tray, Greystone pulled off his glasses and spoke to her.

"Tell Harry to get the carriage ready. I'm going out tonight."

Alexandra schooled her features to show no surprise, though it was late to be going anywhere, unless it was to his favorite tavern. "Yes, Your Grace."

She curtsied, balancing the tray in one hand, then turned toward the door. Lord Clifton said nothing, but she felt his gaze follow her out.

She breathed a sigh of relief as she made her way back, knowing the duke would be gone when Trenton came.

By the time Alexandra arrived in the kitchen, Mrs. Wright had finished moving the preserves and was taking off her apron.

"I'm going to bed," she announced.

"His Grace wants Harry to get the carriage ready. Shall I go out and tell him?" Alexandra asked. Harry slept over the stables along with his son, who worked for the duke as a stable boy.

"If you would. My poor feet can hardly walk another step."

Alexandra smiled. Mrs. Wright worked hard, and she was a fair, honest woman. "I'll be right back."

Harry was already in bed, but his son answered her knock on the stable door. "Hello, Rory. His Grace would like your father to get the carriage ready," she told him. "And I brought something for you."

A boy of only nine, Rory smiled eagerly, still young enough to enjoy the occasional treats Alexandra saved for him, yet old enough not to clamor about her skirts.

"What is it?"

"A whole handful of scones with fresh strawberry jam inside." Throwing back her shawl, she revealed the handkerchief that held these treats.

The boy's eyes went wide with pleasure. "Yer the best, Alexandra."

Alexandra smiled. "Just don't tell Mrs. Wright I gave them to you, or she'll blame me if we come up short tomorrow."

"I wouldn't tell that old bag anythin'."

"Rory!"

Alexandra's chastening tone provoked a scowl. "Well, she made me scrub behind my ears this mornin'."

"No doubt they needed a good scrubbing." She laughed and ruffled his hair before returning to the house.

Mrs. Wright was gone when Alexandra entered the kitchen. She sat down to her sewing, but was interrupted again when Harry came in.

"The carriage is ready. I'm taking it around front now," he told her.

Alexandra started up to the study to tell the duke, but by the time she arrived, he'd already gone. She heard his voice in the entry below, just before the door closed behind him. Had Lord Clifton gone, too? She passed through to the balustrade to see for herself, but when she looked down at the front door, she found the marquess standing there, staring up at her.

She gave him an uncomfortable smile before hurrying back the way she had come, praying he would retire soon. Trenton was coming in less than two hours.

Alexandra entered the kitchen just as Clifton came through the green baize doors. "My lord, is there something I can get you?" she asked, more than a little surprised that the marquess would venture into the servants' domain.

Taking a seat at the table, he asked, "Why do you avoid me at every turn? Abbey or any of the others would love to trade places with you."

Alexandra sat across from him and took up her sewing as she fished for an appropriate response. She wasn't Abbey or any of the others. She didn't care about the marquess's position in society or his money. She was already in love.

Alexandra gulped at this admission. Was she in love?

How could she deny it when the mere thought of Nathaniel left her breathless?

"My lord, we are not well suited," she said. "You've mentioned before the difference in our social status. That is reason alone."

"But I am willing to overlook that. Such things only matter in a wife."

"And I will be nothing less than a wife." She tried to return to her work, but being alone with Nathaniel's half brother made her nervous.

"A mistress is treated better than a wife," he insisted. "You have none of the demands placed upon a wife, only the benefits. If you weren't interested in me, why did you come here?"

"I told you. I needed a job. Unlike you, I must work for my living."

"You could have worked elsewhere."

"I was having difficulty. I'd met you before, and I hoped Lady Anne would let me work off the dress I took from her. How many times must I explain? Why do you persist in making it more complicated than it is?"

"What about the earrings?"

"What about them, my lord? I've tried to give them back to you, and you won't accept them. What am I to do?"

"Are you hoping for words of love? Would that soften your virtuous heart?"

Alexandra stood at the sarcasm in Clifton's voice. "I'm sorry, my lord. Gifts can't buy my affection. Not for anyone. Not even for you. Now, if you will excuse me, I'm going to bed."

She tried to brush past him, but he blocked her path to the stairs. Pulling her to him, he bent his head to kiss her, but she twisted in his arms so that his lips brushed her cheek instead.

"My lord, what are you doing?" She squirmed out of his grasp.

"Call me Jake. I want to hear my name on your lips. I want to convince you."

"Convince me of what?"

"That you want me as badly as I want you."

Alexandra couldn't hold back the laughter that burst from her. "I have no feelings for you whatsoever, my lord."

The look that suddenly descended on his face frightened her, making her wish she could reclaim her hastily spoken words.

"There will come a time when you will beg for a crumb of my attention," he vowed, and he struck her across the face.

Alexandra stumbled back, surprised and momentarily dazed. "My lord, I never meant to offend you." She reached out to put her hand on his arm, but he jerked away, and she fell silent.

Giving her one last smoldering glare, he turned and stalked out, leaving Alexandra rubbing her cheek in astonishment.

Alexandra reached up to touch him. Her fingers skimmed through his hair, making his blood stir and his heart pound. Mesmerized, he reached out and hooked the small of her waist, pulling her to him. Her arms encircled his neck, and her lips parted in invitation as her eyes fluttered shut. Nathaniel quivered to feel her breath on his face, but just as his lips were about to drink from hers, Alexandra's sigh became nothing more than the fetid exhalation of the man sleeping next to him, her fingers, the cockroaches that slithered about the place after dark.

Nathaniel shivered, leaving the dream unfinished as his mind returned by degrees to full awareness. He was sharing a narrow bunk with another man aboard the creaking, stinking hospital ship—one of the hulks reserved for those too ill to work, where dying men were sent, but from which they rarely returned, receiving too little medical help, too late. Still, it was an improvement. There were no chains, and the fare, though mainly broth, was better than the slop served on the other hulks. The doctors were unfeeling, perhaps numbed by the great number of patients they lost, but apathy was preferable to antipathy.

At least they weren't like Sampson. Because of him, Nathaniel had already spent more time in solitary confinement than any other man in the history of the *Retribution*, but it was the last few days that had nearly broken him. Riddled from the flogging they had given him when he attacked the guard, his back refused to heal, and a raging infection had taken hold. Finally the chaplain had intervened and had the guards move him to the hospital.

Since then, he had tossed miserably about in his bunk, breathing the stale air so common to the hulks. Mold and mildew combined with the pungent body odors of the other sick men, who were never bathed, until he would have traded his last meal for one breath of fresh air.

The voices of the doctors hovered above him during their three routine visits each day. Though the sores on Nathaniel's back oozed pus and blood, he had hardly felt them until today, which was why he imagined himself to be getting better. At least he knew that he hurt, and he knew where.

Squeezing his eyes shut, Nathaniel fought his awakening and tried to recall the dream, but it was gone. He could remember those things Alexandra did or said, but he could not conjure up the feel of her, not like it was. So he channeled his thoughts to her letter. At least that was real.

Prisoners' mail was unreliable and heavily censored; it was not uncommon to receive only a portion of one paragraph, or half a page at most. In fact, Nathaniel had received just a few lines from Alexandra:

> . . . *am living in Berkeley Square with your beloved father . . . found you as Trenton and I planned and am doing all I can . . . it shouldn't be long now . . . Trenton is coming soon . . . stay alive and well . . .*
>
> *Alexandra*

Nathaniel groaned. As if he didn't have enough on his mind, Alexandra was now living on Berkeley Street with the duke and his half brother—which was like sticking her head into a lion's mouth. Still, she might not have found him otherwise, and he was infinitely grateful that someone knew of his whereabouts. That was the only thing that helped him to hang on, to fight Sampson's cruelty a little longer.

His thoughts having made a complete circle, Nathaniel sighed in frustration and shifted to his side. He was damp with sweat, his back pained him no small amount, and a constant hunger gnawed at his gut, which the watery broth did little to relieve. Sleep was ever more appealing than consciousness, for only then was his misery forgotten—if not completely, then at least it was merely represented in some strange or fantastical way in his dreams.

Today, however, something more concrete disturbed him and kept him from returning to that blissful labyrinth of sleep. Though sickness and fever dulled his senses, danger signals penetrated his brain: hushed whispering, a number of men moving as a group, and, finally, the voice of Sampson, the clerk.

"Watch that, you fool . . ."

In the next instant, three men rushed him. One carried a black bag; another, a strong, thick rope; and the third, what could only be a knife. Nathaniel caught the gleam of its blade a split second before someone forced his head into the bag and bound his arm to his body.

The sharp prick of metal at his back confirmed his first impression. They had a knife.

"Take it easy now. Struggling will only get you killed," Sampson warned.

"Isn't that the idea?" Nathaniel asked, but he didn't fight. His limbs felt as though they were made of wood, and the knife at his back provided a convincing deterrent.

"If you so choose, I wouldn't mind," the clerk whispered, "but you're too smart for that, eh? Now move."

Half pushing, half dragging Nathaniel from his bed, the three men hauled him through the corridor and up the companionway. It was cool and soggy outdoors, and Nathaniel pictured a delicate, low-lying fog moving on top of the water like shiny white satin. He'd seen it a million times before, but he couldn't see much now. Only vague shapes and deeper shadows. He stumbled again and again until a familiar voice halted their progress.

"What goes here?"

It was the chaplain, Reverend Hartman. Nathaniel was sure of the soft, almost effeminate voice.

"Father, what are you doing about at this ungodly hour?" Sampson demanded.

Nathaniel nearly fell as the clerk's beefy arm shoved him back behind the others, but he knew he was much too large to escape notice. No doubt Sampson was betting on the reverend's mild manner, and more than that, fear. Chaplains generally held considerable power in the hulks, second only to the overseer's, but not on the *Retribution*. Here the pecking order was clear. Reverend Hartman was allowed to go about his business of saving souls only so long as he did not interrupt with discipline or any other weighty matter. No one dared thwart Sampson.

"There's a man who's dying. I promised I would sit with him," the chaplain explained.

"'Tis a rare man indeed who takes his job so seriously, Reverend," the clerk mocked.

"It's no more than you would do. I see you have already begun the vigil of caring for another brother who is similarly afflicted."

"Mind your own business," Sampson snapped. "Things that go on here are best left as they stand—for your own good."

"So I've heard," Hartman replied calmly.

Then Nathaniel heard the sound of his retreating steps.

No help there, he thought in despair.

The prick of the knife at his back prodded him into motion once more. He blindly struggled to keep his footing on the grimy deck, despite the ropes and other obstacles that lay in his path, until Sampson stopped him at what had to be the ship's side. Someone bent to lift him over a shoulder, grunting with the effort, then began to carry him down into what Nathaniel could only assume to be a dinghy.

After lowering him partway, whoever struggled beneath his weight dropped him. He fell about eight feet to land on his shoulder, and winced in pain as the clerk cursed his companions.

"Would you capsize us, you idiots?"

"He's a heavy bugger," a voice grumbled from above.

Nathaniel managed to right himself as the others climbed aboard.

"How much time have we got?" someone asked.

"When is he coming?"

"Midnight."

"Then we're fine."

"Good. Let's get us out of here before the doctors make a stink."

The others took their places, and the slap of the oars on water resounded as the boat began to move. Nathaniel, tense with worry and anticipation, wondered what was happening and why. He knew Sampson's voice, and recognized one other as the guard who had clubbed him at the Warren on the day he had seen Alexandra, but he couldn't identify the third.

Three. He considered the meager possibility of self-defense. He was sick and weak and outnumbered.

The boat reached the shore, and two men hauled Nathaniel out. They pulled the lighter out of the water, half dragging him through the soft sand to the pavement where he could walk more easily. Straining his eyes, Nathaniel tried to see beyond the black fabric that covered his head, but the dark night kept all except a few pale shapes from his perception.

He stifled a groan of frustration. When would they remove the blasted hood? He could do nothing without his eyes.

Sampson and the others stopped, and a key turned in a lock. Nathaniel guessed they were entering the building in which the prisoners picked oakum by day.

As they shoved him inside, the smell confirmed it. Since the prisoners rotated between stacking shot and picking oakum, he had spent many days in the shed already.

"Shut the door." Sampson's voice echoed through the cool, damp room. "Now we wait till he comes."

Someone lit a candle.

"Until who comes?" The guard Nathaniel recognized as James voiced the question clamoring in his own mind.

"The Duke of Greystone, no less." Sampson kicked Nathaniel viciously. "That name mean anything to you?"

Unable to mask a groan, Nathaniel teetered for a moment before regaining his balance. His leg throbbed where Sampson's boot had landed. He attempted to ignore the pain and concentrate instead on what he could do to escape before his father arrived—before they added any more strength to their numbers.

"Why? What's happening?" Nathaniel demanded, when he could speak.

Sampson pulled the hood from Nathaniel's head and jeered into his face. "How should I know? His Grace has paid for the opportunity to speak to you, and we're accommodating him. Simple as that. But if you try anything, or refuse to cooperate, it won't be so simple anymore."

"He's a strong man despite that funny arm," James warned. "He almost killed me the other day."

"I can handle him easily." As if to prove his words, Sampson pointed the knife he carried toward Nathaniel's heart and gave him a menacing glare. "And the temptation might yet prove too great."

"I don't want this to get bloody," the third man complained. Judging by his clothes, he was also a guard, but he must have come from one of the other hulks; Nathaniel had never seen him before.

"You've killed prisoners with your club easily enough. What's the difference?" the clerk scoffed. "So I use a knife instead."

"Cut me loose, and we'll test your prowess." Nathaniel focused on Sampson, hoping he could goad the clerk into a fight before the duke arrived. In a way, this little meeting boded well. It meant that Greystone hadn't yet found the guns, and it got Nathaniel on shore, without chains, for the first time since his arrival.

"I could cut you to ribbons." Sampson's eyes blazed with the desire to do so.

"Words mean nothing, right lads?" Nathaniel looked to the two guards. "Let's put your fearless leader to the test."

"Do you think I'm a fool?" The clerk lashed out, quick as lightning, and sliced Nathaniel across the chest.

He laughed when Nathaniel's jaw clenched in pain. "What? You're not going to scream?" Sampson's mouth hung open in a wicked grin as he laid the blade above the flickering flame that danced at the end of a single candle. "Oh, I forgot. You never show any sign of weakness. Perhaps we should see just how far you can be tortured before you do."

Despite the evil glint in Sampson's eyes and the blood pouring down the front of his coarse gray shirt, Nathaniel tried to keep calm. The wound was not mortal, though the pain was severe. He needed to buy some time. His hand worked frantically, straining against the rope that held it fast as he tried to reach the knot. The bands were weakening, but Nathaniel doubted they would give way soon enough.

"How much is the duke paying you? A few guineas perhaps? I'm worth much more to him than that." Nathaniel's long fingers continued to work nimbly. For once, having only one arm worked to his advantage. The guards had been sloppy when they tied him, at a loss to know how to secure his hand without another to anchor it to.

Sampson scowled. "He'll give us what we ask. He's getting a bit eager to be done with you. Seems someone held him at knifepoint last week, looking for you."

Worry for Alexandra living with his father lanced through Nathaniel as effectively as Sampson's knife, strengthening his resolve. He had to get her away from Berkeley Square. Her letter had promised him help, but if Greystone ever suspected a connection between them, she would not be safe.

"Why bother with him when you're already making a fortune by cheating starving men out of their rations?" Nathaniel asked. "Tell me, how big of a cut do you give the overseer when you use the government's money to buy inferior meat and clothes for us and pocket the difference?"

Sampson coughed, nearly choking on his surprise.

"Do you think I don't know how you have gained such a hold on the overseer's heart?" Nathaniel raised a mocking brow. "You line his pockets with gold, and he gives you whatever you want."

"Hold him." The clerk lifted the knife from the flame. "The blade's ready."

The guards glanced uncertainly at each other, and their hesitation gave Nathaniel the extra second he needed. He tugged one last time on the knot that bound his arm, and the rope miraculously loosened. Then he exploded with all the force left in his body, shoving James back at the same time he kicked Sampson in the groin.

James landed on his backside. Sampson crumbled to his knees. The last guard's face met Nathaniel's fist. Jarred from the impact, the man crashed onto his back as Nathaniel sprinted for the door.

"Get him," Sampson yelled as they scrambled to their feet.

Nathaniel stopped just long enough to throw the bolt and swing the door open, but the few seconds it cost him were too much. James pulled him back by the collar before he could escape, forcing him to turn and fight.

Swinging with a strength born of panic, Nathaniel sent the guard skidding across the floor into Sampson, then leveled another blow at the unknown man's chin. But he was exhausted in mere seconds, and he knew it was only a matter of time before they overwhelmed him. He had to make a run for it.

Following one last blow with a high kick to James's gut, Nathaniel turned to flee, but Sampson managed to grab his arm and pull him back onto the point of the knife. Nathaniel felt the blade slice through the skin of his back, as smoothly as through bread pudding, just before he fell to the ground.

It's over, he thought, as something warm seeped beneath him and Sampson's blood-covered knife came into view.

"You're dead," the clerk jeered, bringing his hand back for the final thrust.

"That's enough. If you value your own life, you will spare his." Reverend Hartman stood at the entrance, his robes wet from a hasty passage. In one hand he held a gun.

Sampson gaped at the chaplain before a self-satisfied smile split his face. "He won't do it, boys." He waved them forward. "A man of the cloth could never commit cold-blooded murder."

Neither Hartman's hand nor his eyes wavered from their target. "I would consider it an act of humanity. I've never killed a man before, but then, I don't consider you much of a man. Now, tell them to get back and let that prisoner up."

"You don't know what you're doing. You're not thinking," Sampson insisted, waving the guards back.

"Now drop the knife."

The blade clattered to the floor as Nathaniel tried to stand. The people around him seemed out of focus and a buzzing filled his ears, but he managed to find his feet. He stood, swaying unsteadily as he surveyed the situation.

"Look at him. He probably won't last the night. You did this for a dead man," Sampson shouted.

The chaplain glanced Nathaniel's way. "No, I did this for me. It was the only moral thing I could do. I'm taking him back to the hospital where he belongs—"

Nathaniel's mind cleared a bit as Reverend Hartman's words sunk in. The chaplain was taking him back to the hulks. He would die there. He had to do something.

Lunging forward, he took the reverend off guard. Slamming him into a heavy table, he easily retrieved the gun, and turning, he squeezed the trigger before Sampson landed on top of him.

The blast deafened him as the clerk cried out in pain, the ball penetrating his gut.

The reverend gaped in astonishment. "They'll hang you for this," he whispered as the guards backed away.

"They'll have to catch me first." Nathaniel waved the priest toward Sampson and the guards. "I'll have the key to this place, please."

One of the guards quickly handed him a metal ring on which hung a single key.

Nathaniel felt the cool metal and took as big a breath as the pain in his torso would allow. "I'm sorry, Reverend, but my life wouldn't be worth a farthing if I let you take me back."

Forcing his body to move despite the pain, he trained the pistol on the group that huddled around the bleeding clerk and backed outside. Then he locked the door behind him and hurried away. He had to make it to safety, and to a doctor, before it was too late.

Alexandra blew out the lamp and sat on the last step of the stairs in total darkness. She couldn't stitch anymore. Lord Clifton's visit had destroyed her peace. All she could do was wait—wait and think about Nathaniel. Did he long for her as she longed for him? Did he close his eyes and picture her face as automatically as his apparition blocked out the darkness behind her own lids? Did she haunt his thoughts and dreams as persistently as he paraded through her own?

What was he doing right now? And the biggest question of all, how could she help him?

The kitchen clock chimed eleven and then each quarter hour until midnight finally approached. Alexandra stretched her neck and rolled her shoulders, thinking her nerves had never been so taut. At least the duke was out, and Clifton, it seemed, had gone to bed. If she moved quietly enough, no one would be the wiser about Trenton's visit. At least she hoped not, for all their sakes.

Alexandra carefully lifted the latch of the back door a little ahead of the clock. She couldn't wait a minute longer.

Moving as silently as possible, she headed through the gardens and sheds, past the stables and beyond, into the mews with only the moon to guide her.

When she arrived, Trenton wasn't there.

Standing on one foot and then the other, Alexandra waited against the back wall of the stables. She could hear the horses inside, whinnying, but Harry was gone. The footmen slept in the basement of the house. Only Rory was anywhere around, and he was probably fast asleep.

Footsteps on gravel made Alexandra turn. A man approached, leaving his horse several houses down.

"Trenton." Alexandra whispered his name as she flew to meet him. Throwing her arms around his neck, she nearly bowled him over.

He laughed softly and hugged her back. "This is quite a reception, considering you're the girl I helped to kidnap."

Alexandra gave him a fleeting smile, but couldn't wait to share her news. "I know where Nathaniel is."

Trenton sobered. "Where?"

"He's in the hulks at Woolwich."

"How do you know?"

"I saw him there. I watched a guard beat him." She winced, the memory too painful to relive. "How do we get him out?"

Trenton shook his head. "I don't know. Perhaps a bribe or two might motivate the right people to turn their heads."

"What about the guns? Have you done anything with them?"

"I sent the duke a letter offering to trade them for Nathaniel, but he scoffed at me. I've never met a more arrogant bastard. He doesn't think we can hurt him, no matter what. I've since written to the Lord High Admiral. Now I'm waiting for him to respond."

"I'd better stay here until Nathaniel is free," Alexandra said. "I'm afraid Greystone will catch on to my reason for coming in the first place, and cause something even worse to happen to Nathaniel. But I don't like it here. Lord Clifton is—" She stopped.

What was the use of explaining the marquess's behavior when Trenton could do nothing to stop it? "Never mind. I'll be fine, for the time being. Just hurry and do something, and let me know what that something is."

"I'm going to Whitehall in the morning to see if I can meet with the police commissioner. Mayne might listen to us if we threaten to take our story to the *Times*."

A sound near the house made Alexandra jump. They fell silent, waiting, but heard nothing besides the horses in the stables. "I'd better get back," she said, uneasy. "Send me word."

"I'll be staying at Marley House if you need me," he whispered.

Nodding, Alexandra headed back. The house was dark and silent, and despite her nervousness, all seemed as it should be as she made her way to her bedroom. She snuggled beneath her covers, anxious for the rest her body craved, and sleep came in an instant.

But she was awakened long before dawn.

"Alexandra." Someone tapped timidly on her shoulder. As the sleep cleared from her eyes, she blinked to see Rory, the stable boy, standing above her.

"Rory, what is it?"

He motioned for her to be silent and beckoned her to come with him.

Puzzled, Alexandra rose quietly from her bed and followed the boy back down the stairs. "What is it?" she whispered again when they reached the back door.

He shook his head, refusing to answer until they were outside and well away from the house.

"Tell me, Rory," she pleaded, mystified.

He turned and took her hand, pulling her toward the stables. "There's a man out 'ere. 'E's bleedin' awful bad, an' 'e keeps callin' yer name. 'E asked me to get ye an' to tell no one else—"

"A man?"

The boy nodded rigorously. "'E's been stabbed, I think."

"Did he say who he was?"

"Aye. 'Is name is Nathaniel Kent."

Chapter 19

Alexandra found Nathaniel crouching in the straw of an empty stall, shivering. In the dim light of the lantern that swung slowly overhead, she could see a dark, sticky substance on the back of his shirt. Blood? Her pulse began to race as she bent to touch it. Sure enough. It was fresh, and it was warm.

His eyes fluttered open. "Alexandra—"

"What happened to you?" She started to lift his sopping shirt, but he moved his arm to stop her.

"I think my father feared the hulks were too pleasant a home for me."

"Greystone did this? That's where he went tonight?"

"Not him." Nathaniel swallowed. "Someone he hired."

Alexandra could see the sweat popping out on his forehead and tried to suppress the panic that made her hands shake. "Why did you come here? They'll kill you if—"

"This was the last place they'd expect me." He closed his eyes and shook his head. "And the only place where I'd find you."

"But Lord Clifton didn't go with his father." Alexandra looked anxiously behind her, through the open stable door toward the house. She glanced at Rory, who was watching them in awe. "Never mind. Don't try to talk anymore. We must get you out of here."

"What 'appened to 'im?" Rory whispered.

"This man is a friend of mine, Rory, and you were right. He's hurt very badly. I need your help. We must get him away from here before your father returns with the duke."

Nathaniel's head fell forward, and Alexandra bent worriedly over him. "Nathaniel!"

"I'm here," he mumbled, his voice thick and slurred.

Alexandra turned to the stable boy. "Rory, can you get me a mount? We need to get him on a horse and take him to a doctor."

Rory gave him a skeptical look. "Don't look like 'e can stand."

Alexandra steeled her nerves so she wouldn't snap at the boy. "We don't have any other choice. Will you get the horse?"

While Rory went to do her bidding, Alexandra clung to Nathaniel's hand. "Hold on, Nathaniel. Please."

To her surprise, a wry grin twisted his lips as the blue of his eyes lifted to her face. "I thought you hated me."

"If you die, I will hate you. I'll hate you forever," she told him.

His eyes closed again and the smile disappeared as he leaned his head on the wooden planking.

"Hold on," she whispered, smoothing his dark hair off his forehead.

Rory had a bridle on a horse in a matter of minutes but didn't bother with a saddle. He led the chestnut gelding out of its stall, stopping a few feet away.

"Thank you. I owe you all the scones you can eat," Alexandra said. "Now we must get Mr. Kent up and onto the horse."

The boy's brows rose as he looked at the huge man huddled at their feet. "'Ow do ye suppose we do that?"

Alexandra stooped and pulled Nathaniel's good arm around her shoulder. "Like this: Nathaniel!" She made her voice low and sharp, trying to cut through the cloud of his delirium.

Nathaniel lifted his head, but it fell back again almost immediately. "Nathaniel!"

A groan was his only response.

"On the count of three, we're going to help you up. You need to stand, do you hear? You're too heavy for us to carry."

"After what I've eaten, I should be as light as a woman," he mumbled, and Alexandra had to smile. He was still there. He was still fighting.

"One, two, three—"

"Going somewhere?"

Alexandra nearly collapsed under Nathaniel's weight as Lord Clifton strode into the light. She felt Nathaniel's muscles tense and realized that he, too, recognized his half brother.

"My lord, please." She set Nathaniel gently back down. "He'll die if I don't get him some help."

The marquess laughed, pulling a gun from his belt. "And that's supposed to move me? Throw that pistol away." He motioned toward the gun tucked into Nathaniel's breeches. "Over there," he said, waving at the far wall.

"A dying man would garner sympathy from anyone who had a heart," Alexandra replied as she took the pistol and tossed it a few feet. "Look at him. Haven't you done enough already?"

Clifton kicked the weapon farther from the two of them. "What about me? What about this?" He waved his handless arm in her face. "I can scarcely ride or shoot. I'm no more accomplished than a three-year-old with a sword. And you've seen my writing. It's hardly legible. But you don't care about that, do you? You only care about him."

"Jake—"

"It's 'my lord' to you, remember?" He pointed the gun at her.

"No," Rory cried, rushing forward.

Nathaniel tried to stand, but fell weakly back. "Leave her out of it. This is between us, remember?"

The marquess ignored him. Turning to Rory, he indicated the stable door. "Go. Get out of here. This man is a thief."

Rory hesitated. "Shall I wake Mrs. Wright and have her send for a constable, then?"

"No. Go back to bed. I'll handle this myself."

The boy shuffled toward the door, hanging back.

"It's all right, Rory. You go up to bed. Everything will be fine," Alexandra said encouragingly, afraid of what Lord Clifton might do if the boy disobeyed.

Rory threw Alexandra one last furtive glance as he shut the door, his face revealing confusion. Alexandra hoped he would go for help, but deep inside she knew that Rory would never defy the marquess's authority to that extent.

When the boy was gone, Clifton turned to Nathaniel. "Now, where are the rifles?"

Nathaniel staggered to his feet but swayed dangerously as though he might fall. He shook his head, his eyes on Clifton's pistol. "I'll never tell you."

"Then I'll find them on my own. Bristol is not so large a place." Setting the barrel of the gun on his forearm, the marquess awkwardly attempted to aim it. By his own admittance, he couldn't shoot well, but at such close range, Alexandra didn't see how he could miss Nathaniel.

"My lord." She stepped cautiously toward him.

"Stay back. I'm going to kill the bastard, like we should have in the first place."

"No, my lord, listen. I'll give you anything you want if you'll spare him. Anything. Do you understand? He'll likely die anyway from his injuries."

Lord Clifton glanced at Alexandra, a lascivious smile curling his lips. "So this is what it takes to melt the ice maiden. Did you hear that, big brother? Your little doxy has just offered me a sample of her charms."

Nathaniel tried to move toward him, but he succeeded only in pitching forward. "Stay away from her," he groaned as he hit the dirt floor.

Clifton laughed. "I think not." He waved the pistol at Alexandra. "Perhaps a little torture is in order for your lover. Take off your clothes."

Alexandra swallowed and glanced at Nathaniel, sensing his awareness despite his semiconscious condition. She unbuttoned her white cotton nightdress until the curve of her breasts gleamed beneath the lamp.

"Now, that's a beautiful sight," the marquess breathed. He reached for her, bent her backward and licked her face. "Damn, she tastes good. Nathaniel, you don't know what you're missing." He grinned devilishly at his half brother. "Or perhaps you do." His mouth moved down her neck, spreading sloppy, wet kisses along its path.

Alexandra bit her lip so she wouldn't scream. Rory's sleeping loft was just above them. Surely her cries would frighten the boy. She didn't want Nathaniel to know how badly Clifton hurt her, either.

"Oh, this is nice," he said, burying his head in her cleavage.

Alexandra's mind raced as she tried to decide what to do. She'd only managed to buy them a little time, nothing more; she had no illusions that the marquess would spare Nathaniel because of her.

She glanced over Clifton's head to see Nathaniel inching his way toward the rack of Harry's whips, directly behind him.

Moaning as though she enjoyed Clifton's caress, she pulled the marquess down to the ground with her, running her fingers though his hair and clinging to him so he couldn't look up.

"Jake," she breathed. "Jake."

Clifton's ardor increased at her response, but by then, Nathaniel had the whip. Alexandra watched as the pirate captain strained to reach his pistol with it, then slowly began pushing the gun toward her.

She moaned again and arched her back, reaching through the hay. The marquess covered her mouth with his, and stuck his tongue so deeply into her throat she nearly gagged.

One last circle with the handle of the whip brought the weapon within Alexandra's reach. She could feel Clifton's gun pressing into the flesh of her backside. He couldn't angle it to shoot anyone now if he wanted to—but then, neither was she far enough away to fire Nathaniel's pistol at him.

Instead she turned the smooth, ivory handle of Nathaniel's gun and grasped the steel muzzle. Raising it behind Clifton, she used all of her strength to bring it crashing down upon his head.

Nathaniel's half brother jerked. For a moment, Alexandra feared the blow hadn't done its job. But then his eyes rolled back, and he collapsed on top of her.

"Are you all right?" Nathaniel's voice sounded raspy to her ears.

"I'm fine." She shuddered as she struggled to escape from beneath the marquess's heavy body.

"Give me the gun." Nathaniel motioned weakly to her. He'd used the wall of the stables to help himself rise, and leaned heavily against it now. But his voice was steadier than it had been since Alexandra found him.

Eager to be rid of the weapon in her hand, Alexandra did as she was told, but her breath caught in her throat when Nathaniel raised the gun and leveled it at Lord Clifton's prostrate form.

She stared at Nathaniel's face. It was intense, focused. Horrified, she clasped her hands over her ears, expecting the blast to make them ring.

But the gun never exploded. Alexandra opened her eyes to see Nathaniel tucking it into his pants as he shuffled toward her.

"Let's get out of here before I change my mind," he said.

Nathaniel knew he wasn't in the hospital ship. The air was too clean, and there were no groans from the other men. Perhaps he was at sea on the *Vengeance* then, his stay in the hulks only a terrible nightmare. But the ground was stable beneath him; it didn't rock as a ship would. And the pain was most definitely real.

He opened his eyes. Sunlight filtered through a crack in the draperies of a long dormitory-like room, but his mind was too fuzzy and slow-moving to place his semi-familiar surroundings.

Someone's head lay next to him on the bed—a woman, from what he could tell. No one else was in the room.

"Alexandra?"

Alexandra's head snapped up. She was wearing a simple calico dress that looked a bit large around the neck. Her hair was disheveled and her face marked from lying on her arms, but her voice was filled with relief. "Nathaniel!"

He had never thought her more beautiful. The fantasies that had entertained him in the hulks rose unbidden to his mind, causing a physical reaction in his body, despite the throbbing of his head. "I can't believe I found you. That you're here, with me. Part of me thinks it must be a dream. Have I lost my mind after all?"

She smiled, took his hand and kissed his palm. "No, but I thought I'd die when I saw the prison guard hit you with that club. It felt as though he were striking me." Her voice broke. Swallowing, she glanced away.

Nathaniel turned her face back toward him, so he could see her eyes again. "My brave Alexandra. Why did you go to the duke's? Don't you know what he is capable of doing?"

"What else could I do? We had to find you." She nuzzled against his hand, and he longed to pull her to him. If only he were stronger.

"Thank God you did." His gaze fell to her lips.

She must have known what he wanted because she leaned toward him until their mouths met. Her lips were as soft as he remembered, and tasted better than he'd dreamed. "Where are we?" he asked, surveying the room again when she pulled away.

"We're at Dr. Watts's—"

"Oh hell!" He sobered instantly. "We've got to get out of here."

"What?" Alexandra jumped to her feet. "We can't leave. You need to rest—"

Nathaniel's head swam when he tried to sit up, but he dared not lie back. "My father knows of this place."

"How?"

"Rat—" He leaned over, hoping the dizziness would soon pass.

"But you're in no condition to go anywhere."

"My father will come here." He managed to find his feet while Alexandra hurried around the bed to support him. "This time he'll take you, too. We'll not get a second chance to escape."

Alexandra looked up into his face and saw something there that convinced her. "You sit here, then," she said. "I'll check the back and make sure it's clear. At least your wound has been cleaned and bandaged, and we've got some decent clothes."

Decent clothes! Nathaniel looked down at the pants he wore. They had obviously belonged to someone several inches shorter than he, and the shirt must have been a castoff from someone much wider. Only the shoulders fit. At least he was rid of his prison garb, though.

"Where's the gun?" he asked before she could leave.

Alexandra shook her head. "I don't know. Dr. Watts took it somewhere before he left."

"Where did he go?"

She shrugged. "Probably out on a call."

"How did you explain all this?"

"I didn't. When he saw your back, he thought it might be better if he didn't know."

Nathaniel considered this. "And the horse?"

"I let it go. I didn't want to be caught with it."

He nodded. "Go, then, but be careful . . . and hurry," he admonished as she darted away.

Supporting himself by leaning on the furniture in the room—the bed, the washstand, the wardrobe—Nathaniel moved into the doctor's office next to the dormitory. He could hear someone upstairs banging around in the kitchen as the enticing smell of bacon wafted through the house. So it was morning yet, he thought, grateful that not too much time had passed.

Digging through the drawers of the doctor's desk, Nathaniel searched for the gun. Where would Watts have put it?

When his search yielded nothing, he moved to the examination room.

The front door opened, and Nathaniel heard the doctor speaking to someone he brought in with him. "I didn't know what to make of it, but I thought it should be brought to the attention of the constabulary."

"The Duke of Greystone came to Whitehall just this morning with a description of the same man," a voice replied. "He said Mr. Kent hit his son on the head and stole a horse from his stables."

Nathaniel's heart began to pound as he peered out of the room. A constable followed Dr. Watts back toward the dormitory. Dressed in duck trousers, a blue swallowtail coat and a top hat, the man carried a pistol, which meant he was more than a mere constable. Only inspectors carried guns.

"You will investigate the entire story before pressing charges against this man, am I right?" Watts asked. "He certainly doesn't seem like a criminal. And it appears that he's been quite abused—"

"If this is the man I think he is, he deserves more than a mere flogging. He deserves a noose around his neck."

The doctor stopped and turned back. "Certainly there are two sides to every story."

"Dr. Watts, a man escaped from the hulks last night, a very dangerous man. And the duke has witnesses to say that this same person tried to kill his son, and stole one of his horses. If Mr. Kent is the one, we're going to string him up from the gallows. Now, where is he?"

The doctor frowned and moved ahead, but more slowly. "They're both back here. He and the girl he said was his sister."

Nathaniel prayed Alexandra would not return at that moment. He needed her to stay in the alley until he could manage to get out of the house himself.

"They're gone," Dr. Watts said, his voice a mixture of relief and surprise.

A creak on the stair and Tutty's voice interrupted. "Doctor? Is that you? Oh . . . I didn't realize we had a visitor."

"Tutty, this is Inspector Striker. Do you know where Mr. Kent and his sister went?"

"No. They're not here?" As the housekeeper spoke, Nathaniel's strength nearly gave out on him. He had to shift his position so he could lean up against the wall, and his movement drew Tutty's gaze through the doorway. Her eyes widened and her mouth opened to speak, but Nathaniel pressed a finger to his lips in a wordless appeal.

She looked back at Dr. Watts and the inspector. "Have they done something wrong?"

"Well, I'm not sure, not sure at all," Dr. Watts admitted. "I was a little unsettled by the terrible marks on Mr. Kent's back . . . thought they should be reported, you know. And Inspector Striker here seems to think that he's a dangerous criminal who tried to murder the Marquess of Clifton."

Tutty blinked in surprise. "Oh, I'm sure you've got the wrong fellow, sir. Mr. Kent would never do a thing like that."

"He hardly seems the sort," Dr. Watts agreed.

Inspector Striker's voice held disdain. "And you are a professional in criminal matters, Doctor?" Without waiting for an answer, he continued, "Mind if I have a look around?"

"Perhaps they went out the back," Tutty suggested, moving forward to herd the two men into the dormitory.

Nathaniel would have been grateful for her attempt to cover for him, except that Alexandra had gone out the back, and he was afraid they would find her. He coughed to gain their attention.

"What was that?" the inspector asked.

"What?" Tutty's voice held a nervous edge.

Dr. Watts cleared his throat. "The fog always seems to give me a tickle—"

"No, the sound came from out there."

Nathaniel heard them come toward the examination room. Reaching for the only weapon he could find, his hand closed on the handle of a surgical knife. He had no idea where the doctor had put his pistol, but now he knew why it had disappeared.

Before the inspector could take more than two steps into the room, Nathaniel grabbed him from behind and laid the knife against his throat. "Looking for me?" he asked.

The inspector didn't move. "Please . . . I'm only doing my job."

"Forgive me if letting you do your job isn't in my best interest. Please set your pistol on the table."

Tutty and Dr. Watts followed the inspector in, the doctor wearing a heavy frown. "I'm sorry, Mr. Kent," he said. "I'm still not sure I was wrong for doing what I did, but I consider myself a pretty good judge of character. I can't believe half the things this man claims you've done."

"I appreciate you giving me the benefit of the doubt," Nathaniel responded. "I don't have the time to explain now, but I am innocent, I assure you, at least of these charges."

"Nathaniel." Alexandra's voice came from the back, softly calling his name.

"We're in the examination room," Nathaniel called back.

She entered behind the doctor and his housekeeper, then gasped at the sight of Nathaniel holding a knife to the constable's throat.

"Hand me that gun. And get some rope," he told her. "We need to tie them up."

Alexandra hesitated only a moment. Nathaniel looked as though he might swoon, and something deeper than reason or thought compelled her to move. She gave the gun to him as he asked, and waited for the doctor to pull some thick cord out of a cabinet by the window.

"I'm sorry," she murmured to Dr. Watts and his housekeeper as she took the cord.

"Don't worry, dear," Tutty said as Alexandra reluctantly began to tie her up. "My niece is expected for dinner. No doubt she'll be along shortly."

To free them. Alexandra understood her meaning. She glanced at Nathaniel to see if he had caught it as well, but his mouth was drawn into a thin line that revealed his pain, and she began to fear he would lose consciousness again. They had to hurry.

"Looks as though you've had experience with such things before," he told her, after she'd finished tying the inspector. He attempted a weak smile as he checked to make sure the knots she'd tied were secure.

Alexandra shot him a look of mock exasperation. "Since I've met you, I've gained a great deal of experience, indeed."

"Not the kind I'd like to give you." He spared her a lascivious grin, then saluted Dr. Watts and his housekeeper.

Alexandra smiled ruefully, her way of saying good-bye, and followed Nathaniel out the back way.

Alexandra helped Nathaniel down the alley, but progress was slow. Sweat stood out on his forehead and ran down his back as he limped along. She feared the jostling and the exertion would start him bleeding again.

"This isn't going to work," she said after they had traversed several blocks. "You can't walk much farther, and we're not moving fast enough. We have to get to an inn or someplace where I can take proper care of you."

Nathaniel grinned as he stared at the top of Alexandra's bodice, which kept gaping open in front. "I like traveling this way. I've never had a better view."

Alexandra clamped a hand over the fabric of her dress. "You're every bit the scoundrel I thought you were."

"If you invite a starving man to supper, you can hardly blame him for salivating at the food."

"You've been issued no invitations." Alexandra bit her lip against a smile. "But I'll take your interest along those lines as a good sign. I thought you were close to your last breath." She glanced around at the rotting refuse that spilled from the gutters on both sides, and wrinkled her nose as they passed an outdoor privy. "I've certainly visited better places. Are you sure we're traveling in the right direction?"

Nathaniel grimaced as a rut in the road caused him to stumble. "We'll blend in far better here in the East End. My father is not so familiar with these climes, I assure you."

"You mean *you'll* blend in," she said, stepping over the feet of a drunk sprawled across their path.

"Are you saying I look no better than yon gentleman?" He quirked an eyebrow at her.

"Let's just say that your clothes fit you about as well as mine do me." She laughed. "Your trousers are equally revealing, but I can't say as I'm thrilled about seeing your ankles."

Nathaniel grinned. "Well, I'll be happy to show you my more exciting parts—"

Alexandra gently elbowed him in the ribs.

"Ow!"

She smiled up at him. "Sorry, did I hurt you?"

He scowled at her, but Alexandra noticed that he didn't bother averting his gaze from her bosom.

"You're incorrigible," she told him.

"So they say."

"Who says? The ladies?"

His grin widened, tempting Alexandra to kick him in the shins.

"Really, you'd think a man on the verge of death would care about more important things—"

"Are there more important things? After a month in the hulks, I'm beginning to wonder."

Alexandra heard the serious note that had crept into Nathaniel's voice, but when she glanced up at him, he looked away. After a moment of silence, he said, "Let's get a room at the first inn we find. I think we've gone far enough."

"Do you not expect me to draw a connection between that statement and several others you've just made?" she asked.

She could feel Nathaniel's ribs shake as he chuckled. "If only I had the strength."

"And how do you propose we pay for this room?"

"Trenton will pay for it. You'll simply have to talk the innkeeper into giving us a room until our friend joins us."

"And why would an innkeeper trust me, especially one in these parts?"

"With a face like yours?" Nathaniel winked. "I have faith in you, my love."

The inn they selected was a small, ramshackle building that sat back off the main streets. The lobby was sparsely furnished with threadbare rugs and dingy draperies. The innkeeper sat behind a tall counter, chewing a soggy cigar butt between rotting teeth. He glanced up from his newspaper as Alexandra entered.

"Good afternoon," she said, blinking as her eyes adjusted to the darkness of the room. She had left Nathaniel outside, hoping a lone woman would elicit a more positive response from the innkeeper. But she doubted anything could influence the hard-looking man she saw before her. With a bulk easily approaching three hundred and fifty pounds, he wore a grease-stained shirt that showed rings of perspiration under his armpits.

He grunted, setting his paper aside and somehow managing to stand despite his incredible weight. "Would ye like a room?"

"Yes . . . however, I have one small problem." Alexandra swallowed hard and gave him her sweetest smile. "You see, I don't have any money—"

"Then ye don't 'ave a room." He heaved his hulking mass back onto his stool and took up his paper.

"I'm supposed to meet a man here. He'll pay you when he comes. He'll be here before nightfall."

The innkeeper kept reading.

"Sir?"

He removed the cigar from his mouth and let it smolder in a crystal ashtray, the only delicate-looking object in the room. "There'll be a premium then, providin' yer man shows up." He looked up. "I don't run no almshouse 'ere. An' if ye don't pay, I'll boot ye out onto the street long before mornin', understand?" His gaze searched her face.

"Perfectly," she said. "I'm sure he'll come."

"That's what they all say." He stuffed the cigar back into his mouth and clamped down on it while he gave Alexandra a gaping leer. With her ill-fitting dress and bedraggled appearance, she knew she probably looked like a girl of dubious character, and his next words confirmed his opinion of her.

"If yer man don't show, I might be able to replace 'im with another uh . . . client, if ye like. Providin' ye work, I'll cover yer room an' board for as long as ye want to stay."

"No, thank you. I'm not what you may think, but I'll take that room you promised."

The innkeeper paused, obviously doubtful, then handed her a key from the wall of pigeonholes behind him. "'Tis just down the hall to yer left. An' don't forget—ye might not like the method of payment I require if yer man don't come through," he said, and his raspy laugh followed her out.

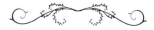

"That wasn't half as easy as you made it sound," Alexandra complained as soon as she reached Nathaniel.

Sitting against the outside of the building, he squinted up at her when her shadow fell across him. "I just hope you got a room," he said, his voice weaker than before.

Alexandra felt a prickle of fear crawl up her spine. Had his wound begun to bleed again? "I got the room. Let me help you up. Do you think you can make it past the innkeeper while I distract him? Otherwise he'll demand payment right away."

Nathaniel nodded.

When they reached the door, Alexandra entered first. She approached the counter and smiled when the innkeeper finally looked up from his newspaper. "I just wanted to be sure you would tell my friend, when he comes, which room I'm in."

His eyebrows drew together, but he nodded, the smelly cigar moving in his mouth as he spoke. "I'll tell 'im—right after 'e gives me my money."

Alexandra moved to the right, drawing the innkeeper's eye with her so he wouldn't see Nathaniel. "That's very kind of you." She lowered her voice. "You know, there are not many men in your position who would have treated me so generously."

He grunted, the kindness of her words obviously throwing him off-balance. "Don't think ye'll change my mind," he rallied. "Yer fellow pays or ye don't stay."

"Of course. Oh, and I was wondering, do you happen to have a porter or someone with whom I could send a message?"

"Not without money, I don't."

"Fine." Alexandra could see that Nathaniel had already made his way down the darkened hallway, so she smiled again, then followed him.

Nathaniel sagged onto the bed as soon as she opened the door. Propping a pillow behind his head, Alexandra swung his feet up and rolled him onto his side to examine the bandage. There was little fresh blood. He just needed to rest.

Breathing a sigh of relief, she turned her attention to the room, which was almost as sparse as the lobby. A washbasin containing gray, tepid water stood near the window, and a chest and a chair were placed on either side of the iron bed. One small rug covered the filthy wood floor. None of the mismatched furniture was in good condition, but it was the smell of the place that offended Alexandra most. Old sweat and camphor balls combined to create a musty odor that prompted her to open the window straightaway. The stench of the open sewer that ran through the gutter outside, made worse by the warmth of the afternoon sun, motivated her to hurry and close it again.

Taking the pitcher from the washstand, she left the room in search of fresh water.

"Pump's at the end of the street," the innkeeper told her when he saw what she carried.

Alexandra scowled at him, wondering why she'd been left with dirty water in the first place. "And some clean linens?" she pressed.

"Yer a picky sort for not 'avin' paid a farthin' as yet." He entered a small room behind him and returned with two towels and a set of sheets.

When Alexandra returned, Nathaniel felt hot to the touch. She took a clean rag, dipped it into the cool water, and dabbed it across his forehead. He didn't move, but he seemed to be resting comfortably.

"You're going to be all right, my pirate captain," she whispered. Then, exhausted herself, she curled up next to him as a vision of the house and children she had always wanted flashed across her mind—the one that came with a husband who was kind and stable.

She had craved such peace and comfort since her mother had died. But when she looked at Nathaniel and felt the warmth of his body next to hers, she was tempted to trade it all away for whatever the pirate captain could provide . . . if only he would ask her.

Alexandra was awakened by a gentle hand stroking her arm. The sun was setting and its rays filled the room with a golden light as she glanced up to see Nathaniel watching her.

"Are you all right?" she murmured.

"You could make me better," he replied, giving her a crooked grin.

She batted her eyelids coyly. "Meaning . . ."

"Meaning it's about time you made good on that offer you made me at Gunther's place. Didn't you say you wouldn't charge me a farthing for an hour or so with your glorious body?" He reached over to cup her chin in his palm and began kissing her neck.

The feather-light touch of his lips made Alexandra shiver. "I was speaking hypothetically," she reminded him.

"Well, the hypothetical is here." He lowered his mouth to where her dress gaped away from her chest and tickled the swell of each breast with his tongue. "I never pegged you as the type to go back on a bargain."

She tried to bat him away, but the attempt was halfhearted at best. "Unlike someone else I know," she replied, lowering her eyelids as desire pooled, warm in her belly. "What was it last time? A trip to shore for a kiss?"

His smile broadened. "Don't worry, I don't plan to cheat you this time. I plan to take my time and give you all you want and more." He slowly undid the buttons of her dress and pushed it off her shoulders to below her bust. Admiration filled his eyes as his gaze lowered. "You're beautiful," he whispered. "Even more beautiful than I imagined."

Alexandra could see his outline in the dwindling light, the aristo-cratic features, the strong chin, the square jaw. She'd removed his shirt before checking his wound, and the muscles of his torso rippled smoothly beneath his bronze skin as he moved. Nathaniel was thinner, but his body was no less defined for all his ill treatment. In repose, his face could look boyish, especially when his dark hair fell across his brow. But when he was filled with hate or anger—or passion, like now—the planes of his face looked chiseled from stone.

Luxuriating in the heat their bodies generated, Alexandra let her fingers travel up his bare arm. He closed his eyes as her hand moved onto his chest, where she spread both palms against him, feeling the softly curling hair that grew there.

"See? I don't bite," he whispered hoarsely. Nipping at her ear, he added, "Not hard, anyway. Do you remember that time I walked in on you after your bath on the *Vengeance*?"

Alexandra nodded. "How could I forget? You looked as though you might eat me for dinner."

He chuckled. "A promise I still intend to fulfill."

"We can talk about the past," she said, "but please, don't let me think about tomorrow."

Nathaniel pulled back to look at her with shocking intensity. "You can't go into this blind, Alexandra. I don't know what my future holds, or when, if ever—"

She raised a finger to his lips. She didn't want to think. She wanted only to relish the way his hand moving over her body made her quiver like the most delicate note of a harp, vibrating on the air. Nathaniel was not the one she had always pictured in her dreams. In fact, he was almost the opposite. He was headstrong, sometimes arrogant, definitely dangerous. His emotions were palpable and often tempestuous. She couldn't see him in the role she had assigned to her calm, steady, imaginary husband.

But she could picture no one else as her lover. No one else could possess her body—and her soul—like she knew he could.

She pressed her ear to his chest to hear the steady thump of his heart until Nathaniel once again lifted her chin and found her mouth with his own. His lips were soft but firm as they moved with mounting pressure. The warm, velvety softness of his tongue slid into her mouth. Yielding, Alexandra let herself be carried away by the passion that swirled about them like a river's strong current, pulling her away from safety to some unknown destination.

Nathaniel left her lips to trail kisses down her throat, stopping only when her hands delved into the thickness of his hair to pull him back for more. The unforgiving muscle of his body, the unique smell of the sweat glistening on his torso, and the budding desire to know him in a way she had never known a man created a heady mixture that put sanity safely out of reach. How long had she imagined this moment? No matter how many times she had tried to force away any thought of Nathaniel making love to her, such visions had encroached on her dreams, slowly ensuring her heart won the battle with her head.

His large hand cupped her breast, circling below it and lifting it for his examination as though he saw some magnificent work of art. He traced its swell from her collarbone to its very tip, then his mouth lowered to take her nipple between his lips and to tease it with his tongue.

Alexandra's stomach did a somersault, and she arched toward him as he moved from one nipple to the other.

Pulling her dress down to her waist, Nathaniel's eyes followed his hand along the flat planes of her stomach.

Alexandra felt a moment of self-consciousness and was tempted to cover herself, but something more powerful wanted no barriers between them. Reaching out, she fiddled with the buttons of his breeches, and his hand quickly moved to help her.

He slid his pants off his lean hips, and Alexandra gasped at the sight of his maleness. Never had she seen a man without his clothes; the sight nearly melted her bones.

"I don't know what to do," she whispered, hearing the wobble in her voice as his hand began to seek out the most private parts of her body. "You'll have to guide me."

"Everything will come naturally," he said, but her words seemed to give him pause. After a moment he lay without moving, as though trying to rein in his desire.

Finally he rolled away, his face set. "We can't do this."

Alexandra stared at him, willing herself to feel something besides a longing so powerful she almost reached out to pull him back to her. The quiet, safe existence she had always wanted seemed less important than having Nathaniel fulfill the promise his body had already given hers. "I want to feel you inside me," she whispered. "Don't stop."

He closed his eyes, breathing deeply through his nose, but didn't speak.

"What's wrong? Don't you want this?" she asked.

Moving beyond touching distance, as though he feared the slightest contact, he sat on the edge of the bed with his head bowed. "I'm wanted by the authorities. It's bad enough that I must leave you in London on your own. I won't deflower you as well. What if I leave you with child?"

Alexandra tried to slow the pounding of her heart by taking several carefully measured breaths. She almost said that she didn't care, that she'd welcome a child of his. But she knew he was right. How would she care for a baby? She had no job, no home. And would she want to bear a child that would never know its father? It was only a matter of time before the duke—or the constabulary—caught up with Nathaniel to take him away forever.

She watched him scrub the whiskers on his face with his hand and nearly drew him back to her, in spite of everything, when a knock sounded on their door.

"Where's my money, wench?" the innkeeper shouted through the panel.

Chapter 20

"Open up!"

Nathaniel reached for the pistol he'd left at the side of the bed, but Alexandra motioned for him to lie back and be silent. Coming to her feet, she threw the covers over him and quickly repaired her clothing before crossing to the door and cracking it open.

"I don't know why my, er, friend isn't here yet," she said, hearing the breathless quality to her own voice. "I'll send a messenger to fetch him right away."

The innkeeper scratched his crotch. "Ye got an 'our." He tried to peer around her. "I thought I 'eard voices."

"I'm alone now, but I won't be for long. My friend should arrive any moment."

"That's what ye said before." He sniffed, apparently reluctant to go. Only when Alexandra shut the door in his face did he finally lumber away.

She turned to face Nathaniel, suddenly embarrassed and uncomfortable in light of what had just transpired between them. "I've got to find Trenton. Do you know where Marley House is?"

Nathaniel threw the blankets back, and Alexandra looked away as he set his gun on the table and began pulling on his clothes. The blackness of his mood showed in the scowl on his face. "That man needs to learn some respect."

"But you are not the one to teach him. We definitely don't need you shooting someone right now," she said.

He fumbled with his trousers. Guessing how difficult buttons would be with only one arm, Alexandra nearly moved to help him, but she dared not get so close again.

"The next time he speaks to you in that tone, I'll shoot him for good measure," he grumbled, but he gave her the directions she needed.

Alexandra smoothed her hair before the mirror. She could see Nathaniel in the glass and felt a sudden impulse to go to him and kiss his brow. Instead, she crossed to the door. "Just be good, for once, all right? I'll be back as soon as I can."

With that she headed out, but Nathaniel called her back. "Perhaps you should take this." He groaned as he reached for the gun. "I don't want you out on the streets alone. It'll be dark soon."

"I wouldn't know how to use it anyway." Alexandra waved the pistol away. "I'll be fine," she insisted, and closed the door behind her, grateful that the obese innkeeper was absent from his post behind the counter when she passed through the lobby.

Nearly two hours passed before Alexandra returned to the inn with Trenton. The trip to Marley House had been quick and uneventful, but Trenton had been gone when she first arrived and she'd had to wait.

"So there ye are," the innkeeper said when he saw her.

"Yes, I'm back. And I've got your money." She stepped aside so Trenton could pay for the room.

"Ye got yerself quite a business goin'." He watched Alexandra closely. "The bloke in yer room can scarcely move, 'e's so tired."

Trenton shot Alexandra a questioning glance.

"You didn't disturb him, did you?" she asked, fear knotting her stomach once again.

The man dangled a key in front of her face, and Alexandra assumed it was the master key to her room. "Took a peek, is all. I knew ye 'ad someone in there."

Evidently reading the concern on her face, he added, "But don't worry, I didn't bother 'im. 'E's sleepin' like a babe, 'e is. I'll tell ye somethin', though. I'll not stand for ye to entertain one gentleman after another under my roof"—he thumped his huge chest between breasts nearly the size of Alexandra's—"without some kind of compensation." He eyed Trenton as if expecting an objection from that quarter, but Nathaniel's first mate only scowled.

"How much?" Trenton pulled a wad of notes from his pocket, obviously eager to dispense with the man so they could get to Nathaniel.

Alexandra hurried to the room ahead of Trenton. Throwing the door back, she rushed inside, calling Nathaniel's name.

He stirred. "Hmm?"

Alexandra let out a sigh of relief. "Trenton's here, but first let me check your bandages." She maneuvered Nathaniel gently to his side to check his wounds, which looked fine, then let him roll back as Trenton entered.

"Nathaniel." Trenton strode across the room to clasp Nathaniel's hand.

Nathaniel smiled. "Am I glad to see you. How's my crew?"

"They're a sad lot without their captain. They all blame themselves for letting Rat escape, but it was my fault. I was in charge. I should have kept a closer eye on him. I'm sorry, my friend."

"You had no way of knowing what he'd do."

Trenton smiled sheepishly. "Or that you'd stay in London so long."

"Something here caught my fancy." Nathaniel shot a glance at Alexandra. "Where's the *Royal Vengeance*?"

"Waiting in Calais. I thought she'd be safer in France."

"Good. And what about the guns?"

Trenton shrugged. "I've kept up with the rent on the warehouse. We just have to go pick them up. I heard from the Lord High Admiral just yesterday. He wants to see the rifles for himself."

"When?"

"Next week. But without witnesses of some kind, besides ourselves, I doubt we can convince him."

"We'll find witnesses. I doubt we discovered the only shipment, which means there are probably others who know about the guns. If we can get the Lord High Admiral to start an investigation, the whole thing should unravel."

Nathaniel smiled. "And if that happens, my father had better enjoy his days as a free man, because he won't have many of them remaining."

That night Alexandra slept on the bed beside Nathaniel while Trenton snored in the chair by the window, but she got little sleep. She was too aware of the pirate captain, and she knew he wrestled with the same desire she did.

Once, as she lay facing the wall, she felt him touch her hair. She squeezed her eyes shut and lay perfectly still until he shifted in the bed and turned away. She longed to feel his arm around her, but at the same time, she knew they'd never be satisfied with that alone.

When morning came Alexandra's eyelids felt as heavy as lead weights, but she forced herself to rise early. She didn't know how long Nathaniel would give himself to heal, and she wanted to take advantage of the time they had together.

She crossed to the washbasin and splashed her face with water.

"Will you take me to a drapers?" she asked Trenton, who was beginning to wake as well. "Nathaniel and I both need clothes."

"That will take a long time," he objected. "We should be leaving in a few days, as soon as Nathaniel is strong enough."

"I'm a seamstress, remember? I'll sew us something in no time."

Alexandra paused near the bed to see that Nathaniel had finally fallen asleep. But he stirred restlessly the moment she moved away.

"Trenton and I are leaving," she told him. "You try and get some more rest. We'll be back in a couple of hours."

"Where are you going?"

"To get some fabric. I don't know about you, but I'd dearly love some clothes that fit properly. So far since I met you, I've worn your half sister's gown, your own clothes, a maid's uniform and Mrs. Tuttle's niece's castoff."

Nathaniel grunted and rolled over, and Alexandra wondered about the pain his wound must be causing him. At least the stripes from the lash were beginning to heal, she thought as Trenton followed her out.

When they returned, both Alexandra and Trenton had their arms full of small bundles: white cotton for a full dress shirt for Nathaniel, serge for Nathaniel's trousers, brocade for a waistcoat and a pretty blue-and-white calico print for Alexandra's dress. Her undergarments were not new, but they were still serviceable, and under the circumstances, she knew she'd be lucky to finish the projects she already had planned.

Nathaniel roused again when they entered, and cocked his eyebrow at the paper-wrapped fabric. "How long do you plan on staying here? Through the winter?"

"I'll be finished before you're ready to go anywhere," she retorted, pulling the chair closer to the light that streamed in at the window.

Alexandra worked the entire day and late into the night. She felt Nathaniel's gaze on her whenever he was awake, but he slept most of the time, and she was glad he was allowing his body time to heal. Trenton remained with them, serving as an unlikely chaperone.

Alexandra took frequent breaks to spoon broth into Nathaniel's mouth. After the food he had been fed in the hulks, he couldn't tolerate much at first. By the evening of the second day, however, he was beginning to want something more satisfying.

"You're recovering quickly," Alexandra told him, stropping the razor Trenton had acquired for her. Nathaniel's stubble was quickly turning into a full-blown beard, and she had immediate plans to shave him.

"Have you ever done this before?" he asked, obviously more concerned with the blade she wielded than with chronicling his recovery.

"I used to shave Willy sometimes, when he was too drunk to do so himself."

"Which means he was too drunk to feel whether or not you did a good job." He smiled ruefully.

"And drunk enough to get mean." Alexandra didn't know why she added that. She had purposely not thought of Willy since the day Nathaniel had asked her about him.

She felt Nathaniel's hand on her arm and glanced up. He didn't say anything, but the look in his eyes was somehow gratifying, as though he empathized with her pain without pitying or blaming.

She offered him a smile. "I don't think about it very often. Neither do I miss him."

Nathaniel brought her hand to his lips. "I'd like to pay him a visit—"

"No." Alexandra shook her head. "He's just a miserable old man. What good could you do? It's enough that I'm away from him. Promise me you'll leave him alone."

Nathaniel watched her thoughtfully. "That's a promise I can't make. The thought of him hurting you . . ."

Alexandra pressed her mouth to his lips. "I'm all right," she said, then lathered the shaving cream onto the lower half of his face and guided the blade around the contours of his jaw. The cleft in his chin proved a bit difficult. At one point, he tried to talk and received a small nick for his efforts.

"Hold still," she told him, "before we have to remove the bandages on your back and use them on your face."

"How am I supposed to stay still when you're so close?" he murmured.

Alexandra glanced toward Trenton, who tactfully pretended not to hear. "You're a rogue, my pirate captain," she said, letting her voice drop to a whisper. "I think my first impression of you was more correct than ever I realized."

"Where you are concerned, I cannot pretend to think only chaste thoughts." His gaze lowered to her breasts while the quirk of a smile turned up his lips.

"Promises, promises," she murmured, teasing him. "You have yet to keep a bargain with me on any count."

His eyes narrowed dangerously. "Don't tempt me too far, Alexandra. I've never been known for my scruples."

Trenton cleared his throat, probably hoping to end their lovers' repartee while in his presence, and Alexandra smiled.

"There," she said, speaking louder as she toweled his chin dry. "With that face you could capture the heart of every woman in London."

"But I want only one," Nathaniel said softly.

The Marquess of Clifton sat in the noisy tavern across the table from Captain Rene Montague of the *Eastern Horizon*. A glass of brandy stood in front of him; the captain had preferred a pint of gin. Clifton swirled the amber liquid, raising it against the light before turning his attention back to Montague.

"The other shipment reached Russia?" he asked.

"Of course. Without one single problem."

"Good. Then why did you want to meet me?"

Montague played with his glass. "We've found the guns."

"You're sure?"

"*Mais oui.*"

"How?"

"I have had my men searching Bristol ever since you told me Nathaniel's ship put in there. We could find nothing at first. I was about to give up when I heard tale of an old couple who were attempting to sell a warehouse full of guns. Their son was recently killed in the infantry. They wanted to move to the country and had no response to the notices they sent their lessor. When I confirmed the details, I knew we had found the rifles at last."

Clifton took a sip of his drink. "And the details are?"

Montague, looking irritated, waved a hand. "They are inconsequential. The important thing is that the guns are in a warehouse just off the docks at Bristol, and Mr. Kent will undoubtedly try to use them against your father, if he can."

"It sounds as though you think Nathaniel's alive despite the knife wound he received when he escaped."

"He has never struck me as an easy man to kill. But I am only going by what you told me—that he did indeed escape. We want the guns regardless, no?"

Clifton swallowed the brandy he had been holding in his mouth, savoring the gentle burn as it descended to his stomach. Alcohol was his only balm against the pain he felt in a hand that no longer existed. He found himself craving more and more of his favorite spirits. "Of course. And we must move quickly, before anything else can go wrong."

Montague nodded. "I'm heading to Bristol at first light. Are you coming?"

The marquess considered the question. If the guns were in Bristol, chances were good that Nathaniel would go there to retrieve them. And Clifton wanted nothing more than a second chance at his half brother.

"I'll go," he said, "for several reasons. First and foremost, I need to make sure Nathaniel is as dead as we hope."

"They fit." Nathaniel teetered near the bed, on his feet for the first time in a week, trying on the trousers Alexandra had sewn for him. His pale face still looked drawn, but his strength seemed greatly replenished.

Alexandra handed him the shirt she was making so he could try it on, too, admiring the way the trousers hugged his long legs and narrow hips. She remembered the fabric she had found in his chest aboard the *Vengeance.* How her fingers had itched to sew for him almost from the beginning. She knew even then that she'd need no pattern. With very few measurements, she had created clothes that fit him perfectly.

Thoughts of Nathaniel's sea chest reminded her of the small picture she had found hidden in the folds of the fabric. She frowned. The lady in that picture had haunted her dreams more than a few times. At odd moments, she worried that he was holding out for that woman, and now that Alexandra knew her time with Nathaniel was coming to a close, she ventured the question she had always wanted to ask.

"You know that portrait you keep in your trunk?"

He glanced up at her and grinned. "You mean I had more than rats going through my things aboard the *Vengeance*?"

Alexandra felt herself flush. She was tempted to explain, except that she *had* been going through his belongings. "Who is she?"

Nathaniel chuckled and arched one brow. "Jealous?"

Alexandra started to deny that she felt anything so base, then shrugged in acknowledgment. "She's beautiful."

"I've always thought so." A far-off look claimed Nathaniel's features. "When I was a child, I used to pretend that smile was meant specifically for me, though I've never seen it, except in the picture. Somehow it made life easier to believe she would have loved me, had she been given the chance."

"She was your mother?" Alexandra asked softly.

He nodded. "Martha managed to acquire the picture from a friend who worked for my father, long after we left. The duke hated her, you know."

"Who?"

"My mother."

"It seems he had no more affinity for his next wife." Alexandra hesitated, wondering if Nathaniel already knew of his father's sexual exploits, and whether or not the knowledge would bother him. "Your father prefers prostitutes and easy women to highborn ladies. At Greystone House, I found a locked metal box that I hoped might contain information on what the duke had done with you. Instead it held a letter from Lord Clifton and Lady Anne's mother, claiming he gave her syphilis, though he didn't seem ill when I was there."

Nathaniel shook his head. "Selfish bastard," he said. "For all his arrogance, he chases barroom wenches about the taverns of London by night, eh? God, my poor mother."

He chuckled, and Alexandra laughed with him, but her mirth didn't reach her heart, which was filled with sadness. The beautiful woman in the portrait could have changed so much for Nathaniel. If only she had lived.

By the time Alexandra woke the following morning, Nathaniel and Trenton had gone out. Where, she didn't know, but that Nathaniel was strong enough to venture beyond the room left her with a feeling of dread. Their time together was dwindling, falling by the wayside like the shavings of a whittler. And like the whittler's wood, Alexandra felt helplessly acted upon, unable to control the paths their separate lives would take.

While grateful for the fact that Nathaniel was getting better, she knew it was only a matter of time before he left to take care of the guns at Bristol. The Lord High Admiral expected to see the rifles in a few days—and she knew Nathaniel would retrieve them without her. He had to. His patriotism demanded that he stop his father, and with the duke shadowing his every move, Nathaniel believed she wasn't safe with him. He thought she might never be.

Alexandra buried her head beneath her pillow, longing for the situation to be different.

A tear squeezed out from the corner of her clamped eyelids. God help her, she loved him. The mere sight of his tall, muscular body, the briefest glance from his blue eyes, the honey-rich sound of his voice in her ear, made her tingle with a response that was as immediate and natural as the pealing of a bell that follows a pull of its ropes. Deep down, she wondered if she could ever feel such an intensity of emotion for anyone else—no matter how steady, no matter how safe, no matter what.

Cursing the vicissitudes of life, Alexandra flung her pillow to the floor and rose from the bed to finish sewing her dress. Could she bear for him to kiss her and leave, without so much as a promise?

Her heart twisted at the thought. She couldn't endure good-bye. She couldn't stand idly by and wave as he and Trenton started off. She had to leave on her own. She had to dredge up the strength to make things easier for both of them. But how, when the very core of her being rebelled at the thought?

Alexandra jammed her needle back into the hem of her dress. A breeze whispered through the open window, carrying sounds from the street outside: the voices of children as they ran about, the cackling of hens, the grate of cart and wagon wheels. It was a humid day, though otherwise mellow—a perfect day to look for work, Alexandra decided as she tied off the final stitch to her dress. Though her experience with Gunther had frightened her, she was wiser now. And she was definitely stronger.

Determined to take control of her mutinous emotions at last, Alexandra paid the obese innkeeper to locate some lackeys to haul water for a bath. Then she hired a small boy, who stood selling flowers on the sidewalk with his mother, to retrieve the clothes she'd sent to the laundress down the street. She'd been wearing the shirt and pants Mrs. Tuttle had loaned to Nathaniel since the day before, and was eager to have her underclothes back.

By midmorning, Alexandra had her hair twisted into an attractive style with ringlets framing her face. Her new dress had a basquine body that was open to the waist, worn over a chemisette, with pagoda sleeves. The perfect fit of her costume made her feel absolutely luxurious as she twirled around in the matching slippers she'd found when she'd purchased the fabric.

She wondered if Nathaniel would appreciate the transformation in her appearance, then attempted to rein in such errant thoughts. She couldn't think about him now. She'd never leave if she did. And she wanted to go before he returned. She had delayed too long already.

Nathaniel was feeling tired and weak by the time he and Trenton returned to the inn. He turned the key in the lock and swung the door open while speaking to Trenton over his shoulder.

"The newspapers make no mention of my escape from the *Retribution*?" he asked, crossing the threshold.

"No." Trenton followed him inside, where they both stopped and turned around in surprise. The room was empty.

"Where's Alexandra?" Nathaniel asked.

Trenton shrugged. "She's probably just picking up our clothes from the laundress."

Nathaniel strode across the room to the bed, where the laundry Trenton had mentioned waited, neatly folded and stacked.

"Our clothes are here," he said, foreboding raising the hackles on his neck.

"Perhaps she was hungry." Trenton's words sounded hollow, as though even he didn't believe them, and Nathaniel strove to keep his face a mask. He was hesitant to show the emotion coursing through his body, to reveal his fear of the truth. Even if Alexandra had left him, there was no need to let his friend know how much she meant to him. He couldn't have her regardless. His father had taken her away from him just as effectively as he had taken Martha. Succumbing to his selfish desires to keep her with him would risk her life. He had no right to do that. And while he was finally willing to give up the personal battle he had waged against his father if it meant a life with Alexandra, the duke's traitorous actions made even that impossible. The welfare of England was more important than the desires of one man—the lives of thousands of English troops worth more than his own. But what would happen to her?

Nathaniel remembered Gunther and his filthy brothel, and felt sick. Alexandra was so beautiful, so innocent. He loved her as he had never loved another woman, and he wanted more than her body; he knew that now. He had refused the temptation of taking her, though she had slept next to him for almost a week. Why? It certainly wasn't a lack of desire. The mere brush of her hand on his arm was enough to excite him. The truth was that he cared more about her welfare: her heart and her mind.

Could he live without her? Did he want to?

Duty. Nathaniel measured the word in his mind. He had served in his country's navy. He had fought in her wars. He had a duty to England and to his fellow countrymen. But if life had ever offered him a crumb of happiness, it was Alexandra.

Suddenly Nathaniel spun on his heel and left the room, leaving Trenton gaping after him. He had to find her. He had to find Alexandra now before he lost her forever.

Alexandra walked quickly, ignoring the men who stopped to gape at her. She didn't care for their whistles or murmurs of approval. She knew only that her heart was breaking.

Biting her trembling lip, she forced back the tears despite the painful lump that had lodged itself, permanently it seemed, in her throat.

I won't cry . . . I won't cry . . . at least, not now.

She had thought of leaving Nathaniel a note, but in the end, had left without doing so. She hadn't been able to think of anything to say. That he was the most incredible man she had ever known was certain, but she doubted the pirate captain would take such a statement seriously. That she loved him was undeniable. Again, a truth that couldn't change anything. Besides, he already knew. She could tell by the way he looked at her, as though he would take her inside himself and hold her there and protect her forever if he could.

Tears streamed down Alexandra's face despite her best efforts to avoid them. *I won't cry,* she sobbed. *I won't cry.*

"Mum, why's that lady cryin'?" she heard a young boy ask.

"Perhaps she's lost something important," his mother said.

Alexandra wiped at her wet cheeks. She had lost something important—the most important thing in her life.

She didn't hear the horse approach her from behind. She was too immersed in her own pain. She stared at the ground in front of her as she walked, until she heard a voice that stopped her cold.

"I know I promised to let you go when we reached London, but I'm not quite through with you yet."

Alexandra's heart leaped. She stopped and turned to see Nathaniel bearing down on her on a large bay gelding, wearing a wry grin.

She tried to keep the joy she felt at seeing him from her face, but allowed herself a shy smile.

"You shouldn't be on a horse, not with your injury."

His expression grew intent. "It's my heart that won't mend. Not if you leave me."

Alexandra swallowed hard. "But what about—"

"Marry me, Alexandra. Marry me and come away with me to the States. We'll be safe in Virginia. It's beautiful country. I visited there three years ago. We could buy a tract of land, have a house full of children . . ."

"You'd become a farmer?" she scoffed playfully.

"No. Trenton would captain the *Royal Vengeance* for me, and together we'd build a shipping enterprise to rival my father's."

Alexandra's heart took flight as she listened. Marry him, he said. Marry him! To have and to hold . . . till death do us part. She'd live in a hovel if it meant she could have Nathaniel.

"Could you ever leave England?" he asked hesitantly.

"Much easier than I could leave you," she admitted, and he swung down to hold her close.

"I love you," she whispered as the band of his arm closed around her.

"Aye. And we'll survive, my love. I just have to turn the guns over to the authorities. Then it's up to them to get to the truth of it. We'll sail to Virginia as soon as we can."

Alexandra's heart reached for the hope he offered her, but she knew turning the guns over to the authorities would not be so easy. Nathaniel could be caught and imprisoned. He could be hanged or shot. Or his father could always surprise them with something else entirely.

She winced. "I'm going with you. I can't bear the thought of you there without me, knowing that you might never come back."

"No, you must stay here—" Alexandra silenced him with a kiss. "I go where you go, now and forever," she vowed.

"Now and forever," he murmured, and the kiss he gave her sealed his promise.

Chapter 21

They traveled to Bristol by train. Alexandra had never taken the train before. She was enthralled with the scenery that flew past her window and the crowds of people who waited on the platform of each new station along the way.

An older woman and her young daughter shared their car, and Alexandra couldn't help but take exception to the way the daughter's eyes darted back to Nathaniel every few moments. The mother, a Mrs. Haws, glanced sharply at the girl each time she giggled in response to something Nathaniel said, but the daughter seemed oblivious to her mother's censure.

If Nathaniel noticed Bessie Haws's interest, he did not give himself away as he talked to Trenton about the Clifton Suspension Bridge currently being built across the Severn.

"Oh, we've seen it, haven't we, Mother?" the girl interrupted, blushing to the roots of her hair when Nathaniel looked up.

He smiled politely. "It'll take a while to finish yet."

"Bessie, perhaps you should rest," her mother suggested, tapping her daughter on the knee with her fan. "You're looking a bit peaked."

Flushed would be a better word, Alexandra thought irritably.

Bessie opened her mouth to refute this charge when the train stopped in Farringdon and several new passengers boarded. A man near Nathaniel's age joined them in the compartment.

"The train's nearly full." He showed white teeth beneath a brown mustache as he smiled. "I hope you don't mind me joining you."

"Not at all." Nathaniel and Trenton moved their legs to make more room as the man took a seat on the other side of Bessie Haws.

"I'm Thomas Madsen," he said, nodding as they each introduced themselves in turn. Alexandra thought him rather handsome with his brown eyes, brown hair, long sideburns and mustache. Smile lines around his eyes indicated he laughed often, and he had an air about him that was pleasantly appealing.

He struck up a conversation with Alexandra while Nathaniel responded to a question put to him by Bessie about the hot springs at Bath.

"Do you live in Bristol?"

"No, I was born in London, but we moved to Manchester when I was so small that I don't remember it."

"I see."

"And you? Are you returning from holiday, by chance?"

Madsen shook his head. "No. My work brings me to Bristol. I'm an inspector with Scotland Yard."

"But you got on at Farringdon."

He smiled sheepishly. "The motion of the train makes me sick. I had to get off the last one."

"I'm sorry. I hope you're feeling better."

"I'm fine as long as I keep myself well enough occupied and don't make the mistake of trying to read."

"Ah," Alexandra nodded knowingly, but never having suffered from motion sickness herself, she didn't truly understand. "Do you enjoy your work?" She caught a subtle glance from Nathaniel and noted a wry smile on Trenton's face. Bessie continued to ply them both with questions, but it was Trenton who elaborated. Nathaniel was too busy keeping her and Mr. Madsen under close regard.

"Sometimes. Other times I find it can get quite drab, usually when I'm filling out the reports." Madsen laughed. "Are you and your husband on holiday?"

"No." Alexandra shook her head, taking the opportunity to avenge herself for Bessie's fawning interest by adding, "We're not married."

"Yet," Nathaniel inserted, staring pointedly at Mr. Madsen. "We're on our way."

"To be married?" This time Bessie spoke, and the disappointment that rang in her voice brought Mrs. Haws's brows into thundercloud position.

"'Tis none of your business, my dear."

Evidently, Bessie heard the steel edge in her mother's voice, because her gaze dropped to her lap. "I was simply asking," she mumbled.

Mr. Madsen smiled genially. "You are very lucky to have found such a lovely bride," he told Nathaniel. Turning back to Alexandra, he continued, "There is no better place than Bristol in which to be married. I was born there and sorely miss it. I wish you both all the happiness in the world."

"Thank you." Alexandra felt Nathaniel take her hand in his own and smiled sweetly at Bessie Haws.

They arrived in Bristol in a little more than two hours. Alexandra, Nathaniel and Trenton bid good-bye to the now silent Bessie and her mother, and waved to Mr. Madsen.

With Nathaniel's help, Alexandra descended from the platform while Trenton rented a cab. They had no bags, and were therefore able to move quickly. They wove through the throng, loaded up and started down the paved road ahead of the other passengers.

Bristol was more crowded than when Alexandra had seen it last. As July approached, and the heat of London became unbearable, many of the capital's citizens fled to Bath or Bristol for a reprieve. Alexandra watched the assorted carriages, carts and wagons that clogged the street as they moved, snaillike, through the melee.

"I wrote back to the Lord High Admiral and told him I am bringing the guns to London," Trenton told Nathaniel. "He's expecting me Monday week. I think it best if I handle it, just in case they believe the duke and the magistrate who sentenced you to the hulks and send you back—or hang you."

Nathaniel frowned. "What about your own neck?"

"I haven't gained sufficient notoriety to be too concerned. Even if they charge me with piracy, it's unlikely they'll hang me."

Nathaniel considered his words. "Newgate is not a pleasant fate."

"So you are the only patriot among us?"

Nathaniel shook his head. "Evidently not."

"Besides, the guns will take center stage."

"I think you're right there." Nathaniel's voice was decidedly neutral, but Alexandra knew he worried still the same, and she couldn't help saying a silent prayer for them all.

It was raining by the time they reached the docks, large drops that splattered when they hit the ground. Nathaniel peered out of the carriage at the darkening sky and cursed the weather. They'd be soaked to the skin by the time they finished unloading the entire warehouse, even if they hired help.

"Perhaps you should wait in the carriage, my love," he said to Alexandra as he descended. "You can watch us from here."

She nodded and kissed him briefly. Nathaniel would have lingered in her embrace, but now that they'd arrived, he felt the need to deal with the guns and be done with them.

"It might be a while," he called, "but we'll hurry."

Alexandra's drooping ringlets gave a slight bob as she nodded her head, and he envisioned having a daughter with the same yellow hair. His fiancée was beautiful, he thought, the only one who could make him whole. Strangely enough, he felt whole already, for the first time since he could remember.

Turning away, he rounded the warehouse and made his way to the alley behind. He easily found the rock beneath which he had buried the key, and dug it up.

"Would you have been able to find it if need be?" he asked Trenton.

His friend nodded. "Aye. The directions you gave were good ones. Shall I hire a wagon?"

"In a moment."

They headed back to the front entrance together amid the crush of people along the wharves. Nathaniel glanced about, hoping to hail a few burly chaps to help, and thought he saw a face he recognized. When he looked again the man had gone, but something about him stirred a memory.

He was likely one of the blokes he'd hired to help him the last time, Nathaniel thought. Turning the key in the lock, he pressed in on the door.

It groaned on its hinges, then swung wide.

Nathaniel stood staring, his jaw agape. The warehouse was empty.

"They've found them." He turned back to push Trenton away. "Let's get out of here."

The two of them began to sprint to the carriage when the familiar-looking man appeared again, a sturdy bloke with bulging biceps. He grabbed Nathaniel by the arm and began to haul him back, as four others separated themselves from the crowd and stripped him of his pistol. They shoved him and Trenton back inside the empty warehouse, and Lord Clifton moved into the light that streamed in through the high windows, one of which was open.

Sailors called to each other outside as his half brother's voice echoed within. "Looking for something?" the marquess asked.

"Clifton, this won't do you any good," Nathaniel said. "The Lord High Admiral already knows about the guns."

The marquess shrugged. "No one will believe my father guilty of treason. But the guns are quite valuable. I must say, I'm relieved to have them back."

The door opened and a gush of fresh air swept into the room as Captain Montague entered with a struggling Alexandra.

"Alexandra, how wonderful to see you." Lord Clifton bowed in mock courtesy. "I feared our paths would never cross again, but fate has been kinder to me than I deserve."

Nathaniel's heart began to race. He glanced beyond the marquess, trying to sense any movement in the shadows. How many men accompanied his half brother?

As if six, including Clifton, weren't enough.

"You're right. The only thing you deserve is to swing at the end of a rope," Alexandra said breathlessly.

The marquess chuckled and glanced above them, where a large metal hook was attached to a pulley system designed to help move cargo around. "Funny you should mention a rope." He gave Nathaniel a meaningful smile, motioning with his head to one of his men. "Charles, I do believe it would be wise to be quick about this."

The man named Charles stepped forward and pulled the hook closer while two others grabbed Nathaniel by his clothes.

"And now we see that my prophecy comes true," Montague said, giving Nathaniel a mocking salute. "You will test the rope long before me, no?"

"Then I'll see you in hell," Nathaniel told him.

Lord Clifton smiled at the exchange. "I saved a few rifles for you." He indicated one of the familiar long, flat crates. "They can provide the stool—a bit of irony I could not resist."

The marquess's men dragged the box forward as Nathaniel's mind flailed for something, anything, with which to gain an advantage. He could think of nothing until a thought surfaced—a memory, really—of Alexandra telling him that his father had syphilis and had given the disease to Clifton's mother. Did his half brother know? If not, would it upset him enough to buy some desperately needed time?

"It's a miracle you were ever born, you know," Nathaniel said, staring defiantly at Clifton as another man started to force him onto the box of rifles. "Syphilis is no small thing. With your father carrying it home from his whores, I wonder that your mother didn't leave him sooner."

His words acted on Lord Clifton like a douse of cold water. The marquess blinked in surprise, and the men who held Nathaniel paused uncertainly. Clifton's brows drew close, and he bared his teeth. "I'll not tolerate such rubbish from the likes of you. My mother might be sick, but she's not gone mad. Her illness has nothing to do with syphilis. And my father has been well for over a year."

"So you didn't know." Nathaniel shrugged, feigning a haughtiness he did not feel. "Evidently it hasn't made itself apparent enough in either parent yet. But it will. It always does."

The marquess's men glanced at one another, and Nathaniel felt the hands that held him lose a bit of their tension.

At his full height Clifton was several inches shorter than Nathaniel. He had to tilt his head back to stare him in the eye, but he did so as he advanced, coming within inches. Nathaniel saw how the marquess's nostrils flared with rage and knew he had hit his target. His half brother had been caught completely unaware.

"That's a lie!"

"Certainly even you can see it's the truth, now that you know." Nathaniel watched Clifton's hand ball into a fist, and prepared himself for the blow. The others stood still, out of surprise or perverse interest, Nathaniel didn't know. "Evidently, he cared little about whose thighs he parted before sharing your mother's bed—"

The marquess's fist slammed into his stomach and Nathaniel doubled over. For the tiniest moment the men's grip on him slackened. Using that moment to twist violently away, he wrenched himself out of their hold.

Nathaniel wasn't as strong as he used to be. He was still recovering from his knife wound, but he preferred to take his chances against a pistol than to swing from a rope.

Two of Clifton's men scrambled to catch him, but with a blow to the chin and a quick kick to the groin, he sent them flailing onto their backs. He lunged for the marquess while Trenton used the sudden distraction to wrest free as well. But they both froze when the man who held Alexandra put a gun to her head.

"Such impetuous actions will surely cost you," Lord Clifton gritted out. "Now you will watch her hang first." He nodded to one of his thugs, who was still gasping for breath.

The surly, muscular man with a rounded paunch began to drag Alexandra toward the rope. Nathaniel's muscles tensed. He remembered the numerous floggings on the *Retribution*, the hunger, the chafing on his ankles from the chains. He recalled the hospital ship with its sick, desperate men, the dampness, the putrid smell of vomit and sweat and the itch of lice. The memories converged upon his mind, all mingling with each other in the same fraction of a second. The marquess was to blame for it all. And now he threatened Alexandra. "If you harm her, I'll kill you before I die," he vowed. "The only way to ensure that I won't is to hang me now."

Something akin to fear flickered in Clifton's eyes. He ordered his men to grab Nathaniel, but Nathaniel had his long fingers about his half brother's neck before anyone could move.

"Let her go," he whispered harshly, squeezing until Clifton's mouth opened and closed like that of a fish and his eyes bulged from their sockets.

Nathaniel felt a surge of strength course through his body, enabling him to squeeze tighter and tighter until the marquess's face turned bright red. "Now! Tell them to let her go!"

The thugs backed away from Alexandra while the one who held the gun leveled it at Nathaniel's back.

"Kill him," Clifton wheezed, trying to wrench Nathaniel's hand away from his throat.

The report of the gun almost deafened them all, but the bullet missed its target by a wide margin. Trenton had lunged at the man, knocking him off his feet, and the two of them were grappling with each other on the ground.

Someone shouted from outside, "They're in here!"

Suddenly Inspector Madsen, the man from Scotland Yard who had ridden the train with them, charged into the warehouse with four constables following in his wake.

"Hold everything," he said, drawing his pistol and pausing long enough to take in the scene.

Nathaniel slowly released the marquess. Trenton stopped fighting, and Alexandra raised her tearstained face in stunned disbelief.

"Well done, Captain Montague," Inspector Madsen said. "You're free to go."

"I don't know where you'll have me go, *monsieur*," Montague replied, his voice clipped. "My life is safe no more."

"You made that choice, not I," Madsen replied, gathering Clifton and his men into one group.

The marquess turned to Montague. "You did this?"

Montague looked away. "I had no choice."

Madsen quirked an eyebrow at Lord Clifton. "Captain Montague was arrested at a pub in London a few weeks ago. It seems he took a liking to a certain actress with a jealous husband. The two were involved in a scuffle, and your friend killed the man. He offered us evidence on the gun runs in exchange for leniency."

Madsen glanced at Montague. "Perhaps it's time to return to your homeland, Captain," he said. Though his words were polite on the surface, Nathaniel got the distinct impression Inspector Madsen didn't like the Frenchman.

"You're a dead man," the marquess whispered to Montague. "Do you hear me? No one betrays me. You can't go far enough. When I get out of this, I'll find you."

"I don't believe you're in a position to be making threats," Madsen said, waving Clifton and his small band toward the door.

"Wait." Clifton pointed at Nathaniel. "What about him? He's the pirate who's been plaguing my father's ships."

Inspector Madsen glanced over his shoulder at Nathaniel. "Sir John told us all about him. Your father's magistrate friend was afraid he'd be implicated in the gun runs as well, so it didn't take much prodding to get to the truth. From what I've heard, Mr. Kent has paid for his crimes."

He stopped as the constables continued to herd the others out. "He does, however, need evidence to prove his identity as the Duke of Greystone's son, I believe." He looked to Nathaniel. "And now you have it. With a bit of persuasion, Sir John agreed to testify to what he knows of you and your, er, father, too."

He grinned, then winked at Alexandra. "Oh, and congratulations again on your upcoming marriage, miss."

Hangings always drew a large crowd, but today's throng was bigger than most. The punishment of one so high in society, combined with the heinousness of his sin, made this execution of particular interest to layman and nobility alike.

Shops closed at midday so their owners and employees could attend. Nearly fifty thousand people clogged the streets. They climbed any tree with a limb strong enough to support the weight, leaned out windows and sat on rooftops all the way to Ludgate Hill along the Old Bailey, north to Cock Lane, Giltspur Street and Smithfield, and back to the end of Fleet Lane. Wagons and carts teemed with people who had paid to stand on them for a glimpse of the action. And more than a few carriages belonging to notable public officials and members of the aristocracy waited at the fore.

The gallows stood ready in the Old Bailey outside Newgate Prison. A temporary roof enclosed the east part of the stage and offered shade to two sheriffs, who sat on either side of the stairs leading to the scaffold. Around the north, west and east sides were galleries for the reception of officers and attendants, and a short distance away, the constables waited inside a fixed, strong railing. In the middle, where the convict would stand, the floor was raised a bit higher than the rest of the platform.

Nathaniel stood watching with his arm around Alexandra as two men shouted to each other, checking and double-checking the apparatus to make certain that everything was in working order. One tested the lever that dropped the trapdoor from under the victim's feet, while the other proved the rope. Originally a notorious murderer was to be hanged today—a man who had killed his wife and cut her into four pieces, each of which had been discovered in a different section of London—but Nathaniel had heard that the prison officials had decided to wait. The execution of a nobleman was already creating quite a stir. Important people were going to be watching, and Nathaniel didn't doubt that those in charge wanted everything to go as smoothly as possible. In degree of seriousness, treason topped the list, after all, creating the common sentiment that the perpetrator of such deviltry deserved to die alone, center stage. It would appease the anger of many, though it must cause the sadness of some, Nathaniel thought, thinking of Lady Anne.

It was a cold day in late September, and snow had fallen through the night, leaving a thin white blanket on the ground that had quickly turned to slush. Nathaniel and Alexandra shivered with the others as they waited for the prisoner to appear, but despite the chill weather, no one left.

Nathaniel's mood was nervous, somber. He did not want to be here, yet he couldn't stay away. He had spent many years hating his father and brother. Now he felt empty. He could scarcely believe what the papers had reported—a wild fervor had surrounded this hanging above all others—though he knew the truth had finally been revealed.

Alexandra gave him a reassuring smile. "Are you sure you want to see this?"

Nathaniel nodded. "But you don't have to stay, my love. I'd rather you not have to witness—"

"We'll see it through together," she insisted.

He could feel her love flowing through him at the slightest touch, supporting him like the wind at his back. How he admired her inherent strength and beauty. He hugged her closer to him. He had thought he didn't know what love was, but he had proven himself wrong. He loved Alexandra with a ferocity that surprised him.

She smiled at him again, and he turned his attention away, focusing on the comments of those around him.

"He deserves what he's getting, that he does," a heavyset country woman said to her friend. "If it was one of us, they'd string us up in two shakes."

The man behind her said, "But *why* did he do it? There was no call to take such a risk."

Nathaniel had spent many long nights wondering the same thing. But he thought he finally understood—as well as he ever would, anyway.

Scanning the crowd, he searched for Lady Anne. She stood near the front, weeping uncontrollably, alone except for her maid. He couldn't help but feel a twinge of remorse at her pain.

Finally two servants forced their way through the mass of people and escorted the duke's daughter back to her carriage. Evidently she could not bear to watch.

Alexandra nudged him. "You didn't do this to her," she murmured.

Nathaniel nodded slowly. Lady Anne was gone now. There was nothing left to see but the gallows.

Inside a small rectangular cell, the Duke of Greystone paced back and forth. He couldn't imagine more outrage than he felt, and wondered if he could bear it. All his life he had been able to take what he wanted, change the rules if need be, break them if they wouldn't bend. And there had been no punishments. He had gotten away with murder, literally. Yet he could do nothing now, nothing to save his son—the one person in life whom he truly loved—despite his money, despite his power, despite it all.

"Just tell me why, Jake. Why did you do it?" he asked, trying to keep his voice from trembling.

The marquess sat in the corner of his cell, slumped against the bars, staring at the floor. His eyes, when they lifted, were filled with contempt. "You still don't understand, do you? You probably never will. You gave me control of Greystone Shipping and assumed I'd run it expertly, like you always did. But I'm not like you. Or Nathaniel. I couldn't do it any other way." The bitterness in his voice deepened. "And I wanted you to be proud of me. Can you believe that? You, who cared no more for my mother than to bring her syphilis from your whores—"

The duke's hand struck almost of its own accord. "How dare you—"

"What? Face you with the truth?" Jake touched his cheek where the blow had left a red mark. "Nathaniel, of all people, had to tell me. Yet I lived with you, nursed you when you were ill not two years past, and all the while my mother grew sicker, alone, in Scotland. That's how gullible and trusting I was. Will you deny that it's true?"

Greystone thought he heard a trace of hope in his son's last question. For a moment he considered telling the boy what he wanted to hear. They couldn't part this way forever.

But he knew Jake's eyes had been opened. The boy could not ignore the steady decline of his mother's health as if he didn't finally understand the cause. Nor could he deny the cursed reason for Greystone's own illness before the disease went into its latent stage.

Nathaniel had truly robbed them at last. "I don't expect you to understand," the duke said.

Jake's lips twisted in a sneer. "There's never been anything to understand but your own selfishness." He laughed—a cold, humorless sound that reverberated in the cold cell. "I thought if I rebuilt Greystone Shipping into the giant it once was, you'd have to acknowledge me as a son worthy of your legacy. Montague claimed he knew how, and you provided the opportunity for the first shipment with the load of supplies you wanted to send to the Turks. It took a bit of doing, but it wasn't a difficult matter to sell the stuff and use the money to purchase guns, from which we planned to achieve a high profit. An investor had to be brought in when Nathaniel interfered, but our banker made a healthy return, like Montague and myself. Perhaps you would have figured it all out, had you not been so busy bringing shame upon my mother and our family."

As Jake's words poured out, Greystone felt as though a knife turned in his gut. Nathaniel was to blame for this, and ironically enough, his own damn patriotism. If he'd never planned to send blankets, clothing and medical supplies to the Turks, his son couldn't have . . .

The duke cut off his thoughts, knowing they did little good now, and closed his eyes to shut out the vision of his son's derision. Jake had been imprisoned twenty-four days since being sentenced to death. By law, three Sundays had to pass between sentence and execution to give him time to repent, and every day had been an agony for them both.

But nothing like this. When the duke had thought Jake still respected him, he could be the doting, blameless father, and could believe, to an extent, the part he was playing. Now he felt utterly exposed, as if his son had peeled back the husks of an ear of corn to reveal nothing but crawling worms.

"Haven't I given you everything?" he asked.

The marquess looked up. "Everything? You've abused my mother's trust, cost her her life. You've ignored my sister, and for years I could garner only the smallest crumb of your attention. In a way, even Nathaniel had more of your respect and admiration than I."

Greystone covered his face with his hands. The fact that he had somehow brought this calamity on himself and Jake, seared him to his soul.

"It's time." The guard outside the cell moved closer. The duke knew the man had allowed them time together only because he had been ordered to do so from somewhere much higher in the chain of command. The Greystone title still held some weight, but it was getting late, and even a duke could stall the wheels of justice only so long.

"I'm sorry, Your Grace, but I'm going to have to ask you to leave now," the guard told him.

Greystone could hardly believe that this horror was reality. Leave so they could kill Jake? His son? His heir? He hesitated. They couldn't part like this.

"Your Grace?"

The duke tried to swallow the lump that threatened to choke him. He wanted one kind word from Jake, who had stood at the guard's request and waited to be led out onto the gallows, one small sign of forgiveness.

"I'm sorry," he said to his son, uttering the words so softly that at first he wasn't sure if Jake had heard him.

The marquess's gaze rose. "Not sorry enough."

As the guard led Jake out of his cell, Greystone tried to do something he had never done before: he tried to take his son in his arms and hold him tightly for an instant. But Jake's body was stiff and unresponsive.

"Don't touch me," he said, and the duke turned away. He wouldn't have a mere guard witness his humiliation. Besides, he couldn't bear to watch his son pass through the door and enter the blinding light of day.

When the trapdoor dropped away, Nathaniel had to avert his gaze. He was sick at the sight of Lord Clifton's body writhing as the life was wrung from it. His half brother had had everything—the money, the power, the family. And he had thrown it all away. For what?

Nathaniel stared at those privileged members of the aristocracy who watched at the fore. Somber and downcast, they murmured to each other.

That one of their own could swing from a rope like any common man struck at the very heart of England's social order. From what Nathaniel saw and read in the papers, they felt sorrier for themselves than they did Clifton.

He would have been one of them, had his life taken a different path. There had been a time when he had wanted to take his place among the gentry, but now they seemed more like the living dead. Worried over a crease in their clothes, or a pudding that lacked a little spice, they were not alive in the same way Alexandra was. Her heart beat strong and true, and she had a mind that knew what mattered.

Nathaniel's gaze came to rest on the woman he loved. Her head was bent; he couldn't see her enormous green eyes, but he knew what he would find in them. Pity. Despite everything Clifton had tried to do to them both, she knew what the marquess did not: that he had never truly lived.

As Nathaniel led Alexandra away, she instinctively buried her face into his coat. They had both seen enough.

Though the crowd resisted his efforts to get through, so enthralled were they in watching Lord Clifton's body swing, Nathaniel insisted. He physically removed those from their path who would not bend to his words until they were finally free and hurrying toward their rented carriage.

Before Nathaniel handed Alexandra inside, he put his arms around her and held her close. She was crying. "How brave you are, my love," he soothed. "It's over now."

They clung to each other until the pounding of his heart slowed with the spasms of her tears. Now that his father's title and lands were not forfeit, Nathaniel knew he would inherit them someday. And his sons after him. But they wouldn't do so in England. No, he would take Alexandra to America and have a family there. And he would teach his sons what it truly meant to be of noble birth.

Epilogue

Three years later a letter arrived at Bridlewood Manor. Addressed simply to the Duke of Greystone, it had come all the way from Virginia. The duke studied the return address as he sat alone at his desk, but he knew who the letter was from.

Finally, with a sigh of defeat, he broke the seal. The delicate script of a woman's hand covered a single page, wrapped around the portrait of a chubby baby.

Greystone set the picture gently to the side as he read.

> *Your Grace,*
> *It goes against my better judgment to write. Nathaniel would tell me that some things never change, but I cannot help but hope they can and sometimes do. Nathaniel and I were married shortly before we left England. He has been heavily involved in shipping since then, and while his empire may never rival your own, he has been very successful. He is a son to be proud of. I have enclosed a portrait of our first child, a boy named Theodore Nathaniel, born nearly a year ago. I felt it only right that you should know.*
>
> *Sincerely,*
> *Alexandra Kent*

Setting down the letter, Greystone lifted the photograph he had placed to one side. He donned his glasses and held the picture close, though he'd grown sick and his hand shook with the effort of doing so. There was no denying that his first grandchild was a beautiful baby, with a ghostly resemblance to his first wife through the eyes, and a strong Kimbolten nose and chin.

His grandson. The heir of his heir.

At that moment, the duke wasn't sure if Alexandra meant to be kind or cruel, but he stared at little Teddy for a long time.

And then he wept.

ACKNOWLEDGMENTS

Heartfelt thanks go to my husband's aunt, Ruth Carlson, and our good family friends, Bonnie Severietti and the late Russell Bilinski, for giving me the kind of support I needed at a critical time while writing this book. Appreciation and love go to my mother, LaVar Moffitt, and my husband's mother, Sugar Novak, for believing in me through the times I scarcely dared to believe in myself. And last but not least, I owe my sincere gratitude to my former agent, Pamela Ahearn, who helped make my dream a reality.

ABOUT THE AUTHOR

When Brenda Novak caught her daycare provider drugging her young children with cough medicine to get them to sleep all day while she was away at work, she quit her job as a loan officer to stay home with them. She felt she could no longer trust others with their care. But she still had to find some way to make a living. That was when she picked up one of her favorite books. She was looking for a brief escape from the stress and worry—and found the inspiration to become a novelist.

Since her first sale to HarperCollins in 1998 (*Of Noble Birth*), Brenda has written fifty books in a variety of genres. Now a *New York Times* and *USA Today* bestselling author, she still juggles her writing career with the demands of her large family and interests such as cycling, traveling and reading. A four-time RITA nominee, Brenda has won many awards for her books, including the National Reader's Choice, the Booksellers' Best, the Book Buyer's Best and the Holt Medallion. She also runs an annual online auction for diabetes research every May at www.brendanovak.com (her youngest son suffers from this disease). To date, she's raised over $2 million.